GAMMA RAIDS I

GAMMA RAIDS I

THE ADVENTURES OF KAT AND LEE

paper flower

R. LYNN HANKS

GAMMA RAIDS I

Copyright © 2025 by R. Lynn Hanks

All rights reserved.

This story is entirely a work of fiction. All names, characters, organizations, places, events, and incidents portrayed are fictitious. Any resemblance to actual persons, living or dead, events or localities is entirely coincidental. No part of this book was created with the use of AI.

Cover Design by Andy Payne
Map by R. Lynn Hanks
Line edits by Noah Sky

ISBN
Ebook: 979-8-9994202-1-3
Paperback: 979-8-9994202-0-6

For Luke,
this one's always been for you.

As denoted by Kat & Lee

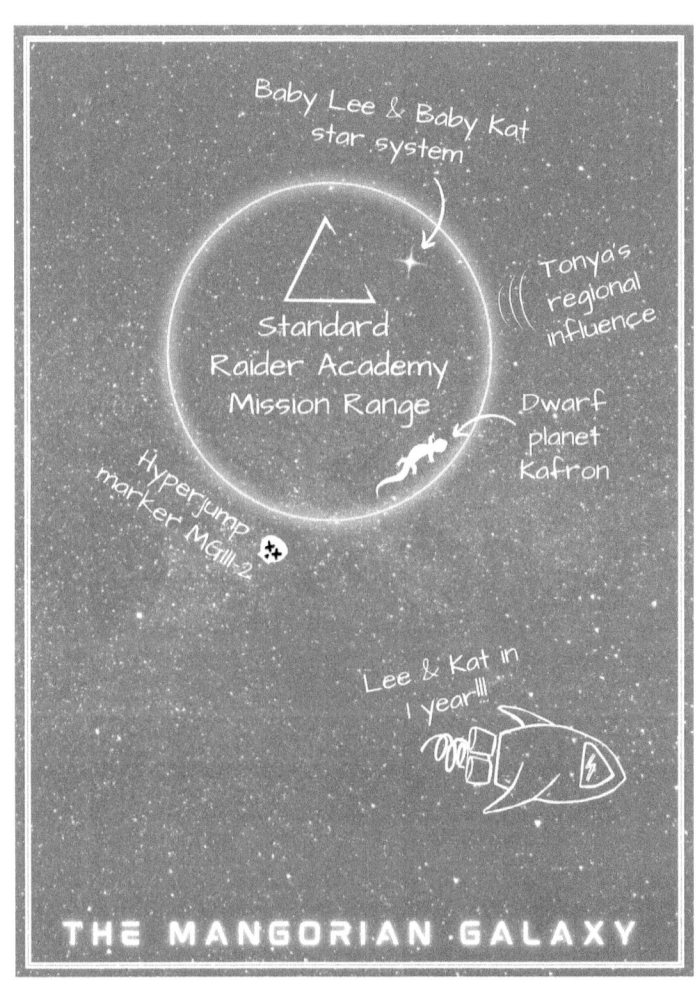

THE MANGORIAN GALAXY

10/06/'31

RAIDER MISSION

AS DICTATED by the Academy bylaws, with respect to the Raider Program of the AMG, the Allies of the Mangorian Galaxy, the Raider mission is as follows:

To protect and preserve the continuation of <u>all</u> life within the Allied star systems of the Mangorian Galaxy.

CHAPTER 1: LEE

LEE WATERS was a raider.

Although, crouched down beside a flowering epiphyte with sweat pooling beneath the polymer of his all-terrain suit, he was probably more akin to one of the dwarf planet's amphibious creatures. The initial raid reports had warned of predatory wildlife. Thankfully, his squadron had yet to encounter anything larger than a salamander in their trek through Kafron's dense understory this morning.

Lee double-checked the blaster at his side. Wiping some of the muck from his gloved hands, he pulled a glass tube from his pack and gently kneaded a few drops of the yellow-green nectar from one of the air plant's flowers. They'd bring the samples in for testing later.

A dark radiation plagued their galaxy. They didn't know its origins, and due to its insoluble nature, it could only be detected when its planetary interactions triggered their radiation sensors. And even then, their labs required physical samples to confirm the dark rays' presence.

Their role in all of this was minor; another particle of space dust in the AMG's galaxy-wide Preservation Initiative. Engineering the grunt work for the scientists and decision-makers came with the territory as raiders—and cadets of the Academy. Like their assignment this morning with Kafron: they were to fly in, extract what they needed, and fly out. But he'd take this over running case studies back on the ship any day.

He scrawled out a quick label before sliding the sample back into his pack with the others. Digging his hands into the mossy soil, he rose to his feet. The cosmic threat was known to leave destruction in its wake. But that wasn't what greeted them here today.

The rainforest planet was like a cave of stalactites, the canopy above vibrant in shades of sapphire, amethyst, and tourmaline. It was a bit overgrown, with the higher branches looking like they wanted to strangle one another, but the sun managed to peek through every couple of meters in glittery pockets. He hadn't been on terrain this exotic in ages. It had been hard to keep from stealing glances overhead as they'd picked their way through the tangle of root and vine.

A patch of brush rustled behind him. Lee whipped his head around, hand instinctively returning to his blaster.

Finn and Tawnee had come up behind him to rest on a couple of arching roots. While those two clutched at their sides, catching their breath, he took count of the rest of his squadron, the cadets scattered throughout the brush dotting the rainforest floor.

Lee had one year left with the Raider Program. One year of leading these slow-paced training missions, traipsing around with a gaggle of cadets under the Commander's banner. Then he would apply for Placement. And when it came to accepting a position within the program, the universe was his limit.

"Heads-up!" This time the sound tore down from overhead.

His *and Kat's* limit, that is. Lee traced the irreverent holler up one of the strangling vine trunks to where his co-squadron lead clung, still several meters up. As she leaped from its grasp, her helmet caught a pocket of light, rose-gold visor shimmering. She landed on her feet, peering around her as casually as if she were out picking wildflowers.

"She couldn't keep her feet on the ground," Lee murmured to himself, hiding a grin. He had to blink past the brightness as she stalked his way. Kat may be his best friend, but she was also stunning. Disarmingly so.

"Interesting sampling method," he said when she had stalked near enough for him to see her face through the helmet's visor. Some tendrils of vanilla-blonde hair had come loose around her face, curling softly in the humidity that had burrowed its way into their suits.

"I got it, didn't I?" Waving the sample tube in one hand, pale grey eyes laughing, she flashed that teasing grin of hers. The same teasing grin that had been a part of his dreams and his nightmares for years. "I'm just saying, if they wanted us to dig soil samples, they should have smoothed that into our titles somewhere."

3

Lee had to work to hide his smile. He understood it. He really did. But it was fun to hear her say it.

"I thought of another action-hero team name for us," she said, coming up beside him, oblivious to the sparks between them. The line he had toed—and shied from—since the first day they'd met.

"Let's hear it."

"The Treetop Scavengers of the Mangorian Galaxy."

Lee snorted. "We sound like monkeys. I think we can do better."

"Whatever, I like it."

The names were the result of one too many late-nighters and a contraband box of brownies to celebrate entering their final year at the Academy. Adding "Gamma" and "squadron lead" before their cadet titles hadn't been enough. Pretty soon they'd added an entire string to the continued adventures of Kat and Lee. Intergalactic Explorers. Discoverers of Mythical Civilizations. The names went on and on—and apparently now included "Treetop Scavengers."

Lee drew up a map of the dwarf planet from the hyperband on his wrist. They were on a timer today. But even with the heightened gravity and the added pressure on their lungs, they'd already traversed roughly two-thirds of the terrain. "We're making good time."

"Perhaps on our way back we can swing by—" Kat trailed off when they heard a *thwump* from behind them.

It was followed by a female's breathy voice through the common communication channel. "Um, guys, I think Finn passed out—"

Turning, they doubled back around to see what had happened.

Finn was indeed lying on the ground, blue-faced, the angle of his helmet askew.

"Don't tell me he was messing with the atmospheric filtration system?" Kat demanded, kneeling down beside the unresponsive cadet and resealing his suit.

"We only meant to shut out more of the smell." A wide-eyed Tawnee wrung her hands.

"The filtration is there for a reason. Mess with the chemical ratios, and you'll melt." Lee dropped his pack to the ground as he rifled through in search of a stabilizer-pack and a tonic. "How far off is he?"

"Nearly back," Kat murmured, recalibrating Finn's filtration system. "We're lucky the atmospheric levels are nearly compatible."

"Here." Lee squatted down beside her, dumping the supplies on the ground while he helped her carefully maneuver the cadet onto his side. And as she applied the stabilizer, his eyes met Kat's.

Don't say it. He could see the irritation and the amusement, the steam building there.

Her eyes flashed. He so desperately wanted to hear what was going on in that restless mind of hers, but they held their tongues, conscious of Tawnee standing anxiously at their shoulders while they waited for the pulse to regulate on Finn's hyperband. Lee reluctantly got up when the rest of the cadets drew near, having finally caught on to the commotion caused by their ignorant compatriots.

The Raider Program was prestigious—and competitive. Only a fraction of the cadets who applied were accepted, and even fewer received an offer afterward. And for cadets like Finn and Tawnee... let's just say they had quite the uphill trek ahead of them. Lee would do the best he could to prepare them, but by the time it was their turn to apply for Placement, he'd be long gone, hopefully established near some outpost in the far reaches of the galaxy. Or beyond.

While Kat tended to Finn, Lee sat the rest of the cadets down and made them go over basic alien atmospheric principles. Only once he was satisfied there would be no more repeats, did he set them going through the entirety of the samples they had collected thus far to make sure everything had been stored and labeled properly.

For the next string of minutes, the only sound was the scratching of ink on toppers as the squadron worked through their collections. His annoyance mellowed out, watching as Tawnee dutifully weighed the lobed palmate genome in her hand. Beside her, her fellow cadets did the same, strewn about the ground wherever they'd been able to find a semi-dry place to sit.

Lee remembered what it was like going out on those early raids. The total exhaustion—and the pure exhilaration. The realization that the galaxy was quite large. Large enough to want to try things that may have been a little reckless...

He stole a glance back over at Kat and Finn. The cadet had finally begun to stir. Kat attentively monitored the soft wheezing noises as she issued the tonic directly into the cadet's suit.

"I'd give Finn some extra saline solution as well." Lee nodded towards the rest of the squadron. "All of you." The last thing they needed was another cadet passing out from dehydration or the like.

"Can you believe this was us once?" Kat asked when Lee came over with the saline solution.

He waited for Kat to finish up on the cadet before handing her the backup solution. "Oh, this was never us."

Kat huffed a laugh, eyeing Finn again. The cadet's face was still tinged azure, but at least he was conscious.

The other cadets had finished up with their samples and begun drifting back to their feet. "Did you see how much further we have?" Kat asked, biting her lip.

"A good three kilometers, give or take." Lee stole another glance down at his hyperband. They still had two hours left before they had to be back on their ship, but at this rate, they would need them. "Tell you what. How about you go on ahead and take the rest of the cadets, and I'll bring Finn along with me in a few."

"You sure?" Kat glanced between him and Finn, then up through the trees, scanning the untracked terrain ahead of them.

"I've got him."

Lee watched her duck under a low-hanging branch with the rest of the squadron. Giving Finn a few minutes to rest, Lee poked around the busy rainforest floor. The faintest hints of rot crept into his suit—was this the smell Tawnee had mentioned? Or was this something new?

He approached a pocket of sunlight where the tiniest of blooms peeked out from under a drooping palm. Its petals were almost translucent, its coloring soft and fine as moon dust, with just a smattering of fiery red pollen at its star-shaped center where it claimed a glimmer of sunlight for itself. It was a bold statement for such a tiny whisper in Kafron's vegetation.

He knew someone like that. Someone whom he sometimes suspected was made of moon dust herself. Or some other cosmic phenomenon, governed by rules and laws entirely her own; a whisper, fighting for sunlight in the ever-expanding universe.

His warrior.

Without a second thought, he slid a glass tube from his pack. Strictly speaking, this was outside their mission objective. But Lee had never been too concerned with bending the rules. Kneeling beside the delicate flower, the sampling tube steady in his hand to not disturb its thin stem, Lee made the cut. A single leaf. Then he rose to his feet.

He wasn't even sure the flower would grow outside the dwarf planet's ecosystem. Wasn't sure how it had survived the dark rays' initial movements. But it was worth a shot.

Pocketing the sample, he wound his way back over to Finn.

The cadet's face had regained its usual color, but he still looked a little shaken. They would have to take this slow. Helping Finn to his feet, he made sure the cadet had found his balance, before they set off, roving once more through the understory.

The rest of the squadron was easily out of hearing range by now, but they had a general direction. They'd catch up next time Kat halted the group for sampling.

They'd trekked a few minutes before Lee stopped, wrinkling his nose. "Do you smell that?" The rot was much stronger in this direction. Steaming tar and curdled milk. Spoiled grapefruit.

He slapped a hand to his blaster as some other horrible notes thrust themselves up his nose, the sickly perfume threatening to gag him.

Finn was dry-heaving at his side. "Stay close," Lee called, ignoring the squelching itch along the collar of his suit. *Why was it so zapping hot here?*

They'd gone another dozen meters, rounding a fallen tree, when Lee stopped abruptly.

That explained the stench.

He ignored Finn's sputtering coughs, forcing himself to push past the *void*-awful scent assaulting his brain while he studied the amphibious body lying on the rainforest floor.

The creature likely weighed as much as he did. Or it had. The straggling fronds of the surrounding brush half-devoured the felled creature, but from what he could tell, it appeared to be more or less whole, its thick claws yellowing. Like its insides had begun to decay long before its death, too rotted through to feed another.

Was this the result of starvation? Or had the dark radiation caused this too? With Kafron's lack of wildlife, it could be either.

Acknowledging Finn's latest round of coughs, they opted for a wide perimeter away from the creature, putting as much ground as possible between them and its lingering stench.

Kat's blonde ponytail had bobbed into view up ahead when he noticed a fresh set of tracks in the mud. They were more like gouges than footprints, and they were only just beginning to fill with moisture. Whatever creature had made them had come through very recently.

Keeping one eye on Kat, Lee made a quick sweep of the dense foliage. High above him, the canopy cast its jewel tones along the leafy fronds, creating with it the illusion of privacy. Was the creature still out here, somewhere, watching them? Or had it moved on?

His eyes continued to dart around as they edged forward, his breathing easing a bit when he could make out the rest of the squadron crouched in various positions as they collected another round of samples. He sent Finn on up ahead to join them.

"Lee, what's going on?" Kat asked as she padded towards him.

"We found a fresh set of tracks, I thought that maybe—"

And then there was movement in the brush. A soft *thrush* as the fronds swished violently. Flicking the safety off his blaster, he drew a second from his pack. The familiar thrums of energy pulsed through his hands as the devices powered up.

The fronds went still.

Tiptoeing at first, he scoured the understory with Kat at his heels, but there were too many shrubs, too many vines, too much *zapping* vegetation.

And then he heard it again. The *thrushing* sound. His hands froze against the metal of the blasters, and his heart seemed to stop, leaving his ears hollow.

He flicked the setting on his blaster for a quick-release stun.

And as the fronds behind them rippled, he whirled, hurtling his body towards the movement, desperate to place himself between Kat and that thing.

The blast rang out through the trees. The thud echoing up through his joints as he dropped to his knees, and something sizable joined him on the rainforest floor.

For a few heavy heartbeats, there was silence around him. The only sound the pounding in his ears as his head caught up with his heart. Kat was okay. They were okay.

Brushing off his knees, Lee tucked one of the blasters back into his bag. Keeping the other out as a precaution, he crossed the last couple meters to where the thing now lay twitching atop a spiky-flowered shrub, its dilapidated body temporarily paralyzed.

Like the carcass he'd found before, this creature seemed one missed meal away from collapse. It must have tracked them here. Desperate enough for food to risk the foreign raider party.

Kat was at his elbow a second later, her own blaster drawn. She wrinkled her nose. "A stun-shot? Really, Lee? That thing tried to kill us."

Only she could scold him after pretty much saving their lives. But her eyes were bright as they took in the beast's diaphanous hide and its scrawny body.

"Poor spinescent flower," Lee muttered, gently prodding one of the spiky flowers from the depressed plant with the barrel of his blaster. Poor Kafron, really.

Kat let out a shaky laugh. The rest of their squadron was split between various stages of morbid curiosity and outright shock as they came to investigate the source of the blast.

"And that thing was...?" Tawnee asked.

"Something we'll want to be on the lookout for," Kat said, having mostly regained her cool composure.

"You think there are more of them out there?" The cadet's wide-set eyes weren't blinking.

"Maybe," Lee said, softly, still studying the beast on the ground. It had its own ghastly complex of claws and teeth, shuddering to draw breaths in its deteriorated state. Finally looking away, he informed them of the creature he and Finn had encountered earlier.

"I'd wondered about the smell..." Kat mused.

Whatever its direct effects, the dark radiation had taken its toll on the majestic planet's inhabitants. It was only a matter of time before the rest went too. He gazed upwards once more to the glittery canopy above them.

They were raiders. Their entire mission was grounded in the protection and preservation of life—of all shapes and forms. But even with all the latest tech the AMG provided them, what good could they do to protect life against a threat like this? What could anyone do?

As the creature continued to twitch, the cadets packed up their samples, continuing the loop back towards their ship. But this time, Lee walked beside Kat, her blaster still gripped tightly in her hands. She gave him a weak smile. And just for her, he said, "We could add 'Rainforest Survivors' to our list of names."

"I'll think about it." They trudged forward a meter. Then she added, "I like 'Slinking Monster Defense' better."

"Walking targets," Finn murmured.

Lee gave a low cough, motioning for them to keep going, while Kat turned to yell at Finn for disrespecting their superiors.

"So," he said, as they walked off into the heart of Kafron. "This beats the time you nearly led us over the edge of a cliff."

"That only happened *one time*." She grinned. "You remember the speeder chase incident?"

"Don't remind me," Lee huffed, his lungs still resetting after the adrenaline.

"You guys are insane," Tawnee grumbled.

But Kat continued on talking as if she hadn't heard the cadet, "And I think it was your idea to bribe our squadron lead with a bottle of that Cryo stuff!"

Lee was laughing now. "I still can't believe she didn't give us both a write-up after that..."

They could handle a bit of radiation. If anyone could figure out an edge, it was them. They were raiders.

CHAPTER 2: KAT

A FEW days after the excitement on dwarf planet Kafron, Kat Hanneman found herself lounging back aboard the Academy in a flex-backed chair inside one of the ship's application rooms. She was sitting in on one of Lee's training courses, Theoretical Exo-planetary and Environmental Concepts. They were Gammas now, which meant in addition to leading squadrons out on raids, they had also taken on the responsibility of training the younger cadets.

As Lee began outlining the parameters for today's hypothetical scenario, she swiveled, tossing her ponytail over her shoulder to peer around at the anxious faces of the younger cadets. She had opted to join him partially because she was bored and had the hour free, and partially for the pure enjoyment of seeing the cadets' terrified expressions. At least being a Gamma had its perks.

They had spent the last couple of afternoons up to their elbows in plant tissue, preparing their raid samples for testing under the speculative eye of the greenhouse attendant. How Lee managed to volunteer there on the weekends, of his own free will and for zero credit, was beyond her. Because if Kat had to grind one more *zapping* pedate leaf—or was it *pinnate*? She couldn't keep them all straight—she was going to burn the whole greenhouse down, Preservation Initiative or not.

Lee finished on the parameters, flicking through the holotech mounted on the wall behind him to a hologram outlining their mission objective. And as the first cadet set off on a dry, overly-exhaustive plan, she tuned his voice out, eyes drifting over instead to the angular windows cutting into the eggshell-colored wall panels on the far side of the room.

The Academy ship was stationed on the outskirts of one of their quadrant's central star systems. And beyond the ship, lay stars. So many stars. Each fleck out there was a planet with microorganisms just begging for discovery. And saving, if their latest mission directive was any indication. Maybe she'd been too hard to judge Kafron, with its climbing vines and slippery creatures. Although, she also wasn't too keen to relive that again.

She leaned over the hyperband at her wrist, scrolling through the updates. Their latest rankings had been posted. She grinned smugly when she saw her face at the top. Still number one, as expected. The number two rank holder stood about a meter away, patiently waiting with arms crossed, his bright green eyes alert, despite the cadet droning on before them. Some small part of her still questioned if Lee let her have that spot. Not that she didn't deserve it, or that he'd ever own up to it.

She flicked through holotech to their schedule. They had seamlessly resumed their morning training sessions with the younger cadets after the raid. A couple of months into their Gamma year and she'd barely bothered to learn her schedule...

It appeared she was leading a holotech advisory this afternoon at 15:00 hours. She scanned further down the schedule, searching for Lee's name. Maybe they could squeeze in an extra workout before then. They'd only been back on the training ship for three days, and already she couldn't wait for their next assignment. Somewhere. Anywhere. Even the ever-present whirring of the air-recycling vents overhead was urging her to go, go, go.

The cadet finally finished his raid proposal. Kat sat back and crossed her arms over her chest, ready to watch the mastery. Lee as her friend was one thing. But Lee as the instructor—well, that was another experience altogether.

"Nice work. That was very thorough, except we are missing one key component. Who can tell me what that is?"

No one spoke at first. Then, a cadet seated near the middle of the room slowly raised her hand. "I think we need to first identify the threat?"

"Elaborate," Lee said.

The lavender-skinned cadet swallowed. "Without a clear indication of what is targeting the species, there is no way to protect against the toxin. So we need to first rule out any external factors to identify the source. Pathogens in the water. Parasites. As well as any existing toxins or unfavorable conditions in the air."

Lee nodded in her direction. "Exactly." The cadet beamed, glancing shyly back down at her notes as Lee went on to expound on her point. His explanations were comprehensive, and as clear as if he were simply explaining directions to access a file on the hub.

Lee was one of the better instructors at the Academy. A reputation he'd gained for not only his patience but also his innate attention to detail. He continued on with his instruction, and despite the outlandish approaches presented, he never mocked. And his focus never wavered from the cadet at hand, or the class listening in; his explanations were as sure as breathing.

Of course, her friend had also unknowingly earned himself a second reputation as the years had progressed. Gone was the awkward, gangly tween of yesteryear. Like most of the guys here, Lee had packed on a significant amount of muscle, his build still lean but stacked in all the right places. He was wearing his hair longer these days too, and his sweet, boyish face soared to new heights in this toned body.

She peered around the room again. Lee might not fully appreciate the second reputation, but the cadets before him sure did. There were a couple of female cadets and at least one male drooling after him.

They went through another handful of cadets' proposals before Lee wrapped up the class. He turned away to collapse the holotech on the wall behind him.

Kat was on her feet when one of the cadets approached him. The lavender-skinned female. Her inky dark hair hung

17

down in wisps on either side of her face where they had pulled free from her ponytail.

"Excuse me." The cadet's voice was surprisingly low and pleasant-sounding.

"Oh, hey there. What can I help you with?" Lee paused gathering up the holotech. He didn't look all that surprised to see her standing there. "Nice work today, by the way."

The girl ran a hand through her hair, a blush staining her cheeks a deeper shade of violet. To give them some space, Kat turned away, flicking instead through her hyperband again.

"You mentioned with one of the proposals the importance of trusting your instincts and not getting distracted by your surroundings... How do you know when you're right?"

Lee seemed to consider his words for a few seconds before he spoke. "Mostly that'll come with time and experience. But what we can work on is making sure you always leave yourself options. Because even the most carefully articulated plans tend to have a way of going off-course. We had a run-in just the other day..."

While they relived Kafron, Kat scrolled through the latest info sent down the pipeline. Apparently, the AMG was cracking down once more on shadow-market activity. With the dark radiation at the forefront of everyone's minds, there'd been an influx of unregulated defense experiments cropping up, supplied by the illegal markets—those in verinity production must be having a field day, since the stuff was at the core of it all. But Kat couldn't even begin to fathom the volatility of the experiments if it was bad enough to warrant the AMG stepping in.

The Allies of the Mangorian Galaxy. While their leader at the Academy, Commander Blanche, was a former raider herself, Kat didn't know that much about the Commanding General of the AMG, except that he led the military and raider units, and that he was responsible for the latest advancements in energy tech. She supposed she ought to get used to reading through these reports. Pretty soon, they'd be answering directly to his General-ship.

Kat glanced up as the girl let out a peal of laughter. There was that pleasant voice again. Too pleasant.

"What happened?" The girl didn't seem in any hurry to leave. It was easy to gauge the girl's interest from her body language; the way she was leaning into him, hanging on to every word Lee was saying. The way she had to keep fussing over those dark wispy hairs.

Kat found herself inspecting the grated floors as Lee explained the creatures they'd run into on Kafron. What was it to her if the girl flirted with Lee? Girls flirted with Lee all the time.

He was her best friend.

Plus, they worked well together. They'd always worked well together, which was how she'd known for years they'd choose each other for squadron leads when they became Gammas. Just like she knew they'd apply together for Placement next term.

She wouldn't let anything come between them and that future.

Besides, she was sort of seeing someone right now. If it could even be called that. It definitely wasn't serious or anything, the whole thing was mostly to skiff some stress. But it had been fun…

She peered down at her wrist as a message came through. Speaking of fun…

> Zane: lightning track tonight?

That had been their thing from the start. Two human beings of a mutual understanding fulfilling a basic primal need. And he certainly had a way with her body. But as long as they were both on the same page about things…

> Kat: I'm in
> Kat: see if u can keep up

> Zane: we'll see who needs to keep up, baby girl

Oh, they definitely would. She had all but lost sight of the instructor-student thing going on before her as her toes curled in her boots—

"What are you smiling about?"

"Oh, nothing." Kat looked over to find Lee standing there, the girl having left and taken her pleasant voice and her smiles with her. "How much I could use a tomato sando right about now."

Lee looked confused but gestured to her hyperband. "And how are the rankings looking?"

"I don't know what you're talking about."

"Sure, sure." Turning away from her, he started gathering up his things.

"You do know that cadet was flirting with you, right?" Kat asked, redirecting the attention towards him instead as she casually tightened the band of her long white ponytail.

"Who, Levy?" Lee looked up, backpack in hand. "She was just clarifying a point from the application today. A point that would've served us well on that last raid, mind you." He paused to collect himself, seeming to add for his own sake, "Besides, she's one of my VLs."

Kat gave him a pointed stare, stifling her laugh while she waited for Lee to catch on. VL stood for Visible Light. Signifying the halfway point in their years of training as cadets. Radio, Micro, IR, VL, Ultra, X, Gamma. But every cadet at some point in their Academy years made the 'Virgin Lips' joke behind leadership lines.

"You don't have to prove anything to me. No judgments here." Kat grinned. She knew her way around Lee's mind so well it was almost too easy.

"It's not like that. I was just helping her."

"And Zane is only interested in my push-up form."

"I still don't know why you're even with Zane," Lee ground out, shaking his head. "All the cadets you could have chosen, and you pick him. The guy takes himself too seriously, thinks he's better than everyone else. I can't stand him."

"I'm not *with* Zane. We're just hanging out. And he's got a lot going on right now." Kat frowned. She thought she knew his mind, but this conversation was taking a turn. Kat cast around for something. "I couldn't stand Cassie when you were with her."

"Cassie completed the program."

"Not my point."

"Isn't it?" Lee crossed his arms over his chest.

When he just looked at her, Kat ran her hands through the hanging strands of her ponytail. "I just think you could do better, that's all."

"With whom, Kat? Who could I do better with?"

The freckles stood out across his nose as she was made infinitely aware of how compact the air had gotten.

Her hyperband buzzed. She ripped her gaze from his as a reminder notification came through about the events coming up this weekend. When she looked back up, the intensity in Lee's gaze had lessened, and with it, some of the previous tension.

He nudged her. "I knew you couldn't stand Cassie."

But before she could come up with something more to say, Lee motioned to the door. She followed him through on strained breaths to the rest of the training levels.

There was no way their conversation was over. Just—paused, for now.

More eggshell-paneled walls met them as they headed around to the stairway.

"Whistler." Lee nodded somewhat tersely as one of their fellow Gamma cadets came down the stairs towards them, a rolled mat clutched under one arm. Kat was straining to remember, but couldn't actually recall the long-haired cadet's given name. They'd always just called him Whistler.

"What up Lee, Kat—or should I say Kat-fron!" He and Lee slapped hands.

"Whistler," Kat echoed, shooting dagger eyes at Lee, the light in his eyes dancing. She silently dared him to laugh at the recycled joke. It hadn't been funny the first time Whistler had told it, when they'd run into him outside the labs, swapping horror stories, the day before.

"Gotta take advantage while the sun is fresh," he shifted the mat in his hands. Whatever that meant. Without waiting for further response, Whistler continued his leisurely stroll back down to the lower levels of the training floors.

Lee was trying so hard not to laugh he was shaking, Kat had to bite down on her lip to stifle her own.

There were the cadets who cared about things like rankings and Placement. And then there was Whistler, with his weird solar allegories. He didn't actually seem to care about the Academy, so why was he even here?

They were up a level before Lee let anything slip. "Kat-fron. It's growing on me." He busted up laughing.

Kat crossed her arms across her chest. "Ha ha." Forgive her if she didn't share in that particular merriment.

And despite her feigned attempts at batting him away, he slung an arm casually across her shoulders. "So, Laser Rounds this weekend," Lee began, changing the subject over to the monthly competition. He'd obviously gotten the notification as well. "I'm thinking it's about time for the Queen to be dethroned."

"Are you kidding? As if." She squeezed his arm hard enough to show some tenacity. She'd been on a bit of a winning streak lately, racking up enough credits between the Rounds and their routine accrediting activities to keep her on top. At least for now.

Rankings could change in a matter of days. Especially if Lee or Zane got rather ambitious with their time. Although, Whistler was also up there with them... that was something.

These Rounds would be interesting to see, though. To the best of her knowledge, most, if not all, of the Gamma Squadrons were off-raid and around the ship this weekend.

The rotating levels that made up the ship's training facilities had mostly emptied for lunch, aside from the stragglers like Whistler, who were taking advantage of the empty training rooms down below. And she and Lee, Kat supposed. She could hear the soft thuds of their boots as they rounded the grated floors of the meticulously polished hallways.

If the Canteen was out of sandwiches by the time they got there on account of Lee's hospitality towards the lavender girl...

They had reached the lower skywalk that bridged the ship's three training levels to the main Heptagon. Standing alongside one of its walls of windows, clad in the usual raider-black, and looking as formidable as ever, was Zane. Like Lee, Zane's body was muscled and hard in all the right places. But where Lee's features took on a certain lightness, a romanticism to them, Zane's dark features gravitated towards cold-hard steel. His posture, like his military upbringing and his dad's rank within the AMG, was rigid. And his onyx hair, buzzed tight on one side of his golden-brown head with the Academy's broken triangle symbol shaved into it, only enhanced his strong jaw.

The broken triangle represented a prism diffracting light, symbolizing their raider mission. It had something to do with correcting the broken paths within their galaxy, or some poetic crap like that. She'd have to ask Lee about it again next time she thought of it.

Just maybe not right this moment.

Zane looked up from his hyperband as they approached. She shouldn't be surprised to find him here. The entire Academy had morning training on these floors.

"Hey." Kat brushed off Lee's touch, coming up to stop next to Zane.

"Am I interrupting something?" Zane asked coolly, addressing her alone.

"What? No. Lee and I were just talking about the Laser Rounds. I've got ten on Sean going down first."

But it seemed Zane wasn't in the mood for friendly wagers. "Anyone can beat Sean. He's short-sighted, only thinks about himself."

"He's not the only one." Apparently, Lee wasn't up for a wager either, the shift in his mood was about as subtle as the latest model of blasters the Academy had purchased.

As Zane whipped his head towards Lee, Kat became aware of exactly how small this bridgeway was for such large egos. "Are you accusing me of not taking my Gamma role seriously?"

"Zane, he's not—" Kat tried.

"I've heard talk," Lee said nonchalantly, "How's being ranked number three, by the way?" So he had seen the rankings after all.

Kat rounded on her best friend, "Lee, that's not helping—"

"You don't know anything," Zane said, ignoring her completely as he took a step towards Lee. "At least I have the guts to go after what I want."

"Guys," she pleaded. Yes, she knew they'd been at each other's throats for most of their years at the Academy, but did they have to have it out now?

"What's that supposed to mean?" Lee ignored her, matching Zane's step as he met him head-on.

"Come on guys, seriously, let's just go grab lunch—" Kat said, her head starting to throb as she wedged herself between them. Cadets were beginning to gather at the opposite end of the domed and windowed skywalk.

A bitter laugh. "Oh, I think you know." And for a heartbeat, Zane seemed to relent, body going slack, as he addressed Kat instead. "Have fun with that, *recreant.*"

"Say that again to my face." Lee squared his feet.

"Fine," Zane said, grinning coldly. "*Coward.*"

"Zane!" Kat hissed, but she was shoved out of the way as Lee launched a fist straight for Zane's face. "Lee!" Kat screamed, the blood now pounding in her ears as well as her head, her vision starting to go streaky.

Zane sidestepped out of the way, parrying as Lee rolled his shoulders with a smirk that said very clearly, *you're about to get it.*

26

Scrambling between them, Kat placed a hand on either guy's chest, shoving as hard as she could. "Enough!"

She rounded on both boys. "For *void*'s sake, take it out in the Laser Rounds." She turned first to Lee. "He's just goading you." Whipping her head around, she shot Zane a glare. "Get your act together."

Closing her eyes, she took a deep breath. And only when the lights behind her eyes had faded and her breathing was no longer heavy, did she open her eyes again. "Now, if you two are done with your little pissing match, I'm starved. I will see you in the Canteen."

She meant to spin on a heel and get out of there.

But she wasn't quick enough to miss Zane's firing remark, "I'll see you in the Spectrum, *Leland*."

Nor the finger Lee flipped back in response; Lee muttered something about forgetting something in one of the training rooms earlier. Whatever, it was a lousy excuse and he knew it.

She ought to go after them.

But later. She really was hungry.

CHAPTER 3: LEE

THE ARENA was cool and humid this morning, despite the hour. The sweat and aggression from the previous matches hung dormant in the air like a sleeping beast.

The benches lining all seven sides of the Spectrum were packed, the faces of the younger cadets alight with awe. Their cheers grew deafening as they reverberated off the massive multi-story windows lining the upper half of the arena, inviting the starry galaxy beyond.

Lee adjusted his stance, his boots digging into the turf of his floating island as he surveyed the spray of neon-lighted vests—beacons in the thick darkness that smothered them.

The arena was made up of roughly four dozen islands, each a couple of meters wide, suspended by magnetic fields, and spaced at uneven intervals throughout. The majority of the islands were occupied—for now, visible only by the glow of their vests and the stacks of holodisks at their feet. And below them: roughly fifteen meters of nothing. A void.

But neither the darkness nor the arena's perfected synergy could tame the roaring rising up around them.

The weekend had arrived. And with it, the Laser Rounds.

The rules were simple: The Laser Rounds were a free-for-all. Every cadet for themselves. If your vest was hit by another cadet's disk, you were out; the lights on your vest would go dark, and you were required to jump down immediately. If you fell off one of the islands, you were also out. The last cadet standing with a lighted vest was the winner.

It was tactical brilliance and a chance at bragging rights. Alliances were formed—and broken. And with the Commander often in attendance, it was one more opportunity to show her what you were capable of; impress the Commander, and you had the best missions at your fingertips. And after a morning spent congratulating victors and flipping coins, the Gammas were finally up.

Lee flashed a grin towards the Gamma cadet atop the island nearest him, the blonde ponytail he could barely make out from the glow of her violent yellow vest. He'd been intimidated by her when they were younger—although never enough to stray far.

"You gonna go easy on me today, Waters?" Kat called over, toeing the holodisks at her feet. There was that teasing, cocky grin again.

"Oh, always, Hanneman." Lee ran his hand along the rim of a stormy blue disk, the collection of manipulated waves that would regenerate should it leave the grid. Maybe taking out a cadet or two with it.

He flicked his eyes towards the opposite side of the arena, to the half-shaved head in electric green.

Timing in relationships had never been their strong suit. Whether it was him with someone, or her. There'd always been something. But now with Zane... He didn't know what in the *void* was going on there.

Kat may have found some common ground with Zane over the past couple of months, the details of which he hadn't cared to scrutinize. But Lee? He still had a score to settle.

Of course, there were a handful of cadets between him and that score. They would be collateral damage. Sean, they had already established, would be no issue; combine him with another two Gammas, and Lee would have himself a hat trick. He'd have to keep an eye out for Neha—as Zane's co-squadron lead, there would be an alliance there, and Neha was known for her wicked curve shot.

Coward. Sure, the timing for he and Kat had sucked over the last year or so. But he'd rather fly things solo than engage in whatever sham of a relationship Zane thought he had going with her.

A low tremor sounded far below them, like the groan of the beast at last awakening from slumber. The industrial fans at the base of the arena began churning their steady stream of cool steam. That would be their safety net, the steamtrap powerful enough to catch the falling cadet. But it still made his gut dive-bomb, every single time.

The holo-screen hovering overhead began its ticking down from 00:00:10. With every second on the clock, Lee began the descent down towards that cool, collected place within himself. The raider. For those couple of seconds, everything was quiet.

The calm before the lightning storm. And as the tension began to crackle again, the anticipation at its zenith, the clock blared.

It was time.

Various colored holodisks shot through the arena in a technicolor chaos. Time seemed to bend as he sank into a comfortable rhythm. Whip. Whirl. Dive. It was a dance in which they were the principal athletes. A whip; Lee sent a disk spiraling through the air. A whirl; he spun, dodging an errant throw. A dive, and he collected his neon holo-weapon all over again.

The Gammas held on longer than the Ultras, or even the Xs had in the Rounds before them. But even they eventually started to drop off. With a low hissing, the fallen Gamma cadets were caught by the cool steam down below.

Lee struck out Sean, the cadet's vest going dark. In its wake, the darkness seemed to pulse around him. As he heard the low hiss of the steamtrap, he whipped his head around, already claiming his next target.

Kat pirouetted through the air in a flash of violent yellow as he sent a disk zipping her way. "Think fast!"

"You'll have to do better than that!" With a quick catch and release, Kat sent the holodisk whizzing back toward him, but Lee was already moving. He crossed his island in three strides. The familiar sensation bubbled up in his gut as he pushed off, gravity tearing at his feet as he arced through the air—

And then his boots met turf. Lee landed lightly on his feet, scooping up a disk with the motion. He didn't have to look around him to know that the *whoop* trailing along would be

Kat, claiming a new island for herself. Nor that she would be wearing a grin to match his own. They lived for this.

"So you never told me," Kat called, sending a disk winging towards the opponent at her back. She and Lee had inadvertently placed themselves at the heart of a skewed triangle. Always keeping things interesting. "What is it about what Zane said yesterday that set you off?"

Lee dove, making the catch on his back, only panting slightly. "This may not be the best time..." Shooting back to his feet, he intercepted a second disk. This one he tossed Kat's way.

"So you can pick a fight with the boy I'm seeing, but you can't even tell me why?" Kat caught his disk, sliding her hands along the edges as she frowned down at the neon glow.

"So now you're seeing him?" He swore she fumbled the disk she was holding. But he could have just imagined it with everything going on around them. "Look," he said, backtracking, in between breaths. "It seems like you guys have enough to figure out between the two of you without me adding to things. The guy's just a dick."

Lee had to chuck the disk in his hands to miss the zinger Kat hurled at his head. The disk degenerated as it skittered beyond the unmarked grid. "Okay, too much, I admit it," he said, but a grin pulled at his lips. "Truce?"

He was on his feet, readying for her rebuttal when his eyes snagged on a couple of figures hovering along one of the upper edges of the stands. Their light-colored uniforms were a direct contrast to the dark, all-terrain suits of the cadets. It wasn't hard to identify the willowy form of their Commander. But the figure next to her—

The flicker of a disk careening towards him from the corner of his eye had him whipping back around. He snagged the holodisk out of the air before looking back around.

The officer's uniform, with its neat alignment of badges, could belong to any member of the AMG's commanding body. Although why he would be here on the ship, where he held very little jurisdiction... Lee scanned the rough features, the sharp, hardened dark eyes...

"Oy, you still with me, Waters?" Kat hollered.

Lee sent his disk careening at random towards one of the other cadets as he tried to rid the rarity of the officer's appearance from his brain. But he couldn't remember for the life of him what he and Kat had been talking about mere moments before.

Lee stretched his arms across his chest. "You ready to end this thing?"

"After you." She kept her tone light, but across the gap from him, her posture had straightened, her every movement calculated—which in Lee's experience, usually meant she was about to kick some ass.

They were down to roughly a dozen cadets. A few still surrounded him and Kat. Zane was up ahead, along with someone in a vibrant purple vest, whom Lee would guess was Neha, judging by her last couple of throws. Whistler was up to their left a little way, mid-aerial, as he dueled it out on several of the higher islands with a couple more cadets. Lee had to hand it to the guy—though it was no secret that Whistler used the Laser Rounds as his own personal playground, he was definitely leveraging today's match.

While Kat dueled with the cadet at her immediate left, Lee parried the ones behind and to his right, just waiting on the mistake that would break them.

The first misjudged the radius of her island, coming down from a sloppy defensive maneuver. The second, Lee struck out with a disk to the chest. Another hiss as another cadet dropped down out of the arena. Kat's cadet went dark around the same time.

Stealing a moment to catch his breath, he peered around to see Zane having moved upwards and going toe-to-toe with Whistler. There was a battle he'd like to watch. Whistler was brilliant, but Zane's intensity was its own force.

Another cadet moved towards them, but there was no sign of Neha, so maybe she'd also met steam—

And then purple blurred on the island directly above them.

"Move!" Lee hollered. He threw himself to the ground, rolling across the island. Her gasp and scuffle was the only sign that Kat had heard him.

"Sorry to interrupt, lovebirds," Neha's silken voice split the darkness between them.

Lee scrambled to his feet as a couple more disks flew towards him at once. He slapped down the first. And as the second skimmed past his right side, Lee snapped it up. He chucked the lime-colored disk, striking Neha square in the chest. Her vest went dark. Whistler was struck out shortly after. A direct hit from Zane.

Although Lee had missed the actual battle, he did look up in time to catch Whistler's swan dive as he arched right over the side. Lee thought he picked up a rise in the tumultuous cheering following the hiss that was Whistler's demise. Although, it was all starting to blur together. The whistles and hollers. The drumming of hands on benches. The hissing as the cadets were eliminated one by one from the competition. A live percussion ensemble.

Zane dropped back in; now only a couple of islands stood between him and Lee. Most of the cadet's sharp features were shrouded in electric-green-tinted darkness, but as Lee marked Zane, he caught the shift in Zane's face as the intensity faded into something infinitely scarier—an unreadable mask.

Lee rolled his shoulders, squaring his feet. He'd been waiting years for this moment. Or at the very least, the past two months.

Kat's exasperated sigh was audible over their whirring safety net below as she collected a couple of holodisks from the turf. "Play nice, boys." But she turned away from them, instead matching up with the fourth and final remaining Gamma.

In Kat-language, that was pretty much a blessing.

Scooping up the forgotten disk from Neha at his feet, Lee took a running leap, swiftly bridging the gap between islands.

Zane fired first, sending one of his disks sailing toward Lee's chest, but Lee saw that move coming. Flipping backward, Zane's disk sliced right under him. He didn't have time to duck when Zane hurled the second. Flinging out his own disk with deadly accuracy, he nicked Zane's from the air, sending both holodisks flying off into the darkness.

The disks regenerated at their feet around the same time. Snatching his up, Lee started sprinting, moving to higher ground. Zane did the same, with Kat pulling out the stops down below. Kat had the advantage as her opponent's throws tended to hang wide...

Feigning angling for the upper hand, Lee kept going, pushing himself as he claimed island after island. Zane could only follow as Lee positioned himself. Positioned them.

And then Lee hurled his holodisk at Zane. A distraction. *Goading him*, as Kat had claimed the day before.

He was probably insane.

But as Zane sent his disk soaring back towards him, Lee leaped straight off the island.

He swallowed back the rush, the plummeting feeling in his gut, right before he landed back on the centrally positioned island below. To intercept the loose disk from the cadet facing Kat.

A dive. A whip. A whirl. He sent the disk sailing unexpectedly back up towards Zane.

Zane's lights went dark.

Lee didn't even care when he felt the subtle zap on his shoulder as either Kat or the other remaining cadet struck him out. His vest went dark as he left the match.

He was lying in the steamtrap at the base of the arena when the violent yellow vest rounded on her final Gamma opponent. The cadet was knocked clean off their island.

Out.

The cheers and the thrumming in the Spectrum soared deafeningly loud once more—and all of it was for Kat. Lee threw his fists in the air, pumping them victoriously.

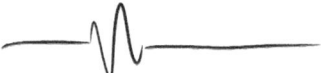

A soft knock on the long, circular door of his dorm room had Lee sitting up in bed. He checked his wrist. 01:12. Groaning, he slid on a pair of jogger pants, not bothering to find a T-shirt in the dark. He slapped a hand to the plated glass sensor by the door. Kat scrambled through a few seconds later.

They stood there another couple of seconds, the dimmed light that lit the hallways at this hour stealing in from the concealed phosphorescents overhead. Lee tried to get his bearings as he blinked back sleep. Kat's arms were pebbled under the hallway fans as she fiddled with the hem of her oversized T-shirt. Zane's T-shirt. He tapped the door shut behind her.

"Here." Stepping blindly toward his desk he grabbed the hoodie from his chair, tossing it to her. "I don't need all his pheromones getting on my stuff."

"Ew," Kat cringed. He could just make out her nose scrunching up.

"That came out wrong," he said, correcting himself. But she was laughing, which was a good sign, and after a second, Lee couldn't help joining her.

Still, she remained, hovering by the door in the couple meters of floor space the dorm allowed, his hoodie in her hand. She was quiet, too.

"Do you want to talk about it?" Lee asked finally.

Kat shook her head. "No."

Grabbing a shirt from the ground, Lee busied himself about the tiny desk near the head of the bed. He'd been working through a couple of follow-up reports for the Kafron raid earlier that evening. The faint starlight from the bay window illuminated his empty water cup and the wrapper from one of the half-eaten power bars he'd abandoned earlier. He tossed them both out.

Kat pulled his hoodie over her head with the faintest rustling, then crawled over to his bed. Making herself comfortable, she perched against the back wall, hands wrapped around her legs. Her long, toned, bare legs...

Lee forced himself to look away, to stare up at a spot on the ceiling. "Sorry if it made things worse for you guys, me taking out Zane today."

A pause. And then, "No you're not."

Lee couldn't stop the breathy laugh that slipped out. "I'm really not," he agreed, stealing a look at her face. A ghost of a smile lay there. Lee made himself look away again, giving her space.

When he looked back, he found she had turned her attention to one of his plants, the aloe in the window. "You know, you're the only one I know on this whole ship who even keeps a plant."

"And it comes in handy." He nodded towards the aloe, where he had torn a piece off one of its succulent leaves only the night before to treat a laser burn. But Kat had moved on, picking up the mini-action hero figurine that sat next to his plants. She laughed softly. "I remember when you got this little guy."

Lee grinned, sliding onto the bed and settling against the wall beside her. "Tonya thought it would remind me of home." He watched her turn the figurine around and around in her calloused fingers, running her thumb over its mini blaster. "I've kept it this long, not really any point in getting rid of it now." He peered over at Kat. She was still staring at the childhood hero in her hands. The very one that had spun their own chain of action-hero names.

"You were right," she said, the words barely a whisper on her lips. "What you said earlier. About us having a lot to figure out..." Her long legs were coiled beneath her, her form lithe with strength and power. And yet, Lee thought she looked small, somehow.

"I didn't mean that as an insult, okay. You, with him—it just gets to me sometimes."

When she continued to stare at him, to look at him with those vulnerable eyes, all vacant and honest, Lee felt his heart crack. He'd do anything to make that look go away.

She pushed herself to be invincible—it was her safety net. He'd seen it that first day with the transports, and every day since. Kat didn't have loved ones outside of here rooting her on, not really. The Academy was it.

But she had him. She'd always have him.

"You're my best friend. I just really don't want to see you get hurt," he said, finally.

She seemed to accept that. She was quiet again, anyway. Lee held in his breathing for a couple of seconds, clamping his lips together. He released it a second later. "Are you guys going to… figure things out?" The question lay raw between them. He thought for a few seconds about telling her what Zane had said earlier that had set him off, about Lee not having the guts to go after what he really wanted. Which apparently everyone knew what he wanted. The conversation they'd started down just the other afternoon…

But that wouldn't be fair to Kat.

She sat up a little, studying his face in the darkness, like she was searching for some answer to his question there on his face. Lee wasn't sure what she saw there, but then she chirped brightly, "Yep."

But the flatness hadn't left her eyes and instead seemed to settle over her. And when she pivoted, laying her head in his lap, Lee slumped down beside her, cradling her head in his arms.

At some point Lee flipped on some music—chill vintage rock, the last album he'd been listening to. If Kat had any opinion about the band, she didn't say anything. Not as they lay staring up at the ceiling as the night crept on.

Minutes or hours later, he didn't know, he felt Kat stir beside him. He felt her body tense up, stiffening, before she relaxed once more, curling into him. Her friend.

Right now that was what she needed him to be. So he was.

CHAPTER 4: KAT

KAT DIDN'T know how it had even happened. But she and Zane had gotten into a fight last night after the Laser Rounds.

You always put Lee first...

It's like I'm being used...

No loyalty...

I need more...

She had been upfront with Zane from the start about what she wanted. It wasn't exactly her fault if the lines got blurred. Which they hadn't.

Maybe they had.

She didn't know anymore.

Still, each accusation Zane had flung at her had stung, like another neon disk into the fractured abyss that was her heart. They had chased her around the hallways and through the dorms until she had found herself at Lee's door.

Call it one in the morning. Call it bad judgment. She shouldn't have come here. Except she always did. And he always let her in.

Lee was dozing in the bed next to her, his breathing light. She ran a finger, feather-soft, along the arm he had subconsciously draped across her middle.

Not even talking with Lee had been enough to fend off her own, internal self-accusations. The wounds were sharper than any Zane or Lee could ever inflict. It was those accusations that had poked and prodded at her all night long. They had tossed and turned her about, winding themselves tightly around her like the blanket she had kicked off desperately in the night. She had shoved them down, down, down, to lay with the blanket now tangled at her feet.

Zane wasn't wrong. She needed Lee.

Just not in the ways he thought she did.

Lifting her arm gingerly so as to not wake Lee, she silenced the hyperband buzzing at her wrist. It was still early, and the hallways outside were quiet. Maybe if she got up now, she could fit in a workout and clear her head a little before breakfast.

Rolling slowly onto her stomach, she let Lee's arm drop back down onto the bed. She listened to his breathing. So quiet and carefree—like a winter sunrise. Extending first a leg, and then an arm, she crawled across his chest. She was easing her other leg over him when a groggy voice stopped her.

"Going somewhere?"

She glanced up. He hadn't even opened his eyes yet and that boyish face of his, the freckles over his nose crinkling, smirked at her. She wanted to smother those freckles. Instead, she let her feet drop down to the floor. Turning on a heel, she sauntered across Lee's unreasonably clean dorm to the closet she knew he kept well-stocked.

"I didn't want to wake your sorry ass. But since you are already awake..." She ripped open a new box of Lee's high-end, energy protein bars, pulling one out in a flash of bright foil. "Thank you!"

His eyes were open now, and trailing her. "You are fine to keep the hoodie—"

"Nah." She shed the extra layer before he had a chance to finish the thought. "I'll be fine. Someone packs on a ton of body heat." She tossed the hoodie his way, and Lee snatched it out of the air with one hand. With a wink, Kat placed a palm to the plated sensor on the wall and sashayed out the portal door.

Despite her assurances, it was chilly in the hallway. The grated floors were cool underneath her bare feet; her arms and legs dotted as she padded past the showers separating their dorms.

On the bright side, they both had dorms on the same level. And so did Zane, who now stood beside her door, his weight distributed evenly between both boots as he vigorously tapped something into the hyperband on his golden-brown wrist.

It seemed she wasn't about to get that workout. Kat took a deep breath, grounding herself. She'd really wanted that extra time to think things over before having this confrontation. It wouldn't change anything. But—just, more time would have been nice.

"About last night—" she said, trying anyway.

"Where have you been?" Zane demanded, cutting her off. "I've been messaging you all morning."

"All morning—it's barely seven," Kat muttered, even as she flipped over her wrist, now scanning through the half dozen alerts waiting on her hyperband. Ah. Five of the messages were from Zane. At least two had come in since she'd silenced them on her hyperband earlier.

"Hey, can we talk for a moment?" She tried again, even as the contents from the latest message finally registered. "A briefing? But we just got back. There was nothing on the schedule... I wonder if Lee knows. The invite must have come last night while you and I..." Kat could feel her face burning. Rather than let her body betray her, she looked down at the message again, a sheet of her tousled hair shielding her as she read through the original message from the Commander.

"I'm sure pretty boy knows all about it," Zane said coldly, guessing correctly where Kat had run off to after leaving his room last night. "In case you missed it, the briefing is at 07:30." Zane made to turn, but stopped himself, smirking. "Nice shirt."

Kat had only a foot through her portal door. But at his not-so-subtle reminder, she wrenched the T-shirt over her head, chucking it at his feet. Bare skin or otherwise, his shirt was the last thing she wanted touching her right now.

She read through Zane's messages in her room while she got ready, the tones of his messages having progressed as they went from sweet apology to cautious defense, to purposefully spiteful.

Fine, he was sorry about what had been said. But that didn't change the fact that he'd said it. Whether he was sorry or not. And now he had to go and turn this thing between them into a *zapping* soap opera.

Whatever. They'd get through this morning's briefing, come out from the raid looking like rock stars, and then maybe she could put all this behind her.

By the time she had slipped into her all-terrain suit, teasing the crown of her hair to add some lift to her ponytail, and applied a threatening slash of black liner, she was the spitting image of *so-over-it*.

She departed her dorm, heading out through the upper skywalk and into the stairways of the Heptagon. But then she paused.

There would be three squadrons in attendance for the briefing. Three squadrons, all vying to impress the Commander with this next assignment. Rock stars or rankings, she may as well get a leg up.

It was just a feeling, really. But instead of taking the stairway up to the briefing, she headed down. She still had a good twenty minutes before she was expected to report, but it would be tight... She took the rest of the stairs, two at a time.

They'd looked up the General's photograph yesterday to confirm after Lee had spotted him during the Laser Rounds. Commanding General, Marion Narron. Neither of them had even met the AMG's military leader before, let alone shared breathing space with the guy. Had he even set foot onboard the

Academy since they'd joined the program? It wasn't until now that she'd thought to check for his ship.

She slowed her pace as she cleared the central skywalk to peer into the Commander's private hangar. But only the Commander's cruiser met her there. The visiting spacecraft that she'd been hoping to find, belonging to one Commanding General, was absent.

However, a quick chat with their favorite aviation operator over in the main hangar, who was friends with the operator in the Commander's private hangar, yielded some rewarding results.

Only then, after confirming those results, had Kat peeled back the foil from Lee's power bar, savoring the bites of lemon zest, before hauling back up the Heptagon and over to Mission Assignment and Briefing.

She arrived two minutes early.

There were already four Gamma cadets present when she got there. Zane, thankfully, had his back to her while he spoke quietly to Neha. Whistler was also there, his red-brown hair tied back in an elegant French braid this morning. His fingers flew across the holo-keys of his hyperband as he typed out a quick message.

Kat walked right up to Lee's side. "Thanks for the heads-up on the briefing this morning, by the way."

"I thought you knew," he said, bemused. "Besides, I'm fairly certain you were the one who skipped out on me. You didn't exactly leave us any time to talk." She didn't miss the way he was studying her elevated breathing and her flushed face, an inquisitive look on his face that read somewhere between *what in void's name have you been up to* and *you know something, spill.*

She stole a glance at the other cadets to ensure no one was paying close attention; Zane bored a hole into the side of her head with his glares, but was still conversing with Neha, so Kat drew her eyes back to Lee. "It's an interesting choice, putting us all on a mission."

Lee again scrutinized her face, but he waited, patiently, for her to finish.

She let her voice drop a sound bite, "I mean, it couldn't be coincidence, could it? That a mere day after seeing who may very well have been, the Commanding General attending the Laser Rounds, we all get called last minute to the same raid. Any old squadrons might be passable, it happens. Sure. But to put all of us on it?"

"Us, Zane, Whistler..." Lee nodded, ticking them off on his fingers, subtly checking that the other cadets were still otherwise occupied. "Whistler though," he said quietly, "an interesting choice."

"He's number four with the Academy. His scores and recent performance make him one of the top cadets."

"Oh I know, and I agree. It's just interesting, that's all." Lee had a point. Sure, they were always butting heads with Zane and Neha. They had very different ideas about how to run a squadron. But with Whistler—the guy didn't even care, although his cadets always seemed to like him quite a bit.

Whistler's co-squadron lead, Ciela, showed up, her pale hair ghostly in these overhead lights. There was nothing particularly remarkable about the Gamma, aside from her near-translucent features. Unlike Whistler, Ciela didn't have the brilliance or likability to back her, whatever the motivation. For a raider, she was average.

Kat nodded at Ciela, before looking pointedly back at Lee. She waited a moment or two, pasting a vague smile on her face. "I paid a little visit to our Commander's private hangar. It's exactly as you expected."

Lee's eyes narrowed.

And because she couldn't resist, Kat added, "It's a good thing too, because I was starting to think you'd imagined him."

Lee flicked her nose. "Coincidence or no, I still can't get it out of my head. What was General Narron even doing here?" While their missions originated from the General of the AMG, their assignments came directly from Commander Blanche.

"Perhaps our auspicious leader was simply bored," Kat offered.

"I'm sure. The General *of the zapping AMG* simply had nothing better to do on a Saturday morning," Lee said dryly. But they didn't have time to say anything more. At exactly 07:30, the Commander's secretary, Nolan showed up. He scanned his hyperband over the plate by the door, and the cadets filed inside.

She leaned in close to Lee. "Was Nolan there yesterday?"

"I don't remember," Lee breathed.

The briefing rooms were all standard, featuring the same eggshell-paneled walls and polished, grated floors as the rest of the ship. The only difference was being completely devoid of windows and furniture. The exception was the holoblock, spanning the length of the front wall on which it was mounted. Trailing along with the others, Kat claimed a spot in the middle of the floor between Ciela and Lee.

They didn't have to wait long. Kat had stood there respectfully all of thirty seconds, forward-facing with her hands tucked behind her back, when the Commander swept into the room.

Commander Yvette Blanche. Six pairs of eyes tracked the ecru leather boots and the matching pants and jacket as the woman approached the front. There was not a red hair out of place. Even if the badges on the Commander's chest hadn't marked her rank, the calculation behind her blue eyes and the prowess of her stance would do it. She was power; she was their law. Kat could barely breathe whenever the woman was in the room.

The door slid shut behind them, and the cadets stood there, silent, awaiting instruction.

"Good morning, cadets," the Commander began, eyes marking each of them in turn.

"As dictated under statute 4A of the Academy bylaws, with respect to the Raider Program of the AMG, the Allies of the Mangorian Galaxy, I have recommended your squadrons for the following mission." The Commander turned to the holoblock behind her, drawing up the representation of a foreign star system. "At 03:56 hours the previous morning, our roaming, military-grade sensors detected spikes of radiation just outside the Anova star system. The spikes encircle what appears to be a rogue asteroid with elevated levels of magnetism from the nearby Argursian toroidal belt. As part of your assignment, your squadrons have each been given coordinates to one of these activity points. At this point, it's unclear whether the recent fluctuation in radiation is organic, or due to its proximity to the asteroid, but we suspect dark radiation..."

Kat blinked. She'd have to double-check on a star map, but if she was correct, the asteroid's star system was beyond the usual range given for any Academy-level mission.

"Your mission is to investigate the radiation, collecting enough samples to help identify any possible sources that fall within range."

She knew what was coming next...

"You will be making the jump through hyperspace at galactic marker MGIII-2," The Commander confirmed.

Kat's heart stuttered. A hyperjump.

Forcing herself to refocus beyond her fluttering heart and the looming jump tomorrow, Kat tried to grapple with the information their Commander presented in their briefing.

"As these rays are highly charged and extremely dangerous, there will be a time allowance of twenty-four hours to support the shields on your spacecrafts. We expect you out of there before then. Any questions?"

Of course, no one had any. And even if they had, they wouldn't have voiced them. Not with the other squadrons in the room. "Academy Secretary Nolan will go over the details. Good luck cadets." The Commander took her leave.

Quadrant III. The galactic marker for the hyperjump had confirmed it. They would indeed be traversing their galaxy well beyond the usual mission range. This explained why the Academy's top cadets had been enlisted for an otherwise standard emissions raid—all the signs pointed towards dark rays, the quadrant was riddled with it, they just needed to confirm its presence.

Nolan waited until the door had closed behind the Commander before addressing them.

"Raid files for each of your squadrons have been added to the hub. Please submit your squadron list for approval by 14:00 hours. Cadet health surveys will be expected by 21:00 hours with a full mission report by no later than thirty-six hours following mission completion. You will be notified when your ship has been assigned and scheduled for departure. You are dismissed."

The Commander's secretary finished their detailing and followed them out. He didn't bother glancing their way as he headed for the stairway and back up to the Command wing, to do whatever it was he did for the Commander with the rest of his time.

For a few moments, no one spoke as they stood there. Processing. Then Zane broke away from the group. "We'll see you guys out there." He and Neha turned away.

"Tomorrow should be fun," Ciela said, shooting her and Lee an attempt at a hopeful grin, although the look came off somewhat off-kilter with her signature wide, non-blinking eyes.

"Or something," Kat murmured, as Whistler also turned towards them.

"Yo—nice win on the Rounds yesterday." And with a wave, he and Ciela also headed off.

"Later," Lee called as Kat shrugged off the compliment. He nudged her shoulder. "It *was* a nice win yesterday," he said, echoing Whistler.

If he was aware she was on edge, he didn't let on, giving her space to sort out the thoughts in her head as they made their way back down through the Heptagon.

Sometimes she thought he knew her better than she did.

CHAPTER 5: LEE

THE EVENING after getting called in for their briefing, Lee and Kat sat huddled around one of the cafe-style tables near Kat's favorite juice bar. They had their personal holoblocks out on the table and open to half a dozen holograms each as they combed through the raid files once more in preparation for tomorrow.

Well, Lee was combing through raid files. Kat, it seemed, had given up a while ago on the notion of gleaning anything more from the pages of reports that had been added to the hub for them. Instead, she sat shooting cran-nuts into his plastic cup from the opposite side of the table.

They'd gotten their ship assignment earlier that afternoon and would be taking out one of the skimmers alongside the other two squadrons at 08:00 hours the following morning.

He raised his eyebrows in mild amusement as another cran-nut arched through the air, before plunking down into his cup. He knew he ought to have been suspicious earlier when she had selected the healthy option from the vending machines. Eyeing the cup dubiously, the handful of cran-nuts now floating among the icy dregs of his drink, he pushed it to the side.

The raid files included all the usual suspects, a star map of the distant system and coordinates, cadet health surveys, and a copy of the brief detailing and roaming sensor report. But what had kept drawing his eyes back, was the quadrant flyover, and more specifically, its statistics.

"What do you think is out there?" He asked aloud. Granted, their raid coordinates for tomorrow were only borderline Quadrant III, but there was so little known about that third quadrant. The star systems and the radiation levels, they knew. The quadrant itself would be devoid of life thanks to the dark radiation present. But as to its former ecosystems and its other life forms—all of that was unknown. The majority lay untouched and forgotten by the rest of the galaxy.

"What's out where? In Quadrant III?" She flicked her eyes up thoughtfully, the pale grey catching some of the white light from the holograms. "Asteroids. Radiation. Verinity. Perhaps if we are lucky... a planet made entirely of brownies..." Mischief danced in her eyes. Lee wished he had his own package of cran-nuts just so he could sprinkle them back over her right now.

He'd walked right into that one. But it was nice to see her spirits up again, as she'd been somewhat subdued all day. "I suppose we'll find out tomorrow."

Was that what awaited their quadrant, too? Aside from the brownie planet. Given the patterns for which they'd identified the dark radiation recently, they still had time before the threat was imminent. But was that the only solution, to watch and wait for it to come upon them? Under the AMG's Preservation Initiative, there were hundreds of defense projects being funded to shield and deflect against the dark rays. But even with the advancements in energy tech to fuel them, the funds being allocated in that direction, they were no closer to finding a more permanent solution. And what if they didn't find a viable solution in time, what then? Unless the plan was for them all to jump ship and flee to a whole other galaxy—at least they'd be fleeing with energy efficiency. But would it be any better out there?

He pictured dwarf planet Kafron again, the haggard-looking creature who'd looked to be just a few days shy of joining his desiccated friend. They still knew so little about the dark rays plaguing them.

He and Kat had always planned to end up somewhere distant and exotic after Placement, exploring star systems on the outer reaches of their galaxy. The prospect of picking up his life didn't scare him. But what about those who lived outside raider constraints? Those whose day-to-day wasn't based around planning the next errantly dangerous mission. Those like Tonya?

He was so wrapped up in the goings-on of the Academy, that he rarely thought about life outside of here. But his mom's whole world revolved around their home star system. Around Lee. If Tonya only knew where he was assigned to fly in the morning...

Lee picked up his cup, absentmindedly swirling the bits of ice and cran-nuts around.

They had commandeered the table hours ago, but the Hideaway had only begun to empty in the last hour or so, the cadets drifting off to whatever evening activities and shenanigans occupied their time. Lee knew where he would have been: the wind tunnels. He and Kat had been planning to surf with a couple of the other Gammas, a favorite pastime of theirs, before tomorrow's mission had taken over their night.

A couple of cadets, probably in their IR or VL years, sat at the next table over, swigging down murky purple juices. One of them smiled tentatively when she caught Lee looking her way. Her friend looked over too, calling out a hasty congratulations when she noticed it was Kat sitting across from them. But Kat didn't seem to hear them. Having finally run out of cran-nuts, she had turned her attention back to the holograms before her.

He didn't know what was stressing her more, the thing with the General and their upcoming hyperjump, or whatever had gone down with Zane. They'd been lucky enough to evade the Gamma for most of the day. Gamma and *co-squadron*, he supposed, as they had technically been called to the same mission. Although even thinking about sharing the raid made his veins spark with ferocity.

Lee waved the cadets off gently with a couple of fingers, pushing the flyover quadrant report aside to go over the brief again until it was burned into his brain. Of course, the cadets would have been there to witness the Gammas compete in the Laser Rounds. Everyone at the Academy had been there.

Had anyone else noted the presence of the AMG's Commanding General, or had they all been too distracted by the event before them? Surely if they had, word would have circulated.

Maybe it was all just a coincidence with General Narron's visit, the timing of the raid, everything. The AMG would have needed explicit permission from Commander Blanche to assign Academy raiders to a mission of this range. But the General could have done that through the usual communication channels...

Lee cleared his throat to run this by Kat.

She ignored the sound. Her eyes hadn't lifted from the hologram before her, but her fingertips had curled, nails digging into the coated metal table.

Lee peered around the near-deserted Hideaway. He didn't have to look far. Zane stood at the railing in the center of the room, by the opening that looked down on the Canteen a level below. He stood beside a female cadet—and it wasn't Neha.

As Zane pushed away from the railing, his eyes met Lee's, a cool smirk grazing his lips. He and the female cadet stopped a few strides shy of their table. The female, short and younger, looked bored.

Lee didn't have to steer his gaze away from Zane to know that Kat was now sitting ramrod straight; even her ponytail looked taut as Zane turned his smirk on her, instead.

"Neha and I finished our preparation hours ago." Zane flicked his eyes from Kat to Lee. "Thought I'd go hit up, I don't know—the *Lightning Track* before calling it a night."

"Good for you," Lee said coolly, rotating his wrist. He didn't bother to volunteer anything else, and Zane didn't linger.

Without losing the smirk, Zane slipped an arm around the female at his side, and they slunk off.

"Should I even ask what he did that's bothering you?" Lee asked once Zane was out of sight. "Like, am I cool to talk crap on him again...?"

Kat hadn't wanted to talk about it last night, and after the Commander's little surprise this morning with the briefing, he was sure nothing had changed. But he tried again, anyway.

Except Kat didn't crack a smile like he'd hoped. She just looked sad.

"He didn't *do* anything." She sighed. "Just leave it, okay Lee? I will deal with it."

Pain flared in her eyes as Kat dipped them back to the hologram she'd been staring at. She flexed her fingers before letting them fall back down to the table. Apparently, dealing with it meant ignoring the situation completely. But if he could go back to loathing Zane in peace...

"Fine by me," Lee said, kicking back in his chair once more. But he wasn't about to back down. Not entirely. Not after he'd seen the flashes of the emotion she'd been unable to shield. "But, I mean, I don't think it would hurt if we completely showed their squadron up tomorrow."

His comment had the effect he'd hoped.

This time when her eyes flickered away from her holoblock, there was a little bit of that spark in her eyes, some of that mischief he was used to. "Our list was approved, right? Let's go over our cadet roster again. Who do we have?"

"We've got our Xs, Nikola and Rian," Lee said, Kat nodding along. "Our Ultra, Dax—" Lee chuckled as Kat wrinkled her nose a little. "He's good when he wants to be." When he wasn't blabbing his mouth off. "And then Levy."

Kat resumed her nodding again, seeming to be keeping a carefully straight face. Levy was their wildcard. And a VL. That had been his suggestion. While all cadets in their VL year or higher were permitted out on raids, they were novices and typically reserved for basic missions.

From what they'd gathered from talk in the Heptagon, both Zane and Whistler's squadrons were bringing mostly X-level cadets for this raid; Whistler and Ciela had selected an Ultra. But neither were bringing along any VLs. For Zane, that was not unexpected, everything was about status to him. But where Whistler had also recruited up, perhaps he and Kat weren't the only ones overthinking tomorrow's mission. Maybe word of the General's visit had spread after all.

True to form, Lee and Kat had made sure to add both an Ultra and a VL to their roster; they'd show the others everything wasn't about appearances. It was a step up from their usual selection method of throwing darts and accepting the first available cadets. But there was something to be said about mixing things up.

Both Nikola and Rian were quick on their feet, and more than adept with the spacecraft tech. Dax, even with his loud mouth, could put his head down and produce results. And Levy—she may be young, but he'd noted time and time again, throughout the term, the insights she brought to light, and the focus she carried to every theoretical scenario. Let everyone make what they wanted of their selection. This wouldn't be the first time they pulled a 180 on everyone.

Who knows, maybe having someone impressionable would be an asset for them out there.

Their lists had been approved, and their cadets notified. Now all they really had left was to get through tomorrow. He was decently pleased with the team they'd pulled together.

They'd spoken with Whistler and Ciela that afternoon to compare coordinates. The squadron would be working some couple hundred kilometers from them. It wasn't exactly prime leap frog distance, but they'd have their radios. Neither had spoken with Zane and Neha, but Lee would wager on them also working at a similar distance.

Kat had tucked her feet up under her legs, having gone back to staring down at nothing, but at least she no longer looked like she would shred through the table.

"You sure you are up for this tomorrow?" Lee asked softly.

"I'm always up for a raid." And there was no hesitation, even if her eyes were beginning to drift back towards the railing in the middle of the Hideaway.

"We'll be on separate ships, working at different coordinates, and barely communicating on the same radio frequency," he said. And he knew why he said it. For her, of course. "But being out there together, in the same middle-of-nowhere, *hole-of-nebula* star system they are dumping us into tomorrow... it may even be too much for me. It'll definitely be too close to contain his cocky ass."

Kat laughed. "You know, Zane called you pretty boy, earlier."

"Now he's in for it." Lee again carefully watched as she tipped her head back a little, narrow shoulders rippling as she laughed. "But seriously. If you want to hang back, take it easy. I don't mind taking point on this one. It's not like any huge brawls will be breaking out between ships..."

He let some mischievous light into his eyes, as he entertained the possibility for a moment. The chaos of facing off with Zane again, only with spaceships this time...

Kat was grinning broadly when he met her gaze. "I'll let you know, Waters. But that has never really been my style."

"Well, the offer always stands." Sitting back, Lee waved a hand, clearing the remaining holograms. "I say we call it a night, actually get a good night's sleep for once."

"*Void* knows we could use it." Clearing her own holoblock, she stood, rocking between toe and heel.

He did the same when he stood up to get the blood flowing again. They must have been sitting hunched over that table for hours with how his feet now tingled. He waited while she pulled the band from her ponytail, running a couple of sweeping hands through it, her long vanilla hair cascading down behind her. The end of the day. The only time he ever saw her slow down.

"So an asteroid tomorrow, huh?" Lee asked as Kat grabbed her holoblock, and they started walking back up through the ship.

"I mean, it's no dwarf planet Kafron." Kat grinned. They took their time climbing the winding staircases of the Heptagon, lingering when they got to the end of the upper skywalk.

A lot was riding on the raid tomorrow. A lot of pressure for results. And yet, he felt oddly okay with it all. Lee and Kat—Defenders of Quadrant III. Together, they could conquer almost anything.

They parted ways, Kat going to the right. Lee to the left. He turned back to bid her goodnight, but Kat had already disappeared around the bend.

CHAPTER 6: KAT

KAT COULDN'T sleep that night.

She had intended to, Lee's notion of getting a full night's rest sounding so wonderful and all.

Until her portal door slid shut. And the thoughts their conversations that evening had stirred up began swirling. How she had let things fall apart with Zane, and inadvertently dragged Lee into it without his knowing. How she was terrified of something like that ever happening with Lee. She couldn't lose him. She wouldn't let herself lose him, no matter the costs...

Then there was the revelation of another potential threat to their galaxy awaiting them in Quadrant III. Not to mention the jump to hyperspace. They'd start out towards her doom in roughly—she checked her hyperband—eleven hours.

She'd shed her all-terrain suit for a pair of cotton shorts and a T-shirt, but that was the most she bothered to pretend she'd be sleeping that night.

She wasn't about to smooth anything over with Zane. And dwelling on the hyperjump wouldn't help her. But as to Lee and the mystery with Quadrant III, the dark radiation that potentially awaited them tomorrow... Maybe she could help them both.

Shoving the piles of clothing and juice cups from her desk and onto the floor, she cleared a space. Then, plopping her holoblock right down in the middle, she got to work.

There wasn't all that much to find, at least with what was accessible to the public. The AMG's raider files would probably have a little more, but as mere Academy cadets, they wouldn't have access to the majority of those files. It was nearing 05:00 hours when she finally decided she would allow herself a few minutes to try and get some sleep.

She awoke what felt like seconds later to a message from Lee.

Lee: grabbing drinks at the canteen. see u soon.

With a groan, Kat sat up, pulling her all-terrain suit back on. She really needed to start getting some sleep again soon. She vowed she would figure things out with all the men in her life by the next time they were back at the Academy. *Boys.* She corrected herself. There were no men in her social circle. Although with Lee's offer last night, to run point and give her space to sort out all the mess with Zane... she appreciated him more than he would ever know.

Lee was waiting for her along the central skywalk, a skinny aluminum can in each hand, his smile fading as she drew close.

"*Void*, Kat. Did you sleep at all?"

Kat extended a hand in response, accepting the power drink Lee offered her. She was aware of how bad she looked. She had avoided glancing in a mirror this morning for that very reason. And even then, she had still caught a hint of her red-rimmed eyes and the dark circles underneath them from the reflection in one of the stairway windows on her way down through the Heptagon.

She popped open her power drink with a soft *chink*, Lee following suit a couple of seconds after.

She tried her best to rein in her distaste for the stuff as she drank it down. It wasn't that they tasted all that bad, equal parts nutrition and caffeine, they just felt like empty calories. It was a principle thing. But they had become a part of their little pre-raid ritual to help with the nerves.

"I did a little research into Quadrant III," she said when she'd finished a good portion of her drink.

Lee's eyes widened in surprise. Whatever he'd expected her to say, it wasn't that. "And?"

Kat shrugged. "Let's just say, any public operations out to the quadrant were abandoned a century ago."

"I see." Lee tipped his can, studying the liquid inside. Kat could picture his thoughts swirling along with the murky liquid within. From what she'd been able to gauge, no one had been sent out there in close to a hundred years... at least no one reported in the common records. And yet here they were.

But they could get into that later. There were more pressing things at hand.

Beyond the skywalk, the main hangar was a bustling hot-spot. Three spacecrafts were going out this morning. Dock workers and systems crew-members alike darted between the skimmers, which had been brought forward to hover on their landing gear just inside the hangar doors.

She wasn't surprised to spot Whistler underneath one of the skimmers, personally overseeing the preparation of his spacecraft. Both his parents were mechanics. Ciela would likely be along soon, if she wasn't already in there. Although she was a little surprised she hadn't run into—

"You look like shit."

Glaring, Kat looked up to see Zane and Neha stop midway through the skywalk. Neha was straight-faced as she glanced right past them, anxious to get to her spacecraft.

Zane narrowed his dark eyes. And for the few seconds they looked at each other, Kat thought she glimpsed a hint of concern there, and something that could resemble sorrow.

Schooling the flutter of surprise, Kat looked away. She could take care of herself. "Shit who is going to show your ass up this afternoon. We'll see you guys out there."

Zane shrugged off the obvious dismissal, and Kat pretended not to notice the look he shot Lee. The obvious implied meanings of *you sure you've got her?* But then Zane and Neha walked away.

Lee knew better than to question her current mental health or where her head was at. Instead, they downed the rest of their drinks in stilted silence, before heading in to join the thrall.

"I'll check on the lineup," Lee murmured, peeling off as they entered the hangar.

"Meet you on the skimmer."

It would be a race with all three squadrons going out today. Each squadron wanted to be the first one out there to start cracking down on the radiation and reporting back to Command.

"Whistler." Kat nodded towards the Gamma squadron lead parked just inside the loading ramp as she passed. He lay on his stomach with his tools in hand while he adjusted something with the engine.

"Sup." Whistler glanced briefly her way, before turning back to the systems crew beside him. "The compression ratio with the hyperdrive is loose. Let's make sure we are tightening that. Don't want to go too hard on Lyra..."

Whistler and Ciela would have the advantage today. At least in reaching their coordinates first. Once they were all out there, however, then it would be fair game.

Like Whistler and Ciela's skimmer, her and Lee's spacecraft was sleek and minimal, built for speed rather than comfort. They could make the route in a fraction of the time this way. This also meant they'd be making the jump that much sooner as well.

Edging around their own mechanics, Kat did a quick walk-through of the ship. It was an extension of the Academy with its eggshell panels and bright polished surfaces. The holotech system for the observation deck was mounted along the port wall, with everything up to code. The mini-fridge was stocked.

Emergency supplies and extra bedrolls were packed away in the cabinets on the starboard wall with the RIM vehicles. Two sets of bunks had been squeezed into the tiny dorm in the back by the loading ramp; that would be fun. At least it was only for one night. They would be a little cramped, especially at maximum occupancy, but they would make it work. They'd done it before.

She was checking on their shields and energy levels up in the cockpit when Lee joined up with her.

"We got our call number—we'll be second. Whistler's going out ahead of us."

No surprise there. Plus, it could have been worse.

Nodding, Kat ran her fingers lightly along the controls. This would be the spacecraft carrying them through space-folding distances at mind-numbing speeds. She'd only made the jump to hyperspace two other times in her Academy years. Once during flight training; a mandatory pass at the end of their IR year before being permitted on raids. Then again a couple of years later, for the odd mission assignment to the neighboring quadrant. Both times she had managed to hang on to consciousness, but she had come within breaths of insanity. The very essence of who she was screaming as the squeezing began. The deafness in her ears. Her life spiraling out of her hands once again... She let her fingers slide off the controls, wiping her sweaty palms against her legs. They could do this. *She* could do this. Nothing was being stripped away from her this time. She was in control.

Swallowing, she turned away to find Lee leaning against the port wall of the cockpit. But he wasn't watching her. Instead, he was studying the control system with interest. He directed his chin to the dashboard behind her. "I was looking into the updates to the hyper-flight control system for this latest skimmer line. One of the residual effects."

"Oh yeah?"

"May I?" Pushing off the wall, Lee brushed past. She caught a waft of teakwood and cedar, like the musky planter boxes she might find down in the greenhouses.

"During the synchronization process, they re-wired the system to account for the changes." He touched a finger to the smooth surface of the control panel, letting it slide to one of the controls near where she had laid her own finger seconds before. "But what they didn't anticipate was the interactions it would have on the acceleration compensator. Supposedly it acts like a second damper." He let his hand fall, tucking it into the pocket of his dark suit. "Some of the reviews say that when they took it out for trials, the jump to hyperspeed, it only felt like they were pulling a couple G's." Hand still tucked into his pocket, Lee turned, strolling back past her. She stared after him in amazement.

"Hey Lee—"

"Yeah?" He paused, looking back.

"Thanks."

"I don't know what you're talking about." Smiling slightly to himself, he continued his stroll the short length of the ship, over to where the mechanics were beginning to close everything up.

A second damper, huh... She could get on board with that.

The systems crew finished up with their inspection a few minutes later, walking them through everything before bidding them a safe voyage. All that awaited them now was the arrival of their cadets and the go-ahead from the aviation operator.

Taking up a spot near the mini-fridge, Kat gave herself a couple of minutes to breathe while Lee skipped through some anthems, building them a raid playlist.

"So you really were up researching our third quadrant last night?" Lee asked, turning the volume up a little as he stepped back from the holotech's audio connection. "I understand why you didn't get much sleep."

Kat shrugged, resting her elbows back on the counter behind her. "I wanted to know if that brownie planet was actually out there... And I was hoping there'd be something to tie in with our mission today." Other than the sheer amount of sampling raids they'd been on lately and today's space jump hiccup, their Gamma year was turning out exactly as affadelic and amazing as she'd always imagined.

Were they really so lucky as to do this, just her and Lee, for the rest of their lives?

"What was the verdict?" Lee asked, dragging his fingers along the crown of his head, re-tousling his brown hair. Her favorite of his freckles caught the light.

"I really couldn't find all that much. There have been reconnaissance missions in the past to see how long our shields could survive out there. And there were some commissioned projects in the late century before ours where they went in deep and actually attempted to harness the dark radiation. But then nothing; operations of both of those natures just ceased. Like they decided the risk was too great or something."

"What risk was too great?"

Kat flipped her head around, tracking the tenor voice to the golden-brown-haired cadet coming up the loading ramp.

Nikola.

The cadet wore his signature black rectangle-framed glasses, which if Kat recalled properly, weren't actually for sight, but to protect against certain molecular compounds found in the air. If met directly, the compounds could apparently 'dull his eyes' full potential'. Or something to that nature.

"The risk of sending cadets out to highly radioactive areas for extended periods of time," Lee lied smoothly. The kind of debate the kid might expect of his squadron leads before a big raid. No need to inadvertently throw the rest of the squadron into a panic right before a mission.

"Oh, sure." Nikola seemed content with that explanation, turning to check out the rest of their ship.

Lee caught her eye, shooting her a wry little grin. *I've got you.*

Dax showed up next, sweeping his hair from his eyes as he stopped beside Lee, making some too-honest joke about being picked for all the tame raids. They were still two cadets short, and already the cabin was feeling constricting. Kat was this close to getting the Ultra a hair tie as he swept his shaggy waves from his eyes for the fifth time.

Kat found herself almost hoping Levy would be late. But their VL strode up the loading ramp, prompt and polite, with eyes sparkling eagerly in the skimmer's bright overhead lights. They were roughly the same height, although Levy seemed to shy away from her gaze. Kat had to remind herself that she was reading too much into it when Lee struck up a conversation with the girl. After all, it was either chat with Levy or entertain Dax.

Rian joined them last, looking put-together as usual with her straight hair tied back behind her head in a no-nonsense knot. Kat was happy to pawn Dax off to her while she familiarized herself with the various tech mounted along the observation deck one more time.

But annoyances aside, there was an excited energy in their cabin. They didn't get opportunities to venture this far out from their quadrant all that often.

They got their five-minute warning, ushering everyone to find their seats. A set of three lined either wall outside the cockpit.

As their cadets strapped into their harnesses, she and Lee gave them a brief overview of their mission this morning.

"You should have all received the mission assignment yesterday." Kat paused, waiting for nods before moving on. "Good. Then you will know that the AMG has tasked us with the investigation of dark radiation. I think it goes without saying, but if it's out there, we intend to find it."

And despite the routine nature of the rundown, Levy had sat up straight, at the edge of her seat, nodding along to their instruction with bright eyes. Was the girl always this eager?

Kat stopped caring as Lee crossed his arms over his chest, the squadron lead incarnate. "I'd add, as a conscious reminder, that there will be two other squadrons out there with us today." And he let a hint of menace creep into his words at the end there, the implication only too clear as he met each of their stares. *Don't even think of letting us down.*

When he looked back over at Kat to see if she had anything to add, she shook her head, her insides sparkling with wicked delight. "I think that about covers it."

He cleared his throat. "Alright then. Let's go kick some asteroids."

Kat and Lee slipped up to the cockpit. They were strapping into their own harnesses when operations radioed in. Their ship was up to blitz. Dawning his headset, Lee answered the call. "Roger that, Skimmer A-02 moving into position."

He started the engine as Kat raised the loading ramp and landing gear. Headset still in her hands, she turned to Lee. "I didn't think you had it in you back there."

He shrugged. "I told you I'd take point. Besides—a little intimidation never hurt anyone."

"You never cease to amaze." Grinning, Kat slid her headset over her ears. And for a moment they were IRs in their third year again. A Gamma breathing down their necks as they sat in the cockpit, about to pilot a spacecraft for the very first time.

"Hey Lee," Kat called out, her voice ringing clearly through their headsets, "How do you get to Gemini?"

She didn't need to look over at him, didn't need to meet his gaze or see the slash of his smile to know he remembered those exact moments she was remembering. The words he had blurted out in a panic all those years ago. The nearly-flopped piloting test. And her auto-response to rescue him, her forever co-pilot. The words they repeated with every single flight afterward.

"Go for 30, Kat."

It took them a couple of hours at hyperspeed, even with the skimmer, to reach the galactic marker for their hyperjump. A couple of hours of dread sloshing about Kat's stomach as she tried to mentally prepare as best she could for those torturous few moments...

She hated the squeezing that accompanied the jump, and the loss of control. That feeling like everything she knew and everything she was, was about to be sucked away from her.

Conversation had been somewhat stilted. But between Dax's endless stream of commentary and Levy's occasional questions, the younger cadets had more than compensated for Kat's lack of input. That, and Lee's carefully curated playlist. Kat had been able to lose herself a little in the guitar melodies of the art rock. And critiquing them.

"This song has legit been ending for seven minutes."

"It's a drum solo. It's telling a story," Lee said.

"What is it saying, then?" Kat swiveled in her chair, waiting.

"It's saying, that it is not for the uneducated."

"You have no idea," she accused.

"I don't know, I think I'm with Lee," Dax chirped up from the cabin behind them. "It's a solo of defense and passion..."

Kat lost track of Dax's explanations as a marker appeared on the radar, their checkpoint too quickly approaching.

"You still with me, Hanneman?" Lee's voice cut through the headset again.

Kat swallowed. Her head was starting to spin.

"Preparing to make the jump," Lee called out again. Kat could only watch as the cadence played out. A beautiful symphony of buttons and switches, while Lee prepped the systems' hyperdrive.

"We're jumping in three. Two. One..."

Lee calibrated the navigational computations. The last motion as they switched into hyperdrive. It felt like they were moving in slow motion as the ship accelerated—her heart was a distant echo in her head as she felt the familiar squeezing and popping in her ears. And yet—lost as she was, she was still able to retain some consciousness as her eyes clung to the control panel on the dashboard like she could see that second damper in motion—her lifeline.

Everything around her flashed brightly.

And then it went back to normal again, her senses returning to her as her heart resumed its normal volume. They had done it. They were through.

She let out a breathy laugh, her tear ducts working on overdrive as she blinked back the dryness there. She could hear the gasping breaths behind her, followed by a low whistle. "Alright!" Dax was cheering.

And Kat couldn't help the slight smile that escaped her. They were through, it was behind them for now.

When she could master herself enough to look over, Lee met her gaze, raising his brows a little. *You okay?*

Kat gave him a little nod, and then that slight smile again from before, which Lee returned. She hadn't noticed if Lee had adjusted the music, or turned it down for the jump at all. But she was all too aware when she heard Dax's overloud voice singing along from the cabin behind. She bobbed her head along just a little.

She gave herself a few minutes to adjust and regain full control of her body. When she was sure her legs could carry her weight, she rose to her feet to check on the cadets in the back and grab the sedatives. Taking three of the berry-colored pills, she split them in half, passing them around the group.

She wasn't surprised to find Dax in full spirits, what with the bawdy singing that'd been floating up to the cockpit. He swallowed his sedative immediately, chasing it down with a large gulp of water. Rian held her usual composure, taking it evenly while Nikola rambled off some random study involving the sedatives, that she didn't care to imbue into her brain at the moment. Levy, however, appeared a little shaken. Some of the eagerness from before had faded.

"Not so bad, huh?" Kat said, reining in her own experience of the last few minutes as she forced some brightness into her voice. "Here, take this. It will moderate your heartbeat and prevent arrhythmia. The levels tend to rise and then slow dramatically with a jump like that."

"Oh. Thanks." Levy accepted the sedative and water bottle Kat handed her way. Of course, having an immediate task to fulfill helped moderate the emotional strain. She assigned Levy the collection of plastic once the other cadets had finished with their drinks.

Kat returned to the front. Resting a hand against the headrest of her seat, she handed Lee a bottle of water with one of the sedatives. "Bottoms up."

Screwing the lid back onto her bottle, she picked up her headset but didn't slide it back over her ears. "Sorry I was no help back there." Her inability to master herself was unacceptable. And the way her body shut down, every time, after all these years...

She kept her gaze locked straight ahead of her as she replaced her headset, sliding back into her seat.

But Lee's voice came from beside her instead of through the headset, as he tipped it down. "Hey, we did it though. We made it through. You did hyperspace, Kat."

"Yeah," she murmured. "We did." And now wasn't the time to dwell on it. Or think on the return flight. According to their calculations, they had a little over an hour before they would reach their coordinates. She replaced her headset, sinking into the gentle thrum of the spacecraft.

They were within range when Lee fired up the reverse thrusters, dropping the speed of their skimmer down to a low cruise. He was frowning as he stared down at the radar on the dash between them. "That's odd."

"What's up, errant meteoroid?" She leaned in, hands already going to the controls as she scanned for some potential obstacle in their path. Their radiation shields could handle the smaller debris, but anything of sizeable dimensions...

"Not a meteoroid," Lee said quickly, eyes flickering between radar and windshield. "But according to the report, given the elevated levels of magnetism the sensors picked up, there should be an asteroid straight ahead."

Tearing her eyes from the system on the dash, Kat squinted off into the distance. There were bits of rock and dust spaced here and there. But nothing directly in line with the ship. And definitely nothing large enough to be an asteroid. "It's got to be a mistake. We would see it by now."

Lee just shook his head. Somehow, she had a feeling Lee wasn't about to dismiss the asteroid that easily.

And then the dashboard stuttered, the lights flickering on and off as the system glitched. It was only for a couple of seconds, the spacecraft seeming to stall before the system came back on again.

"Switching over to manual," Lee muttered, one hand gripping the controls while the other switched off autopilot. Kat gripped the arms of her seat, standing by in case something else went out next.

The lights on the dash flickered a couple more times, the spacecraft oscillating a little as Lee completed a recalibration effort, but it was more or less a smooth transition.

"We are coming up on coordinates." Lee coaxed the spacecraft, increasing the thrusters until it came to a stop. "Aaaaand we're here." He killed the engines.

Kat dropped their chief shield into place, waiting while it locked into place. "Counting down from 24:00:00."

And for a few seconds afterward, everything was still as they gazed out into nothingness.

A couple of their cadets had come up to peer out of the front windshield and into the barren space the asteroid would have occupied. "I don't see it," Dax murmured. On Dax's other side, Nikola was silent.

Then a low female voice spoke from behind them. Levy. "What happens now?"

CHAPTER 7: LEE

THE ASTEROID'S absence had thrown them. And with the system glitching... There was already more to this mission than Lee had anticipated. But the clock was running, and they had an uphill battle as it was. Asteroid or no asteroid, they had a job to do. "Let's get to know this fancy, high-grade tech of ours."

"And the asteroid?" Dax asked.

"Let me worry about that."

It wasn't exactly a solution. Not yet anyway, but it would get them moving.

"Okay, guys. You heard the man, let's get to work." Jumping to her feet, Kat whipped her head around, ponytail slicing through the air. Lee knew to duck. Dax and Nikola, however, weren't so lucky. With a hiss and a groan, the cadets followed Kat back to the main cabin. Kat spouted instructions, seamlessly taking the lead, while Lee started down the post-flight operations. "Rian—you and Dax take the sensors. Let's get a read on what levels of particles we are looking at."

"Things better be crazy out there," Dax muttered, looking away quickly when Lee caught his gaze from up in the cockpit.

81

But Lee was thinking the same thing. For all the trouble they'd gone to with a system's failure, and getting them out here, they had better find something.

"Nikola let's have you get started with one of the RIMs. Starboard Wall, fourth cabinet." The X cadet snapped into action at Kat's command, shuffling up the grated aisle with Rian and Dax. The latter took up spots facing the port wall observation deck, while Nikola went right past them to get started with one of the mod-vehicles.

"And me?" Levy asked Kat, her voice cool as ever. Despite her uncertainty upon their arrival, Levy seemed comfortable out here, as much so as any of the more seasoned cadets.

"Have you ever operated one of the mod-vehicles?" Kat asked.

"The RIMs? Only in trainings." Raiding Interstellar mod-vehicles, the standard issue AMG drones, most commonly used in the collection of hazardous or otherwise unattainable matter. Of course, the mod-vehicles had also served other, entirely unrelated purposes for Academy cadets in the past... Lee shook his head, smiling to himself as he double-checked the cabin pressure and airflow. Good times.

"The same principles apply, minus gravity. Follow Nikola's lead." Grabbing one of the RIM vehicles from the aforementioned cabinet, Levy took up a seat at the small table tucked into the wall opposite the observation deck. Setting the tech down on the table facing Nikola they drew up the mod-vehicles' holograms for programming.

Kat seemed to consider, before addressing both Nikola and Levy. "Keep them close to the ship while we check for glitching. I want to see how they hold up against the magnetism out here. Let's give them an initial range of, say, fifty meters."

"Yes ma'am," Nikola murmured, head down and cranking.

Lee made it through the post-flight systems checklist. The cabin behind him was quiet, but not in a tense way. More of a flutter of anticipation. Rian and Dax had the sensors buffering; they would have their first snapshot of the radiation levels within minutes. Opposite them, Levy and Nikola had their heads together as they went over parameters.

They were really doing this.

And now for the part he'd been putting off. Connecting to the system's transmission, Lee sent a message out to the other squadrons.

> *Skimmer A-02 has arrived at coordinates. Not reporting any visual of the rogue asteroid.*

A message came back from Whistler's ship a few minutes later.

> *Ditto.*

Zane and Neha were still en route to their coordinates and hadn't yet appeared on their radar. But they'd have the skimmers' messages waiting there for them when they arrived.

Heading back down the aisle, Lee had to squeeze past the others to reach the magnetometer on the far end of the observation deck. Kat had tucked herself atop one of the neighboring countertops while she flicked idly through their raid files.

Typing a code into the mounted tech, Lee scanned his hyperband. He took a step back, crossing his arms over his chest while he waited for the magnetometer to power up. "Nice perch."

"I thought so," Kat said.

"I appreciate you waiting on me to get started."

"Oh, I'm sorry, did you want help? I thought the asteroid was yours to worry about." Closing out the file she'd been skimming through, Kat kicked her feet out and jumped down.

Lee shot her a flat stare, but he stepped to the side to give her a clear line of vision as he began programming a template. The magnetometer would help them locate the magnetic field of the object that had been captured in the initial AMG report.

Coming out here today, he'd planned on more or less dismissing the actual asteroid. It could take its magnetism back to the toroidal belt, for all he cared, so long as they could gather their samples and sensor data. But where this one was apparently invisible... His eyes flickered back up to the front, where the ship's window opened to the vast empty space out there ahead of them. *Where are you?*

He finished setting up the template, his fingers hovering a couple mills above the keypad that would hopefully get them some answers where the magnetic field was concerned. He pursed his lips. Here goes.

Tapping that final key, Lee crossed his arms over his chest to wait.

They had rough coordinates for the magnetic field from the AMG report. But without a visual, they'd be relying on the magnetism readings to help them create that image.

They were waiting for the magnetometer's results when the sensor data came in.

"Um, guys, you might want to see this," Dax said. Lee caught Kat's eye, before taking the couple of steps up the aisle to the Ultra cadet. They'd heard that one before.

Lee stared back at the too-flat graphic data the sensors were collecting. There were minor dips and hills, some variance in the wavelengths and amplitudes of the energy waves coming in, but overall the landscape was far too uniform.

"And this is everything?" He shook his head. The radiation levels were nowhere near the reported spikes from the AMG's sensors.

Then a series of resonant beeps announced the magnetometer's initial results. "Here we go," Lee breathed, steeling himself as he rejoined Kat.

He did a double-take when he saw the readings the magnetometer tech had spit out. With its scattered crux points and sporadic interactions with the axis, it looked like a first-year Micro cadet had written the program.

"I'm going to check the template and run it again."

Kat frowned, but didn't say anything as they adjusted the programming.

A few minutes later, the follow-up results from the magnetometers came in.

They were as nonsensical and all over the place as the ones before. Lee ran a hand through his hair, bracing it on his scalp while Kat leaned in to get a better look at the results.

"Something is definitely screwing with the tech," she concluded.

"Probably the same thing that was screwing with the ship." Lee ran his hand through his hair again, glancing from the magnetometer's latest haywire results to the sensors with their consistent waves rolling through. He didn't know yet what to make of the lack of radiation spikes, nor the elevated magnetism. Or if dark radiation was even at play. But he was now convinced they had everything to do with whatever was going on with that magnetic field.

But if it wasn't an asteroid, then *what-in-the-void* was out there?

Despite his convictions and the confident front he and Kat had presented thus far, nothing about this raid was going according to plan.

He didn't dare take the ship in deeper, not with the risk of getting stranded out here. Even if one of the other squadrons miraculously managed to pull them out, they'd never live it down. And with their magnetometers rendered useless, their only options for gleaning anything from the former radiation disturbances lay in their sensor tech and the RIM vehicles.

The sensors appeared to be entirely unaffected by whatever strong forces were messing with their ship and the magnetometer tech. However, there was also nothing of interest to note from them, either. The radiation landscape was dormant. They took it in turns, monitoring the sensors, and even expanded the scope to the point that they were now recording everything within a hundred kilometers' range—any further, and they'd be capturing rays bouncing off the other squadrons' ships. But the likelihood of anything exciting occurring out there seemed less and less likely as the afternoon wore on.

Their RIMs' collection of space debris, on the other hand, was the one good thing to come out of the day. While the vehicle communication appeared to lag the further out the vehicles went, they were able to thoroughly canvas at close range. And as it turned out, Levy was pretty good with her hands. Between her and Nikola, they'd already gone through a good third of their storage materials, and expanded the RIMs' initial ranges thrice already. And while they operated the mod-vehicles, the rest of them assisted in securing and labeling the radioactive debris the RIMs brought back to the hatches. Assuming those spikes of radiation had actually occurred out here, they'd find evidence recorded on their sample matter.

Late afternoon faded into early evening. Lee waited until Levy and Nikola had returned the RIMs with their latest batches, before pushing his way over to join them.

"Hey guys, go ahead and power down. Get some food, and I'll grab someone to switch you out."

Cutting a quick grin to Levy and the hint of pride grazing her lavender cheeks, Lee slipped back up the grated aisle to grab a quick meal for himself. Kat again sat perched atop the counters. "Spinach and rice, or white bean?" she asked, drinking from her own nutritionally balanced and optimal caloric food pocket.

Lee wrinkled his nose. Raid food. "Is that all that's left?"

"Cadets get first dibs on the stroganoff meals."

"Generous of you." He eyed her own white bean food pocket.

Kat shrugged, as much concern as she'd let show. "It's been a long day."

As he went to reach for the handle, Kat slung a leg over the mini-fridge, holding it closed with the heel of her boot. "Remember, spinach or white bean."

Lee's eyes narrowed. *And you're going to enforce this?*

Kat simply raised her eyebrows. *Try me.*

With a huff, Lee let his hand drop. "I promise."

Satisfied, Kat slid clear of the fridge door, letting both limbs hang freely once more.

Lee relieved Dax and Rian next, taking their place before the sensors. He watched the energy waves roll across the holotech as he cracked open his white bean dinner pocket, squishing around the mush inside. At least this one had green chilis, so there would be a kick. A little one, anyway.

Kat abandoned her perch on the countertops to help pass out drinks to the cadets who'd crowded around the little table. Then she grabbed up one of the RIMs herself.

She put up a cool front and pretended not to care. But she'd always had his back. She'd do the same for her cadets—even at the expense of herself.

He watched while she powered up the mod-vehicle, rubbing her eyes with a hand, before sending the RIM vehicle out.

If Lee hadn't already known Kat was tired, he might not have been able to tell. She could push through anything; they'd done sleep-deprived all-nighters before. And maybe this seemed like a little more than a breakup or Academy stressors. But she'd been here before, she'd sort through it, right? Whatever Kat was going through was Kat's business. He wasn't about to get into it. Yet.

He was still seething from the memory of Zane this morning. Even *he* had noticed.

Kat was his best friend. If she ever did cross that edge, he'd be there for her, he'd know. He just hoped it never came to that.

"What's the verdict?" He asked, when her mod-vehicle made it back from its first outing.

Kat rolled her shoulders back, releasing a tight breath. "It gets dicey out there with the magnetism. I'm mostly worried about the vehicle cutting offline too long and facing collision and damage."

"Your call. We'll set a border limit."

Kat nodded faintly, eyes already setting on a new target. He knew that look.

While their cadets finished their food pockets, Lee began completing their health surveys. The 21:00-hour deadline would be upon them before long. "Anyone feeling nauseous?" He asked the cabin at large.

"I will if I have to eat another one of these," Dax joked, squeezing the rest of his dinner pocket into his mouth with an exaggerated grimace.

Lee raised his brows. His stroganoff. But then Nikola started off on a long and enthusiastic tangent about how the dinner-pockets were perfectly formulated to provide maximum nutrient combinations to avoid bloating or excessive hunger, and Lee turned his full attention back to the cadet health surveys.

They swapped Kat out after the other cadets had finished with their dinner, tasking Dax and Rian with the RIMs, while he and Kat drafted a quick update for the other squadrons. There wasn't much to report. And they had very low expectations of hearing back anything of value. But they sent it out anyway.

There wasn't all that much more they could do for their mission. Their best bet lay in collecting as much data as they could over the next fifteen or so hours, and hoping they'd be able to make something of it later.

Around 21:00 hours, they had each of the cadets draw straws, deciding who would get the first shift before dividing up for the night. The lucky ones were ushered off to sleep. They'd all need their stamina if they were going to keep this up into tomorrow.

"This means you as well," Lee said when he saw Kat still lingering out in the main cabin.

"I'm fine," Kat said, swaying on her feet.

He placed a hand on her arm to steady her. "I've got this." And when she opened her mouth in objection, he winked. "Go get some sleep, you really do look like shit."

Shaking her head, Kat flashed him a crude gesture. "I'll be up at two," she called behind her as she headed back to the bunks.

He was still grinning when he turned to begin the first shift.

"Down to just you and me, man," Dax joked.

Indeed.

CHAPTER 8: KAT

KAT COULD hear light snoring coming from the bunk below hers when she awoke at 01:55.

She'd been more than happy to get some shut-eye despite giving Lee a hard time, and had fallen asleep as soon as her head hit the pillow. The long nights were finally starting to weigh on her.

Even now, her eyes were still heavy with sleep. She could have closed them and slept another six hours—three times that —if it wasn't for the squadron lead still awake in that main cabin who hadn't yet had the chance to close his eyes. Lee would likely still try to protest and pretend he wasn't tired. He probably would've even taken the entire night shift himself, if she had let him.

Low voices drifted in from the main cabin, the sounds barely carrying through the door.

"...I'm glad you were able to grab some rest, it takes some getting used to. Raid sleep quarters are never the most comfortable."

It was quiet for a second, and she could hear the soft ruffle as someone stirred in their bunk. Then she heard Lee ask, "How is everything going?"

"Good—really good. I'm learning a ton." That would be Levy.

"We've assembled a really solid squadron," and Lee paused, before adding, "You're pretty good with those mod-vehicles."

"It's nothing."

"No really, you should be proud. The RIMs can be tricky to get the hang of, it takes a certain skillset and intuition. You'll have to ask Kat about them sometime, she went through this phase where she was obsessed with mastering them. She and I would race them up and down the Heptagon."

Kat wondered if Lee was smiling right now too at the memories.

"I'd been hoping I would get to work with you. You and Kat are legends. Word of your raids and your adventures started spreading when you guys were only Ultras. I mean, Kat is practically invincible, and you're..."

The girl's words trailed off. Kat could imagine the faint blush creeping along her cheeks. The pause seemed to draw on forever. She wondered what the girl had been about to say. Kat was about ready to climb down from the bunk, but then Lee laughed. "I'm sure we did our part to propagate those stories..."

When he spoke again, his voice was softer. Milder. "She really is something. Best not tell her I said so, though. It'll go to her head."

"I'll remember that."

It was quiet again for a second, and then Levy spoke again. "I think it's impressive what you are doing out here. Having the confidence to lead a raid like this..."

"What's impressive would be actually finding some answers."

"Do you still think this could be the work of dark rays?"

"I don't think I'd dare rule it out yet." And then he added, "I think much of the cosmos is still a mystery to us."

"Well, I trust you."

Lee laughed again, a soft, comfortable sound. The sound was barely discernible from the other sleep sounds and gentle thrums of the ship around them.

Kat checked her hyperband. *Void!* It was time to be up. Running a quick finger under both of her eyes to catch any loose smudges, Kat rolled to the edge of her bunk, dropping down lightly on her feet. Tapping a hand to the plated glass beside the door, she slipped through, before closing it again behind her.

The main cabin was dim; the bright overheads had been replaced by strips of low lighting that fanned out over the countertops and along the grated floor, marking the aisle. The table in the back where the pair sat was shadowed, lit only by the colorful blips coming from the observation deck's holotech.

Lee rose to his feet as Kat came up beside them.

He roved over her face with tired eyes—tired, but clear. She silently dared him to even try to take the next shift. But amusement just peppered those eyes. "I sent Rian off to sleep."

Kat nodded, eyeing Levy, who sat on the bench across from him. The girl was bright-eyed and looking much too cheerful for the *zapping* middle-of-the-night. "Anything new?" Lee would, of course, have awoken her if there was. Still, she had to ask.

But Lee shook his head.

"We kept the parameters where we'd left them," he said by way of explanation. And from the tightness in his voice, it wasn't hard to gauge just how much this was irking him.

He didn't need to walk her through the last few hours' worth of sensor readings. They'd be more of the same. But maybe with a little more nightly data behind them, they'd be able to identify some trends.

Raising a couple of fingers to his brow in salute, Lee left them, disappearing through the door to the dorm.

This left only the quiet, with an uncertain Levy playing with one of the delicate beaded bracelets on her wrist. The night was already off to a fantastic start.

Sighing, Kat nodded towards the observation deck. "Let's go over some of this tech and see what you can do." If she had to be awake with the girl, they may as well get some instruction in.

It was nearing 03:00 hours before they spoke about something other than the ship's holotech. The VL turned out to be quite adept for her year. They'd covered most of the tech in a little under an hour.

"Are they always this—taxing?" Levy asked. She sounded calm and collected, despite the sheer number of systems they'd just gone over.

"What, the raids?" Kat snorted. She'd expected this question to come up at some point, it always did with the younger cadets. But she had expected "tedious" or "boring". Taxing was a new one. "Some more than others. It's the research-nature. You can find value in them, though. Lee always does."

For a few more minutes, only the beeping of the sensors carried over the soft thrushes of the sleeping spacecraft. And when Levy spoke up again, there was a new tension in her body.

"Were you two ever a thing?" Levy managed to keep her voice neutral, but Kat could sense the anxiety buried beneath her question.

"Who, Lee and I?" Kat sucked in a breath. "No, of course not. Never," she added, surprising even herself with her honesty. Because she and Lee... They were not an option she'd allow herself to entertain.

"He likes you though," Levy observed.

Where was this heading? Whether from the girl's intimate observations or to see how Kat would react, she didn't know. But she picked through her next words carefully. "Lee likes everyone."

"He doesn't like me."

Kat searched the girl's lavender face, with her eager eyes and even-tempered smile. There was no sign of the foolish, starstruck cadet she'd expected to see; the cadet only interested in ogling all the hot Gamma boys. The cadet Kat had hoped to see.

Turning away, Kat faced back toward the holotech on the port wall. "Don't underestimate yourself."

An hour later, she dismissed the cadet.

Invincible.

Levy's words echoed around her head like the empty cabin encompassing her while she waited for the next cadet to emerge and claim their shift.

She used to feel invincible. Like if she pushed herself hard enough and ran fast enough, nothing could touch her.

And she may still appear invincible to others. But it had been a while since she'd felt that way. And lately, trying to outline this thing between her and Lee—she felt more vulnerable than ever.

Invincible? Not even close.

CHAPTER 9: LEE

THE SHIP was quiet when Lee awoke the next morning. Slipping from the dorm, he leaned against the doorframe, letting his eyes adjust to the low lights overhead. Nikola hovered beside the observation deck, tinkering around with some of the ship's other tech while Kat paced up the grated aisle.

"I'm guessing I didn't miss anything?" Lee asked.

Kat started, peeling back around.

"Morning," he grinned, pushing off from the doorframe.

He didn't bother with the main lights yet as he slid onto one of the benches of the small table. Kat slid onto the bench opposite him. He could hear her restless legs as she kicked them outwards, continuing her pacing motions underneath the table. "I don't like this," she said.

Lee glanced past Nikola to the sensors, with their ever-present wavelengths rolling through, then back to Kat. "I don't want to return empty-handed."

"Technically, we aren't," Nikola said, still facing the holotech of the observation deck. "We've got a hatch full of space debris."

Lee looked back over at Kat, meeting her pale grey eyes, and the restlessness also present there. But she pursed her lips, pulling her legs up under her to keep them still. "He's not wrong."

While he hated the idea of passing the job off to someone else, it didn't look like there were all that many options left for them, either. He ran a hand through his hair. "Can we expand our range again for the RIMs? Gather even more?" It was all they had left to do. Keep gathering data and evidence, and hope in the end, that they'd gathered enough to tell the Commander a complete story.

As the morning progressed, they switched out the low lights for the overheads once again, the bright lights a shock to his system. The remainder of the cadets filtered out to join them until they were all crammed once more into the main cabin and power drinks littered the countertops.

They took it in shifts to send out the RIM vehicles, and were coming tantalizingly close to the end of their allotted time extension when a message came through from Zane and Neha.

Field is dormant. Skimmer A-03 is calling it.

Their message was followed by Whistler and Ciela.

Skimmer A-01 also calling it.

It was down to them, then. The last ones standing.

Lee caught Kat's eye. Sidestepping around Dax, who had begun a series of hold-lunges down the middle aisle of the

99

cabin, and Levy, who was practically bouncing on her toes, Lee motioned for Kat to join him up by the cockpit.

They needed a plan, they were just grasping at stars now. With roughly two hours left on their shields, they really couldn't afford to linger out here much longer, and definitely not without good reason. But he couldn't shake the feeling that they were missing something obvious.

Behind him, Dax and Levy had engaged in a full-on, one-legged balancing competition. With their steady hands gripping their ankles, and their cores drawn, it could go either way; however, due to Dax's boisterous nature, and Levy's focus, he'd put his money on her.

Sure enough, Dax toppled over first, head shaking and mouth running as he demanded a rematch. Lee had to look away to hide his grin as he turned away from her triumphant smile.

He thought back to his conversations with Levy this past week. What options had they left for themselves this time, how many answers had been left unturned? And what about the asteroid? Was that simply a distraction from the importance of their mission with the radiation? Or was the radiation the distraction?

He was peering out the front window of their ship when Kat joined him. "The Commander said in our briefing that they suspected dark radiation, right?"

"She did, and we have the samples. But there's not exactly a planetary object out there to complete the sequence."

"No, there isn't," Lee agreed.

Kat turned to peer out the broad window with him, as if she might catch a couple of shooting stars, spelling out the path for them. "There's nothing else out there for us. We've already run the scans and collected a wide array of space debris."

He tore his eyes away from the window. "Not from everywhere." And since they were down to the wire anyway... "Can you get a mod-vehicle out there?"

She met his gaze, eyes slanting up the handful of centimeters to meet his. "You really think the magnetic field is connected to the radiation spikes?"

"Call it instinct." Call it creating options. He'd had his eye on that void since they'd arrived.

He waited for her while she silently ran over the potential consequences and what they stood to gain. Or lose. One word from her and he'd abandon the entire notion. They'd flip the ship around and fly right back with Zane and Whistler, game over.

But when Kat lifted her chin, it was intensity and defiance that glinted there in her eyes, in her smile. *I'm in.*

That was all it had taken. One look, and he knew she was on board. That she'd back him up to the very last pulse of their radiation shields. They always seemed to run on the same wavelength, anyway.

With a slash of a smile, Lee turned to face the rest of their cabin. "We're gonna need a couple more samples."

Kat trailed a half step behind him as he pulled Levy over to join them with the mod-vehicles. Levy's eyes widened as he explained the new assignment, but to the cadet's credit, she didn't appear to balk; not as her grip latched tightly around one of the vehicles' controls. No, there was nothing uncertain in Levy, instead, there was a spark in her dark eyes and a fierceness he'd never noticed before. An expression mirrored in the squadron lead holding the other set of controls.

Conscious of the limited time left on their shields and the backward ticking on the clock, Lee addressed them both. "We have just under two hours. I really don't want to have to go retrieve any AMG equipment. Let's make this count."

Kat and Levy set to work immediately without so much as a glance outward to the undefined magnetic field at least a hundred kilometers out.

They would make it.

It would take a few days for the Academy's labs to process the space matter afterward—who knew if the samples would even yield anything of value.

It was a bit of a long shot, but it was all they had now.

Running through the wording a couple of times in his head, Lee squeezed back up to the cockpit to prep the ship for flight and send out one last transmission.

Skimmer A-02 will be along shortly. We've one more angle to exhaust.

Zane and Neha shot a message back not thirty seconds later.

Watch your shields.

CHAPTER 10: KAT

"REMIND ME never to doubt you," Kat declared, tipping back the contents of her second green juice that evening. She was sprawled out across Lee's bed with his hoodie tucked tightly around her arms, forcing herself to stay awake while they worked through their post-raid write-up. The full report wasn't due back to the Commander for another day and a half, but Lee liked to get them completed early while the raid was still fresh on his mind.

She frowned, peering up into her empty cup. She couldn't even count how many of those vile power drinks she had downed over the last day and a half. That and meal pockets. She'd never been so happy to hold a plastic cup in her life.

"And she's getting loopy," Lee said, leaning back to cradle his head with his hands. He had his feet propped up on the desk and his holoblock in his lap as he eyed her juice cup somewhat warily. That he was tolerating her having a drink near his bed at all was a sign of just how mentally drained they all were after the events of this last raid.

Their mod-vehicles had made it out to the edge of the magnetic field and back with only minutes to spare on their shields. A rush of adrenaline and flashing lights had propelled them home. She just hoped something would come of it.

Some of that ecstasy had lingered when they'd finally made it back to the Academy. Heads held high, with bins full of the space debris they'd collected over the past day, they'd dropped everything off with the labs for storage before grabbing a quick bite. She had even let Lee talk her into a little sparring match before coming up here, where she'd collapsed on his bed, with zero intentions of moving anytime in the near future.

They hadn't run into any of the other squadron leads yet, although Zane had messaged her about an hour ago, checking in on how things had gone. She'd left that one to hang in the cosmos. He could read about it tomorrow afternoon with the rest of them when the raid reports came out.

Whatever was going on between them was over as far as she was concerned. Should never have been a thing to begin with.

"You know you could just sleep," Lee said, coming over to stand beside her. She must've been staring up at the ceiling for too long. He snatched the plastic cup up, pointedly, from her hands and tossed it clean into the bin.

Kat stuck out her tongue.

Chuckling, Lee scooped up his holoblock once more, getting back to their write-up.

She flipped over to her stomach, breathing in time to the soft whispers as Lee typed, reading it out loud as he went, with Kat occasionally chiming in on the very detailed findings he already had in place. She could strive for years, but she would never possess Lee's concentration.

Or his instinct.

Maybe there was some correlation between the magnetic field and the radiation, the spikes were often a sign of dark radiation. But until they heard back from the labs, they really had nothing to show for the past day and a half.

Either way, though, it had been an adventure of the likes Kat didn't wish to repeat anytime soon. She was over hyper-space jumps as travel, no thank you.

"You know," Lee said thoughtfully, the whispers halting. "We may need to add a new action hero name to our list..."

"Oh, I've already thought of a couple." Kat pushed herself up, sitting on her legs. In between space-passage karaoke with Dax, and distracting herself from the looming return jump, she really had thought through some. "I'm pushing for either Toroidal Belt Flat-liners or Sub-zero Archaeologists."

"Whichever one you like." Lee smiled faintly, still off on whatever thread had woven together his last thought.

She traced that smile with her eyes. The quiet confidence and joy that had always seemed to come easily to her friend.

She'd never asked Lee what it was for him, why he wanted to become a raider. Not outright, anyways. Every cadet who came to the Academy, who endured the vigorous training and education requirements, had their own reasons to be here. Some reason worth fighting for. The reason they would cling to on the most tiring days and the longest nights.

Realizing she'd been staring, she glanced away, toying with one of the sleeves of Lee's hoodie. Her hair was in tangles; she hadn't had a chance to run a brush through it in over thirty hours. She knew for a fact that if she peered in a mirror, she would see the smudges of the black liner that was nowhere near her eyes.

She was a wreck. In more ways than what was visible on the outside. She'd built a name for herself with the Academy as a raider, and she fought every day for that name; she and her aunt both relied on the financial support the program afforded them. She knew how quickly everything could be taken from her... And some days that foundation felt as fragile as the life she'd had before.

And what about Lee? If they ever did try to start something, would it even work out, with a mess like her? It was a truth she'd been fighting against for years.

"What are you thinking about over there?" Lee had paused his typing again. Had he asked her opinion on something?

Kat shook her head, blinking back her thoughts before glancing up at him once more. "Nothing."

His brow was scrunched, like he was weighing something in his head. But he just smiled again, turning away from her once more. "Whatever you say, Hanneman."

She went back to listening to the deliberate whispering of his fingers and the pleasant undertones of his voice, basking in the familiar scents of teakwood and cedar.

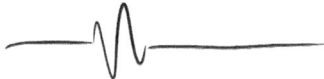

Kat sat up suddenly at the abrupt change in lighting. "What is it? Did we find anything?"

She had to blink several times to see anything at all; the room was bathed in darkness. When her eyes finally adjusted, she could make out the faint outline of a closet, and then a desk. The shape of Lee beside it, peering over at her. "Sorry, I didn't mean to wake you," he said. The rollers on the bottom of his chair squeaked as he nudged it backward.

Lee's room. She was back in Lee's room, and they had recently returned from their raid. It all came flooding back to her; their findings with the asteroid; the jump to hyperspeed; their write-up—

"Here, I will take a look." She leaped up, rubbing at her eyes, trying to prepare them for what would undoubtedly be a flood of light when she re-opened the report. Had she been asleep for hours, or just minutes?

"Sleep, Kat." Lee's teeth flashed brilliant white in the darkness. "I just sent it out." Yanking teasingly on her ponytail, Lee crossed the space in two steps, collapsing onto the bed.

She stood there a moment, counting her breaths. She traced the shadows from the window until the light creaking of the mattress at her back had stilled.

Almost robotically, Kat turned, crawling back in after him and curling into his side. She fell right to sleep. She knew, because when she awoke the next morning, the room was quiet once more, and she was alone; a blanket had been draped across her and tucked neatly at her chin.

She remembered to check her hyperband for messages this time, but there was nothing there. And she was warm. So she closed her eyes and went back to sleep. She'd deal with everything another day.

CHAPTER 11: LEE

THE TRAINING levels were empty this morning. Likely due to the buttery scents of warm biscuits and greasy faux-sausage wafting throughout the Heptagon—*was it already Friday?* They'd been back from their raid for two days now. But with everything that had happened over the last week or so, he'd lost all sense of time.

He'd have to push himself extra hard this morning.

Lee had awoken this morning feeling agitated. Despite the early hour, he'd pulled on his all-terrain suit and slipped out of his dorm, heading down here. No surprise, he'd had his pick of the levels.

Lee dropped his bag onto the floor of the matted training room, facing each of the humanoid targets in turn. He settled on one towards the far end of the room. "It's you and me."

Squaring his feet up and facing his vinyl opponent, Lee drew in a breath, steeling himself as he started off through the motions.

Jab, uppercut. Hook.

Beginning with the basics, Lee took it slow, really sinking into the punches. After a few minutes, he added in the kicks, using the rhythmic strain to dull the edge and clear his head.

He was usually more settled after a raid. First, from the liberation and exhilaration of being away from the Academy and actually doing something meaningful. Then, upon the return and finding closure in the follow-up report.

Not to mention, Kat had all but admitted that she and Zane were no longer a thing... Granted, they'd all been pretty *zapped* the last couple of days. But Lee would be willing to bet the next Laser Rounds' winnings that it was Zane who'd been messaging her the past couple of days, and Kat had barely batted an eye.

But even that elation wore off as the lights in the hallway shifted from dusk's dim to dawn's bright, and he let his aching muscles take over.

It wasn't normal for him to have something linger with him this long afterward. Then again, it also wasn't normal to find whatever anomaly they'd faced out there. And he couldn't shake the feeling that the answer to all their questions had been staring him right in the face.

Jab. Knee. Sidekick, sweep. Cross.

They'd completed their mission and investigated the radiation. And while they hadn't uncovered an actual viable source, they hopefully had enough evidence coming, in support of the dark radiation, that would recommend further investigation of the elevated magnetism. His part in all of this was just about over.

Lee could get on board with it; he was ready to move on.

The door slid open and someone strode in, stopping just inside the door. It was just as well, Lee was about done in here anyway. He was ready to enjoy his biscuits and gravy.

Wiping his brow, Lee turned around.

Zane stood on the other side of the room.

Lee tensed, locking eyes on Zane as they sized each other up. But the air between them was already much too taut for this to be anything other than confrontation.

"You found something," Zane said.

Not a question. But Lee shrugged anyway, releasing some of that tension from his stance. The gesture was anything but casual. "We'll see."

"We're on the same mission."

Again, not a question. Zane's tone had enough privileged demand inked into it, that it almost hid the undertone Lee was picking up on. Confusion. And curiosity, maybe. Was the Gamma cadet anyone else at the Academy, Lee might have given him some partial explanation; at least the parts from his mind that he'd fully digested.

But this was Zane. And he had now ruined Lee's morning.

Lee let a cool smirk settle on his face. "Like I said. We'll see." Sauntering the rest of the way across the room, Lee went to collect his bag.

"Your squadron stayed out a full two hours longer than the rest of us," Zane said bluntly, rounding on Lee. "Relying on your shield that long—you put your spacecraft at risk and everyone on it."

"Our shields held just fine." Lee knew the risk of stressing out the radiation shields; the chance of collapse. But they'd still had minutes left on their time allowance, and that was only for the warning. He'd monitored the shields' levels right through the very end.

"You can play with your own safety all you want. But when it comes to her—"

"Leave Kat out of this," Lee hissed, the agitation from that morning flaring right back up again. Especially as Zane's lips turned up in a smirk of his own—something colder.

"Oh, but that's right, I forgot," Zane said with that frosty smirk. "*She* won't play with you."

Lee was done with this conversation. "You have a problem with the way we're running our squadron, you take it up with the Commander." He narrowed his eyes. "It's like I said. You can read about it with everyone else when they release the lab reports."

This time Zane took the dismissal, storming out the door.

Lee remained there for a few more minutes, willing himself to relinquish his anger and clear his head a bit. When his heartbeat had steadied, he slapped a hand to the wall, leaving the training room behind.

He didn't care about what Zane had said about the radiation and their remaining there with their shields. They'd done it before and they'd do it again. They'd been perfectly in control that afternoon. But as to what Zane had said about Kat...

"I was just looking for you." Kat crossed the lower skywalk, bright-eyed and bossy-faced. "It's biscuits and gravy day."

112

"You just missed your boyfriend," Lee grumbled.

"Who? Zane?"

"Who else?" Lee shot back, Zane's final comment reverberating around his insides like acid.

"I thought we were past this. He and I aren't even talking."

"Whatever. It's your business." Lee didn't realize how dismissive and cutting his words were until Kat's face plummeted.

"Who peed in your cereal." She started right back the way she'd come, swinging her head around so fast and with enough of a slice that her ponytail actually looked lethal.

"Kat—Kat!" He called, catching up to her. He stretched a hand to her arm to stop her. "I didn't mean it, okay?"

"And that's *your* business," she said, brushing him off and hurling back his own words with every ounce of bitterness he'd tossed her way.

He wished she'd yelled at him. It would have been better than this. Anything would have been better than this. Better than Kat, standing there looking hurt—furious, too, her eyes were flashing, but mostly hurt. He had caused that pain, and for no reason other than Zane's useless remarks. Because he'd let them get to him. Again.

She swallowed. "Look, I will see you later, Lee, okay?" There was still a hint of bite in her words. But he deserved it. The damage had been done.

He let her stalk away before making his way slowly up to the showers. It was going to be a long day.

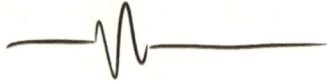

The day was made even longer by the fact that Kat was refusing to speak to him. Totally justified, in all fairness.

Not that he had all that many opportunities; they both had full schedules. But she wasn't answering any of his messages. And the couple of times he passed her in the hallway, she blitzed right past and out of sight again.

It was lunchtime before he had any real free time. He waded through the flood of cadets clambering to get to the Canteen, but there was no sign of Kat's vanilla-blonde ponytail. Ignoring his growling stomach, he sidestepped around a group of cadets gabbing about the hallway temperatures, and headed, solo, up to the dorms.

Why couldn't he have run into Zane now, when he was ready to slam faces to the ground?

He swung by Kat's first to check, but his knock was met only by silence. Either she was there and didn't want to see him, or she actually wasn't around, and likely didn't want to be found.

He waited a couple of extra minutes anyway, before following the curved hallway around to his dorm.

How could he have been so careless with the words he'd tossed back at his best friend? Of course, he cared about her business. He was thoroughly invested; that was why any of this even mattered, to begin with.

To distract himself, he opened up his holoblock.

They'd submitted their space debris samples for testing three days ago. And while it wasn't unusual for them not to have heard anything back yet, the Commander had made it sound rather urgent during their briefing that day...

Scrounging up a protein bar, Lee drafted a quick follow-up email. They'd been getting to know the lab managers quite well lately, perhaps he could flex that relationship a little. There was at least three squadrons' worth of raid work to be processed, in addition to the other squadrons who'd gone out this week on separate missions of their own. He'd see if they couldn't push their stuff to the front of that pile.

He checked his hyperband again, just in case Kat had sent something through. But when he didn't find anything new, he closed out his holoblock.

He didn't run into anyone on his way back down through the Heptagon; the rest of the cadets were well into their lunch hour. But that suited him just fine, he didn't need any interruptions. He had one more thing he needed to do.

The greenhouses were located on the lower levels of the Heptagon, a stairway below the lower skywalks that connected the training levels to the rest of the ship.

Lee stopped before the jagged doors to scan his hyperband. And when they split apart, he stepped into warm, loamy paradise.

A myriad of aromas greeted him. From the warm soil and burrowing roots to all manners of fruiting vines and trees, all of it topped off nicely with the staining finish of the greenhouse attendant's homemade, nutrient-rich solution.

The greenhouses were therapy. As effective as his workouts were on his physical health, the greenhouses provided him with a sort of mental restoration and wellness. It was a sanctuary.

The majority of the plots were devoted to hydroponics and the cultivation of fresh produce from the ship's residual food waste. But there were also community plots in the back, the beds left open for cadet research and experimentation. It was to these plots that Lee now strolled.

Eyeing the faint blue-green of the lights that warmed the soil below, Lee leaned in close. A slow smile spread across his lips.

It had only been a week and a half since he'd uncovered the species on dwarf planet Kafron. But during that week and a half, the concentrated energy from the lights had performed miracles. Where a single clipping of a thin-stemmed leaf had hinged, maybe a centimeter away from wilting to its death, a small plant now sprung. It was a young sproutling, barely shooting from the soil. But if he were lucky, it wouldn't be long before they got a bloom, with petals the soft color of moon dust.

He looked over out of instinct to the greenhouse attendant strolling, with her ambling walk and gravelly voice, the second aisle over. Every meter or so, she'd dip down to check on the Academy's plots.

She looked up with a knowing smile, and Lee gave her a nod, dipping his head in respect.

He owed Ilan his gratitude. He'd left careful instructions with her while he was preoccupied and away for their latest raid. And when he'd returned, he'd found this.

Ilan finished her inspection of that aisle's plots, coming towards him next. She stopped when she reached him. "When you're ready, Leland, plot nineteen needs our attention."

"Yes ma'am." Accepting the assignment, Lee retrieved a pair of gloves and a small trowel from the back wall, only turning his back away from his warrior flower temporarily.

It had worked. He'd made the cut on Kafron on a whim, entirely unsure if the pH or the nutrients in the soil would be compatible. And yet, here it was, alive and well; possibly even thriving.

It wasn't Kat's fault she had mixed with Zane, or that the timing was always wrong. Or, if Lee was being honest, that he couldn't man up and just tell her what he felt. What he'd felt for her all of these years. Because it always came down to that same gossamer truth: was he enough for her?

But if he kept faulting her for it, he might really lose her.

Like with the moon dust flower, there were 8.515 x 10^{13} km, nearly 9 light-years of reasons why this thing between them might go nowhere. But if he took the risk, and finally went for it, for once... Maybe their stars could collide.

And that chance of collision was everything.

CHAPTER 12: KAT

KAT HAD been ignoring everyone. The billions of messages from Lee. The reminder from her aunt about overdue utilities. The obnoxious chat function on their latest hyperband updates, providing the younger cadets the opportunity to pester Kat incessantly about meeting together at the juice bar for green drinks...

Oddly, she hadn't received anything else from Zane. Not since the other night. Maybe that meant he'd finally moved on from her and whatever short-fused relationship they'd entertained over the last couple of months.

She stared at the blank wall of metal facing her, the smooth surfaces around her thrumming from the generators below. There were no eggshell panels down here.

It was a place she liked to come. The little antechamber was barely large enough to accommodate a couple fully-grown humanoid figures. It was noisy, and with the whole system seeming to teeter on overdrive, the generator was constantly in a whirl around her.

And it was warm. Unlike the industrial fans that seemed to blow across every other meter of the ship, in here there were no outside forces to interrupt the circulation of the heat from the generator. Kat would slip down here whenever she needed to think. Or be alone. Or even, simply, exist. The steady noise and heat formed a little cocoon around her, a cacophony for which her mess of a mind could sing.

She was surprised at how quickly the day had slipped away from her. The days following a raid were usually quite the drag of exhausted responsibility. She'd squandered some of the afternoon doing yoga, and surprisingly, the slow pace agreed with her spiraling mind.

She'd only left the studio behind when a group of her cadets came by to join. At any other time, it was an opportunity she would have delighted in abusing and misusing with her favorite co-conspirator at her side. But alone, without him, her heart wasn't in it.

That was when she'd ducked out to come down here.

Lee probably could have found her if he'd wanted, she'd shown him her spot a few years back. But he was giving her space.

A lot of space, apparently. His last message had come in hours ago. He'd likely gotten distracted obsessing over something. The thought alone brought sunshine into the dim antechamber of her mind. She'd head up to see what he was up to and smooth things over.

Soon.

Kat leaned her head back against the buzzing metal, letting her eyes close. The warmth muddled her thoughts in a mechanical fever.

Light footsteps joined the caucus. Kat's eyes flicked open as she tracked the subtle creaking to the rungs of the ladder, followed by a sharp intake of breath.

"Oh." A round, lavender face peered back at her with equal surprise.

"Levy?"

Kat frowned, feeling horribly disoriented as she struggled to put her thoughts together. "Did Lee send you down here to find me?"

"Lee?" The other girl asked, confused. "No—I didn't think anyone else came down here—I can come back some other time..."

Kat stared at Levy for a couple long seconds; the girl was barely blinking. Relaxing her position, Kat leaned back against the wall and patted the surface beside her. She let her breathing find its peaceful rhythm again, closing her eyes to block everything else out as Levy leaned back against the wall beside her.

She could feel the shift in the air as Levy adjusted her position, conscious to keep their knees from bumping in the narrow space.

And then there was stillness. The only static, the ever-present churn of the generator.

"This is nice," Levy murmured.

Kat grinned, not opening her eyes.

She could hear the stutters in Levy's breathing as the girl lifted her head, probably to check what Kat was doing and make sure she wasn't the only insane one. Kat let her smile remain so the girl could see it. And then Levy let her head fall back against the wall again.

After a few minutes, Kat spoke, opening her eyes again. "An entire ship basically at our disposal, and we find ourselves crammed into an airshaft."

Levy laughed, "Although to be fair, it is a top-of-the-line gear cutter 580 model. They don't make them cleaner than that." Levy paused, likely thinking through something, before adding, "I only come down here when I need to get some space."

"Who would you be hiding from?" Kat mused aloud. Not caring enough to keep her thoughts to herself.

"Everybody. Jerkoff Xs and Gammas who think too highly of themselves."

Kat coughed pointedly.

"Sorry. I didn't mean—you aren't—"

"It's okay." Kat peered over, appraising Levy. "You aren't afraid to say what you feel." It wasn't a question, more commentary, but—

"What, too soft to be a raider?" Levy attempted a laugh, but it came out shaky.

But Kat surveyed Levy again. Like the other night on the raid, their early shift on the skimmer. Maybe she was starting to figure out the girl a little bit after all.

There was nervousness in her, yes. But also a strong sense of desire to do right—even at the expense of one's self. And stubbornness. It reminded her a bit of herself. A version she very well may have been three years earlier. And she didn't know what to make of that.

"I get it," Kat said, leaning her head back against the wall. "It can be tough navigating the Academy dynamics." She was staring straight ahead. "And the older cadets *can* be assholes."

She was collecting her breath, about ready to climb back to her feet when Levy looked over at her.

"How did Lee know to linger out there with the magnetic field?" she asked.

But Kat could only shake her head. "That's Lee for you. He doesn't miss anything—and we had some personal stakes in the mission this time around."

"With the other squadrons."

"With the other squadrons," Kat confirmed. While she was okay with Levy asking her these questions, that didn't mean Kat was about to clue the girl into all her private dramas.

"They are just intimidated by you—the pair of you," Levy confided. "Everyone is. You are a power combo. Everyone knows you guys will get first pick when you are done here, with Placement, missions, you name it."

Funny. The girl had told Lee something similar the other day. But the girl's assumption wasn't wrong. They'd had their names at the top for years. But thinking of life after the Academy made her think of Lee and their petty fight that morning.

The last comments they'd hurled at each other were only too fresh in her mind, and she was missing her better half.

"I've got to go take care of some personal business. But I'll divert anyone I see heading your way." She made to slide back down the ladder, but paused with her hands on one of the rungs, sighing. "And Levy?" She said quietly. "There is nothing wrong with being soft."

Kat disappeared down the other side of the generator. Back into reality.

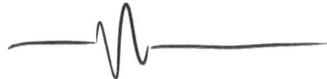

A cloud of excited chatter hung outside the Canteen where Kat had come in her eagerness to make things right again with Lee. The chatter seemed to thrum and grow the closer she got to dinner. Did they not feed these cadets enough?

She stepped through the open doorway. Her eyes widened as tumultuous noise rained down on her. And for a few seconds, the decibels seemed to crest, before settling over her.

"Miss me?" The rain dissolved as a familiar, medium-brown head appeared above her left shoulder. He nudged her head with his chin.

"Exactly the one I was looking for," Kat said. A grin pulled at the corners of her lips as she caught the smudge of dirt on his cheek and the easy smile on his face. She let the smile take over but held Lee's probing stare, his green eyes. They'd still have a talk about this, but—had she ever noticed how green his eyes were? It was like bathing in mineral pools...

"Void, Kat." Lee laughed, tucking her into him. "I thought you might have been down there, but if I'd realized it was this bad, I would have come and found you earlier."

"Let's just get some food, I'm starving."

"I'm sure you are." Lee was still chuckling as he led them into the Canteen and through the line, filling her tray with everything she pointed at.

They were almost to their table when a shadow fell over her, blocking out some of the concealed overhead lighting. A pair of boots swam into her vision, the laces tied with all the care of a military brat.

"Ugh, Zane," Kat groaned. She was vaguely aware of Lee's arm tightening around her shoulders in warning. She looked up to see the disgusted look on Zane's face, right before he bailed.

"That was weird," Lee said, before taking the last couple of steps to their table. "He seemed off this morning, too."

"He spends way too much time on his shoelaces." Wait, this morning? Kat flicked her eyes over to Lee. Did some of that weirdness have to do with Lee's fun little outburst earlier? But where she expected to see some level of residual irritation there, Lee's face was carefully blank.

This was turning out to be quite the interesting post-raid hangover.

Lee set her tray down on their usual table. "About earlier..." he began, cutting himself off with a little chuckle and catching her as the tabletop rose up to greet her. "You sure you're doing okay?"

She nodded, but her head was still swimming as he glanced down at his hyperband. Maybe she had spent too many hours down there. The wavering amusement slid from his face as he read through the latest message that had come through.

"That doesn't make sense," Lee murmured.

"What doesn't make sense?" She could've sworn her carton of carrot-lemongrass juice was slowly collapsing inward.

Lee scanned and re-scanned the message. He flicked his eyes away, staring at nothing before dropping back down to his hyperband. "I followed up earlier with the labs about the material we submitted. It says here that there was an error with our submissions..."

"An error, like how? Like something we did? We've been submitting similar material for months now."

But Lee shook his head. "The entire batch is under internal review with the Commander."

"Internal..." Kat processed aloud, "What does that even mean? For how long?"

"Doesn't say. I'm sure there's a limited period of seizure. But even so..." Lee was frowning.

Nikola spotted them, then from across the room. He had that excited look on his face that she knew all too well from that latest raid. That look that told her he'd recently uncovered the latest secrets of the galaxy and was dead set on sharing them. His rectangle lenses caught the light as he made for their table.

"What do we do?" she asked, her voice dropping down an octave. Or five. Her lips had begun to move in slow motion by the time Nikola reached their table, seconds away from imploding. "Not now," she groaned impatiently.

"What do we do," Lee repeated, a joyless smile crossing his lips. "We pay a visit to the Commander." He jumped up from the table, his tray of food long forgotten behind him.

"Can you even do that?" Nikola asked, peering after Lee and having seemingly only just realized he'd walked into something.

Kat shot the cadet a look. It wasn't a question of "if". They were doing it.

Although how, exactly...

She caught up with Lee, matching his pace as they strode back out of the Canteen and up the length of the Heptagon.

Commander Blanche kept quarters on the highest levels of the Heptagon in the Command wing directly above staff. But beyond that information, Kat was completely in the dark. Not even Gammas, raider squadron leads, had access to the rooms beyond this particular set of zagged-cut double doors.

Lee didn't bother to slow his pace until they'd reached that top level.

Kat pulled on his arm, but Lee ignored her, only stopping when he stood facing the doors. He held up his hyperband, dictating a quick message. "Gamma squadron lead, Leland Waters, would like to request an audience with Commander Blanche regarding Mission AX13-AR."

He finally looked over, meeting her gaze. Kat raised her eyebrows pointedly.

Rolling his eyes, Lee lifted his hyperband once more, adding, "And he's accompanied by squadron lead, Kat Hanneman." He peered back at her wryly. Fully satisfied, Kat nodded.

With a huffed laugh, Lee sent off the message.

And now, they waited.

Thirty seconds. A minute. "What's taking them so long?" Kat murmured.

Lee just peered over at her. *You shouldn't even be talking, Miss too-many-hours in the airshafts.*

She stuck out her tongue. "This was your idea."

Huffing another laugh, Lee tucked his hands into his pockets.

They stared back at the doors to the Command wing in silence.

"I've always wondered what was through these doors," Kat said. She studied the jagged split down the middle and the security panel, then around her at the windowless, paneled walls.

"More industrial paneled walls. Some portal doors—albeit with slightly higher security."

She reached over and pinched his arm. Lee laughed, rubbing his left forearm.

"But has anyone *you know* ever passed through here?"

Lee appeared to think for a moment, letting his arms drop down by his sides again. "We'd be the first. And before you say it —no, we aren't adding this to our list of names."

Pretending to be mildly offended, Kat meant to turn away from him, but she got distracted by the smudge staining one of Lee's cheeks. Shaking her head a little as she hid a grin, she sidestepped around him. He stared back at her warily while she leaned in with one of her hands to get the dirt.

"Ack!" Lee hissed, batting her hands away. "What are you doing, *mom*?"

"You've got dirt on your face, *lycophyte*."

"Club moss? Ha ha. Very clever," Lee said, still leaning a fraction away from her.

"Tsk. Whatever. Just hold still." Kat lifted a hand towards him once more. This time, Lee allowed her hands near his face, only cringing back a little when she went to lick her finger. "Tonya would be so proud of me," she sang.

"Tonya would freak if she saw you lick your finger to get the dirt," Lee muttered under his breath. "But she would appreciate you stepping in."

He sighed. "She worries too much."

"It's because she cares about you," Kat reminded him. "And me. In fact, your mom may even like me more."

"She actually might," Lee agreed, tensing up again as Kat reached for his hands, but he allowed her to lift one up as she examined the dirt under his fingernails.

"You should probably hide your hands, *assuming they ever bother to let us in*." She directed this last part to the door, still as motionless as when they'd arrived. Maybe Nolan hadn't gotten Lee's message.

Lee glanced carelessly at one of his hands, before brushing her off.

A minute later, the doors split open and the Commander's secretary, Nolan stepped out. Only he wasn't alone.

"Whistler?" Lee asked.

Kat could feel her brow narrowing in her confusion. She wanted to say something. She wanted to gape. She wasn't sure what her body was doing instead, but their fellow Gamma didn't stop or look their way. He didn't seem to hear them at all as he passed by, brow scrunched, and lips pressed tightly together. This was probably the most emotion she'd ever seen Whistler express, apart from the Laser Rounds.

What was in the air today?

Kat met Nolan's gaze. Or she tried to—Nolan wasn't meeting either of their eyes, presently too distracted by something on his hyperband. "This way," he said to neither of them in particular, turning on his heel.

Kat glanced over at Lee, who looked as dumbfounded as she was. But the two of them followed after him, and the doors slid shut behind them.

Nolan led them down a broad hallway, its eggshell paneled walls and zagged-cut doors gleaming on either side of them. Exactly as Lee had predicted. But neither Kat nor Lee said a word as they passed.

Turning down a side wing, Nolan stopped before a door without markers denoting its purpose. But scanning his hyperband to the plate on the wall, the door slid open, and they were beckoned inside.

The office was neat. And much smaller than anything she'd expected to find through these doors.

A narrow, white desk extended off of the nearest wall, with a set of chairs arranged neatly to one side; a holoblock sat in the middle. It was as neat and blank as Lee's dorm on the weekend.

Nolan gestured for them to sit, not bothering to wait before stepping around the desk, sinking into his own flex-backed chair, and adjusting the armrests.

Both she and Lee remained standing.

She'd never actually spoken to the Commander's secretary outside of a briefing, and definitely not from behind these doors. He had one of those plain faces, where he could have been about their age, or several years older. She wondered vaguely at his qualifications and resume, given his status and rank.

Finally, Nolan looked up, glancing at them for the first time that afternoon. "Now, what may I do for you?"

"I'm sorry," Lee said, a little too politely, "but this is a matter pertaining to Mission AX13-AR. A matter of which we would prefer to address with Commander Blanche directly."

"Commander Blanche is unavailable at this time. As such, I have been given specific instruction to address any dissatisfaction or concerns with regards to the raid in question."

Kat could feel her blood beginning to boil. It was all she could do to remain silent as Nolan motioned unceremoniously with a hand for them to sit once more. "Now, what may I do for you."

CHAPTER 13: LEE

DISSATISFACTION. CONCERNS?

Lee's first reaction was rage. A red-hot blaring thing that charred the edges of his vision, churning in the pit of his gut. They weren't here lodging petty complaints about childish issues. There had been a mistake with their labs. A mistake that now impacted their mission assignment.

From the tense way Kat was clenching her palms, she was even more irritated than he was. But she held her cool and remained silent at his side.

Taking several deep breaths, the edges of his rage dulling, Lee sank down into one of the chairs. A couple breaths later, Kat eased herself nimbly into the other.

Lee'd had his fair share of dealings with the Commander and her pantsuits. From standard briefings to her appearances at the Laser Rounds and at the Advancement Ceremonies every year. He knew her to be a fair and just woman. Strict, sure, but also fair.

But this—sitting here facing Nolan—this was something new.

"There's been a mistake with the labs," Lee said, bluntly.

"I'm assuming we're still speaking regarding mission—" Nolan drew up the holographic message on his holoblock, reading off the alphanumeric mission-code, "AX13-AR?" He glanced back up at Lee.

Kat jumped in, "The space matter associated with the labs would have been filed under Leland Waters and Kat Hanneman, Nolan." Her voice took on these weirdly low undertones as she leaned in a little, batting her eyes unnecessarily often.

But Nolan had already glanced back away. There was another stagnant pause while he pulled up the labs associated with their specified raid and whatever access secretary-to-the-Commander bought him.

Lee shot Kat a sidelong glance, incredulous. *What are you even doing?*

She glared back. *We have to try something.*

Still indignant, Lee turned back to face Nolan. The Commander's secretary appeared to have located the lab material in question.

Nolan's face was devoid of emotion when he glanced back up at them. "There's no mistake, but I will make note of your concern."

"That's not possible," Lee said coolly, allowing some of his frustration to burn to the surface. "We aren't novices when it comes to lab protocol. The proper processes and procedures were followed exactly, and the submission records were confirmed by us three days ago."

"I can verify. I have the documentation to prove it," Kat dropped all niceties as she addressed Nolan this time, although a slight blush still colored her cheeks.

"I will repeat to you what I have said to your fellow cadets," Nolan said, speaking slowly as if he were addressing insolent children. But when he paused to draw a breath, his eyes appeared to sharpen. "There was an error with the submissions. All space matter and resources associated with the raid in question have been claimed by Commander Blanche for Internal Review." It was the most direct he'd been all evening.

And then he dropped his gaze, the image of boredom as he swept a hand back through the holofiles to clear them. "I have noted your discontentment, to be shared with Commander Blanche at her earliest availability. Now, if you will excuse me, I have business to attend to."

Robotically thanking the Commander's secretary for his time, he and Kat were hastened from Nolan's office, where they once again found themselves on the wrong side of the Command wing's zagged doors.

"'Oh, Nolan?'" Lee goaded, batting his eyes, the moment the doors had fully closed behind them. "What in *Nebula's Galaxy* were you even thinking?"

"I was thinking," Kat said, smacking him on the shoulder, "that we weren't getting anything out of him. It was worth a shot."

"Try harder next time." Lee frowned, rubbing at his face like he could get this irritation, this frustration out of him that way. "What even was that?" He threw his hands down, starting to pace the grated floors. "Claiming the labs for 'Internal Review'. And the Commander is suddenly 'too busy'—oh wait, what was the word he'd used—'unavailable' to meet with us." Of course, there'd be specific language in place so Command could do whatever the *void* it was that they wanted. More AMG secrets.

"If that's what they're calling it these days." Kat didn't bother to try to talk him down, as he walked the stretch between the doors once more. "None of it makes any sense."

Lee didn't know what more could be done on the subject. They'd gone straight to the source—and then been spat right back out. The longest day ever. And yet he didn't want it to end on that note. "You want to go somewhere else?" he asked, finally. *Anywhere else.*

They meandered back down through the ship, stopping at one of the vending machines in the Hideaway to grab some food. Kat's red-rimmed eyes of that afternoon were mostly back to normal, her vulnerability replaced by some of the grimness he imagined mirrored his own.

They found themselves back down on the lowest floor of the training levels.

"I wonder..." Kat sprinted up ahead of him, slipping through a set of doors.

She poked her head back out of the door frame. "It's free." The anti-gravity chamber was miraculously not in use tonight.

Sliding onto one of the benches alongside Kat, Lee swapped his combat boots for a pair with suction soles and pulled one of the full-body spacesuits off of the wall. The bulky suits were a little warm, conditioned for free-standing space temperatures, but at least they were easy to don over their all-terrain suits. He slid into his, then waited for Kat to hold her ponytail out of the way before zipping her in.

Yanking on her ponytail teasingly, Lee led the way into the main chamber.

Starlight greeted them, filtering in from the contoured floor-to-ceiling windows set in the wall. They left the chamber's lights off, allowing the celestials to guide them as they found their bearings.

However, despite the suction-soled boots on their feet and the helmets in their hands, neither Lee nor Kat showed much willingness to seal off the chamber. Not just yet. Instead, he took up a spot against the wall, sinking down to the floor. Kat did the same, setting her helmet on the floor next to her. Her scent of wild azara and orange blossom flooded his senses. She truly belonged among the treetops or somewhere deep in the galaxy, like that canopy back on Kafron.

And for a moment, they just sat there, side-by-side, with the crush of the cool walls at their necks and the churning of the air vents up above.

"I'm sorry, about this morning," Lee said, playing with the little rose-colored visor on his helmet. It felt like all they did was apologize these days.

"It's fine." Kat's head dipped down onto Lee's shoulder. "I forgave you hours ago."

He angled his head so he could see her face. The hint of a smile grazed her lips. "No, it's not fine." He nudged her with his shoulder, the bulky material of his suit caressing her own. "Kat, it's not fine."

Her pale grey eyes lifted to his, and he held that gaze, not willing to lose that contact—even for something else. Something better...

"Look, I like that you care. That you watch my back. I know I'm always watching yours." He could feel her knee through their suits as it dipped against his. He peered down at their two bodies, constantly touching; her pale hair seemed to absorb the starlight.

He wanted to tell her everything that was on his mind. About them. About her. Those words danced around in the air between them, teasing him. Taunting him...

But he wanted to tell her on his own terms. Not when they were both buried in worry. Not with the mess of their labs hovering over them.

The words were still trying to escape as he swallowed them back down. Later. After they got all this raid stuff sorted out.

He would do it then.

"Zane has nothing on you, you know," she said a moment later, addressing his knee.

"Yeah?"

"Yeah." She itched her nose against his shoulder.

"Are we talking like a couple centimeters or like—"

"Stop right there," she squealed, slapping a hand to his chest as a laugh tore itself from her lips. It was a breathy, wild, at-your-wits-end sort of thing. But he loved it. He couldn't make himself look away. He clutched her hand to his chest, while the ripples of laughter scattered themselves around the room. The air suddenly felt lighter as some of the day's tension dissolved among their laughter.

And then they heard voices behind them, as someone stomped their feet outside in the anti-gravity chamber's antechamber.

"Oy. We're in here," Kat hollered, pulling her hand free to bang at the door behind them.

The noises behind the wall stopped. "But it hasn't been scheduled..." a younger cadet was whining.

"Room is occupied," Lee yelled back. Kat was grinning at him. Her grin grew wider.

"Come on." She leaped to her feet, extending a hand to yank him up with her. "Be weightless with me!" Flipping her long ponytail behind her back, she plopped her helmet jauntily onto her head.

"Are you serious? No way, I was up training at the gym all morning."

"Baby."

"Nope."

"Zane would do it..."

The last of his restraint exploded. Riding that ire, Lee slapped a hand to the keyed button beside the door, sealing off the portal. He threw on his own helmet, sliding the visor into place. The room was bathed in the golden-pink undertones. "The things I do..."

Kat flicked the rose-colored visor over her own eyes, hitting the switch.

The familiar sensation of weightlessness crept through him; the whizzing of one thousand sparkflies in his stomach. And when the sparkflies settled, Lee kicked off from the floor.

He was floating in space. With the raised ceiling and the window, he could have been anywhere amongst the cosmos. Just he and Kat, alone in the galaxy. He drifted for a moment, and when he reached the wall, he kicked off again.

Somewhere out there, she laughed, that wild sound again. He shot towards her, intercepting her path as she careened through a series of hoops edging overhead. And as they intercepted, he looped a hand around her waist, sending them spinning. The whole world—time itself revolved around their axis, with no forces to pull them down. Up. Anywhere, except for where she went.

He caught sight of her eyes. Those laughing eyes—dazzling him through her visor. He would do anything for her. Be anything she needed. She'd always been his anchor in their orbits, anyway.

They laughed until their heads spun and their session ended, gravity pulling them down once more.

"Let's go again," Kat grinned, lifting her suction boots from the floor with a squelch.

Lee chuckled as he took in her bright eyes and the exhilaration written all over her face. She really would skyrocket through space forever if she could.

And he'd be right there along with her, if she needed him.

"One more go," he said, groaning softly as he jumped to his feet. "But after that I'm out. My muscles are wailing. And before you try something, it isn't going to work next time." It had really, truly been a long day, and he was all sorts of drained.

"Whatever you say, Waters." Squelch-stomping, she trod over to the keyed button once more. And as gravity diminished around them, right before she pushed off, he caught the waggled eyebrows and the edged, "But wait until you hear what I'm going to suggest. I promise it won't have anything to do with working out..."

Unsticking his own boots, Lee adjusted his helmet, and entered the cosmos once more.

CHAPTER 14: KAT

THREE TIMES.

She had convinced Lee to be weightless with her three times —although the last was only to spite the reoccurring banging of the impatient cadets waiting in the antechamber. But poor Lee, even she had been exhausted by the time they unsealed the portal door. Leaping off the ceiling sure took it out of you.

Thankfully, it was an off-week for the Laser Rounds. They'd gotten to sleep in a bit and enjoy a rather quiet and leisurely Saturday. Things almost felt like they were back to normal. But with Lee back up in the greenhouses this afternoon, Kat had instead made her way down to one of the matted training rooms to keep the endorphins flowing.

It was casually full today. She took her time warming up, before weaving over to an empty corner.

She and Lee hadn't talked today about the raid or the issue with the labs. Or about last night, the two of them in the anti-gravity chamber, floating...

It was getting harder to deny her feelings for him. There'd been something budding between them for a long time, now.

She knew he felt it too. And last night, there'd been a moment... The physiological cues had been all there. The speechlessness. The constant need to be always touching. The hyper-intent focus and gentle dip of his eyes... This thing between them was as real and tangible as the gravity that had held them there that night. Until it hadn't.

She was terrified to take that next step with him. But she was even more terrified of taking that step and then having it not work out, and losing him. Lee was everything to her.

She'd waited last night for him to make a move. To let her know he saw her. That he accepted her, and that he was willing to take that risk.

And he hadn't.

But he had stayed.

And that had to count for something, right?

Tuning out her relentless brain, she let herself breathe through the other cadets' jabber while she pushed through set after set of crunches. Apparently, Whistler had moved on recently from some cadet named Ty, but the breakup was mutual, and if Ty was okay with it, one of these cadets was interested.

She ought to give Whistler a heads-up next time she saw him. Let him know Ty's friend was available.

Kat lay back on the mats while she let her heart settle again. She was only now starting to feel the burn from all the reps. Perhaps she'd go take a spot at the juice bar after this and wait for Lee to emerge again with another status update on the Academy's rare botanical hybrids.

She was envisioning her green pineapple soother when her hyperband buzzed. Maybe it was Lee. Lifting it up to eye level, she quickly scanned the message.

Then she sat up, ignoring her shaky stomach muscles while she stared back at her hyperband.

Security clearance has been upgraded.

Void. So no green juice, then.

Savoring one more long breath to pull some oxygen into her muscles, Kat stood up. She may as well get a move on in getting cleaned up. If she knew two things about the Academy, it was that nothing happened without a reason, and that timing was everything. And in this case, she had zero doubt more information would be arriving very shortly.

She wasn't wrong.

She'd barely gotten out of the showers and was pulling her hair into a fresh band when the invite arrived. Only the message hadn't come directly from the Commander, it had come from the Commander's secretary.

Her hyperband buzzed again.

Lee: Coming to find you.

Not an hour later, they found themselves back outside of the Command wing and staring at the thick, split-paneled doors.

"Twice in one week," Lee whistled, answering her unspoken thoughts.

"We're starting to become quite the regulars." They'd been back and forth enough lately, that she was starting to get whiplash. "Watch," she murmured. "Next we'll get upgraded suites."

"Pretty sure you're getting ahead of yourself."

"Do you think it'll come with my own bathroom? Maybe I'll get a walk-in!"

Lee was just watching her, amused. "You done?"

"Almost." Kat nodded along. This was becoming even more fun with his insolence. "What if they let us install some of those, like, neon party lights. And then you could handle the music..."

"Here she goes again."

Kat was grinning. "Okay. I'm done now."

Bemused, Lee turned back to the doors. "Shall we try this again?" Instead of waiting for Nolan to let them in, Lee walked right up alongside one of the doors and flashed his hyperband towards the glass panel on the wall.

The doors split apart. Their newly acquired security clearance was definitely working.

With one last glance behind them, they strode through the doors. They found Nolan waiting at the corner where they'd turned last time. And like last time, he led them down the side wing, holding his hyperband up to the plated glass on the wall, until they stood once more in Nolan's office. Lovely.

This time, however, the Commander's secretary didn't immediately close the door behind them. Kat and Lee had barely taken up spots along the back wall when Nolan was out the door again, and out of sight as he headed back up the hall-way.

"You didn't check who else was on the invite today, did you?" She asked tentatively. It hadn't occurred to her earlier to even look. She'd assumed it would be a follow-up from the previous afternoon...

Maybe a minute later, they heard footsteps coming towards them. Lee met her gaze with raised brows. And seconds later, Whistler strolled through the door, his hair tied back in a fishtail braid, walking much quicker than seemed possible with his casual gait. And a couple steps behind him—

Oh *void*, no. It *zapping* better not be—

Zane stiffened as he rounded the doorway. He acknowl-edged Whistler with a curt nod, glancing right past both she and Lee, as Nolan rejoined them. Like her, Zane didn't bother to take in their surroundings.

He had also been here before.

"Are we waiting on the Commander?" Zane asked abruptly, his voice clipped.

"Commander Blanche is unavailable," Nolan said, closing the door behind him. It was just the four of them, then.

So maybe no walk-in. And no party lights.

No one spoke as Nolan took his time settling behind his desk.

Kat's eyes narrowed at the blatant display, his obnoxiously proper posture. Never mind her insolence. Her memory of yesterday's impromptu meeting was all too fresh in her mind.

Then, Nolan finally deigned to address them. "Early Friday morning, a processing error was made known regarding the lab samples associated with Mission AX13-AR. Until we can confirm that the physical samples are still viable, the space debris in question has been claimed by Commander Blanche for internal review." Kat had to physically restrain herself from spouting expletives at the not-so-subtle reminder. "As this is a time-sensitive matter, and the Commander is otherwise engaged, she has requested that her top cadets lead this review."

What?

Kat's eyebrows shot up. That would explain their new security clearance. And if she'd wanted only her top cadets, that would eliminate Ciela and Neha. But still—what?

First, they were flagged for incorrectly processing the raid samples. Now they were being asked to conduct the review? She was thoroughly confused.

"For reference, you will find everything you need on the hub with your new clearance. Your regular training schedules have been suspended, and your cadets are being re-assigned as we speak." This was really going to be a thing then. The four of them. Working together. Like together-together this time... She wasn't sure she was down for this. "Any findings should be sent directly to Commander Blanche and myself. She expects to hear from you very soon."

Kat was gaping. She couldn't help it. Even having closed her mouth, she probably looked like some bulging-eyed parasite, not yet discovered, from one of the watery planets.

They were dismissed. Kat was still struggling to form coherent thoughts as she trailed the others back out through the Command wing. And just like that, they were back on the other side of the doors once again.

"What just happened?" she asked nobody in particular, firing her question into the void.

They'd barely been back from the last raid for four days. She'd blinked, Nolan had happened, and then here she was, once again, being grouped together with these two.

Her gaze splintered reluctantly between Zane and Whistler. The latter's expressions were unreadable, but Zane was clearly fuming. She knew that tension all too well. Hated that some of the same tension was rippling through her.

"I need a break," Zane muttered.

Lee crossed his arms over his chest. "We need a plan."

Zane also crossed his arms over his chest, the muscles in them taut as he braced himself, looking very much like he was going to push back. But he didn't.

"After dinner," Whistler cut in, his voice coming through a little hoarse. He cleared his throat. "We'll meet up again down in the training levels at 19:00 hours."

To do what, they didn't know. That they needed space, however, was perfectly clear. "Deal," Kat said, lamely.

"Fine," Zane agreed, not waiting around, before peeling off down the hall. Whistler also extracted himself, giving Zane a couple meters head start, before following after him.

Kat wasn't particularly hungry, but she let Lee talk her into a table down in the Hideaway, accepting the Green Pineapple Soother he slid her way.

She twirled the little blue straw around the bottom.

"You should drink it," he urged her. Kat met his green eyes, surprisingly clear for all that had been going down recently.

"How come you aren't more pissed?" she asked him, still ignoring the juice on the table. "Nolan is literally trying to tell us we don't know how to do our jobs correctly. Even if we are now also the ones to review it..." She frowned. It didn't make any more sense now, than when Nolan had first said it. "But, of course, *Commander Blanche*, who couldn't be bothered to meet with us personally, expects to hear from us soon." Kat slung the title with as much venom as she could muster.

"She's head of the Academy," Lee shrugged, gripping his drink with his fingertips. As if that explained anything.

"Answer me honestly. Do you believe we made a mistake with our submissions?"

"No." Lee was wide-eyed as he closed his hands more securely around his cup. He studied the concoction inside. Something with strawberry in the title. "But maybe there's more in the works here than I initially realized."

She heaved a sigh, snatching up her pineapple soother. "I hate when you're more level-headed than me." But she flicked her eyes up to his to let him see the compliment in them. Even cranky, she had to admire his perspective, his ability to see the bigger picture.

All her level-headed musings dissipated as they departed the Hideaway an hour later.

"The idea was to meet up for a workout, right?" Kat stopped them just outside the Hideaway doors.

"Oh no." Lee frowned in a meager attempt to pull the power before her idea was out of the hangar. But it was too late.

"Come on, it'll be fun." Flashing the smile she knew drove him mad, Kat tugged at his elbow, pulling him upwards through the Heptagon, until they came to a stop alongside the starboard doors fringing one facet of the Spectrum.

Snapping open the hidden panel from along the zagged doors' inner edge, Kat began reordering a couple of the wires. All cadets beyond their initial years onboard the Academy were familiar with the rudimentary schematics of ship systems. She and Lee just had a more intimate understanding.

She counted in her head, three... two...

"Okay, okay." Lee sighed, glancing around them, to make sure no other cadets were passing through. "But if we're gonna do this, you'd better be on your best behavior."

She flashed him an angelic smile. *I don't know to what you refer.*

She let him shoo her aside, his fingers working quick as lightning to deactivate the locks. Then, stepping back for her to pass, she sashayed through the dimness and into the vacant arena.

Whistler and Zane met them at the edge of the steamtrap. The abandoned islands dotted the floor before them.

"We shouldn't be here," Zane grumbled, his dark eyes shooting to Kat, despite the fact that the message to meet here had come from Lee.

Whistler didn't protest out loud, but he also glanced around the Spectrum with discomfort.

"We needed a plan, right?" Holding Zane's glares, Kat strode to the switchboard behind him, cranking down one of the levers. The sunken islands began to glow as the neon holodisks re-generated across their surfaces.

"Come on," Whistler relented from behind her. He followed Kat over to the wall, accepting the magenta-lighted vest she handed his way. She didn't wait to see if Zane would follow, before sprinting off into the darkness to claim an island.

Lee set the timers, climbing onto an island equidistance from her and Whistler. The warning *buzz* sounded. And as the fans began whirring, Zane hurtled onto an island.

The islands rose, letting magnetism claim their course until the Gamma cadets levitated fifteen meters in the air. And then the timer began counting down overhead.

Tonight it was every cadet for themselves. No alliances. No audience.

Tonight the point wasn't to win. They all had scores to settle.

The clock blared. And for those initial minutes afterward, they went hard. Catch. Release. Destroy. Hurl.

There was no dancing tonight. Not as they painted the arena in streamlines of electric-lemon and scorched-and-filetedreds before anyone even bothered to do more than launch their disks out into the darkness.

There would be no getting out of the Commander's assignment, whether her ladyship was present for it or not. And pointing fingers at one another would do them no good. As far as the Academy was concerned, they'd all been called out with the lab business.

Requesting a different squadron was also out, for the same reasons they'd all ended up in this position. They'd broken something with whatever they'd done or found on the last raid. And now they had to figure it out. Because apparently, everything else had been put on hold until then.

Kat hurled a disk high above Whistler's magenta vest. Instead of staying on his island, Whistler took the running leap, rocketing up high to catch her holodisk from the air. When he came down, he kept the momentum, arcing between islands in a loose aerial.

He was ready to play.

Kat grinned. They could finally have some fun.

Sprinting, she also leaped from her island, arcing over towards Whistler. They dueled and whirled, until Lee also came over to join them, pulling out all the silly little survival stops they drilled into their cadets every morning.

Tonight, for the few minutes they were able to get away from Academy politics, with no one here watching their every move, tonight was for them.

They were battling it out, going full acrobatics, when a disk came tearing through the gap between them. Whistler actually lowered his arm, the disk he'd been about to throw, while she and Lee just turned to track the source.

The fourth player, who they'd all but forgotten about.

"What's your problem, man," Whistler called out, glancing down at the disk still in hand.

"If this is about how we ended things..." Kat began.

"To put the record straight, I ended things. You were too big of a coward to even have that conversation." Zane shook his head, snorting. "You guys really are perfect for each other." He turned away, then stopped himself. "But do you really think me that petty? That I would let some silly relationship get in the way of my performance as a raider? A relationship, I might add, that you are clearly not mature enough to handle."

Kat had tucked her hands under her arms, squeezing so as not to holler right back at his face.

Tagging himself out, Zane leaped down off his island.

Lee glanced between her and Whistler, before following Zane over the edge.

This left only her and Whistler standing there, staring. He shrugged, and flipping sideways, barreled out of sight.

Kat rolled her eyes, following them down.

They shut off the islands, walking back up through the darkened benches. They were nearing the starboard doors when Zane finally stopped. But this time he directed his comment to Lee. "You guys lied. After that last raid, with the labs. You guys lied."

"The Commander claimed those, we haven't even seen the lab reports yet. We'd be right back here anyway," Lee said slowly, staring back at Zane, point-blank through the darkness.

"She claimed error in all of our labs. But that's not it." Zane shook his head again. "I asked you specifically after the raid what had given you cause to linger. And you said nothing. You admitted nothing. We could have figured this out—we should have figured this out. There is obviously something we missed. Instead, we all look like incompetent fools."

Kat wanted to fire a retort back. Wanted to berate Zane for being so *zapping* difficult to work with. Instead, she looked away. Looked anywhere else. Looked at Whistler, who tracked the whole thing like volleys from a space court. But she'd also never seen the cadet more serious in her life.

"We should have figured this out," Lee said, finally, letting his words hang in the air between them; his words flickered like the degeneration of the holodisks minutes earlier.

Placing two fingers to his wrist, the lifeblood running through his veins, Lee looked back at Zane. "No more lies."

"No more lies," Zane agreed, bowing his head.

A temporary camaraderie, then. They would see how long this would last—she wasn't holding her breath.

CHAPTER 15: LEE

SUNDAY MORNING, Lee picked his way through the still-deserted line in the Canteen. It was early, but he'd wanted to squeeze a workout in. They were meeting up at the PARC in a few minutes to get started with their 'Internal Review'. Whatever that would entail. This thing between their squadron was as fragile as the tofu-scramble hot breakfast he was bypassing this morning.

There'd been no whisperings regarding their shenanigans in the Spectrum. At least none that he'd heard. Of course, they'd also cleaned up after themselves and had quite a bit of experience with hiding their tracks.

Skipping right to the end of the line, he settled on a black plum and a granola bar, tucking the latter into his bag for later. He was strolling out of the Canteen when a low female voice washed over his thoughts.

"Hey, Lee."

He looked over to see Levy standing by the door, her dark lips and lavender cheeks turned up in a little smile. He'd been so completely engrossed in his own stuff, that he hadn't even noticed her. "Did you get your updated schedule okay?" Levy would have been one of those cadets who'd been reassigned to another Gamma for his usual lecture. He couldn't remember who she'd be working with.

"I did." She squinted. "I think I've got Flyn for Exo-Planetary concepts."

"Good." Lee nodded. Flyn was decent.

"Any word yet on the labs?" she asked, "I'd heard there was an issue or something?"

"Yeah—we're still trying to work through that. To be determined..." He tried to make a joke of it, but everything was so up in the air, that he was having a hard time finding humor in their situation.

He felt a little bad. He wanted to say more. He wanted to explain why they'd had to switch things up again and what was going on with the labs. After all, Levy had been on that initial raid. But he wasn't sure at this point how far into his security clearance this latest assignment fell.

Fumbling through a quick, "Well, I'll see you later," Lee walked away, heading up through the ship. The whole exchange had been somewhat dissatisfying, but he didn't know what more he could have even said to her without giving something away.

More and more cadets trickled through the stairways as he climbed higher up the Heptagon to the PARC. He could get used to this, his first taste of life after the Academy, with his days designed around his leisure and his next great assignment.

The Planning and Research Collaboration rooms grouped alongside Mission Assignment and Briefing were typically reserved for Gamma raid use—although he and Kat usually opted for their preferred table in the Hideaway.

He stopped outside the first door on his left. Scanning his hyperband at the plate by the door, Lee strode in.

Zane was already there and sitting near the head of the long table that ran along the middle spine of the room, a set of holofiles open before him.

Clearing his throat, Lee headed for the opposite side, some midway down. He set the plum and granola bar down on the table, slinging his backpack off his shoulders, before kicking it under the table, mentally preparing for a day digging through radioactive data. He didn't bother to spare Zane a glance as he turned to peer into the glittering expanse of holodata his fellow cadet had pulled up.

"What is all this?" Lee asked.

"The lab reports."

"The—what?" Now he glanced over. But Zane gestured with a golden-brown hand to the holofiles before them. There were pages and pages of line items included with the lab reports. Possibly enough to encompass three squadron's worth of sample data... "I'd assumed that they hadn't been able to process any of our submissions. This was all on the hub?"

"Accessible only with security clearance. But yeah," Zane muttered, flicking through another couple of files. "That's not all that's there either."

Lee had only begun sifting through the other files on the hub, when Whistler arrived, with Kat hot on his heels.

"Morning," Kat said, breezing right around the table by Lee. She actually had the gall to appear disappointed that they hadn't flipped the place upside down yet.

Whistler came to a stop at the head of the table, scrutinizing all that had been drawn up. "What the..."

"What are we looking at?" Kat demanded, peering up the length of the table towards Zane and Whistler.

"See for yourself." Stepping back to give Kat some space, Lee scooped up the plum he'd abandoned on the table a few minutes earlier and stared into its black-purple skin.

"This can't be what I think it is. These aren't supposed to be ready," Kat said.

Lee studied the plum in his hands, taking a bite.

That wasn't even the half of it.

It was barely 14:00 hours, but Lee was already exhausted. And mentally drained. Story of his life, lately, it seemed.

They'd spent the morning sifting through the files on the server. Everything was there. Everything. From the lab reports to the actual skimmer sampling logs. There were even copies of each of their sensor and magnetometer observations from the raid, each piece uploaded, labeled, and compiled neatly into a folder on the hub for them.

They'd started combing through the line items of the lab reports, too, comparing them to the sample logs. And so far, they'd deduced no signs of cross-contamination or mislabeling, with nothing flagged by the lab managers or any other assisting personnel. And aside from requiring an official sign-off from the Commander, everything appeared to be complete and in pristine shape.

It was all starting to feel eerily like a setup.

They broke for a bit to clear their heads and stretch their legs, but really it was a sanity check. No one was anxious to push this newfound alliance between them.

Zane mentioned fitting in another workout, and Whistler took off to scale the Wall with some friends. And Kat—she was insisting she get her green juice, which honestly sounded amazing right now. All he'd had yet today was that plum and granola bar from this morning. He promised to catch up with her in a bit. But first, he had a toll to pay. The mom tax.

He'd been putting off this latest call for about a week now, hoping things would settle down for them. But with all they'd dipped their hands in, maybe it was better that he get their call out of the way.

He did a quick once-over of his dorm, peeling open one of his energy protein bars while he waited the token blips for his mom's call to connect. He was going to have to restock soon, Kat had also been devouring them lately. Maybe he could get his order in before the next transport arrived...

"That doesn't look very hearty."

"Hi, Mom." Lee grinned, setting the foil aside as the hologram of Tonya Waters' reality merged with his own. "Hearty, no. But it does the job."

She still appeared slightly concerned, smoothing a manicured hand through her bleached-blond waves as she peered around the virtual space they had opened.

"Are you staying ahead on laundry? Your pillowcase looks like it could use a press."

Lee just smiled, reining in his retorts. Leave it to Tonya to find something to reprove. If she could only see Kat's room...

"I will swap out the pillowcase the next chance I get," Lee quickly assured her. "Is that a new product?" he asked, redirecting the conversation away from the state of his room and gesturing towards the vivid pink she wore on her lips. "I like the fuchsia."

"Oh, why thank you." She fluttered around their stainless steel kitchen towards a neat little stack of boxes on the counter. "I'm trying out Solar's latest collection, they call it *Tropical Explosion*. Aren't they fun?"

Lee nodded, smiling vaguely when she opened up a few of the boxes to show him the various fruit-inspired hues of the products. Shortly after Lee had joined the Academy, Tonya became a consultant for the beauty boutique; she now had clientele across one of the minor star systems. The whole operation was a little ridiculous, and most of the empty space in the house went towards housing the zillions of boxes of cosmetics, but it kept her busy, and she seemed to be really good at it—if the metallic pink plaque above the butter dish was any indication.

"Could your friend Kat use a couple? I could send her Pineapple Sensation? Except, maybe Iced Dragon Fruit would do better with her skin tone..." Tonya considered. "Would you say she's more of a spring or a winter?"

Lee had to fight to hide his grin as he tried to picture Kat sporting the bright yellow or pink lipsticks, but he shook his head. "None of the cadets here wear much makeup. I think you'd be better off targeting a different kind of girl."

"Oh. Okay." Trying not to appear too crestfallen, Tonya busied herself re-stacking a couple of the boxes.

"How's dad?"

"Your father is doing really good." Tonya grinned as she stacked. "He's been busy with work. He had a patient call in just the other day who'd been exposed to some toxins that made his secondary hands turn this shade of violent green..."

Lee nodded while his mom gave him all the updates on his dad, the house, and her closest friend, Bri, who'd also taken up consulting around the same time. His dad was a medic for the Allied Medics Star System Service and was often away for days at a time. Probably another reason she had gotten so involved with Solar Cosmetics after Lee had left.

"You seem happy," Lee commented, watching her. Silly as it may be, his mom clearly loved all of this.

"Thank you, sweetie." Tonya smiled; it made her eyes sparkle. Lee wondered how often they sparkled these days, or if she was too busy pretending not to worry about him and his dad. "But enough about me, tell me all that has been going on with you. What's Kat up to? She and I haven't talked in forever."

Lee rolled his eyes. Even with everything his mom read about the goings-on in the galaxy, he still sometimes got the impression that she pictured their raids as big, intergalactic field trips. But he supposed it was better this way. There was less to worry her.

"Kat's fine—we've both been busy. We received a special assignment recently, us and some of our—friends." He had to bite past that last word. But it was close enough.

"How wonderful! I still remember how excited you both were to go out on your first raids. Have you been keeping up with that space farming? You know your great-great-grandfather was a pioneer of the times..."

Lee had to resist rolling his eyes again; his mom referenced his early ancestor every time the subject came up. As raiders, they were allowed to divulge their status and rank, as to their actual missions, those were generally kept secret as detailed by the Commander.

Space farming had been one of his earliest alibis for how to explain what they did when they went out on raids. Tonya already knew it was an interest of his, and it honestly wasn't that much of a stretch with all the dark radiation sampling they'd been doing lately.

"Uh, yeah. Hey listen, Mom, I've got to run," he said quickly, cutting her off before she had the chance to inquire after more details he'd have to fabricate; he barely knew what to feel about everything right now, let alone how to lie about it. It was like with Levy earlier...

"Oh, okay. I love you, sweetie. We'll set something up again soon, alright? And bring Kat next time."

"I'll do my best." Lee smiled. "Love you, mom."

He ended the call with a click, once more alone in his dorm.

It was always a nice reprieve to be a part of Tonya's little bubble for a few minutes. They were simple calls. But they tied him to humanity. Reminded him that actual lives were being led out there beyond the ship's walls, beyond the next raid.

All of their business with the lab samples and the radiation spikes... It was all lightyears away from Tonya and Solar Cosmetics. Even from his dad, with the expanse of the Allied Medics. And Lee would do everything in his power to keep it that way.

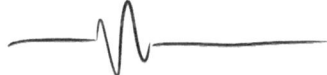

"How is Tonya?" Kat asked when he caught up to her in the Hideaway. Her green drink was down to its last few sips.

"She has some weird colored lip products for you if you want them—Drunk Pineapple or Tropical Vomit, or something."

Kat wrinkled her nose. "I'll pass."

Lee hid his smile. He really ought to figure out a way to loop Kat in next time. His mom would love that.

"Thank her for me, though, will you?" Kat asked, sincerely, curling her legs up under her.

"Of course." And while Kat finished her drink, Lee used the table as a medium to channel his anxieties.

What was it he'd told his mom earlier—that she'd be better off targeting a different type of girl?

Maybe he would, too. Even just sitting there, curled up, Lee could see that Kat was a force of her own. As unpredictable and sought-after as a shooting star. She could take on any galaxy, and very likely win.

Even if the galaxy these days was just getting in their way.

"It was weird though," Lee said, tying up his thoughts. "Trying to explain to Tonya everything that's been going on right now, without like getting into this latest assignment."

"She understands, though. We've always had to keep this part of our lives a secret from her."

"Yeah. But something about this time—it just felt a little different. A little more—invasive, almost, to keep it from her." Not to mention, nothing about this last assignment or raid felt normal.

They stretched their break out as long as they could, Lee trying desperately to shake the unsettling feeling in his gut. But he could feel the hour on his hyperband burning a hole in his wrist.

Reluctantly sitting up, he nodded to Kat. "You ready to dive back into the fire?"

CHAPTER 16: KAT

THEY'D SOMEHOW made it through forty-eight hours as a squadron—and with only minor burns to show for it.

Kat blamed Zane. Had they really needed to draw up every single observational report that Nolan had included on the hub? But they'd accidentally overloaded the PARC's holoblocks that first day, and when things got fiery, Whistler'd had to go beg one of the tech managers to set up a replacement—with a higher photon limit.

One good thing had come of it, though. In the process of re-drawing up all of their holo-files, they'd isolated the samples in a way that led to them uncovering the altered radioactive signatures. They were, in fact, dealing with delta-grays. Dark radiation.

But that still didn't explain the seemingly random radiation spikes... Or why the radiation had flatlined. That was today's objective.

Rolling on her feet from heel to toe, Kat peered across the glittering star map of their former mission coordinates that hovered over the table between them. The dotted holo-representation was a similar star map to the one the Commander had used in their original briefing, except they'd started adding in the coordinates where each of their space debris samples had been found. They were looking for asterisms that might help them understand the dark rays' latest activity. And what better way to find those patterns than through a literal map of the star system in question.

Kat bounced on her toes a few times while she tried in vain to locate the couple of samples she'd been plotting. She'd been on her feet for the past several hours—and not in the loose, got a nice workout kind of way. Problem was, the line items were all starting to look the same. Between the three sets of reports from their prior squadrons, they had quite the range of space debris to cover before they could come up with any concrete assumptions. She longed to go back to the days of collecting plant samples and calling it good. She would even scale the *zapping* blank cliffs again, cracked fingernails and all, if it meant getting them out of this latest assignment.

"And we had to do pink?" Zane groaned as a fresh debris sample plot appeared on their star map.

"It's cerise." Kat frowned. "And it stands out." If only the answers they sought could also show themselves in vivid color.

"Starting down another one," Whistler murmured, clearing a space before him as he drew up a fresh set of lab reports. Between the cerise star map and each of their holo-files, at least a dozen holograms glimmered over the table between them, its surface littered with a random assortment of water bottles, snack bags, protein bars, and a couple of Lee's black plums. The smell of charred smoke had, thankfully, long since been filtered from the room. All in a day's work.

She'd located the coordinates for the samples she'd been plotting before, when something else about them caught her eye. "What do we make of these?" she asked.

Lee popped one of his lazr-pods from his ears as she expanded the sample data so they were large enough for Whistler and Zane to see opposite them. The altered radioactive signatures, evident of the dark rays, were, of course, there with the samples. But that wasn't what had caught her attention.

She studied the radioactive isotopes before noting their relative location on the star map. Their *central* location. One from which she herself had piloted a RIM vehicle to collect samples during those pivotal hours.

Both samples had been collected hundreds of kilometers from any of the radiation spikes. One might even call them obsolete... Except—

"Wait a second," Lee leaned in closer, eyes darting between the two samples. "These aren't the ones we collected out by—"

"The asteroid," Kat confirmed with a faint smile when he looked back at her suddenly.

"What asteroid?" Zane asked.

Lee took a step back, running a hand through his hair as he explained their situation with practiced patience. "Each of these samples was collected near the magnetic field. They appear to indicate that there was both dark radiation, and a mini radiation spike present—at least at some point in time. However..." He frowned, stepping closer once more to scan the hologram.

"There was no asteroid or planetary object there to trigger that radiation spike?" Kat nodded. "It's just like with the coordinates that triggered the AMG sensors."

"And that's not all," she said, expanding the sample data once more. "Do you see the pattern with the isotopes? It's almost like they've been altered a second time..."

Lee turned back to Zane. "Could you pull up one of those data points near the radiation spikes? I want to see their radioactive signatures."

Wordlessly, Zane did as demanded. They compared the isotopes side-by-side. "They aren't an exact match," he said slowly.

"But they're pretty damn close," Whistler agreed, shooting her and Lee a sharp slash of a grin.

"How's that for an asterism?" Kat sang, to which even Zane gave the slightest hint of a smile.

There was no sensor record of a spike in radiation around the magnetic field. And yet, there they were, sharing the same, twice-altered radioactive signature. Something was definitely out there.

They did more comparisons with their radioactivity data for the next couple of hours, identifying similar patterns from the isotope samples collected near the other radiation spikes. They were all connected. The spikes. The magnetic field. Whatever was out there with the dark rays had left its own unique radioactive signature.

If only there was a way for them to procure more data and samples from that magnetic field...

166

And as she stared up into the freckled pink star map before them, the new evidence taunted her, like the beginnings of a lightning cloud just gathering friction.

Hours, and what felt like days later, Kat collapsed into her chair, straddling it backward. She pawed at her face with her hands. Then, remembering she'd actually put eyeliner on earlier, she dabbed frantically under her eyes to clear away any smudging. She didn't know why she even bothered. Could the day be over already?

Wrinkling her nose at the remaining energy protein bar left sitting on the table, she glanced over Lee's shoulder to see the hologram he was reading through on his lap. "What are you up to? That doesn't look like our radiation sample logs..." She leaned around her chair to get a better look.

"Academy bylaws," Lee murmured, not lifting his eyes. She watched his green irises scan line after line, while he read further down the hologram. How had he even learned to achieve that level of concentration? After a day spent plotting, and the other half squinting, her eyes were burning.

Further up the table from them, Zane was up to his elbows in isotopic decay data. He had a power drink open before him with his usual, I'm-going-to-do-pushups-on-your-face scowl.

Their line of insights had gone dark after the radioactive signature. She was about ready to put this assignment to bed. And yet—with what they'd been able to accomplish thus far, it truly seemed like the four of them might actually survive this project and see it through completion—provided there were no more fires. But beyond that? She studied the tension in both Lee and Zane's postures, their calculated attempts at appearing relaxed. It wouldn't be long before the stress got to someone.

She glanced across the table to Whistler. He'd tied his red-brown hair in a knot at the base of his neck. The style made him look more mature, with some of that seriousness from the other night. He'd turned out to be easier to work with than she'd expected. Had he ever gotten around to contacting Ty's friend?

"Okay, here we go," Lee said, glancing up. "'Internal Review grants Academy Leadership exclusive access to claimed material for a limited period for the sole purpose of quality control with regards to maintaining the AMG's records.'"

"We're still missing the quality control part," Kat said, glaring up at the cerise results of their flawlessly intact radioactivity records.

"I don't know why, but I wanted it to be more than that," Lee frowned, skimming through the bylaw once again.

She extended a hand, patting him lightly on the shoulder. "It's okay."

He pinched her arm. "But I mean, why would they bother to go through all this work for a handful of radioactivity labs? Even with what we uncovered with the signatures today." Sitting up, he pushed the bylaws to the side, sifting through the other holograms spread over the table between them. "I guess technically, that would also include the sensor data. The magnetometers... but to what end?"

"Commander Blanche."

"Sorry?" Kat asked. Her eyes shot across the table to where Whistler watched them debate with narrowed eyes.

"You asked why they would go through all the work," Whistler said impatiently. "But it's not the Commanding General; it's not the Commanding Council. The bylaws specifically refer to Academy leadership, which is Commander Blanche."

It took a few seconds for his words to click in her head, but she got there. She groaned. "That's what Nolan was trying to tell us."

Lee was nodding. "Both times we were in there, Nolan was very particular with his wording."

"He was being such a dick about it too..." Kat muttered.

Whistler grinned.

"It was the same for me." Zane looked over from the holodata he was sifting through. He waved a hand towards Lee and the Academy bylaws still open across his lap. It had been a good catch, with the wording and all. "Whatever this is, she knows what she's doing. But what I'm struggling to understand with all this, is why? Why does she want this information kept secretive? It's not like we haven't all encountered dark radiation before."

"And why loop us in?" Lee nodded, catching Zane's drift. "That doesn't exactly make it a tight secret."

Kat didn't call them out on the fact that this wasn't exactly normal dark ray behavior. They had larger stars to align.

"It keeps it within Academy walls, though," Whistler said, a moment later, warm brown gaze drifting over their star map again.

"Then, maybe, it's not a question of why. But from who," Lee murmured.

But at this point, Commander Blanche could be hiding the secret from anyone. The AMG. The galaxy in general. Things in the public eye had already gotten crazy out of hand. Kat had read barely a week or so ago about all the fear-induced experiments fueling the shadow-markets. She shook her head as she flicked her eyes over to her hyperband, checking the hour. She started mindlessly scrolling through the latest pipeline's news and updates at her wrist.

She scrolled past another article on regulating defense experiments, then scrolled back up as she processed one of the sub-headlines.

Commanding Council Called to Session to Address Illegal Shadow Sales

"Our Commander has a seat on the council, doesn't she?" she asked quietly.

"Sure," Lee said.

Kat read them the headline from the report on her hyperband, slumping down again into her seat. "If she was trying to hide these reports from someone within the AMG, I imagine she's had a hard time of it. She's been in session with them all week."

A few seconds later, Lee joined her. "This is getting fun, isn't it?"

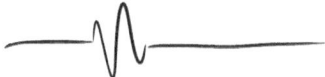

"What'll it be tonight, a bag of chips, or a power drink?" Lee joked as they made their way down into the Hideaway, having finally broken for the night. They'd missed dinner for the third night in a row, which meant it was either raiding the vending machines or another one of Lee's energy bars. And since they'd had those for lunch…

"Don't make me laugh." But despite their missing dinner, the night was still young, and most of the tables in the Hideaway were already in use.

"I'll go get food," Lee said, peeling off.

Kat went to perch at the railing in the center of the room, stretching her arms across her chest as she looked down over the darkened Canteen. Apparently, this was what their lives were reduced to now.

"Another interesting day." Whistler came up to perch beside her at the railing. She supposed they would all be wandering around here somewhere.

Kat huffed a laugh. "Sure was."

"Is it just me, or was it weird to see those two actually getting along today?"

"Zane and Lee?" Kat snorted. "It's painful to watch, right? You're not alone." But she shook her head, glancing across the room towards Lee's medium brown head by the vending machines. "He's trying. They're both trying."

"Well, as long as they don't start making out in front of us..." Whistler grinned, then seemed to consider. "Although, that doesn't actually sound all that bad..."

Kat snorted, tilting her head as she studied her fellow Gamma. She'd heard he was open to both genders. Whistler with his laid-back manner. The crooked grin that hooked up on one side.

They weren't friends. Not really. She'd only ever considered him a potential rival; someone to steal the good Placements.

She'd never stopped to question if Whistler was even charting for that future.

Lee came back around the railing, then, holding out a skinny aluminum can in his hand. "They were out of the chips you like, so I got you this instead."

Kat just stared at it. Her stomach was ready to eat itself. But she was pretty sure she'd rather go hungry than drink that tonight.

She was daring herself to be the bigger human and grab it, but then Lee pulled the can back, tossing her a bag of chips from behind his back.

"The machine spat this out by mistake." Lee shrugged, cracking the energy drink open with a *chink*.

"You don't really have to drink that. I'll share my chips." Kat tore into the bag.

Lee took a swig. "I've had worse."

She eyed Lee suspiciously, before offering the bag to Whistler, instead. "You getting anything?"

"Nah. I've been snacking all afternoon. I'm good." Whistler waved to a couple friends across the room. "I'll see you jokesters *a demain*."

"Hey Whistler," she called out as he turned to leave. "I like the base-knot." She nodded towards his hair.

Whistler winked, shooting her his crooked smile once more, before heading to meet his friends.

"I can't believe you are really drinking that," Kat said, turning back to Lee.

"It's not that bad." Lee elbowed her in the ribs.

"It is. Those things suck *asterisms*." Kat waggled her brows at the callback to their findings this afternoon. "Too soon?" She teased.

"Too soon," Lee agreed.

A gaggle of noisy and giggling cadets flopped into the Hideaway. Rather than linger to learn more about who was doing who, she and Lee edged their way back out. One of the cadets in the pack turned as they passed, waving a lavender hand at her and Lee.

"Hey, Levy," Lee called.

Levy smiled, cheeks blushing profusely as she called back, "Hey, Lee."

Kat frowned after the girl as they turned away. What was that about?

"You know, this hasn't been all bad working with Zane and Whistler," Lee commented as they made their way up to their dorms.

She eyed him suspiciously. If they had to keep these niceties up in their free time too, however scarce...

"Don't get me wrong. I still can't stand them," Lee corrected himself quickly when he caught the look on her face. "But overall, it's been okay."

Yeah yeah. "I'll see you later, Waters." She stuffed the rest of the chips into his hands. Maybe their thin diet lately was getting to his head.

"Good night, Hanneman."

CHAPTER 17: LEE

COINCIDENCE, OR correlation?

That was what Lee was thinking about as he made his way up to the Command wing the following morning.

It was definitely a correlation, that both their squadron and Whistler's and Zane's squadrons had ended up out on that last raid. The Commander wanted to send out her best. And as much as he wanted to believe it was also correlation, that the samples he'd had them linger that day to nab from the nearby magnetic field had turned out to be essential to their mission, it was also entirely possible that it was just coincidence.

He pictured their glittery cyber-unicorn, "cerise" map they'd compiled. The cosmic trail the galaxy, or rather its groundskeeper, had left them had also brought along a whole slew of new assumptions to play with.

They'd gotten lucky. An educated-lucky, but lucky all the same.

But where they'd received the invitation from the Commander for a briefing, barely a day following their breakthroughs with the dark radiation signatures, was that correlation? Or another coincidence?

He supposed he'd learn pretty quickly here.

He scanned his hyperband at the doors, still somewhat in awe of the new clearance he now held at his wrist.

"—we know the drill, Nolan."

Lee had to reign in his laugh as the feisty vanilla-blonde ponytail came into view. Nothing like Kat telling someone off first thing in the morning. She was still huffy from dealing with Secretary Nolan when Lee assumed his usual spot at her side.

Whistler and Zane were both there already, as well. That was no surprise. Lee had known this time around to check the cadets on the invitation in advance.

Nolan, thankfully, refrained from repeating his script, instead nodding curtly at Lee. "It will be just a few minutes."

"Yes sir," Lee said, ogling Kat's ever-so blatant eye roll.

"What's the worst that happens, they kick me out?" she stage-whispered.

Whistler smothered a grin, adjusting the band that held his hair in a knot at the nape of his neck. There was something a little different about his fellow Gamma lately, or maybe it was just seeing Whistler so serious. But both Whistler and Kat appeared to be in pleasant spirits this morning. Apparently, she and Whistler ran on the same mood-schedule these days.

"Actually, did you ever know Gunnar?" Kat asked Whistler, clutching at her arm as she angled herself away from Nolan's retreating figure. "Almost got kicked out during our Ultra year —cocky as a *zapping* astro-bull. He had quite the temper too..."

"Laser licker," Lee muttered, after ensuring that Nolan was truly out of earshot.

Whistler choked on a laugh.

"And that's putting it mildly," Lee added darkly.

"Lee didn't like him," Kat said.

He glanced at her sidelong. "If I can recall correctly, you didn't either. I believe the words 'sloppy' and 'tongue wash' came into play."

An expression somewhere between amusement and disgust flickered across Kat's face. "But anyway," Kat said, shrugging matter-of-factly, "I heard he actually mouthed off to the Commander towards the end of his Gamma year and lost all of his offers for Placement."

"Where did he end up?" Whistler asked.

"He accepted some minor role within the star system," Zane said, not bothering to glance over in their direction from his position beside the door.

"I always thought his parents would've pulled some strings," Kat said thoughtfully.

"I think that's how he was able to land that position. Big loss of honor," Zane said. Lee didn't add that Gunnar probably wouldn't have had very many options, even with his connections. The cadet's rankings had been okay, but his work was second-rate. As, apparently, was his game when it came to girls.

His mind was dredging up other memories from Ultra year when Nolan returned on crisp steps, and they were escorted inside another unmarked door. Like their regular briefing rooms alongside the PARC, this one was bright and devoid of furniture.

Then the Commander strode through the door, with her usual dominating presence and the trailing air of expectation. Lee straightened, hands shooting behind his back as the door slid shut. She was back. His eyes snagged on her commencing figure—maybe it was a trick of the light, but was that a crease in her jacket?

The Commander reached the front, and as she turned towards them, a thin slice of red slipped over her cheek. Quick as lightning, she'd shifted, tucking the loose strands back into her usual immaculate hairdo.

He adjusted his stance. What was going on?

When she addressed them, however, their Commander was as fierce and unyielding as ever. "Good morning, cadets. Academy Secretary Nolan is processing your findings with the Internal Review. In the meantime, we have another assignment for you. As dictated under statute 4A of the Academy bylaws, with respect to the Raider program of the AMG, the Allies of the Mangorian Galaxy, I have recommended your squadron for the following mission..."

She turned towards the holoblock at her back, and Lee couldn't help the spark that shot up his veins. The crackle at his fingertips. Lee was more than ready for this next assignment; maybe they'd finally get the chance to finish what they'd started. It felt like ages since they'd been sent out, rather than a mere week.

Squadron, though. He could sense that hesitation in the other three bodies standing along either side of him. Were they going to be able to keep this working together thing up?

The Commander drew up the holographic representation of the now familiar star system. "Our sensors have once again detected spikes of radiation as of 18:24 hours yesterday afternoon. While the exact coordinates have varied, their relative location is the same, falling along the Argursian toroidal belt just outside the Anova star system. And although we have since learned there is no asteroid, be wary of the elevated magnetism levels..." While Commander Blanche spoke, Lee traced the coordinates on the star map with his eyes. The radiation spikes once more surrounded the magnetic field, which was denoted this time by a series of connecting dots. "Your mission is again to investigate the radiation and its relationship to the magnetic field, as well as any other possible sources that fall within range."

At this point the Commander paused, turning fully away from the holographic map at her back. "This next instruction comes directly from me. Uncover what you can and report back via the usual channels. But you are not, under any circumstances, to engage, despite what you may find out there. Is that clear?"

More than one breath caught. The crackling in his bloodstream, smothered, in a single sentence. Engage... What exactly did she believe was out there?

The Commander continued, "You will again be making the jump through hyperspace at galactic marker MGIII-2. Assemble whatever squadron you need, but I will caution you again, take care with this assignment." There was the briefest of pauses during which Lee swore he saw a hint of that fear, and that concern cross her eyes. And then she was continuing again where she had left off. "To accommodate for size, you will be taking out one of the cruisers. There will be a time allowance of ninety-six hours to support the shields on your spacecraft. We expect you out of there before then. Any questions?"

A larger ship and better shields. And with her allowing them to recruit additional cadets to the squadron...

She intended them to stay until they found something.

"Academy Secretary Nolan will go over the details. Good luck cadets." Lee had finally adjusted to her presence when the Commander took her leave, the room feeling suddenly too large, and their raid too looming. In her place, Nolan addressed them, starting down the usual detailing.

"Raid files for your squadron have been added to the hub. Please submit your squadron list for approval by 19:00 hours. Cadet health surveys will be expected each night by 21:00 hours with a full mission report by no later than thirty-six hours following mission completion. You will be notified when your ship has been assigned and scheduled for departure." Nolan's eyes dipped. "In the meantime, take care as you make the *rounds*. You are dismissed."

Was that a warning?

They were back outside the zagged doors of the Command wing before Whistler turned to him. "You don't think he some-how knows about the Laser Rounds the other night?"

"Oh, he definitely knows," Lee said. A glance at Zane and Kat confirmed they were thinking the same thing. And yet, there was no hostility in anyone's eyes, either. Instead, there was shock. Shock and confusion.

The radiation spikes had returned, and the Academy was sending its top cadets back out to investigate. That part was clear. But as to what had come of the Commander's meeting with the Commanding Council this past week, and Nolan's little role in their dark ray findings… Lee didn't know how those played into any of this.

Correlation or coincidence?

The others didn't have much to add, either, perhaps having been drawn into their own thoughts as he had; a swirling haze of uncertainty. They talked very little as they headed back down through the Heptagon.

Zane excused himself as they reached the upper skywalk. "Meet up later."

Whistler turned off a couple stairways later at the Hideaway doors, with little more than a wave.

They were down to only Kat and Lee when they wove through the Canteen doors. They still had a good half hour before breakfast would be cleared away, but the hall was already deserted; the majority of cadets studiously in the training levels awaiting their first lessons. Rather than linger there, exposed, especially after Nolan's subtle comment about their happenings in the Spectrum, they took their trays up with them to the Hideaway.

They'd rounded the first stairway before Lee tackled another thought on his mind. Their squadron list.

"I'm going to recommend Levy."

"For the raid?" A laugh burst from Kat's lips. "Be serious."

"I am serious."

Kat stopped so abruptly that he thought she'd missed a step. Balancing her tray on the railing, she whipped her head around to face him. "Levy is a VL. A *VL*, Lee. She's still in her training years, a fact you yourself pointed out just the other day."

"And *you* said that having a VL on our squadron would do us some good," Lee shot back.

"That was before." Kat shook her head, her vanilla-blonde ponytail lashing behind her.

"Are we really back on this? Levy is a good raider. And you and I have never cared about status."

"It's not about that." Kat flicked her eyes away.

"Then what is it about, Kat?"

"I just... I want to be sure you only want her around for raid reasons, that's all. We have a lot on the line," she amended.

Lee could feel the heat coursing through him, the sudden flare of irritation rising up inside of him. "On that last mission, she kept pace; she didn't utter a single negative word or put up any resistance as far as I could tell. Not to mention, she was one of the best cadets when manual override took over. She earned her place here."

He meant to turn away, to keep walking, but he couldn't help himself, couldn't let himself walk away quite yet. "I thought you liked her."

"I did—do. I just didn't know how much you did."

Lee studied her, blinking through his incredulity. He didn't need her permission to recommend Levy. But, really. Really? He didn't know what to say to any of this. He was too frustrated to even form coherent thoughts.

Because there was no possible way that Kat could be feeling threatened right now. *Kat*, who was at this very minute, the top of their class, which meant she was also at the top of the Academy. *Kat,* who for no reason, other than sheer boredom and total disregard for Lee, had likely made out with half the guys in said class and several from older classes in the past. *Kat,* with her long, toned legs and that absurdly cocky grin. The insatiable blonde ponytail whose length she kept running her hands through absentmindedly as she tightened it. Lee was shaking his head he was so furious.

"I don't even know what to say right now," he muttered as Kat ran a clenched hand through her hair once more.

He pictured Levy, with her wide, innocent eyes... Yes, Levy was a *VL,* for *void-sake*. A VL who very likely didn't even know who she wanted to be yet. And if she had Kat scrutinizing her, stacking that additional pressure on her this early on in her career...

Lee waited until he'd calmed down and regained some composure before he tried to speak again. "Look, let's just go find a place to sit down and eat something, okay? My blood sugar is low. We'll figure out the list later."

Directing his chin to the level waiting for them at the top of the stairs, he averted his gaze. But he waited for her to join him before they started back up the stairs.

CHAPTER 18: KAT

SHE WASN'T jealous.

She wasn't.

Because that wouldn't be fair to Lee.

Even if she hadn't exactly seen the girl coming…

But apparently, it didn't matter. Three days later, despite the urgency presented in their briefing, they still hadn't heard anything back from the Commander on their ship or their squadron list.

They'd bartered and haggled that first afternoon, whittling it down, until they'd put together a short and succinct list of cadets; they'd settled upon ten. Six cadets and four squadron leads. Zane and Whistler were each bringing two cadets to the squadron. She and Lee each got one; as co-squadron leads, they technically shared raid experience across their joint pool of cadets.

Ten cadets, to uncover the source behind the mysterious radiation spikes. That is, if they ever got sent out to actually do the *zapping* thing. But at least their latest mission assignment got them away from the PARC. After days spent cloistered around that research table, it was just nice to be roaming the ship freely again.

Just to keep up appearances, they'd participated in a blaster showcase with the younger cadets, where they'd further solidified their places at the top of the Academy, as if it should ever be called into question to begin with. The rest of the cadets had all dispersed by now to enjoy their weekend, leaving the four of them to claim the corner of the blaster range.

"What if we just contacted our cadets anyway?" Whistler asked. He stood at the edge of the zap-line, taking aim with the latest blaster model that had come in. This particular model boasted a long-range frequency well over the usual strength for its size. A low whistle escaped his lips as the weapon decimated its target on the far end of the range.

To her left, Lee sucked in a breath as he tracked the blast. She'd give it two minutes before Lee abandoned the blaster he was holding to get his hands on the same model. "We'd be going against the Commander," he said, his eyes still drooling after the blast's wake. "Which basically means going against the AMG, as well. Not to mention, it wouldn't reflect well on our rankings as Gamma cadets."

"Yeah, but when has that ever stopped us?" Kat winked. Powering up her own blaster, she fired with deadly accuracy, annihilating her target. So what if *Nolan* called them out again.

Zane lifted his golden-brown chin towards Lee. "I'm with him. We've got Placement coming up. This is one line we shouldn't cross." The looks that passed between them afterward, might have been considered as gratefulness, were it anyone else—solidarity, even. Except this was Zane and Lee. The best she could describe it was a degree warmer than usual.

For a few minutes, the only sounds were the *zingings* and *zaps* as they took aim again and again.

"Why are they dragging this out, though?" Kat wondered aloud, barely bothering to aim as she fired off her blaster with very low interest.

"With all the repeat activity surrounding Argos..." Whistler was nodding.

"I'm sorry, what?" Kat laughed, cutting through the noise from the blasters.

"Argos? The magnetic field near the Argursian Toroidal Belt, formerly believed to be an asteroid? It's a bit of a mouthful to keep repeating all of that..." Whistler explained.

Lee huffed a laugh, peering down with admiration at the fresh, long-range blaster for which he'd swapped his other. On Whistler's other side, Zane offered a weak grimace, which was basically a smile for him these days.

"Argos it is." Kat grinned.

"Whatever we're calling it," Zane commented, dropping his grimace altogether, "I'm wondering if the delay could also be related to the Commander's meeting with the Commanding Council this last week. She sure appeared to be having a rough time of it when we saw her."

"I ran into Nolan when I was coming up from the central skywalk the other day," Whistler observed. Whatever work the Gamma had been doing on his beloved Lyra. "You don't think the Commander would've been called away to meet with them again, do you?"

Commander Blanche had definitely looked wearied when they'd gone in for their briefing. Enough so, that Kat had almost forgiven their Commander's ask with her 'Internal Review nonsense' over the course of the past week.

They hadn't heard anything from Nolan, either, in the days since the briefing. Not with more cryptic messages for them to wrack their heads over, and not in response to their research and the internal review they'd been conducting.

Kat ran her hands over her ears catching the flyaways. "I haven't seen any more official council meetings on the pipeline." Not that it meant all that much. Who knew how much of the AMG goings-on were actually broadcasted their way.

Zane voiced as much. But his guess was as good as hers. "Whatever she's been doing, she wants us to be the ones out there."

"Her best." Kat studied Zane's face as he flicked his eyes to her. The lack of distance there. It had been a while since she'd seen that annoying smirk he often carried surface.

"I'm still curious as to why, though. Why go through all of this, why keep it a secret?" Lee asked, feigning ignorance of the exchange between her and Zane. Or displaying real ignorance. There was no acting involved.

There were still a bunch of answers they were missing.

Their mission back out to Argos would be its own beast. They'd need to be prepared, going in, if they wanted to succeed.

Which meant they'd need to make sure their squadron was also fully onboard and ready...

"We don't need approval to instruct..." Kat murmured, watching as Whistler pulverized the prospective target on the wall for the umpteenth time in a row.

"I don't follow?" Lee asked, his green eyes skipping from the target to her.

Even Whistler lowered his blaster with interest, a slow grin already forming on his face.

"I mean, we can't *officially* brief them with the raid details without approval, yeah, there's a line we probably shouldn't cross. But, I mean, no one could stop us if we happened to be hanging out on the training levels at the same time as our cadets, doing the same drills and exercises..."

"Just a little extra coaching from their Gamma mentors." Whistler nodded, catching her drift.

An unofficial squadron.

Lee's eyes flashed. *I know exactly what you're doing.*

She held his stare with her own, awaiting the verdict. "It would be *under the radar*, of course," Kat clarified out loud, just to make sure everyone was on the same page.

"I don't know..." Zane said, slowly.

"Well, I'm down." Whistler was grinning from ear to ear. "We've been sitting around, killing time for three days now. Squadron approval, or not, we need to be training together. We need to make sure everyone is prepped and up to code."

But Kat still had her eyes trained on Lee. His was the only endorsement that mattered in her mind. "We know this has something to do with the radiation signature we found. It has to be. And with all the secrecy the Commander has put us through... We've got one shot, one more chance to get this right and figure things out. I doubt they send us out a third time."

Lee took in a couple of long, drawn breaths. She could see the conflicting thoughts warring there in him, and the opposition, whatever it may be. But this is what they were trained to do. They obeyed orders, yes. But it was also instilled in them to go above and beyond. To complete the mission. "Whistler's right. We do need to be ready. And if this is what it takes..."

Let's see what you've got, Hanneman. The unspoken words, meant only for her, flashed in his eyes.

Kat beamed. It felt like they were back on track, despite their little hiccup the other day. Yes, she still didn't entirely understand his fascination with the VL girl, why it had to be her out on the raid. And yes, to win him back, she'd played in a little to the self-sacrificing, for-the-good-of-the-universe crap that always rang well with Lee. But at the end of the day, she had his back, and he had hers. She was determined to support him.

"I'm in, too," Zane relented at last.

And with the four of them now onboard with the new plan, Kat turned back to face one of the targets on the wall with renewed focus. "Who's up for a rematch?"

A rematch or a recharging. Maybe that's what everyone had needed all along. Maybe that was all she and Lee had needed.

Letting their competitive natures take over, they started yet another contest to determine who was the best. It would very likely end in another four-way draw, with more than one bruised ego.

But it worked for them.

CHAPTER 19: LEE

THE UNDERCURRENTS of rebelliousness and excitement guided them as he and Kat wound their way down through the darkened stands of the Spectrum the following evening. Like with Whistler and Zane the other night, they were taking a risk in meeting their squadron down here tonight; Nolan's warning only amplified that risk. Someone could walk in right now and report them for breaking into the Spectrum, incinerating their squadron plans before they could even get them off the ground.

Of course, tonight could also be epic.

It hadn't been difficult over the course of the day for the four of them to covertly make contact with their cadets—Sunday was another free day. Lee hadn't minded at all swinging down to the training levels when he saw Levy heading there after breakfast. And seeing the surprise and slight mortification on her face as he'd fallen into step beside her had only been a perk.

They'd passed the same message along to each of their cadets: *23:00 hours. Blackout Galaxy. Starboard doors.*

They'd know what it meant.

They were a little early, but even in the faint starlight filtering in through the windows high above them, he could make out Whistler, with his long hair braided into a knot behind his head. He stood at the base of the stands talking animatedly to someone. He looked over as they cleared the last bench.

"Hey guys," Whistler said, running a hand through his hair. "Have you met—"

"Hanna." Lee nodded towards the X cadet. There was a knowing glint in her hazel eyes as Hanna turned towards them. She sized them up with a disinterest that was betrayed by the heightening of her darkened brows. Beside him, Kat wore what Lee could only describe as a roguish grin. The three of them had gotten into a bit of a scuffle a year ago, an indirect result of the cadet's holographic design abilities and a set of flagged IDs...

"You know each other?" Whistler asked, glancing between them.

"It's been a minute..." Lee shot her a slash of smile.

"Created any fake identities lately?" Kat inquired, grin still in place.

"I've learned a few new tricks," Hanna said, again feigning disinterest as she inspected a set of manicured nails.

They were discussing some of the other cadets they had in common from past raids, when Zane slipped up beside them. He took up a semi-casual stance, facing into the stands as a pair of fair-haired cadets clambered towards them from the opposite side of the Spectrum. Those doors definitely hadn't been unlocked before...

Whistler had insisted they bring both twins onboard; Lee had heard this from other Gammas as well, that if you could get them, you wanted them on your squadron. But as the twins came up beside Whistler, sandwiching him between them, Lee wondered idly, and not for the first time, whether Whistler didn't have kinky reasons of his own for wanting them both there.

One of the twins had her hands in her pockets, fair hair poking out in wisps from the tiny knots on either side of her head. The other wore hers loose with a black choker around her neck. They had faint smiles on their faces as they glanced from him to Zane, and around at the gathered faces, feeling out a weak spot. Those grins turned maniacal as they landed on Hanna.

"Nice nails," the twin with the choker said. And Lee braced himself for some sort of catfight.

"Thanks, they can cut wire," Hanna said, flicking her eyes up and baring her teeth in a grin of her own. So the cadet did have some grit to her.

The twins shared a glance between themselves.

Lee flicked his head away to hide his amusement, catching Zane's gaze instead. They would be trouble. Distrust flashed there—or disgust, it could have been either. Maybe both. But Lee held that look, nodding subtly. They could work with this.

A couple more cadets made their way down through the stands. One held a portable video game poking out from under his arm with dark hair that hung in his face; he slouched as he walked. Lee didn't miss the way the cadet's eyes gravitated over to Kat, seeming to latch on as he came to stand a couple paces from the others. Lee eyed him a moment, before dismissing him; it would be fine. Especially as Levy came over, a shy smile on her face.

He felt bad. He'd barely spoken to her in the days since the last raid. Not since the, 'Hey, Levy,' he'd said in passing the other night. The youngest cadet to the squadron by two full years, and yet she belonged here every bit as much as they did. She held her head high, black hair shining, as she joined the small group, nodding her hellos.

"Levy, this is Hanna and—" Lee motioned unwillingly to the second cadet, his hand edging toward his gaming device.

"Jed," the cadet said simply.

"Jed." Lee gritted his teeth, matching a name to the disdain already forming around the kid's entire personality. Kat hadn't yet seemed to notice his attentions, still glancing between the twins and Hanna with interest. Zane had better have a good reason for including the cadet on the squadron.

"Levy and I go back at least a month, right, Kam?" One of the twins said to her sister, the pair of them exchanging a look before peering over at her.

"We are impressed to see you down here tonight," the sister agreed. And when she shifted, Lee noted a septum piercing glinting at the twin's nose. At least he'd be able to tell them apart.

Lee watched to see how Levy took to the challenge, if she was aware of the year discrepancy of their gathering squadron. But Levy seemed more or less unaffected, giving the twins a polite smile as she turned to Lee to explain. "We did a challenge together down at the energy rings a few weeks back, Kiara, Kamata, and I."

It was his turn to be impressed. He couldn't suppress his smile as he looked around at the alliances and bonds already forming. They would need those alliances; they planned to push their cadets. Which meant tonight was already off to a much more successful start than he could have anticipated.

It wasn't long before Nikola drifted down through the stands, looking as if he'd been swept in by accident. But he seemed excited as he peered about, like everyone here was part of one of his scientific studies. Lee supposed, in a way, they were.

Lee joined the other squadron leads, Zane looking dutifully on, with one eye keeping watch on the doors above them, while Kat stared down their cadets, basking in the superiority of their position, and Whistler, just along for the ride. The four of them stood there a moment, sizing up their assembled squadron. Shadow infractors of the vacant arena.

"We have all ten of us here now," Lee murmured, the empty benches around them seeming to absorb his voice.

"We'll see if it's enough to face-down Argos," Whistler said, softly, drawing out the words, reminding them what it was they were up against. It was a seemingly large number for a squadron mission to do what he anticipated would be more standing around hundreds of thousands of light years from here. But on the gut chance there was more going on with Argos than it seemed, the only chance Lee and the others really cared about at this point, they wanted to have their best. What could they say, they'd been molded after their Commander.

"Let's make this count," Zane said, eyes still on the starboard doors above them.

Drawing in closer so they could better see each other in the starlight, they started through introductions once more on lowered voices. It was all posturing, really, over who brought what to the table. And amidst the excitement and expectancy glinting in all of their faces, Lee managed to identify a couple more cadets, matching names and skills to faces. Jed was supposedly a brilliant programmer under his careless facade. And the twins, Kiara and Kamata, were well-versed in quantum mechanics. And although he'd since identified that one of them had a piercing, he couldn't for the life of him, remember which was which.

When it got to his and Kat's turn to introduce their cadets, Kat merely nodded toward each of them. Nikola. Levy. But any subtlety or nonchalance was dismissed by the ferocity and pride in her pale grey eyes. Just the fact of being invited here tonight was a testament to their excellence. Hiding his grin, Lee tipped his head back towards her to bring this home.

To *the void,* with whoever or whatever it was that was currently messing around with the Commander and their raid approvals. Whistler had said it best last night, if they planned to succeed, they needed to have everyone prepped and training together as a squadron.

Kat cleared her throat, and nine pairs of eyes skittered her way under cover of darkness. "As you have probably guessed by now, we can't officially brief you. But as part of our unofficial mission, we have your first assignment."

She met Lee's eye as she paused for dramatic effect. She was very much enjoying her theatrics this evening. Lee winked.

"We are going to train," she went on. "Starting tomorrow, with every free moment and second that we have. We are going to push the limits beyond what you even thought our tech capabilities possible. Our mission will be—*complicated,* at best. But we want you to be prepared for every possible scenario so that there will be no surprises when we get out there. Any questions?"

It was almost scary how similar her voice sounded to their Commander right then. But nods made their way around the circle shadowing her words.

"And as an additional parameter to this assignment—" she paused once more, letting the gravity of the situation sink in. "All of this stays between us. Our meeting tonight, the training to follow, nothing gets back to Command. No one can know what we are doing."

The twins had gotten those maniacal smiles again. Was that a normal occurrence? And Jed, the poor guy, seemed even more enthralled by Kat than before. Was she really the one he wanted to tangle with? The cadet probably couldn't handle her if he wanted.

"Instructions will be forthcoming. Watch your hyperbands," Zane said, a hint of foreboding in his tone that made his face even more menacing than usual.

With their promises of discretion for their new assignment and a thank you on his part for their willingness to come out tonight, they broke for the night, and any formality evaporated with it. But no one left. Not right after, anyway. The others seemed as content as he to bask in the lawlessness and exclusivity of the evening.

More than content; Kat was sure enjoying herself. He didn't see if she'd initiated the interaction or if she'd just been drawn in, but she was in raucous conversation with one of the twins, one of them demonstrating something that he suspected had to do with the Laser Rounds arena. Like-minded souls, they were; he could already see it. He shouldn't be surprised.

Whistler and Hanna also stood nearby, chatting, although from the way Whistler's eyes kept slipping with each sputter or snort from the trio beside them, one of them was clearly less invested. Lee could see a mini attention tantrum brewing as Hanna's eyes shot daggers in Kat and the twins' general direction; a girl used to owning the spotlight. Maybe this was one cadet who would actually get behind some Solar Cosmetics...

"Hey," Levy said. He hadn't noticed her bright eyes and dark smile weaving around the benches until she was right next to him. She batted the dark hair from her eyes with a dainty hand.

"Hey, yourself." Lee grinned, tracking the movement. He had never seen her wear her hair down before. "Thanks for coming tonight."

"You said that earlier," she said smoothly.

"Did I? Well, I meant it." Lee cast around for something fascinating to tell her, but he was coming up blank.

"This is cool," she said, glancing around her. "I've never been in here after hours."

Lee glanced around as well. "I'm not saying this from prior experience or anything..." he let his voice trail off. "But if one wanted to find certain contraband items, they might check here on Tuesday evenings."

"Tuesday," she repeated, laughing. "That's oddly specific." She had a warm, rolling laugh; her curious eyes seemed to glow with the sound. Lee made himself look away while he shrugged it off, just so he'd stop staring. He felt oddly comfortable when he was around her.

His eyes snagged again on Kat's long ponytail a little ways over. And just from the jaunty way it swung, he could tell she was saying something that was equal parts obnoxious and intoxicating. The twins had abandoned them by now, so it was just her and Whistler. Whatever he was telling her now couldn't be nearly so interesting as his hair this evening. But she tipped her head back in laughter. She looked really happy. Almost satisfied.

"That must suck."

"Sorry?" Lee turned, remembering Levy standing next to him. He shot her a look he hoped she'd take for the apology it was.

"Having to watch your best friend get with every guy at the Academy." Levy shrugged, her turn to look away.

"She hasn't been with *every guy*." Just the ones that drove him crazy.

"Okay, whatever, my mistake." Levy peered around at the grouped cadets.

"She's not with Whistler now, though, right?" Lee asked, quietly. Clarifying. He'd been a little preoccupied with all the research and getting their new squadron off the ground to notice when that had started up.

Levy laughed. Her voice was calming, he decided. Like the warm breeze after a storm. "I don't know. But I could find out for you?"

"What, like ask him?"

"I was thinking the twins, actually. They know Whistler pretty well." Levy shrugged.

He considered saying yes to her proposition for a moment, wherever the twins had scattered to, before realizing how ridiculous this was. He was a Gamma, for *void's* sake, and she was his best friend. He would just ask her himself if it came to that. So he waved a hand. "I'm sure it's nothing."

"Okay." She shrugged again.

"Do you know the twins well, then?" he asked then, determined not to obsess over what was definitely not happening between Kat and Whistler.

"Only from that one occasion, only in passing. I've actually only worked with you guys and Nikola, before," she admitted.

"You'll do great. You belong here," Lee said, and he meant it. With her aptitude and her perception, he stood by what he'd told Kat the other day. Having someone like Levy out there could very well be the key to this mission.

"Well it's late, I'll see you later, Lee," Levy said.

"Have a good night," he said, waving her off. He watched her start up through the benches before glancing around once more for Kat.

She and Whistler had drifted over to perch along one of the benches at the base of the Spectrum.

He was sure that they were just friends. She was just enjoying herself, making light of the energy and the moment. They'd all earned the right to enjoy themselves tonight. They'd been wound up much too tightly as of late, both with what they'd put themselves through with that last assignment, and with what was coming...

He made his way toward them.

"Sup, Waters."

"Whistler," Lee said, nodding toward the Gamma as he drew up close.

"Not a bad turnout tonight, huh? I was just telling Kat, I think we've got ourselves a good crew."

"Lots of big personalities," Lee observed, spotting the twins again as they started back around toward the opposite doors of the Spectrum.

"They're harmless enough," Kat said, following his line of sight and catching on to what he was getting at.

"I can vouch for Kiara and Kamata," Whistler said. "As I'm sure Zane would for the others."

Zane it seemed had already left, and with the twins heading out too, it left just the three of them out tonight. "An unofficial squadron," he voiced. It was the first time he'd admitted it aloud. They'd all be expected to do their part and put aside differences to make this work.

"So, tomorrow…" he mused of the full day awaiting them.

"Tomorrow," Whistler agreed, gaze divvying between them, eyes seeming to linger a second longer on Kat. But then he held up a hand in farewell, heading over to catch up with the twins. Lee had little doubt he'd be seeing a lot of Whistler in the upcoming days, he just wasn't quite sure yet what to make of him.

Shaking his head to clear that last thought, he peered out over the empty arena. From this angle, he could just make out the edges of the grounded islands from the starlight overhead. There *were* a lot of big personalities in their squadron. But if they could wrangle everyone together they had the potential, like any of those islands out there, just waiting for the right physics and the right conditions to raise them high.

"Tonight went well," he said, nudging her arm when all she gave him was a faint smile. "Nolan hasn't sniffed us out yet."

"Thank the *void*," she laughed, but it was a hushed sound, short-lived as she went back to staring off into the arena. "Levy seems like she's getting along," she said, her eyes carefully trained on the line of lighted vests.

"I think she'll do alright." He studied the way she seemed to sink into the grated floor here, resigned to only the ghosts of tonight's excitement. A trail of silver starlight lined her hair and down her face, making each flicker of her lashes, and dip of her eyes shimmer. Was she thinking about the raid right now? Or something else?

"You good?" he asked.

"I'm just tired."

He felt that. Down to his soul, he felt that. "A few more days," he said. But then he wondered if that were true. Who knew when their approvals would come through. They'd get through the next few days. Get through their raid, and everything would get back to how it was supposed to be.

He was thinking about ways they could make the next few days a little more bearable, when Lee heard a couple more voices trickle down towards them. One of them had a low, rolling timbre to it.

"I hadn't realized anyone was still here," Lee murmured, squinting as he stared up into the darkened stands. Slipping to his feet, with Kat in his wake, they started up towards the starboard doors. Lee could just make out a couple of dark silhouettes. One of them had his arm braced, casually against one of the doors, the buzzed side of his head catching the starlight while he chatted quietly with someone.

"I thought he'd left already," Kat said at his side.

"I thought so, too." He didn't know why those words gave his stomach a weird tumble.

And then he heard the other cadet. "I'm just excited to learn from all of you," she was saying. And her low voice was bright—innocent.

Her lavender face glimmered into view. Lee felt his steps speeding up as his insides froze over, the logical part of his brain at complete odds with his body.

He had no claim on Levy. But he wasn't sure he liked the idea of her with Zane any more than he had Kat with Zane. Kat was much too good for Zane, but at least she was aware. Whereas with Levy—she was naive to Zane's forwardness and charm. And given Zane's more recent history—if he planned to try something with her—

Zane leaned in towards Levy, closing the gap between them, and Lee lost it. All reason and logic splintered from him in a hailstorm of frost and ice.

Kat got there first, rounding on Zane. "Hey, leave the girl alone. She's not another one of your playthings."

"It's not what it looks like, I just ran into him," Levy tried to interject.

"You don't know what you're talking about," Zane said, rolling her off and ignoring Levy entirely as he took a step back. "As if you're one to talk, Kat?" And the implications in his voice. The messy way he slung her name—

Lee hurdled over the last couple of steps as Zane laughed, a bitter sound. "Oh, that's right," he said. "You can tangle, but when things get even a little messy, you ditch."

"Uncalled for," Lee called. Clearing the remaining space between them, he grabbed ahold of Kat with two arms, holding her back, lest she did anything drastic—lest *they* did anything drastic. And despite his own irritation, the daggers in his eyes, he put his back to Zane to talk Kat down. "Look, he didn't mean it like that. Okay? Walk it off." Who was he really talking to, though, Kat, or himself?

"You're insane. Both of you." Body shaking, Zane waved them all off, as he slipped back through those starboard doors, leaving the three of them there panting in the starlight.

Kat gave Zane all of ten seconds head start before also storming off, murmuring something about calling it a night.

Clenching his hands into fists, Lee held the tension before releasing his grip. "Look, they just—sorry." Motioning for Levy to head on out of there ahead of him, he quickly resealed the locks on the doors before chasing down Kat.

It took several flights of stairs to catch up with her, and when he finally did, her face was cold as ice.

He wasn't even entirely sure what had set her off, or if it was the same protectiveness as with him. Zane made arrogant, bigheaded comments all the time, but this time... he'd thought they were past all this. And as for Levy... if she was smart, she would stay clear after tonight. But what did he know, anyway.

Lee sighed. There were bound to be some sort of repercussions after this.

Lee walked with Kat until they cleared the skywalk, and the dorms split off to either side.

"Talk more tomorrow?" he asked.

She nodded, a relenting, stony thing that didn't make it to her lips. And when she slipped around the corner, he let her.

He could fairly safely assume that her reactions tonight had to do with her former situation-ship with Zane. But again, that didn't feel quite right, she'd made it clear before that she was over him.

He felt oddly blinded by his uncertainty.

He'd made it back to his dorm before he noticed he had a message waiting for him on his hyperband from a new contact.

> Unknown: is kat ok?
> Unknown: I promise it wasn't what it looked like. We were just talking.
> Unknown: oh, and this is levy btw. I pulled your number from the hub.

Smiling, Lee added her name to his personal contacts, typing back a quick response.

> Lee: she'll be fine, don't worry about it—it's just stars in the sky.

Lee bit his lip, debating, before sending back one more message.

> Lee: how's that for a functional squadron? ;)

She sent her response back swiftly.

> Levy: oh, this is already the best squadron I've ever had.

Best squadron, huh? He'd see about that. He shook his head against the imagery forming of the curiosity behind Levy's long-lashed eyes, and the boldness in her shapely, dark lips. She was a good one. With the right training and the right people behind her, she definitely had the potential to go far with the Academy.

Kicking off his boots, Lee sunk back onto his bed.

He had been careful not to linger this morning, not wanting to draw too much attention to his interactions with Levy, or with any of the cadets. And maybe it was out of attachment for their newfound squadron, but a burgeoning part of him wondered what it would be like to actually have time to hang out with someone like Levy, someplace away from the raid pressures of wandering eyes and tattling ears.

The night had surely taken a turn. Although as to which direction, he didn't yet know. But all in all, tonight had gone infinitely better than he could have hoped. The squadron's camaraderie was tangible—for the most part. As tangible as the electricity that had pulsed through the empty Spectrum tonight.

And despite his exhaustion, the anxiety beginning to creep back in, he began planning out a couple training session ideas for the next few days that might help the squadron formulate an even stronger bond. If they were going to do this, they may as well really do this.

They were going to be a secret squadron.

CHAPTER 20: KAT

THE ALARM on her hyperband blared overly loud when she awoke the following morning. The air vents in the hallways were too cold. Her all-terrain suit chafed. And the smells from the griddle nearly overpowered her stomach as she stumbled down toward the Canteen. But she brushed past all of these as she slipped through the Canteen doors. They had a squadron to train.

Lee was already up. And despite the gnawing nibbling at her insides, there was a certain spark in her gut when she saw Lee standing there dutifully in the line, his tray in hand. So much mystery had been built up around Argos and their upcoming raid assignment; maybe they were in over their heads. She just hoped it wasn't too much longer before they could get out there.

Lee let a handful of cadets go ahead of him while he waited for her to join him.

She took up a tray but made no plans to fill it.

"Interesting night," Lee commented. He kept his tone light, conscious of those around them.

She wanted to follow suit but gave up mid-breath. "How bad were we?" She stared straight ahead, bracing herself for the facts. She knew they'd overreacted last night. But she just couldn't let it slide. Not right in front of her face, not with Levy, and not after just having seen her down there with Lee...

"I really wouldn't worry about it—the guy's a dick. Nothing new there."

Her stare slid between the freckles on his nose and his green eyes, catching the mild laughter there. Lee was in fine spirits this morning. More than fine. She hadn't seen him this—excited in a long time. "You say that about him a lot."

"And I will probably say it again before long."

She smiled. It was nice to know that some things never changed.

"But if you wanted to talk about it..." he began.

"Nope. I'm good." Not today. Not tomorrow. Not ever, if she had it her way.

Lee backed off, hands flattening in surrender against his tray. They made it all the way to the hot plates before she sighed. She'd meant well last night; even if seeing Zane hitting on Levy was just the cherry topper on a whirlwind of an evening. "It's just, this is a good idea, right? Training in secret?" She pictured the way Lee had looked all cozy and the like, talking with Levy again last night.

"I think you're in your head. It's a brilliant idea. Your ideas always are." He nudged her side with his elbow. He was wearing a little side smile that had her own perking up for a moment.

"Speaking of which, I'm pretty sure that kid, Jed is in love with you."

Kat wrinkled her nose. But she let the expression drop, sighing. "I should probably go apologize to Zane."

"Probably," Lee agreed, piling some eggs and toast high on a plate. "But you could give it a couple hours. Give him time for your passionate words to really soak in there."

Kat snorted, tipping a short stack of eggs onto her own plate.

They took up spots at their usual table. Kat was still trying to work past the bewilderment of their actions the night before when Whistler slid into the spot next to her. "Bad news."

"What's up?" Lee asked, setting down his fork.

"The Academy received a visitor this morning."

"It's not just the Commander returning?" Kat asked, carefully.

Whistler slowly shook his head. "Different AMG ship, voyager. I had Zane confirm just now. One of the passengers was a ship inspector."

"Zane will be right. Guy grew up around these ships," Kat ran her hand through her ponytail. "But why would a voyager be carrying a civilian?"

Wordlessly, Lee also shook his head.

"I went and talked to my guy over in the main hangar," Whistler explained. "The claim he's working through is that the converters we are using on some of our spacecraft' are out of date. Which is completely bogus. Our ships' tech is entirely up to code."

"Which ones are they claiming are lacking?" Kat asked.

"Cruisers," Whistler said.

The tension reverberating with Lee's next inhale was palpable. "Of course they are."

"Someone really doesn't want us going out there again," she murmured.

There was no sign of Whistler's crooked grin. And Kat didn't have any responses or flip sides. This was all starting to really piss her off.

She was still fuming when the twins breezed past. One of them saluted her.

"Aren't they the ones who got busted for amplifying the shocks in the Laser Rounds' vests?" Lee asked, pushing some of his eggs around his plate.

"The very same." She couldn't help the tiny grin that turned up her lips. She watched, then, as Hanna came up to join the twins. She hadn't realized they were friendly.

"So I guess the question now," Whistler said, watching the three of them exit the Canteen. "Do we abort?"

"AMG freely poking about..." Lee murmured, glancing over at Kat, a twinkle breaking past the uncertainty in his eyes.

"Oh, definitely not." Kat grinned, turning back to Whistler. "I'd say we double down."

"I'll post a meetup schedule," Whistler grinned, sliding back to his feet. "See you guys around 14:00 hours."

"I wonder what Nolan makes of all of this, a new ship in his territory while his master is out," Kat mused when it was just she and Lee again.

"I'm sure he knows," Lee commented. But there was enough of a question there, that she decided she'd make *void*-well certain.

They could, of course, just march right into the Command wing and demand he tell them all he knows of those ships. But where was the fun in that? And with their cadets all down in trainings for the first half of the day, they had time to kill. So instead, after they finished their breakfast, she and Lee grabbed their holoblocks and their bags, taking up a spot bordering the upper skywalk, just down from the Command wing.

A stakeout.

They would be reprising their favorite roles of all time. Bored and arrogant space cadets on a secret assignment that wasn't going anywhere. She was fairly confident they could get in believable enough character.

Those first few minutes turned into an hour, turned into her and Lee taking turns slipping back down the Heptagon for green juices. And when even that didn't work, they pulled out their holoblocks.

They were all too familiar with Argos itself, and they needed more data before they could figure out anything more behind the dark radiation spikes and their upcoming mission. But maybe there was something in their raid files that could help explain what had triggered their Commander to go through all this trouble in the first place.

Their upgraded security clearance was still in effect from their latest assignment, and they had access to a whole new set of files on the hub. Hopefully, they'd be able to dig up something useful on Quadrant III that they could use.

She found record of an accident that had occurred a hundred years ago, around roughly the same time that operations had ceased in the quadrant. And while details on the actual experiment were murky, the resulting accident had been catastrophic. The research facilities themselves had imploded, taking out an entire planet with it. One of the reports had mentioned something, too, about the risks of igniting a singularity, but she hadn't been able to find out anything more about that.

"What do you make of this?" she asked Lee, thinking for just a second. "Do you think this could be the reasoning behind why they stopped stationing people out there, it's just too dangerous? I know they've since banned all attempts at harnessing the dark radiation... I don't know. It honestly sounds like the same old-same old. Another century, another fight for humanity. Although, as this operation had been backed by the AMG, it is interesting I've only been able to find this one record..."

"Lee?" she asked again, peering over to see what he was working on. He was reading something on his hyperband.

"Who's that from?" she asked, checking her own hyperband for a missed message.

"Oh, uh Levy. She was just checking in to see when we are meeting."

"Oh, nice." Kat stared right through the holofile she'd been reading. It was too bad that whatever they'd been doing out there in QIII a hundred years ago hadn't succeeded. Maybe then, they wouldn't have to deal with this latest twist.

She was actually about to be pretty disappointed with the Commander's secretary, her bladder screaming to run down to the Ladies', when their star appeared.

"Good afternoon," Lee called out a tad jauntily as Nolan walked past.

"Seen any new ships around?" Kat asked, flashing him the most obnoxious grin she could muster. She fluttered her fingers in his direction. To her delight, Nolan actually scowled.

"Official AMG business," he muttered, disappearing as quickly as he'd come down through the Heptagon.

"Oh he's definitely aware of the ship down there," she said once the sound of Nolan's footsteps had fully retreated.

"I'm betting it's his job to keep an eye on it. Which just affirms our previous assumptions." Lee's green eyes flashed as she met them. "Someone in the AMG is trying to delay us."

It was just before 14:00 hours when she and Lee packed up their things again, and heading over to the highest of the training levels. Whistler had canceled his usual meditative practice. In its place on the Academy's time block, read an extracurricular class description so bland, Kat was almost embarrassed to be seen heading in this direction.

"Preliminary Raider Resources," she snorted, greeting Whistler at the door.

Whistler's eyes sparkled. "One could always use a refresh."

He had reserved one of the larger application rooms; a size and shape that could be reasonably compared to the main cabin of a cruiser...

Zane leaned against the back wall of their makeshift observation deck, arms crossed over his chest as he chatted quietly with Hanna. She seemed to know everyone here—every male, at least.

Kat opted to stand with Whistler and Lee, assisting in barricading the door against wayward cadets while they waited for more of their squadron to show. Not that she was avoiding apologizing to Zane, or consumingly ashamed for letting her own stuff get in the way of the squadron...

When the twins arrived, a few Micros and Rads tried to walk in after them. "Oh, I'm sorry," Whistler cut in, stepping in their path. This is more of a remedial course for those struggling with their core curriculum."

From over her shoulder, Kiara smirked at that last bit. "Struggling?"

Kat broke her stance to join Kiara and her twin. "You heard the man, everyone's got to prove their worth."

Kamata rolled her eyes. "Wherever do we begin?"

They had a full squadron by five after. Starting in with the basics, they covered the inner workings of sensor tech and magnetometers—for theoretical purposes, of course. After everyone had proven competency, they moved on to ship components and maintenance, radio communication, and emergency response. Basically, anything and everything they could think of that might come up over the course of their ninety-six hours in Argos.

Nikola had to duck out during the second hour for a previously scheduled programming credential. And Hanna, for a hologram instruction. Each time someone left, the squadron leads took care to send their cadets on roundabout paths back through the training levels. With someone external onboard the ship and loose about the Academy, they couldn't be too cautious. Who knew how much they knew about their upcoming raid?

When it came time to break for dinner, they slipped out of the room in twos and threes, sitting at separate tables in the Canteen so as not to attract unwanted attention.

"What do you say we tackle blasters after dinner?" Lee asked, twirling his fork about the strawberry-cobb salad on his plate.

"Fun, and educational. Another necessary skill to master," Kat agreed. "Let's spread the word."

The range was busy tonight; many of the lanes were already full when they got there. Careful not to disrupt anyone, they threaded back behind the waist-high barrier denoting the edge of the range. Around them, the *zaps* of blasters reflected off the eggshell panels in a rainbow of color. They took up perches back behind the barrier to wait for a free lane. Jed joined them before long, his dark hair hanging over one of his eyes. He didn't say anything, as he slipped quietly up to lean against the railing beside her.

She was side-eying Lee, promising pain if he said something, when she caught sight of another face coming through the doors. A round, lavender face.

Lee spotted her then, too.

Levy smiled when she reached them, glancing uncertainly between her and Lee. "Um, hey guys."

The blaster lane up ahead of them opened up.

"Perfect timing. Let's see what you've got." Lee nodded to Levy and Jed before swinging his backpack off his shoulders and strolling right around the waist-high barrier to the zap-line. Kat trailed along after them, some of her enthusiasm for the plan fading with each step. Yay. More mentoring.

Jed was fully versed in blasters. He selected a model and took aim with ease. The only thing he lacked was the repetition and practice for accuracy.

Levy, on the other hand, needed more encouragement. She got hung up selecting a blaster from the wall. And then again when she finally stood at the zap-line, frantically tucking the dark hairs that had come free from her ponytail back behind her ears. Gripping the blaster gingerly in her hands, Levy glanced sheepishly from Kat to Lee before turning back to the holo-targets lining the wall.

Part of her grip failed her. It was a common mistake Kat had seen in cadets over the years. She watched Levy fire off a few blasts, before turning to Lee, pointedly. He just stared back at her.

Sighing, Kat pushed past Lee, toward a very wary Levy. "May I?" From the scope of instructor, it was simpler to interact with the girl. And with those two words, she'd transformed Levy into just another mentee and her responsibility once again.

After demonstrating how poor grip affected control, and how a simple adjustment could fix the problem, Kat corrected Levy's hand position and made her repeat the steps back to her to make sure she'd committed it to memory.

It was impossible to miss the approving smile on Lee's face as Kat stepped back to give the cadet some room. She rolled her eyes. Yeah, yeah. And she hated to admit it, but it wasn't all that bad working with the girl. Just as Lee had said, Levy took instruction well. Fifteen minutes later, the girl was still going through the steps to check her grip before each blast.

"She's good," Kat murmured to Lee as one of Levy's blasts struck very near the center of the target. The two of them leaned back casually against the barrier at the edge of the range.

"That she is," Lee agreed. She could see the zaps from the blasters reflected in his eyes. He tracked Levy's fingers as she caressed the blaster in both hands, finding the perfect balance between tight and loose.

And as the soft *zing* bit the air, Levy squealed, whipping her shiny black hair around. "I think I've got it!"

Lee was grinning as he pushed off from the barrier to congratulate her. "That was amazing. Seriously, that's all it took?"

Levy tucked her hair behind her ears again, definitely a nervous response—and one Lee was drinking right in as he angled his body more fully toward the girl. And like last night—

it was an interaction Kat didn't really need to see with everything else going against them.

She needed to get out of here. Stretch her legs, and clear her head for a minute, away from the girl. With barely a flutter of a wave in their general direction, not bothering to say goodnight to any of them, Kat spun on a heel, clearing the range. She was through the doors and down a level before she stopped outside one of the training room doors.

It was just Lee being a good mentor, she told herself as she crossed through the doorway, tapping it shut behind her. The Lightning Track was bathed entirely in darkness.

That's just how Lee was.

But with Levy... she didn't know Levy.

The girl had a good work ethic, she'd give her that.

Kat sat down on the floor at the base of the track, letting her body adjust to the smooth tension of the dark surface below her. She stretched out her calves and the various muscles in her legs. She fully intended to push herself this evening.

The door to the track opened, a sheet of light filtering in. She didn't bother to look who it was before the door slammed shut once more; they would've seen her.

A pair of boots strode towards her on steady feet, stopping at the other edge of the track. She didn't acknowledge them as she wordlessly finished on her legs.

After that night in the anti-gravity chamber... After all of her and Lee's history together... she just assumed it would be their turn. She never stopped to consider there could be someone else. But she'd been invisible in that range, and down in the

Spectrum that night—at least to the only face she cared about. The face now smiling and preoccupied with someone else in another training room.

Forget invincible, she felt completely invisible. As invisible as that asteroid, Argos.

And invisible cadets could do what invisible cadets did best.

Rising fluidly to her feet, she pulled one arm over her head, then the other, loosening up the joints in her arms, and then in her neck. Finally, she peered over at the strong, steel-like body beside hers, what little of it she could make out in the darkness. The track was dim as dusk—and even the void, in sections...

"I'm going to take it hard," Kat warned, pulling at her arms once more.

"Let's see it, baby girl," Zane said, stretching his own arms.

And then Kat was off.

The Lightning Track was designed to train the senses, as well as the body, its course entirely synthetic, with pits and hills that shifted by the hour. Kat hurtled up one such shift as she approached the hilly terrain.

She was fast. Her thin build was designed for speed, her thighs sleek and honed from years of trainings like this one. But Zane was faster.

She felt his presence, hot on her heels; she heard his breathing as he shot past her into the darkness, flying over a dip in the ground. And when all she could make out was his silhouette in the distance, she ran harder. She pushed herself until she was also flying past the pitfalls and obstacles and the blood in her veins was pure adrenaline. And only then, when that other force had taken over, did her mind begin to soothe.

The track was exhilaration. A high that took her out of this world.

And she could get lost in it.

Several loops in, feeling her lungs begin to constrict, and before she could overextend herself, Kat veered off, loping over to the opposite side of the track and easing her steps to a light run. And then a jog. And then, her heart returning to a somewhat normal beat, the euphoria fading into more of a pleased exhaustion, she slowed to a walk.

She didn't know how he'd known to turn off, or if he was listening for her. She didn't know how far he'd run, only to sprint back and catch up with her. But then he was there, matching pace as he came up beside her. His own breathing a rush beside her own moderated inhalations.

They didn't talk as they cleared the remaining distance back down the length of the track. And not as she guzzled down the rest of her water, pulling on her legs to keep her body loose.

"You are insane," he muttered. She just angled her head back.

As always, talking had never been their thing.

Kat didn't remember starting anything, or if Zane was the one to initiate. One minute she was panting in the dark, the sweat rolling off their skin mingling in the organic humidity of the tempered room. And then her lips were at his neck and Zane's hands in her hair. Zippers muffled the heavy dark fabric as it fell away, leaving behind only hot breaths on her skin. His hands were surprisingly cool where they traced the round lines of her hips, a stark contrast to the heat coming from his firm body as it found hers, again and again and again. Forgotten moments and hushed kisses. And stilted breathing; so much breathing.

And then it was over.

Zane left the room first, only stooping once to straighten the laces of his combat boots.

That was one way to do an apology.

Raw and roaring, Kat sank down to her knees. She dug her fingers into the cool track and screamed and screamed until the ringing faded from her head.

And then she, too, stood, wiping her hands on the pants of her all-terrain suit, before stepping back into the bright lights of the hallway. Her head had cleared, but a dark shadow remained, seeping over the dwindling possibility of her and Lee.

What had she done?

She was still blinking past the brightness as she rounded the training level, taking the first stairway she came to.

"Where'd you run off to?" Lee grinned. A tuft of hair peeked out from behind his ears as he looked up from the hyperband on his wrist. He pushed off from the wall. "We were looking for you."

Kat couldn't bear it. The nonchalance. The normalcy of the gesture. She wanted to throw herself on the floor once more and hurl him down with her, if only to feel, for once, even an ounce of what was churning through her head.

But she didn't want to do it here, barely a stairway up from where she'd taken a laser to their frayed chances at a relationship. So instead, she took a breath, steadying herself, and forced a bland little smile onto her face. "Got in a workout." She tipped her head. "Hey, I'm exhausted. Talk later?"

She didn't wait for Lee to respond. And she didn't wait to note the concern that peppered his face as she fled the training levels; it would only make it that much harder for her to keep her words in check.

She didn't stop until she reached her dorm. Slamming the portal door behind her, she collapsed into a heap on her bed.

CHAPTER 21: LEE

IT HAD been another full day.

A good day, though. A really good day. Their cadets were really stepping up and starting to come together as a squadron. Secret rendezvous for the win. Which was important, they would need every trick of the trade they could think of when they finally got out on their raid.

Today they'd gotten creative, building on the cadences they'd started with yesterday, pushing their cadets harder, demanding more. They'd reserved a larger room, actually carting in a little extra tech so they could divide into smaller groups while they took the skillsets to more practical applications.

They were currently cycling through a series of stages involving everything from air leaks to rogue creature attacks, and there was one instance they'd devised where an aerial was required. Anything to keep the cadets thinking on their toes.

He watched as the duo nearest them took on a simulated engine failure to their "ship", the diagnosis made especially difficult by a strange magnetic pull messing with their equipment. Levy caught his eye, smiling back sheepishly as she worked with Kamata to redirect power flow and get the sim component back online.

"Why does heavy magnetism keep showing up?" he overheard Jed exclaiming, rolling his eyes as he tore his gaze away. But he had to smile at the cadet's patience with Nikola's lengthy diagnosis of an approaching vagrant ship and an evasive maneuver plan.

"Why indeed," Lee murmured. He made note to dial up the magnetism even higher on the next stage.

A little ways off to the side from them, Kat stared into one of the angular windows along that exterior wall, appearing completely ignorant of Jed and Nikola's current fight for survival.

Shoving his hands in his pockets, he skirted around the room. "You've been absent today. Everything okay?" It was getting to be later in the afternoon. They'd been in trainings from the moment trainings ended this morning, until late this afternoon, only breaking a couple of times to grab water.

"Don't worry about it," she said quickly, eyes roaming the eggshell-colored wall panels just below the window, before sliding his way.

"Did you ever figure things out with—" Lee jerked his head toward another corner of the room where Zane monitored the emergency responses of Kiara and Hanna.

"We worked it out," Kat said flatly.

"I hope you made him sweat a little, first," he joked, scrutinizing her reactions. Something seemed off.

Kat grimaced. She actually looked like she might be sick for a minute, but then she smoothed the expression on her face. Was that just from fatigue, whatever off-day she was having, or was there more? "You sure you're good? You know, you could take a break for a bit and grab water. We've been at this for quite a while."

"I'm fine," she said quickly. And then a minute later—"You know what, I think I will grab that drink. I'll catch up to you later, Lee." She didn't look back as she slipped out through the training room doors.

Still puzzled, ironically, especially given their present have-a-plan-for-everything environment, he was not entirely sure whether he ought to give her space or go after her. He checked his hyperband. Dinner would be starting soon, up in the Canteen. He'd catch up with her then.

"What do you think," Lee asked, sweeping back around the room to where Zane stood. Crossing his arms over his chest, he motioned for Whistler to join them. "Do we add in a time constraint for additional pressure, or call it a night?" His eyes dipped once back over to the door Kat had just exited through.

"I think they could handle one more circuit," Whistler said.

Lee cut his gaze over to Zane. "You down for one more?" Lee quickly let his arms fall to his side when he noticed Zane had also crossed his arms over his chest.

"Yeah, let's do it," Zane said, adjusting his stance. And when the duos next broke to start a fresh exercise, they met them at their stations to outline the new requirement.

They were tired. Some of them were probably bored. And it had been an anxious couple of days. But there was an eagerness and a determination and a fight glinting through them that brought him pride in the squadron they'd assembled. Official, or otherwise. And despite their histories and personal vendettas, the dynamic of the squadron was working. Even with Zane. He and Zane hadn't gotten into a single spat since they'd started working together on this raid. And as for Zane and Kat—there was some lingering cordiality there, however that had gone down. But like she said, they were working through it.

After another circuit, the squadron broke for the night, going their separate ways.

Lee didn't see Kat at dinner. He even swung by her dorm afterwards, and when she didn't answer, he went back to his to regroup. As much as they'd made the best of their delay with going out on their raid, the stress behind it was starting to really eat into him.

Sinking into the chair behind his desk, he drew up the hub on his holoblock. They ought to have received their list approval and ship assignment by now. Especially if the inspector's claims were as fabricated as Whistler believed. With the AMG ship here, and the Commander called away again...

Someone really didn't want them going back out there. Whatever was going on here was happening behind closed doors. Beyond the Academy's doors. This was bigger than them. And yet, they'd been assigned to the heart of it all.

He drummed his fingers along his desk, clacking a short little rhythm, while he tapped into a folder someone had flagged on the hub. A series of lab reports from prior raids, by the looks of it. They were seemingly random, though. He wondered what the dated reports had to do with Argos.

He checked his hyperband. It was barely 19:00 hours, no one would be asleep yet at this hour.

> Lee: what r u up to?

While he waited for a response to his message, Lee directed his attention back to the flagged files on the hub. He squinted, studying the line items on the reports as he switched through holofile after holofile. What was he missing here?

Screw it.

Back to the PARC for him. He'd get loads more done up there, anyway. He sent out a quick message to the other three squadron leads to let them know his plans.

> Zane: (thumbs up)

> Whistler: solid plan to me

> Kat:

Nothing came back from Kat. It was a little odd she wasn't answering her messages. But if it was anything like the anxiousness he was feeling with their raid, she'd figure it out and be back onboard, full-force by tomorrow.

His hyperband buzzed.

> Levy: well, right now hanna and I are meeting up
> with the twins to go paint the energy rings hot
> pink...

Lee snorted. He had no idea how you manipulated that frequency of energy, but that actually sounded like a lot of fun. The kind of stuff he and Kat used to get into a couple of years back, before all the responsibility had started stacking up... He wondered when the last time was that he'd done something pointless and reckless just for fun.

Next time, he vowed.

With a sigh, he sent back a quick message, promising Levy their secret was safe with him. Then, he gathered up his backpack to endure another long evening in the PARC.

It almost felt like getting back to normal, heading over here —and voluntarily, this time.

No one was using the rooms tonight, so Lee got his pick of location. Scanning his hyperband at the door, he flipped on the lights and ducked into the first door on their left.

Lee had already started drawing up some of the holofiles from the hub when Zane slipped through the door. He nodded, before claiming his old seat on the opposite side of the table from Lee. When Whistler arrived, he went to his former seat as well, until only Kat was missing. Her absence was striking tonight.

Lee cleared his throat, trying to work around the weirdness of not having Kat here with them. "So what are we looking for in here?"

Zane's brow lowered, "What do you mean?"

"I'm assuming one of you flagged this folder with the lab reports?"

"I thought you guys might have," Whistler said. "Kat, maybe?"

Lee shook his head. "She'd have told me. We were looking through the raid files earlier today." But if none of them had flagged them, who did that leave? The Commander? Nolan?

With no guide, they set to work, blindly digging through that folder to see what they could find out.

But thirty minutes later, Lee still had no idea what he was searching for. Aside from learning that none of them had flagged these files, it didn't feel as if they'd made any progress. And the only thing the various lab reports appeared to have in common was the type of tests that'd been ordered. These were all sample testing for dark radiation, all ordered and corroborated by the AMG.

Maybe this had been a mistake tonight to get the other squadron leads involved, and at such a late hour. Not to mention, what Kat would make of them doing this without her.

He checked his hyperband just in case she'd messaged, but there was nothing from her.

"We can't get in trouble for being in the PARC tonight, can we?" Whistler teased, slumping back in his chair.

Zane raised his eyebrows, still conscious of that line they all trod.

Lee flicked through to a fresh lab report, expanding the hologram for his tired eyes.

He expanded it again.

A single notation in the coding had been underlined in precise, light strokes. He knew this notation, it was the delta notation of a radioactive signature. Their radioactive signature.

He studied the lab report. This couldn't be right, though. The dates didn't match up. According to the ship's labs, this test had been ordered weeks and weeks before...

"You find anything?" Zane asked curiously, peering down the table.

"Not sure," Lee said slowly. He flipped to another report, studying the coding this time. Sure enough, underlined in that same, precise laser-marker, was the delta notation. He flipped to another. And another. The same delta notation had been underlined in every report he passed. And each report was stamped and signed at the bottom in the same manner.

Corroborated by the AMG.

Corroborated by the AMG.

Corroborated by the AMG.

He stared at Commanding General Narron's roughly legible signature. It was the same General who'd been in attendance of a certain event onboard their ship earlier that month; an event referenced by Nolan in their briefing a week prior.

In the meantime, take care as you make the rounds.

But what did the General have to do with all of this?

"Have you guys seen this yet?" Whistler asked, expanding the hologram before him for them to see. "I found this communication in the folder—it was mislabeled as another lab report."

Lee had to forcibly drag his eyes away from the General's scrawl on that latest report. He took his time coming around the opposite side of the table.

The hologram Whistler had found was the photon-copy of a communication sent directly from Commander Yvette Blanche to the Commanding Council, requesting she send out another squadron of cadets to investigate the dark radiation.

But that wasn't what made his pulse speed up. According to the timestamp, her message had gone out before the new radiation spikes occurred.

And that wasn't all.

Scribbled below her message, in precise, laser-marker strokes, was a note:

Have you made the Rounds yet?

Raking his hands down the legs of his pants, Lee let his hands pound down atop the table. Their Commander had mentioned at the beginning of their briefing that Nolan was still processing their findings. But was it 'processing' she should've said, or 'having processed'? He'd bet Nolan had been in the midst of making these very notes. "Commander Blanche is not concerned about investigating the dark radiation. She's concerned about investigating it *first*." He looked up. "I know who flagged these files."

"Who?" Zane demanded, straightening his posture to match his tone—the tone of a soldier's son.

Lee drew up one of the lab reports at random, expanding it so they could more clearly see the underlined delta notation. "We were wrong the other day, about Nolan. He wasn't warning us about breaking rules. He was trying to send us a message."

"That someone already knew about the dark rays and the radioactive signature?" Whistler guessed, filling in the gaps.

"And not just someone." Lee drew in a breath as he motioned to the signature at the bottom of the report. Oh, this would be fun. Why in the *void* did Kat have to be going through something tonight...

He said the next words quickly before anyone could interject. "The Commanding General may have been here at the Academy during the Laser Rounds earlier this month."

Zane inhaled, his nostrils flaring. "I'm guessing *she* knows, too." It was impossible to miss who the 'she' was in this scenario. But if that was all the reactions he'd get from them, then maybe this wouldn't be so bad after all. Which was good, because—

"Why, the fuck, did you not tell anyone?"

The forced calm in Zane's voice had Lee tensing as well as any show of muscle or shouting would have. And Lee was grateful, for once, that Whistler was on the squadron. A buffer. Even if, at that moment, Whistler was also not looking too pleased with their having kept this bit of information from everyone.

And then Kat walked through the door.

CHAPTER 22: KAT

KAT HAD just gotten back to her room earlier that evening when she saw the messages come through, first from Lee, and then from Zane and Whistler.

She thought about ignoring them and pretending she was asleep. Or lying down somewhere; wherever it was they thought she'd gone after Lee had given her an out earlier. She really didn't care. She went as far as to lay down on her bed, staring up into the dim ceiling panels.

She'd managed to make herself busy all day going through the motions. She'd done some research and attended their trainings; she'd even slipped down to the airshafts for a bit this morning, before realizing, like right now, that it wasn't her head she wanted to be inside of at the moment.

With a sigh, Kat sat up, heaving her body back off the bed. It felt like gravity had quadrupled in the last four minutes. Tossing her head to get the stray hairs from her face, Kat crossed back over the skywalk and down a level to the PARC.

"Sorry I'm late," she said as she came through the door. She froze as all three boys looked back at her from the same side of the table. "What'd I miss?"

"Fuck you. Fuck you both," Zane muttered. She dared take a few steps over to the opposite side of the table. Ire rode Zane's face, and Whistler shot her a sheepish grimace as she turned to Lee. But Lee's face was unreadable. She slid her chair out with her foot, shrugging her bag from her shoulders as Lee came back around the table, hands in his pockets.

"But seriously," she said, directing her question to Lee alone this time. "What's going on?"

"We think that the files on the hub were flagged by Nolan, and that the AMG—and more specifically, the Commanding General himself—has been searching for Argos." Kat could only blink through Lee's assumptions as he explained about the radioactive signatures they'd found in the dated lab reports. And then he got to Nolan's involvement.

Lee cleared his throat, glancing across the table as he acknowledged Zane and then Whistler in turn. "I also told them about General Narron's lovely appearance at the Laser Rounds the other day..."

"Oh. That," she said. Across from them, Zane scoffed. That explained his little outburst there. "Well, now that that's out there... What do we make of the General and his role in all of this? He's got to be the reason we're still here, right? The one behind the delay with our raid approvals? The AMG ship poking about? It's no wonder the Commander has been looking so frazzled lately."

"He's definitely not making it easy for her," Whistler agreed, having apparently bounced back after their little reveal. "And what about the radioactive signature? Those records on the lab reports go back weeks, months—maybe even longer than that."

"General Narron's entire campaign has been about his Preservation Initiative, with all of the energy developments and his crusade to support life..." Lee said slowly. "All of it is tied to combatting the dark rays. Kafron, our recent raids... Is that a part of this too, or has all of that just been for show?"

"You think he could be using the Initiative as a cover?" Zane asked, finally. Kat could see the betrayal there, even though Zane was doing his best to muscle past it all.

"Maybe not a cover, per se; the dark radiation threat is real. But it could be an ulterior motive," Lee offered, laying his palms down flat on the table.

"It would also give him an inexhaustive amount of resources, which would make it fairly easy to hide something like this," Whistler said, thoughtfully.

It was quiet for a moment. Then Lee cleared his throat and swallowed. "Let's say General Narron was using our samples and testing as an excuse to search for something." He swallowed once more. "Did he find it?"

It was again quiet.

"There's got to be more to learn on this," Zane said, finally. "We've got the clearance, but the guy's a public figure too. At least a part of him has to operate in the light. Maybe he left a trail we can follow."

While he and Whistler started their research into the Commanding General of the AMG, Lee swiveled around to face her. "I didn't expect to see you tonight," Lee said in a low voice.

"No?" she asked carefully, not looking at Lee, and definitely not looking towards Zane, as she instead found a spot on the floor to scrutinize. She pretended to fiddle with something in her bag.

If she showed Lee her pain, he would leap to her side with blasters blazing and fire in those clear, keen eyes. He would see all of the thoughts she'd been squashing down inside of her. And any potential happiness for him with Levy, or anyone else for that matter, would be ruined.

And so she squashed it down further. She could do this. For him, she needed to do this. And after a moment, she looked up at him and gave him a little half-smile.

As expected, he was surveying her. His green eyes were honed from years of standing by her side. But they couldn't pierce this barrier tonight.

Everything good?

She shrugged. *It will be.*

She flicked her eyes away from his, and across the table to the other two squadron leads who'd also both agreed to come up here to work, despite the late hour. No more lies, and no more secrets.

Except for this one.

This time, Kat really did fiddle with her bag, pulling out a bottle of water. She took a drink, imagining the water washing away her actions from last night, and doing her best to pretend that both halves of her turmoil weren't sitting there less than a meter away from her. She started in with the others.

It was a tense hour while they went through holofiles of whatever they could find on the hub and the public domain to see what they could learn about the Commanding General. But the deeper they dug, the more there was to dig; it was overwhelming. His illustrious hands were all over everything. The feat was proving as elusive as the radiation surrounding Argos. And the entire time, the silence seemed to crash into her, in and out in cresting waves.

"All this research and intrigue is making my head ache." Whistler frowned, pushing back from the table. "I need an energy drink, or a snack or something."

"I'm coming, too," Kat said, jumping up. If he could only see what was going through her head.

She'd truly intended to dig her boots in and help tonight. And she was trying. But at the mention of getting out of here, even for a few minutes...

She was on her feet and meeting Whistler at the door before anyone else could steal her getaway.

"To what do I owe this honor?" Whistler teased as they made their way down through the Heptagon.

"Oh, believe me, the pleasure is all mine."

"Seriously, though. You doing okay? You've been a bit of a blur lately." She didn't know if he'd caught something in her tone, or if he'd just been paying attention. But Kat didn't know how to answer that. Instead, she peered further down the stairway. The noise echoing up through the stairways grew louder the closer they got to the Hideaway.

"I know it's not my place to pry, and if it's something else, you can just tell me to shut up," he began.

At that, she grinned.

"But with this squadron, and everything else the Commander has tossed our way, we wouldn't have made it this far if it weren't for you. So whatever is going on, I hope you know we're here for you." He shrugged. "And if you ever need to talk, I'm here."

The kindness on his face was genuine. And she could see he really did mean that. Maybe she could use another friend in her life.

And as they'd escaped the PARC for a few minutes, she intended to make the most of it. "How anxious are you for some processed crap?" They'd reached the Hideaway with its ever-present vending machines. But she stopped him before they could go in, a little grin slipping to her face.

"Guessing I should say, not at all?" Whistler raised an eyebrow.

"I was hoping you'd say that. Cuz I have a better idea."

Both of Whistler's eyebrows had lifted, but he didn't look apprehensive. He looked excited, as a grin slid across his face. "I'm not sure I know what I'm getting myself into—let's go."

The Canteen on the level below was closed for the night, its doors sealed. But a slight detour around the side and some minor hot-wiring had the service door springing open.

"Why they even bother to lock doors around here in the first place..." Whistler laughed as he followed her inside. He peered around him with interest, while Kat led them to the closet at the far end of the kitchens. "You've done this before."

Kat shrugged. "Only when we get really hungry."

They stuffed their pockets with leftover dinner rolls and were halfway back up to the PARC when they ran into the twins heading back down.

"You guys lost?" Whistler joked, but it had to be nearing 22:00 hours...

"We, uh—forgot something," Kamata fudged. She caught her twin's eye.

Kiara nodded, a mischievous grin on her face. "Yeah, yeah. What she said."

Kat snorted. Sure they did. But she let it slide, Whistler doing the same as Kiara began regaling them with a tale from the other night.

"So, you and Whistler, huh?" Kamata winked, pulling her aside. "We've been dying to know. Who is better?"

"I'm sorry, what?" Kat asked, feigning disinterest despite being a little thrown by the dark sparkle in the twin's eyes.

"You know, our Gamma boys. Zane, Whistler, or Lee? Kiara's got a thing for Zane, she loves them intense. But my bet's on Lee. It's always the quiet ones..."

"Oh, we haven't—"

"That's not what Hanna tells us."

Hanna, huh.

Kiara had finished telling her story, and both she and Whistler were looking over curiously to see what they were talking about. Or Whistler was, anyway. Kat had a feeling Kiara knew exactly what her twin had asked her.

Dismissing herself with as much cocky bravado as she could manage under the circumstances, Kat headed back up to the PARC. She wasn't sure she liked this latest rumor.

"So I brought back rolls if anyone is hungry," she said, patting her pockets as she crossed into the room. She took a bite from the one in her hands.

But it wasn't Lee who answered her. Lee wasn't even in the room at the moment. Instead, Zane flicked his golden-brown head dismissively in her direction with a chilly, "No thanks."

Intense? Try irritable.

She came around the table to her chair, clutching the roll tightly in her hands as she stared into the universe of holofiles they'd drawn up before they'd taken a break.

"Hey—are we good?" she asked into the silence.

She didn't glance over to see if he was looking at her, and she definitely didn't care to look at him.

"Yep."

"It's probably best if it doesn't happen again," she said, eyes now on the door to the room, lest someone else walk in.

"Don't worry. We're old news, baby girl. But out of curiosity," Zane drawled, and Kat stiffened. "Does Leland know about last night?"

"No." Her eyes shot right to his, pleading, as she pulverized the bread in her hands. "And you can't say anything."

242

"Whatever you say."

Kat sunk into her chair, unseeing, as she stared back into the holofiles. She'd made a mistake. How could she have been so ignorant? Yes, she was trying to let Lee find happiness. She didn't want to be the one to pull him down with her. And whether or not Zane now realized, he could shatter this whole charade of hers with a single word.

How could she even think about making room for Whistler? She couldn't even handle her own crappy life.

They'd returned to their silence; a *zapping* speeder ship could have crashed right through and neither of them would have acknowledged it.

Lee returned a few minutes later, a bit surprised to see her back already and seemingly empty-handed. "What, no green juice today?"

"Wasn't in the mood," Kat shrugged, swiping into a holofile at random. She stole a glance back to Zane once more, but the Gamma was blank-faced. The ammo he now held rested idly in his steeled hands.

"Interesting, but I can go with that," Lee said, settling in next to her.

Then he chuckled. "Wasn't in the mood, or didn't have time after smuggling food from the kitchens?"

She'd forgotten all about the bread in her pockets, the haggard remains of hers now crumbs on the table. The squished snack was the least of her worries, but she reached a shaky hand into her pocket. "Roll?"

CHAPTER 23: LEE

TWO DAYS later, Lee was coming out from a morning work-out when he found a message waiting for him on his hyperband. He stopped abruptly when he saw the send receipt.

> *Squadron approved. Cruiser A-01 cleared and beginning preparation. Departure scheduled for 08:00 hours.*

The Commander had included no fanfare with her message; no explanations offered as to possible complications or external reasons for the delay—not as if they needed them, they knew better. He didn't know why he'd expected anything different. But the approvals were almost anticlimactic after all their speculations where she and the General were concerned.

They'd spent another day split between trainings with their cadets, and research up in the PARC, trying to learn what they could on General Narron. He was ambitious, and he'd had a swift rise through the military ranks. But he was also well-re-spected; the General had transformed the energy landscape, the efficiency with which they traveled space and dealt in energy. Championing their galactic survival above all else, he was the reason their defenses against the dark radiation were what they were today. And it was these contributions and successes that had aided him both in his rise to Commanding General and in pushing his latest Preservation Initiative through. He was a hero in many eyes.

But Lee could still picture the hardened dark irises that had stared out at them during the Laser Rounds. What were the costs that had made him so?

Costs aside, though, today Commander Blanche had won. Whatever she had done to go around the General had worked, and she was getting to send her cadets back out there, her raiders. And they'd do what they always did. They'd already had their briefing; they had everything they needed to know.

Out of habit, he messaged Kat.

> Lee: *did u hear the news?*

> Kat: *I finally get my walk-in?*
> Kat: *jk. it's about time!*

It was odd. They'd seen each other constantly over the last couple of days, during their secret squadron trainings and up in the PARC. But it didn't feel like they'd actually had a chance to talk, lately. And it was definitely the longest they'd gone, maybe ever, without hanging out.

He checked the time. It was too late to meet for breakfast, but maybe they could meet up this afternoon.

> Lee: *lunch?*

Several hours later, fingers raw, and pleasantly aching, Lee stood waiting beside a stack of trays in the Canteen. They'd agreed upon 12:00 hours, but he was early. He'd snuck down to the greenhouses before this, knowing they'd be away for a few days. He'd only come back up here now to give his fingernails an extra scrub, and to beat the rush on the stairways.

He grinned as the familiar grey eyes and vanilla-blond pony-tail whipped through the door.

"Hey," he said when she stopped beside him.

"Hey," she said, tightening her ponytail with both hands.

"We should probably—" He motioned towards the grow-ing line and the stack of trays at his elbow. When had things become so inorganic between them? Grabbing a couple of trays, he handed one to Kat.

"Thanks." She wrapped both of her arms around her tray, hugging it up against her chest. "So, tomorrow should be fun."

"A lot of pressure riding on us, that's for sure." Understate-ment of the century. "You ready for it?"

Kat blew out a breath, some of her flyaway hairs floating up with it. "As ready as I'll ever be. Who knows, maybe we actually do find something this go around." She said it lightly, but he knew the weight had settled over all of them.

He could see it then. The flickers of annoyance in her brows. In her nose. He'd been waiting hours for this reaction. Days, really.

"The Commander had us start working on that internal review, what, a week and a half ago?" she asked.

"Twelve days," Lee agreed.

"She's had us at her beck and call for twelve days... And all she has to say, is 'Squadron approved'?"

"I wish I'd been with you when the message came in," he admitted with a grin. But he buckled in, he could see she was just getting started.

"So what, she's only entrusting her top cadets—her *best* cadets with a mission that is very clearly close to the vest, very likely involves the AMG, and doesn't have anything else to say about it. I'm over it."

Lee's grin widened. *Void,* he'd missed her dramatics. And her sarcasm.

They reached the servers. Setting his tray down on the ledge, he grabbed some bread and loaded his sandwich with as much lettuce and tomato as he could fit. Then he handed her his tongs. "On to the pocket diet after this."

"Ugh, don't remind me," Kat groaned, loading her own sandwich at least as tall as his.

They sat down at their regular table. Again, he couldn't remember the last time they'd just enjoyed a lunch together. "Let's do something tonight. You and me. We can make a celebration of it or something. We'll call it, 'finally going out on this raid of ours.'" He wanted—needed, to see Kat laughing again. It felt like it had been so long.

"Just the two of us?" Kat asked.

"You and me." Lee nodded. "We could visit the energy rings, or do a run on the Lightning Track? We haven't done that in a while." Lee really couldn't care less what they did at this point, so long as—what was that look about?

He swore a wary, almost lost look had peered back at him, before she'd looked away. "What if we do the energy rings?" Kat toyed with a piece of her sandwich. "We haven't messed around with those in ages."

They'd barely sorted out some loose plans when their lunch party was interrupted; first by the twins, and then Hanna.

"Anyone up for some climbing? Gammas vs everyone else," one of the twins said, plopping right down next to Kat, and grabbing a tomato slice from off the top of her sandwich. Kat didn't seem to care, as her eyes flicked from the twins to Hanna.

"No ropes allowed," the other twin clarified. This one wore a black wire choker—Kamata. Which meant the other one was Kiara. Lee was learning.

"They probably won't want to come," Hanna said. She seated herself with care alongside Kamata, fluffing her hair and checking her nails. But Kat had gotten that spark in her eyes. The spark grew until there was a fierce grin on Kat's lips.

"I'd be down for climbing at the Wall. But only if we make things a little more interesting."

"Let's hear it," Kamata said. There was something just a little rough around the edges with her and her twin, but Kat seemed good with them.

Kat shrugged. "Blindfolds."

Lee huffed a laugh. He'd known something like this was coming.

Levy walked by then, shooting the twins a little smile as they waved her over. She hovered beside them for a bit but didn't sit down, almost like she shied from the Canteen lights overhead.

He smiled at her. Taking that as her cue, Levy came around the table, gesturing to the spot next to him. Lee scooted his tray up out of the way to make a little more room.

She was quiet for a few minutes while the rest of the table talked themselves higher. It appeared this post-lunch event was going to be quite the spectacle.

Levy wasn't shy, at least not from what he'd noticed. She was more of an observer. But at the moment, even that seemed like a stretch.

"You feeling okay?" he asked, leaning over. She still had yet to utter more than a word.

"Headache," she grimaced.

"Do you want me to get you a dose for that? I probably have something back at the dorm. My dad's a medic."

"It's fine, I get these all the time. It should go away on its own, eventually."

He nodded. Levy was tough. Tougher than he'd scanned her for at first glance. But Lee also got the impression that Levy didn't have all that many confidants. And with her easy disposition and quiet confidence, he couldn't begin to fathom why.

"What'd I miss?" Whistler asked, also coming up to their table. He claimed one of the two remaining seats, bridging the gap between Hanna and Levy.

"We are going down to climb, blindfolded. You in?" Hanna asked, batting her extended lashes.

But Whistler didn't care about her eyelashes. He peered sidelong at Kat. "I'm in if Kat's in." Big shocker there. He'd worn his hair in that ridiculous French braid today that ran down the length of his crown.

"You bet your ass I'm in." Kat flashed the grin that would obliterate them all in a few seconds' time. He supposed they'd asked for it. "Oh, hey Hanna—" Kat called out, then, just loud enough to get her attention. "They're all pretty phenomenal."

Lee didn't understand Kat's comment, or Hanna's scowl as she looked away. Some understanding had passed between them that went clean over Lee's head.

But then Kamata was sliding to her feet, and Kat began to frantically stack things onto her tray. "The last one down there has to start the climb one-handed."

Kat looked over to him as she jumped to her feet with the others. "You guys coming, Lee? Levy?"

Lee took one look at Levy, her face paling by the minute. "You guys go on ahead," he said.

"You sure?" Kat asked.

"I'll find you later."

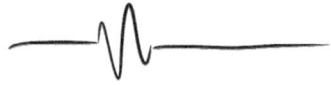

"I feel really bad. You could have gone with them," Levy said, a half hour later. They'd taken their time picking through the leftover morsels of his lunch. The room was almost completely emptied out by the time he picked up his tray.

"It's cool. We climb all the time." They'd reached the stairway outside of the Canteen. "You want to go sit down in the Hideaway? Maybe find a good spot somewhere to recharge before tomorrow?"

"Honestly, I think I may just go lie down. Walk me?"

"Here," Lee motioned upward with his head, toward the dorms above.

The noise of chatter from the various levels of the Heptagon faded the higher they climbed until only the whirring of the fans overhead kept them company. "That's cool about your dad being a medic. I think it's a really noble profession," Levy volunteered.

"It is noble." At least Lee could agree on that. They'd crossed through the skywalk, its star-speckled exterior, before he'd realized she was waiting for him to expound on that. "He's away a lot," he explained. "As a kid, we'd sometimes go weeks on end with just me and Tonya."

"Your mom?" Levy asked.

"Yeah. She's helpless if you're fixing a spacecraft or hooking up holotech. But if you ever want to add the perfect pop of color to your eyes, she knows just the thing."

"What?" Levy asked, sputtering as her warm, rainstorm laugh slipped from her lips.

"That came out much weirder than I intended." Lee laughed. But when Levy again waited for him to go on, he explained all about his mom's enterprises with Solar Cosmetics and how she'd offered to get some for Kat.

There was some sort of emotion in her eyes. Pain, maybe, from her headache. "You and your mom sound close."

Lee shrugged. "I guess. As close as I can be, as a raider. I think I really surprised her when I decided to join the program."

"How so?"

"I think she'd hoped I would have picked some profession where I could stay a little closer to home. Especially with everything my dad's seen, being a medic and all. But my heart was always with the stars."

"My family was surprised too, when I decided to join the Academy," she said quietly. And there was something more in her face that told Lee he shouldn't pry into this one just yet. They all had something to fight for.

They'd reached her dorm. Lee stood by the side so she could scan her hyperband at the door. He'd decided full hall-lengths back that it was really easy to talk to Levy.

She'd set one foot through the portal door when she turned back. He noticed it was tidy in there. He could just make out the soft blue of a folded afghan at the foot of her bed. He wondered what Tonya would make of Levy.

"Thanks for choosing me for the squadron," she said. And when she looked back at him, it was as if the dust had been swept away from his head, and he caught a glimpse down a path he'd never realized he had.

"It was all of us," Lee said roughly, nodding, before he left, turning and heading back the way he'd come.

Lee didn't go down to the training levels for a climb. He didn't even set foot down there until later that afternoon, and even then, it was only to retrieve the water bottle he'd left after his workout that morning, before heading up to the PARC.

In lieu of an afternoon training, the four squadron leads were meeting up one last time to go over details for the following morning.

"Let's see, we've got all the files from the hub?" Lee asked, rifling down through their holo-materials.

"Just dropping them over now," Zane murmured.

"And you confirmed the ship is ready? No weird convertor issue?" He asked Whistler.

Kat snorted. "I can't believe that was even a thing."

"Guy ought to be reported," Zane murmured.

"Verified her myself." Whistler drummed his fingertips along the edge of the long table that ran the length of the room.

Lee began closing out the holograms one by one, the other squadron leads doing the same. Days and days of research and preparation, all compiled for a single instance. How far they'd come.

Whistler had rebraided his hair from this afternoon, and Zane sported a fresh buzz, the previous shaved lines of the Academy's broken triangle symbol barely visible with the last-minute cut. Even Kat had taken the time to smooth some of the errant strays of her ponytail for tonight. A new respect hung over the length of the table between them. And an understanding.

They truly had come a long way from that first night with the Laser Rounds, making lifeblood vows over shaky understandings, to their last squadron meetup yesterday afternoon. He traced the long table, now all but devoid of glittering holographs, and the slightly crooked chairs by the table from the night before; the only remnants of the four of them and the functional-against-all-odds thing they'd formed between them during this last week or so. Somehow they'd managed this.

But they weren't done yet. He truly hoped they were ready.

Lee glanced around the room one last time before they turned out the lights.

"How did the Wall go today, by the way?" Lee asked as they started back down through the Heptagon.

"This one set a new record," Whistler said, coming up even with Kat, and nudging her shoulder, his ridiculous French braid swaying with the sentiment.

"You really should've come," Kat laughed, wrapping her hands around her arms as Whistler echoed the sentiment.

"Really, man. It was such a rush. We should make this a thing. Blind climbing before every raid."

"I'll be there next time," Lee promised, glancing behind them to where Zane trailed a couple of steps behind. Zane had the air of death about him and didn't contribute much as they wound their way downward, but he also didn't break away tonight, either. They all processed the weight in their own way —clearly.

Lee and Kat had planned to split up from the others after this for the energy rings. But as they were passing the Hideaway, he found he wasn't particularly anxious to get away tonight. Kat also didn't seem over-eager to rush off—not as they ran into the twins and Hanna.

They'd stood outside gabbing a good fifteen to twenty minutes over what climbs they were going to hit up next time, before finding themselves back outside the Spectrum once again. The starboard doors were miraculously devoid of locks tonight; a minor mystery for another time.

And then there they were, back where it had all started. Back at the base of the Spectrum in the Blackout Galaxy and engulfed once again in the mystique of the darkened arena.

Jed showed up before long. And Nikola. Even Levy. Her headache must have settled, because she seemed in good enough spirits tonight, striking up a conversation first with Hanna, and then with Nikola.

Tonight the Spectrum was electrifying.

Like the other night, an excitement had settled over them. Only this time, the edge they rode was for the raid. They were finally going out again to discover the unknown. The past few days had been pure bliss compared to what he expected in the coming days.

He fell into conversation with Jed for a few minutes, if only to confirm the cadet wasn't entirely insane. Aside from him being a recommendation of Zane's, Lee still knew very little about the X cadet. The kid wasn't much for conversation, that much was immediately clear. But he'd left his gaming device back in his dorm tonight, so that was something.

"So you're into programming?"

"Uh, yeah."

"Did you pass all the exams yet?" Lee asked, genuinely curious how far his expertise extended.

"I write them."

That actually left Lee a little dumbfounded—talk about unexpected. He glanced around to see if he could use anyone else to get a bit more out of Jed.

A little way along the base from them, Hanna and Zane had been cornered by Nikola. Lee considered rescuing them from factoids for a moment but decided it would do each of them some good.

Kat had that spark again, as she chatted with Whistler and the twins. Were they still on about the Wall, or was this a new venture? Her eyes glistened like starlight as she smiled at whatever Whistler was telling her and the twins—

"Hey, you enjoy yourself tonight," Lee said, cutting the kid free.

He was on his way over to see what could be so entertaining when he glimpsed Levy standing off to the side, alone. Fumbling at his previous resolve and sliding his hands into his pockets, he traced the stands around until he got to her. "Hey, you."

"Hey, yourself," she said. "Thanks again for walking me back this afternoon."

"It was nothing. Are you feeling any better?" He scrutinized the shadows grazing her cheeks, letting his gaze dance across her lavender face.

"I am, actually. A little rest was just what I needed." She smiled. "It's like I said, they always go away eventually. Did you have a nice afternoon?"

"I did. Took it easy. Then Kat and I met with the rest of the squadron leads to do a little prep." He glanced back over his shoulder. The twins had moved on, leaving only Kat with Whistler. Again. He felt the pang in his gut before he could turn his back to them.

"You bring up her name a lot."

"Do I?" Lee asked

"It's okay. I get it."

Lee studied her again, the star's reflection in her dark eyes. Her fluttering eyelashes. "Do you?"

"You guys have this thing between the two of you." She shrugged, her dark eyes falling. "Always have, always will."

This thing.

The dust swirled around and around in his head; the galaxy in a bottle. But maybe he was tired of waiting around for the path to clear.

"Hey Levy," he began, her eyes beaming back up to his, a soft expression lighting them...

And then she kissed him. It was fleeting and hesitant. A question.

As her lips left his and she lowered her heels back down to the ground, his lips parted. He stared down at her for a heart-beat.

And then he kissed her back, testing out this new feeling with her.

She was grinning when he pulled back again, and she looked up at him from under that sheet of shining hair with those curious, dark eyes. "I was wondering if you'd ever do that."

Reaching a steady hand out, Lee pulled her face back up to his.

Somewhere in the darkness, someone hollered. Lee gave them the finger, leaning in to kiss Levy some more.

Yes, tonight was electrifying.

CHAPTER 24: KAT

THE LIGHTS in the hallways were still dimmed when Kat left her dorm that morning. She milled around the central floors of the Heptagon until the Canteen's doors were unlocked.

A handful of cadets trickled in while she picked her way through the line, but she took her time, deliberately and intentionally; she'd never seen the platters so well-stocked. She held up a couple of the power drink flavors, examining their ingredients. It was funny that she'd never bothered to look before now. Selecting one with infused strawberry leaves for Lee, she set the drink off to the side and set about thumbing down another label to find one for her.

Lee had certainly enjoyed himself plenty last night, and she'd all but paved the way for them after her oversight with Zane the other night. She'd tried not to think about it this morning while she'd pulled her hair back and slipped into her all-terrain suit. She'd tried not to think about whose scent Lee would be wearing when she saw him next, or guess what time he'd eventually made it back to his dorm—or if he'd even made it back up there at all. She'd seen the way he and Levy had been intertwined around each other down in the Spectrum.

She'd left rather early, letting Whistler walk her back to her dorm. Everything was completely platonic between them, but he still continued to impress her with his perception and insight, despite his generally easy-going disposition.

She'd thought they'd had a moment as they were standing outside her door, where she'd wondered if he might have liked to come in. But it wasn't Whistler she'd pictured shutting the portal door behind him and stretching out across her bed, teasing her about her dorm being messier than the Canteen on Biscuits and Gravy Day. It wasn't Zane, either. It was a boy. The boy who'd preferred strawberry jam on his sandwich. The boy who'd grown into his nose and his gangly limbs. The boy she could still see shining through the features of her now filled-in, almost 19-year-old best friend.

So she'd thanked Whistler and smiled, before sending him on his way. He'd never really been hers to keep, anyway.

She planned to meet Lee along the central skywalk, like usual, but he caught up to her on her way out of the Canteen.

"You're up early." Lee looked surprised. And maybe a tad tired. Like he'd indeed had a busy night. She ignored it, blasting the thoughts away like another bit of space debris flying too close to their path.

"Here," she said, handing him his power drink. She noted his dubious expression at the reversal of roles. "Yeah, yeah. Don't get used to it."

Lee was still chuckling as they crossed into the skywalk, stopping midway through. Leaning up against the railing with his forearms, he cracked his drink open. She did the same, peering out into the star-speckled eternity.

"You think this is the last time?" She asked.

"That we go out on a raid? Nah. There'll be at least a couple more after this," Lee teased, nudging her with his arm. He didn't move his arm away after, though.

She studied their arms, the strength in each of them. It had been obvious from their early days at the Academy that they made a pretty formidable team. And up until now, they'd been pretty resilient. But with these latest developments, with Levy... Could they still withstand it if Kat wasn't the strength he leaned upon? And he hers? Did she even want to?

She hadn't realized they'd been quiet for so long until she heard Lee swallow beside her. He still hadn't moved his arm. And she didn't lean away.

"Are you okay with today?" he asked. "I realize we never talked about it."

About Levy? Were they really going to do this right here? Right now? She braced herself—but not against the cool railing. She could feel his pulse and the fluttery tightening in the muscles of his forearm where it touched hers.

"The hyperjump will be just like last time, and you may even feel it less. It's been a while since we've been out on one of the cruisers."

A shaky laugh escaped her. The hyperjump. He was talking space travel. She'd been so preoccupied with everything else

261

going on, that she hadn't even spared a thought for the impending jump this morning. Suddenly looming before her, she actually had to brace herself on the railing to steady the quaking feeling in her legs as her heartbeat picked up.

"You've got this," Lee said, catching her gaze and calming the horror in her eyes. "You've got this." He gripped her arm with his other hand, steadying her. And for a moment, his green eyes held her there, wide and searching. She wondered earnestly if this would continue. If he'd still have her back. And she realized how badly she didn't want him to move his hand. She didn't want to move away from this, and where they stood right now.

She held onto that moment as long as she could. But lingering would only delay the inevitable; it wouldn't turn back time. And after a few seconds, she smiled numbly. "Thank you." And finishing up her drink, she pushed away from the railing. "These are still so bad."

"After all these years." Lee drained his as well. "What do you say we go see how much damage Whistler's done?" They chucked their cans on their way into the hangar.

Their cruiser hovered at the forefront of the main hangar with its loading ramp lowered. Some of the systems crew-members exited as they came up.

Both Whistler and Zane were already onboard. Apparently, they weren't the only ones wanting to keep an eye on their best pilot and mechanic.

She greeted Zane coolly as Lee drifted over to observe the mechanics working alongside Whistler. They were running

through all the pre-flight checks. "How are things looking for
—"

"*Starla*," Zane cut in, giving them an obviously pointed
look as he glanced between her and Lee, and Whistler.

"Starla," Kat repeated, biting down on the tail-side of a grin
threatening to spring forward. Nodding at them to continue,
Kat came around the opposite side of the bay, listening in while
Whistler gave them an update on the ship's systems, and the
latest verinity core-cell. With the cruiser's energy capacities,
despite its size, their flight times would be roughly the same as
their last trip out to Argos.

Leaving Whistler and Zane to guide the rest of the inspection, she and Lee did a walk-through to check out their latest
accommodations.

The cruiser was definitely built for comfort—at least compared to the skimmers. The rounded cabin itself was probably
the size of two of the PARC rooms combined. A series of
harnessed, in-flight seats lined both sides of the cabin's contoured windows, with all the latest holotech and sensor equipment arranged neatly around the observation deck in the middle of the cabin. The spacecraft could easily have accommodated twenty cadets. They'd be at half capacity for this mission,
which meant less cramped sleeping quarters and fewer fights for
the ship's two spiral showers.

She trailed Lee back past the set of round, translucent dining tables with their matching chairs, towards the kitchenette
that lined the back wall. The little bar area was situated between
two mini-fridges on either end. "I wonder why they needed

two," Kat murmured, opening one of the doors to investigate its contents. All the usual suspects lined the top shelves, but in the bottom drawers...

Kat took a step back, slamming the door shut as she ran her eyes along the countertops. No one needed that much fresh produce, unless...

She walked reverently towards the beautiful, stainless contraption nestled up against the wall. "Someone loves me. A green juice machine?" She squealed. "Please, please tell me this was you!" She peered over to the side to smile sheepishly over at Lee.

"You've got to be kidding me." He huffed a laugh. "I swear I had nothing to do with this," he said, half shaking his head and half gaping in utter bemusement.

"What's going on?" Zane's cool voice asked. Kat let her gaze shift his way for barely a second as Zane started across the cabin towards them. He dismissed them when he saw what they had gathered around, heading instead up to the cockpit. Never mind him. She turned back to the green juice machine. There must be an instruction manual around here somewhere... She could probably just figure it out...

"We never talked about last night," Lee said. He trailed his hand along the countertop, speaking quietly enough that she could easily pretend she hadn't heard him if she wanted.

She pursed her lips. "Oh?" If he wanted to go here, she sure wasn't going to lead this thing.

"We'd made plans, you and I. I know I'd promised you a night together, with just us." His hand stilled on the counter. "I'm just sorry we didn't get to hang out, you know?"

Kat turned her back to the pretty machine. She'd opened her mouth to say something, before realizing she had no idea what she wanted to say—what she could even say?

She wanted to ask about Levy. But she also wanted to know as little as possible.

She settled on, "It's fine. We can hang out anytime. We're hanging out now." That felt okay enough, right? It matched Lee's tone?

Wow. This was really what they were reduced to now, mimicked tones and forced phrases?

She shook her head. "Really. We're okay." And she smiled. She and Lee would always be okay. They would be. Resilience. To the *void* with her earlier thoughts.

Of course, she wanted to choke on her words a few minutes later when Levy showed up, her lavender skin practically glowing as she floated up from the loading ramp.

She was pleased when Kiara and Kamata arrived immediately after, saving her from that reunion this early in the morning. The twins appeared oddly calm and collected, compared to their usual mischievous demeanors. "We aren't into mornings," Kiara informed her. That made two of them.

Whistler joined them, too, before long, making things a little more lively. In between Kamata and Kiara's wagering over who of their squadron would go insane first if they got stuck out in space, she found herself catching Whistler's eye. She wanted to apologize for last night, for any disappointment he might have had on his part. But when Whistler's lips turned up in that crooked grin, she knew they were okay. There were no hard feelings.

She stole away when Hanna finally decided to grace them with her presence, excusing herself to make sure everything else was on track for them to head out. They had all their cadets, with Nikola having come up, surveying the cabin with that unquenchable curiosity of his, and Jed, slinking around by the bar in the back. Please don't let him be into green juice as well, she really didn't need that right now...

With Zane finishing up the pre-flight checklist in the cockpit, she headed for the loading ramp, where Lee met her at the base.

"I thought you'd be with..." Kat didn't finish her thought, shaking her head as she changed tactics. "Were you just—"

"Checking on status? Yeah. We're cleared to go as soon as everyone gets settled in. They're ready for us."

She followed Lee back up the ramp, rejoining the rest of the squadron. "Hanging in there?" he asked, ushering the rest of the cadets away from the opening as he got ready to raise the loading ramp.

Kat shrugged. "As much as ever."

Lee tapped in the code for the ramp. Its closing was as good of a signal as any. The cadets quieted down, gathering loosely around the observation deck where Zane now leaned. She, Lee, and Whistler, joined him so that the four squadron leads stood facing their squadron.

Zane spoke first. "As of 07:00 hours yesterday morning, we are officially a squadron. We are going out under the Commander's banner and will abide by her rules—all of her rules." Was that warning for her and Lee? Or the Twins? Whistler? The groupings could be limitless.

Striding right past any undertones, Lee followed him, addressing the group. "You should have received the mission assignment. The Commander has tasked us with investigating the radiation surrounding Argos. Starting now, that is the only thing that matters. Put everything else behind you."

Kat's turn. "As you may have learned from the past few days —" a round of smirks and shared smiles met her words. "Our investigation will include a lot of grunt work and will very possibly be dull as shit. Hang in there." She winked.

"Which means," chimed in Whistler, grinning broadly, "we will have to find a way to make up for that where we can. Now, let's blitz."

There was no need to intimidate this time around. The majority of their gathered group were seasoned cadets; they knew what was on the line, and they'd all be elbow-deep in wavelengths and amplitudes before long. They'd all best enjoy these last few hours while they could.

While the cadets picked their seats, the four of them made their way up to the cockpit.

The pilot's chambers were much roomier than last time and included four seats this time. Pilot, co-pilot, systems, and main cabin liaison.

Whistler was the obvious choice for pilot. But as for co-pilot and systems—

"Dibs," she called, glancing sidelong, and daring both Lee and Zane to contest her for one of those seats. If she got stuck back on cabin liaison—

Laughter dancing in his eyes, Lee offered with a sweeping gesture to the seat on their right, while he himself slid into that central role of main cabin liaison.

While Kat reconfirmed the coordinates programmed into the system, Zane confirmed with Whistler that they were all set to go.

"You guys ready for this?" Whistler asked as he slid his headset over his ears. His voice echoed through their headsets as he radioed in to operations. "Cruiser A-01 moving into position."

It was surprisingly comforting to hand over the reins to Whistler and Zane, tuning out everything except Whistler's voice in her ear. It wasn't Lee, but it wasn't a bad second choice.

As Whistler started the engine, she turned back to face Lee, a broad grin splitting her face as she mouthed, "How do you get to Gemini?"

CHAPTER 25: LEE

LEE WAS on his feet before Whistler's tenor voice came through the cabin's speakers. "Good afternoon cadets. This is your pilot speaking. Cruiser A-01 welcomes you to Argos where the local time is—definitely not 12:35, but that is the hour we're going to stick with. Please remain seated until the spacecraft comes to a complete stop..."

Sliding the lazr-pods from his ears, Lee gazed out one of the bowed windows. The space-scape of Argos was like any other he'd stared into for the last seven years. But having confirmed what they had with the dark radiation, and still knowing so little, it felt eerie. Like whatever connected that magnetic field to the radiation spikes was just outside these windows, watching them.

He'd been back and forth between the cockpit and main cabin as the flight had progressed, taking the lead on distributing the arrhythmia pills after the hyperjump. But as they'd gotten closer to their coordinates, he'd taken up a more permanent seat back here in anticipation of Argos' magnetic field's interference.

Like last time, the system glitched. But Whistler truly was a gifted pilot. No sooner had the lights flickered than Whistler had taken over manual control of the ship. Lee hadn't even felt the acceleration of the thrusters as the ship had come to a stop; the guy could model the simulation for the *zapping* auto-pilot program if he wanted.

And now here they were. Their home for the next few days.

He turned away from the window to find Levy had also come to her feet in the seat next to his.

"Can you believe we're already back out here?" She asked.

Lee laughed. "Too soon, right? And at the same time, it feels like it's been ages."

There was a lightness about her, an eagerness. Even now, after a long morning in flight, her eyes were still bright, her cheeks lightly coloring as she laughed.

He wished he'd had more time to just hang out back here. He'd chatted with her and the other cadets a little, in between getting everyone settled back here, but he'd ultimately ended up sliding his lazr-pods over his ears and pulling up some of the reports he'd saved on his hyperband. They had one more chance to figure this thing out, and he wanted to hit the ground running.

He was apologizing to Levy for everything being so busy when Kat emerged from the cockpit. "I never got my green juice," she announced to the cabin at large, as she strode right past them all, her long hair streaming behind her with its ever-present flyaways.

270

Lee sighed. "Excuse me." Turning away from Levy, he followed Kat back to the shiny juice machine. She'd already started to give love to its little dials and knobs when he got back there.

"I've seen simpler controls on a micro-conversion speeder." He leaned back against the counter beside her. He still couldn't believe it, what were the chances?

Her eyes flashed, but he grinned, shoving his hands in his pockets while he waited for her to get the juicer whirring. If it was blood sugar she needed, he'd best not get in her way.

"It sounded awfully quiet up there," he said, once its gears stopped turning.

"Yeah, well, three's a crowd." Okay, that he'd believe.

"I missed your playlist," she admitted a minute later. She lifted the metal carafe from the base, examining the contents inside, before dumping them into one of the little plastic cups stacked on the counter.

"Even the drum solos?"

She considered. "They grow on you."

He stared out across the main cabin. The rest of their cadets flocked over to the observation deck as Zane joined them in the main cabin. It felt so weird to have all this space out here—nothing at all like last time.

He and Kat met Zane at the platform where Zane eyed the green drink in Kat's hands with narrowed eyes. Lee suppressed rolling his, as Kat swigged loudly from her straw. These two.

With motions far too practiced at this point, they drew up their diagrams of Argos. "So we have a little under ninety-six hours on the clock," Lee said, looking to Zane to confirm that Whistler had the main shield locked into place and counting down. "Let's see what we can do here."

"Nikola—let's put you and Hanna on the radiation sensors. I'll be here for backup." He studied the holotech on the observation deck, and the cadets still angling around. "As for collecting samples..."

They'd debated this on and off on the way over whether it was worth expending the energy. They had the cargo space, but the samples weren't specifically requested this round, and where they'd already confirmed the presence of dark rays—

"I still think it wouldn't hurt if we end up being the ones to process the samples again or not," Zane said. "And we may want the evidence."

On that, Lee agreed. Especially if the General came poking after their raid-status again. Plus, they'd already confirmed last time that they were able to guide the vehicles back. Lee motioned with his head, "Kamata, Kiara." He glanced between Kat and Zane, someone would need to keep the twins in line.

"I've got them," Kat volunteered, following them into the storage bay in the back to locate the RIM vehicles. Fair enough.

They tasked Levy and Jed with attempting a reading of the magnetism, to be overseen by Zane.

They'd begin with a general sweep of the area, which Lee was ninety percent certain would yield results identical to last time. And once they'd confirmed that the radiation around them was once again dormant, the magnetism off the charts, then they'd take on the magnetic field and see what Argos had in store for them. It was only a matter of time now.

So Lee stood by as the tumultuous tech booted up around them.

Their initial rounds of data came in. As expected, there was no energy recording of the radiation spikes the AMG sensors had detected. And after also dismissing the magnetometer, which—no shocker—was again malfunctioning, Lee turned to face their diagrams of Argos.

Right on target.

Last time, they'd been searching for dark rays with only the undulations of the cosmic rays to go on. They'd repeatedly observed this slice of the galaxy as a whole. And up until about nine days ago, they hadn't had any reason to do anything differently. However, after learning about the elevated radiation levels surrounding the magnetic field and their uncanny relationship to the radiation spikes, they now had every reason.

He'd been thinking about this on the passage over as he'd anxiously awaited the opportunity to really scope out Argos' magnetic field. Yes, they still wouldn't have the magnetometer to give them exact coordinates. But they had this new assumption to guide them. Dragging his eyes from the loose circle of dots at the heart of their diagram, he set to work.

It took a calculated effort to draw up the new set of parameters, matching the estimated coordinates of the magnetic field to the sensor tech. And then a collective inhale, as they waited on bated breath for the sensors to calibrate the next round of data.

"Here we go," Nikola chattered excitedly, and no one bothered to shush him when the waves on the sensor tech began rolling in again a few seconds later.

The recorded radiation levels were incrementally higher with the narrower scope. And although the levels were still nowhere near comparable to the reported radiation spikes, it was something different. And he could work with different. Something about the magnetic field was interacting with the dark radiation, so now the question was: what?

After days spent training together back on their ship, the squadron churned out results like a well-oiled machine. It shouldn't be long before they came up with something. They started into a dry cycle, alternating between observing the magnetic field from even narrower scopes while they formulated a plan for getting even deeper. There had to be more they could learn from the data, more they were still missing.

The afternoon dragged on.

Just to give the others something to do, they swapped out one of the twins, sending Levy and Jed over to the mod-vehicles, while the rest of them took turns to monitor the sensor tech; the twins had made it into a bit of a contest to see who could collect the most samples in the shortest amount of time.

If the raid continued at this rate, they'd have a roomful of space debris by the evening, and then they'd really have to get creative.

Kat had just ducked over by Whistler to make another green drink when Hanna and the twins started up a conversation in lowered voices. Lee tuned out the start of it, but he started listening in again when he heard Whistler's name come up, and Kat, by association.

"She does seem pretty cozy around Whistler these days..."

"I wouldn't put much stake on it, I think they're both just bunking around."

"You guys do know we're all sitting here, right?" Lee asked, not bothering to flick his eyes away from the holotech.

"Yes, but it's all in your favor," Hanna preened. He could see her dramatic attempt at flattery from up the line in his peripherals.

"Hanna's right. First with you and Zane, and now Whistler, she's hit up all the hot ones—girl's got great taste." This time, Lee made the mistake of looking over. He caught Kiara's wink, her black septum piercing catching in the overhead lights.

"I hope that was worth it," Zane muttered from opposite Lee. Apparently, he wasn't the only one who'd tuned in against their will.

Lee leveled Zane a look.

"I'm just saying, girl can fight her own battles. *Void* knows she likes to start them."

Lee didn't bother to weigh in. It was all futile anyway.

He should have just stayed out of it.

They swapped out Levy and Jed on the mod-vehicles. Lee was getting ready to take his own turn with one of the RIMs when he heard Levy. "Hey—what do you make of this?"

He knew better than to get his hopes up as he and Zane came around the observation deck alongside Levy, her shiny black hair catching the light. "Right here, look at these waves." She motioned to the sensor recording in front of her.

It wasn't a spike—not like the AMG sensors had recorded, and not like the dark rays typically triggered. This was something else, something new.

"Expand that hologram," Lee said, watching the wave move farther and farther down the line. This was closer to a transient disturbance. For a single wavelength, the amplitude of the energy wave recording nearly doubled. And then barely a wavelength later it was back down like before, as if it'd never happened. It was like a measurement on an EKG. Like a pulse.

"And this is the first time you've seen it do this?" Zane asked, tracing down a similar thought pattern. Levy just nodded, Jed looking on over their shoulders.

Lee studied the measurements, willing the sensory tech to replicate the fluctuation—and also apprehensive at the prospect of another one; of there being more. The magnetic field was strong, that much they'd already witnessed, both from its effects on their ship and on their magnetometer tech. But as to this pulse, and what it said about the magnetic field... he didn't know what to make of that. And it was that unknown that worried him.

"Let's keep an eye on this," Zane said motioning for Levy to monitor the recordings, while he started up a report. "We'll let you guys know if we see something like this happen again."

Lee nodded curtly toward Zane. If it had happened once, it could happen again—they'd just have to wait for it.

Lee had snuck away to grab one of the white bean dinner pockets later that evening when he again found himself by Hanna. She leaned against one of the countertops in the back as she stared aimlessly out towards one of the starboard windows. He was just going to nod and pass her by when something in her smile stopped him.

"I still can't believe the dark rays out there. The detectable radiation alone would fry you," Hanna murmured, motioning with her head toward the observation deck in the middle of the cabin. "It makes you sort of understand Nikola's molecular-protection glasses." And when she smiled again, there was no sign of the coquette from earlier. Hanna without her cronies nearby was almost pleasant, charming, even.

"He told you about those?"

"That last night in the Blackout Galaxy."

Lee huffed a laugh. Poor kid. But she was right—about the radiation, anyway. He'd been in deep with all this for so long, it had all just become data on a holochart.

And with that pulse today, it brought him right back there with her. What could anyone do against a phenomenon like this? Not to mention whatever was going on with that magnetic field. When the dark rays eventually crashed down on them, it would be like waves on a beach. And they'd be the sitting ducks.

"Have you ever heard of Solar Cosmetics?" He found himself asking, to lessen the tension a little. He offered to hook her up when they got back. Tonya would be thrilled her son was assisting to expand her empire.

He drifted back over to the observation deck when the twins headed their way, leaving the trio to that blasted green juice machine.

It was a small grace they didn't see another pulse as afternoon turned to evening. They'd dragged one of the kitchenette's translucent dining tables over beside the observation deck as they started down a deep scouring to see if anything similar had shown up in their earlier data. All of their earlier data. Without the narrowed scope, he wasn't incredibly hopeful. But if there was something out here to be found, they were going to find it.

He just hoped four days would be enough.

With no more news of another pulse, the other three squadron leads had taken to dividing up the night shifts, while Lee shifted his focus to filling out the cadet health surveys for the day.

Up the platform from where he worked, Nikola was prattling on about an article he'd read recently on the fourth state of matter, some of the lesser-known properties of plasma. They ought to put Nikola on first shift for the night. Like Lee, he seemed wired.

Lee's brain had been running on an urgent edge all day. Maybe he'd go take one of those spiral showers in a bit, try to calm his mind. If that principle even worked when the soothing water elements were removed from the mix. He didn't know the mechanics, but he was pretty sure the showers up here relied instead on air and energy...

He could sense her lithe body when Levy came over to stand next to him. Lee shot her a little smile, lifting a hand to her head. "I think she's looking a little peaky. Definitely warm," Lee teased, pretending to type something into the survey with his other hand.

Lifting her own hand to cover his, Levy took a step closer, peering into the surveys. "Does your survey ask anything about racing heartbeats?"

"I can't say it does." Lee's eyes met hers. Letting their hands drop, Levy slipped her fingers through his.

"What about difficulty..." she stood up on her toes, her lips grazing his cheek, "breathing."

"I—nope." Lee shuttered, all of the thoughts whooshing from his brain as he struggled to complete his sentence.

Stepping back again, she bit her lip. Lee had to inhale, gluing his eyes to the surveys before him as he tried to remember what *in-the-void's* name he'd been doing before this very second in time.

He stared into the hologram for another second. Two. "I don't really know how to do this," he admitted. He glanced over at her sidelong.

"Do what?" She angled her head. "This?" She squeezed his hand.

Lee swallowed, staring down at their still-entangled hands.

Levy was a quiet force of her own. Strong. And resilient.

He'd thought about kissing her several times today. Thought about just pulling her into the shadows with him, away from the others, and picking up where they'd left off the other night. But every time he'd thought about solidifying things, or continuing things, he'd been pulled away. Something with the ship. Something with the test equipment. Something with Kat.

He traced her face with his eyes in the darkness. When had someone dimmed the lights?

Sighing, he squeezed her hand back, before slowly, and deliberately letting their hands drop apart. "All of this."

"Take your time." She smiled. And it caught him off guard the way Levy was looking at him, all starry-eyed and such. Like there wasn't an entire galaxy just beyond these walls.

He knew that look. He'd seen it reflected on his own face, a time or two. Was he crazy to waste this time? Even for tonight?

His eyes trailed her long after she'd walked away, leaving him standing there with the cadet health surveys.

Lee Waters. Emotionally incapable of leading with a clear head.

CHAPTER 26: KAT

THEY RECORDED two more of those pulses in the day that followed, each as jarring and seemingly unconnected as the last. They'd tried to locate a pattern in timing or amplitude with the rest of their data, but thus far, they'd only been able to isolate these few, making for a grand total of three. She didn't know what to make of that.

"It's almost like the magnetic field is alive," Kat muttered, careful not to disturb the green juice cups spaced up and down the observation deck as she pulled an arm across her chest. She and the other squadron leads had been standing in basically these same spots the entire day, only breaking from the platform to grab snacks or make another round of green juices. She and Whistler had taken to experimenting with flavors in-between shifts.

"A living magnetic field," Lee mused. "What would that make it, some type of plasma-based forcefield?" There was a thought. The whole idea sounded crazy, like something she'd overheard Nikola chattering about earlier. On the other hand, the galaxy was massive. With so many secrets being kept be-

281

tween the Academy ship and AMG headquarters alone, who knew what else was hiding in the farther reaches.

It had been hard to put all they suspected about their Commander and the Commanding General behind them. The idea that he was searching for something—and that whatever was out here could turn out to be that something...

Her eyes glossed right over Levy, to Nikola, who'd also taken up a place in the last couple of hours at the round dining table bordering the observation deck. These two alone, of all their cadets, had remained semi-close throughout the day. Nikola seemed newly invigorated by the pulse findings, and Levy—Kat didn't even want to go there. She was really trying not to let whatever was going on between Levy and Lee bother her, and she'd found ignoring the girl to do the trick. At least for now.

They'd full-on pardoned Jed when his dumb hand-held video game had come out this afternoon since it left them free to focus on the matters at hand. He and the twins were now huddled along the harnessed seats by the windows, playing through a level alongside Hanna's bored hair twirls.

"What if there was a way to test all of these theories at once?" Whistler asked, pushing away from the holotech altogether as he glanced from her to Lee and Zane.

"Now we're talking," Kat said with a grin. She didn't even know exactly what he was implying yet, but if it meant taking some sort of action, she was already on board. She could do with mixing things up a bit.

"How." Zane crossed his arms over his chest. And both Lee and Zane looked skeptical as they glanced between her and Whistler.

"Easy. Blasters."

Easy and safe, it turned out, were two very different parameters for Whistler's assumption.

If the mysterious magnetic field really was some type of plasma-based energy field, it should theoretically absorb their blasts. Of course, there was also the off chance variable of something else occurring as a direct or indirect result of the blasters.

Lee had his reservations, mostly concerning the cadets and their general safety. Kat had to wonder if there wasn't also some newfound protectiveness coloring his judgment, particularly in a light shade of purple... Of course, not too far down her mental conscience, she knew he was right. The safety of the cadets was on them.

Then there was Zane, who wasn't interested in breaking any more rules.

You are not, under any circumstances, to engage.

The Commander had given them her warning days and days ago. But that was before the pulses. Before they'd determined there was something more going on here besides dark radiation. Not to mention, this was also their last chance, and the Commander's only chance, to identify what was out here before the General.

But it was getting late, and they were already heavy into their second afternoon, with only a couple strange, unidentifiable pulses to report back to the Commander. They needed to identify what was out there, and if this was the only way... their mission overruled the Commander's orders.

"I call for a vote," Kat said. They were just wasting time now. They were either in or they were out.

Zane straightened. Whistler nodded in recognition. And when Lee turned, there was clarity in his green eyes.

"There's something out there. That much we do know," Kat said, clearly stating her grounds. "So now here's our question. Do we go find out what it is, or do we stay with what we know now?"

"What do you think we do?" Lee asked bluntly, turning towards her. As the one who'd called the vote, her say mattered.

Kat glanced down at the platform of the observation deck as she swirled her green juice in a circle. It was a fresh cup with carrot and ginger tasting notes she'd made just a few minutes ago when their debate had continued to stall. "I think we don't have a lot of other options. Like last time, our hands are sort of tied, and the clock is ticking." Kat glanced tentatively through the hologram of Argos to Zane and Whistler, then back over to Lee.

"You are sure you can get us out?" Lee asked then, addressing Whistler directly.

"On my role as a raider." Whistler tapped two fingers to his wrist, a slow smile spreading across his lips.

"Zane?" Lee asked. Zane had been quiet as he studied them, the cadets, and the situation as a whole, gauging their best course of action. It was a trait he shared with someone else she knew.

But then Zane sighed. "For the sake of furthering our research. And on the condition that we do what we can to ensure cadet safety first."

"I second that," Lee said, his face set in a hard slash of a smile.

They didn't have much time for small talk after that as they rushed to get everything in place with the blasters. It was almost absurd. Three tiny pulses, barely a blip in their data reports. But that blip had re-routed the entire raid's focus. And within an hour or so, they were ready.

For this round, Zane was sitting back in the main cabin with the rest of the cadets, with everyone seated and strapped into their harnesses; another precaution, should things go to the *void*. Whistler sat in the pilot's seat with his headset over his ears and hands at the controls, ready to maneuver them to safety if necessary with a second's notice. And by some stroke of luck or manhandling, Kat had ended up in the cockpit opposite Lee, each with one of the ships' dual blasters at their fingertips.

The cruiser was not outfitted for full-on warfare. As such, the blasters at the head were only equipped to dislodge immediate obstacles from their path that the shields couldn't handle. Even so, they lowered the strength to its lowest frequency settings. All they needed was to identify that something tangible was out there.

She knew this was a little reckless. Despite their precautions and the measures they had taken to ensure they made it out of this alive, this could still go all shades of wrong.

"Ready when you guys are." Whistler's voice cut through her headset. The slightest edge transformed his usual tenor voice a few keys lower, to baritone.

They were not to engage. But as there was no immediate threat present, they would not technically be disobeying the Commander's orders. These were merely preventative measures...

"I'm a go," Lee said. And as she met his bright green eyes across the cockpit, the familiar sparks of challenge thrummed through her.

She sucked in a breath. "Let's do this."

Three precise blasts to a set of pre-determined coordinates near where they'd traced one of the pulses on their sensors.

She had her eyes trained on the ship's radar. But the blasts crossed the screen too fast to catch—a blink, and they'd gone dark again. The pace of her heartbeat picked up. "Did you guys catch that?" She looked across the cockpit first to Lee and then up to Whistler.

"From my side, they appeared to disappear right around here. Almost like there was an invisible border of sorts..." Lee traced a finger loosely along the edge of the screen. Did magnetic fields have borders?

"Yeah, I'm reading the velocities of the blasts off of the ship's log. You can see them building—and then they just disappear... It's like..." But Whistler's own voice trailed off as well. Then, "Let's go again."

She nodded, if only to psyche herself up.

They adjusted their coordinates, targeting another of the pulse's coordinates before launching again; if there was some sort of border out there, they didn't want to over-stress it and risk a light show prematurely.

Four times they went, adjusting their coordinates each time, with a set of random coordinates for the last.

She'd been watching the radar the whole time, but for this last one, she sat back, training her eyes instead out the window before her. She saw the blasts very clearly as they went out, streaks of scarlet into the darkness. And then, like they were crossing some invisible line, they simply disappeared. No fizzle. No impact. Just—gone.

Magnetic fields didn't have borders. But energy fields could. Like the one around their very ship.

A single word seeped through her brain at the thought.

Shield.

She didn't want to be the first one to voice it. Because with the dimensions they were looking at...

She was vaguely aware of a conversation going on inside her headset; of Whistler murmuring something to Lee. But she caught the gist of it; they were thinking the same things as she.

How could there possibly be a shield out there? That would make the whole thing some ginormous forcefield...

Zane came up to the cockpit, chatting with Lee and Whistler to see what was going on, having been listening in without context. But none of them knew quite what to make of it. Eventually, Zane crossed back out again to inform the cadets and loop them in.

Kat slipped her headset from her ears. Disbelief and shock were making everything a little delayed, she'd need a moment to process this. But they'd done it, they'd really found something.

It was almost like a strange euphoria had settled over her. Not joyous. Just... strange.

Whistler slipped off his own headset, slinging it around the headrest of his chair. He winked over at her and Lee as they climbed to his feet. "Green juices?" There was one way to process.

"I'll catch up with you in a second," Kat found herself saying with a laugh. She toyed with the headset in her hands. Her favorite co-pilot remained up there with her, gazing about the cockpit. Was he as dazed as her with all of this?

They'd hardly spoken this afternoon—definitely not about anything non-raid related. And not because she was avoiding him. Not entirely, anyway. But she'd seen the way he looked at Levy. And if she was being honest with herself, she was jealous. It was the way she wanted Lee to look at her again.

"What do you think, 'Blaster's of Argos'?" he asked with a little side smile, coming around the cockpit and stopping only a head's-width away as he shoved his hands into his pockets. The action looked normal enough, but she thought there was something reserved about his smile tonight.

"We can add it to the list." At her knowing look, he peered out through the front window.

"This is only the start of it. We aren't finished yet."

"Not even close," she agreed. She returned his fierceness with a grin. "But, we could take it easy tonight."

As if on cue, Levy appeared down the aisle to the main cabin. The girl waited just inside, bouncing on her toes, almost expectantly. "You've got someone waiting on you."

"Oh." Lee waved a hand. "It's fine. She's fine. We aren't— not exactly."

Kat squinted as she stared back at him, confused.

But Lee added quickly, "Whistler, too. He seems like he's good for you."

"Oh, Whistler and I aren't a thing. We're just friends." She tilted her head.

"But I thought after that night, after Zane..."

She straightened. "He told you about that?" For the second time that night, she felt her pace quicken. She tried frantically to reign in the panic forming, but the words escaped anyway. "The other night was just a one-time thing. It should never have happened."

"One-time thing... Wait, what?" Lee's face was mostly unreadable as he pieced her words together, but she caught the slight pitch in his forehead when the realization hit him. When it hit her. And all too late, she realized her mistake.

"He didn't tell you. You didn't know about the other night," Kat said slowly as Lee continued to stare back at her, his face unyielding, and growing stonier by the second.

She ran a hand through her ponytail. "This is not how I wanted this conversation to go," she muttered, now raking that hand through her hair. "Whatever, it doesn't matter. It didn't mean anything."

She took a couple of deep breaths to steady herself, glancing back towards the main cabin, where Levy had once more disappeared as she ran through all the words she'd bottled up. All the affirmations she wanted to screech through to the next atmosphere blitzed through her brain.

"I know I'm broken and that I waited too long to tell you, it took me this long to even realize how I felt about you. And I know you deserve better, and, *void*, I don't know if we'll even last if we do get together. But I think you know all of this. I think you've probably already accounted for these factors in that brilliant mind of yours. And if everything is up to the *void* in the end anyway..."

With one last stuttered breath, she gave him a shaky smile. "Lee, you're the one I want to be with. I know it's awful timing, with Levy and all... She's a sweet girl, but... I want to try us." She stumbled through it all, before trailing off.

"You want to be with me?" he asked. And she thought she saw something flicker in his eyes.

She smiled broadly, nodding, letting every last reserve of her affection for Lee shine through, grappling against the shadows in her head. This was it. This was their moment.

And then something cracked in his gaze; a tremor in its usual crystal clarity.

She could feel the tears forming. She blinked past them as she stared back at him.

She'd been ardently mistaken. This wasn't surprise or hopefulness. This wasn't hesitancy. This was irritation—morphed into something infinitely cooler.

He laughed. And it was the coldest sound she'd ever heard.

"Lee—what?" She scrambled to find him as her vision clouded over, the ripples freely flowing down her cheeks now, as everything she cared about seemed to crash down around her in a hazy waterfall. "Is—is it Levy?" It was the only explanation she could think of. She was too late. She had taken too long to finally pull herself together.

Lee was shaking his head, his hands clenched. His whole body seemed to tremble from the restrained anger as he stared at a spot just above her head.

"Lee!"

She lowered her voice as a couple heads from the main cabin turned their way. "Lee," she pleaded, hushing her voice to little more than a whisper. A fingernails-on-steel, shredding whisper.

He lowered his eyes just once to meet hers. This time, the pain was only too prevalent "Why? Just—why, Kat?"

Oh.

She stared back into his green eyes and the heart-peeling agony that met her. She'd caused this.

And then his whole countenance shifted back into the unreadable mask. It was in his posture and the hard planes of his arms and chest. And in his face—there was no sign of the boy she knew in his face.

"Whatever. I'm over it."

He turned away. And with no one there to anchor her, Kat felt herself crumple.

CHAPTER 27: LEE

LEE COULD hear Zane and Jed talking quietly in the main cabin when he came out from the dorms the following morning. It wasn't yet 07:00 hours, but he hadn't been able to sleep. He'd tried for a few hours before giving up entirely.

Even now, dulled and groggy, his recollections from last night cut into his gut with an edge he didn't know how to soothe.

They suspended their conversation as he drew up beside Jed and Zane, their silence only aggravating the growing pang in his stomach.

It wouldn't have been hard to guess that something had gone down between him and Kat. They may as well have streamed it over the ship's speaker system. But after their fight, Kat had gone back and locked herself in one of those ridiculous spiral showers. And when she hadn't emerged again from the dorms, he'd personally taken it upon himself to cover her shift; not that it did any of them any good. He'd stood there staring blankly past their data to the stars outside, ignoring his cadets entirely. If he wanted, he could probably have pointed out every single pinprick of starlight with his eyes closed.

Zane dismissed Jed after a minute, murmuring something about him grabbing a drink.

"Hey, you—need to talk about it?" Zane asked quietly.

Lee narrowed his eyes at him. And after a few seconds, Zane went to join Jed. Even in the dimness, he could read enough on Lee's face to know to leave him alone.

Lee heaved a sigh. He'd waited years to hear Kat say those words. He'd dreamed about them. And then to have them tossed in his face, like a bad power drink... And right after admitting she'd been hooking up with some other guy—again.

I want to try us.

But there'd never been an us. They'd both made *void*-well sure of that. To the *void*, with 'whatever'. Of course, it mattered. It mattered to him because, once again, she hadn't chosen them.

Sure, he was angry. He was frustrated, and irritated... The list could go on and on.

But what was worse was that Lee had seen the truth behind her intentions, the undiluted devotion written all over her face. And he'd still walked away from her.

The repercussions and revelations of that conversation reverberated around him in a volatile waves.

When Zane returned, him and Lee worked in silence, for the most part, to get all their reports up and synced. A couple of times, Zane cleared his throat like he might say something else, but both times he gave up when he saw Lee's expression, instead channeling all his focus into the reports. They switched the lighting back to daylight as the first stirrings of morning came from the dorms.

Surprisingly, Lee wasn't overly upset with Zane's little role in all of this. He was disgruntled, sure; it took two. But the hiding it and the timing... that was all her.

A couple of cadets made their way into the main cabin. One of them was Levy.

She stopped when she saw Lee, waving tentatively. But then she cut away, abruptly, heading for the mini-fridge in the far corner.

That was his fault. Lee had all but blown her off in the aftermath of Kat's confession.

Look, Levy. I can't do this right now. With everything going on with the raid, the drama is just too much for me. I'm sorry.

He'd been encouraging Levy for weeks now. A portion of that was unintentional, yes, this wasn't the direction he'd planned for them to go. But even still, part of that had been him.

And even now, standing here, feeling as bitter about it as he had last night, he couldn't bring himself to take back the words he'd splayed.

He'd meant them. He'd meant all of them. That was the problem.

He glared toward the dorms in the back.

He tried to focus on Argos as the morning went on, trying to force his mind back to the energy fields—or rather, the forcefield they'd accidentally uncovered the night before. But at the sound of the green juice machine's many blades whirring, Lee ground his fingers into the cool synthetics of the observation deck, before abandoning it entirely. He shoved the holograms out of his face, brushing right past the source of the whirring as Whistler came towards them, with his long, red-brown hair braided back neatly, and a drink clutched in his hand. "I'm going to go pull stats," Lee declared to no one and everyone.

He made himself busy, taking his time as he checked out the current levels of their own shields from up in the cockpit. They still had a good fifty-five hours they could remain stationary. At least their shields were in perfect condition.

He peered out the front window to where the invisible energy rays undulated toward them, undeterred except for their cruiser's shields. If it wasn't for those, the dark rays would have fried them, as Hanna had reminded him a day and a half earlier.

A shield implied protection, meaning that there was something that needed to be protected.

But what were the energy fields out there protecting?

Since he was up here already, he pulled some of the recorded data from their radar and the ship's blasts, hoping there were more insights to be gleaned from it about what they were up against.

But the data only reconfirmed what they'd already assumed. That there was some sort of physical barrier out there. Energy field. Forcefield. Shield. Plasma. They could call it whatever they wanted. It was still just as implausible. Not to mention impossible...

Maybe they could've still written this whole thing off as coincidence, even with the magnetic field having screwed up their tech like it had. That was possible.

But with the pulses... And where they now had tangible evidence of the existence of the energy fields.

And the timing...

Both times they'd been out here, there'd been no signs of the reported radiation fluctuations. But shortly after they'd left...

"It's all too perfect," he murmured. He had to tell someone.

He was caught off guard when he came back into the main cabin to find it swarming. Had that much time passed? And as that first vanilla-blonde head turned his way...

Kat stood along one side of the observation deck. She glanced toward him as he came through the door, eyes puffy and swollen.

Lee hated the pleading way her pale grey eyes clung to his, and the way her usually laughing face had turned wan, completely devoid of its usual color and liveliness.

He hated that it was he who was causing her this pain.

He wanted to pull her into his arms and tell her it was okay, that they were okay, and rainbow bridge that strain between them.

But he couldn't.

And they weren't.

"Hey, can we talk?" Her voice was little more than a current in the draft-less room as he blew past, bypassing the holotech of the platform altogether. He was headed for the only place he could think of to get away from everyone on this *zapping* ship.

He made it all of five paces into the dorms before he rammed his fist into one of the steel posts.

CHAPTER 28: KAT

KAT WASN'T sure how long she'd been staring at the wall. It was made up of eggshell-colored panels, like everything else on the ship. All the ships. It was always eggshell.

She hated it.

Except for the green juice machine. She didn't hate that.

"What are you drinking?"

Kat held out her cup robotically for Whistler to taste. She'd been shirking a little from her squadron lead duties this morning, but they could all screw her for all she cared. She'd already messed around with that enough.

"The carrot really comes through."

Eyes narrowing, she let them dip to the side. "What are you doing?"

"I haven't tried this flavor combination before." Whistler pursed his lips, considering.

"You really don't have to do this." Kat drew her drink back in toward her. Outcast, party of one. Taking the straw, she lifted it out a little way, watching as the liquid drizzled back down into her cup. "It was all me."

Whistler actually had the gall to look confused, to which Kat breathed something a little like a laugh, but it came out scratchy. Maybe she was blowing everything a little out of proportion. They still had two days left on their ship's shields. Although, after their findings last night... did that change anything?

"Have there been any new developments?" She asked.

"It's been—quiet," Whistler concluded, turning his back to the green juice machine.

"That's not a good sign." Kat spared a glance around the cabin. It *was* quiet.

Nikola, apparently also had one of those handheld games; he'd finally caved. He and Jed sat across from each other, not speaking, at the round table a few meters from them. Levy and Hanna sat off by themselves over by one of the windows. Judging by the way Hanna's eyes darted away from hers, they'd just been talking about her. Real mature, guys.

There was no sign of the twins, but according to Whistler, and under strict guidance not to send out any actual blasts, Kiara and Kamata had been up tinkering with the ship's blasters. She was alarmed that any of the squadron leads would have let that slide. But apparently, this was the point they were at now with their raid.

She reluctantly stretched her gaze across the floor to the observation deck. Zane stood at one end, Lee at the other, also not speaking, with the holotech spread between them.

Whistler didn't explicitly invite her to tag along, but when he crossed the space toward the observation deck, Kat followed.

She tucked her arms over her chest as she came to a stop near Zane. "Hey."

"She decided to show up again," Zane muttered, glancing from her to Whistler with narrowed eyes.

At least one thing hadn't changed. The dynamic was normal enough that she relaxed a bit. "Show me what you're working on."

Zane expanded the hologram he'd been looking at. It was a compilation of each of the confirmed pulses, as well as a handful of suspected ones that matched the structure of the energy waves.

"Each of these contains so much energy." Kat shook her head.

"And that's only the recordings from the detected pulses..." Zane clicked into one of the smaller pulses he'd been studying. "Say there was even a fraction of that energy coursing around those energy fields. For something of this size..."

"It's got to be, what, roughly two hundred kilometers, give or take?" Whistler agreed from her other side. "There's no way this is stable." Kat could feel her eyes widen. She hadn't actually done the calculations yet.

"There would have to be something in there moderating the energy..." Lee said, not looking up from the sensor data rolling in further up the platform. Something—or *someone*.

She stared into the hologram of Argos spread between them. She'd never heard of any type of shield of this size. Even with the Academy, the ship's high-frequency shields were a fraction of the size, and they couldn't be sustained for more than a few days at a time; and even those weren't guaranteed to hold against a real threat like dark radiation, they'd merely buy them time.

"What would something like that even look like?" she murmured, but her own words came floating back to her. *A living magnetic field.*

Not only would something like that be insanely dangerous in and of itself. But could it even be kept under control? And what of the dark rays? They'd seen the numbers behind those initial spikes. Something about those energy fields had caused them, which begged the question, what else were they capable of? She gnawed at her lip.

"To have something this powerful out here, it must serve some type of purpose," Whistler said, working through deductions. "But there's nothing living out here; nothing can survive the dark radiation. What purpose could it even serve?"

"Or rather, what's it hiding?" Lee asked. Kat's head snapped towards him, but he again kept his eyes carefully trained on the diagram between them. "Let's say you were searching for something, using the entire AMG as your cover; wouldn't something like this be exactly what you'd be looking for?"

He couldn't be right. This was too big. Too major.

"Do we report back?" Whistler asked, the question hanging in the air between them, like mist in a de-gravitized planet.

"Not until we know for sure what we're dealing with," Lee said. He glanced first to Zane, and then to Whistler. And then, relenting, to her.

302

Another pact. For now.

"We've got to get in closer to check this thing out," Whistler was saying. Kat swallowed, Lee having released her with his eyes, to go back to staring at Argos.

"Let's say we were able to get close to this thing. We wouldn't get through it," Zane said.

"You could just drive the ship at it and see what happens," Nikola called from the table in the back, not glancing up as he continued whatever he was doing with his game.

"You want to crash the ship?" Whistler asked dryly.

Across from them, Zane was murmuring something about how, exactly, the arcane-chasing nerk had even made it to his X year.

"We don't know exactly what we're dealing with. If we didn't happen to pass through then, best case scenario, we'd just hit a wall," Lee evenly explained. And no one asked about the worst-case scenario. Worst case wasn't an option.

She was still watching Nikola and Jed, through a narrowing perspective of ignorance. Their cadets had probably tuned them out once more, oblivious to the real world. But if a couple of their cadets could be oblivious, what was stopping the rest of them...

"What if there was a way we could ensure that it didn't see us coming?" Kat asked slowly.

"I don't follow..." Zane said.

"The energy fields must have some resistance, designed to deflect a certain type of matter. But what if we were no longer to appear as that type of matter..."

"Like a camouflage?" Whistler asked, considering.

Lee flicked his green eyes to hers once again. And for a moment there, he held her with his gaze, his brows scrunching.

She wanted to apologize and make things right. Let him know that she hadn't meant to blindside him last night.

And she thought she caught something there in return—the charge of something wanting—and then he flicked his eyes away once more.

Blinking past the thoughts threatening to swarm her, she turned away to where Whistler had drawn up a blank hologram. "It's like this." He expanded the hologram, tilting it, as he worked up a rough sketch of their ship. "With our current situation, our ship is just another obstacle to be blocked. But let's say we were to alter said obstacle's fingerprints—say, the energy waves coming from our own shields, to match those of the energy fields out there..." He glanced over at Kat, to confirm this was what she'd been getting at as well.

She just nodded, her eyes on Lee. His face had gone stony and unreadable again while he considered their proposition. "You want to try to get past the energy fields," he asked, finally.

"Little bit, yeah," Kat said.

Lee swallowed, but he didn't meet her gaze this time. Instead, he scrutinized the hard surface of the observation deck, before turning to face Whistler. "Is that something we can do?"

Whistler studied his sketch, calculating through something in his head. "We'll need Kiara and Kamata."

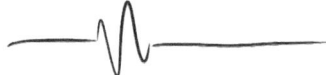

The twins were content to exchange their experiments with the ship's blaster system, for the opportunity to re-calibrate the cruiser's shields. And Kat realized pretty quickly that it was not a question of "if", but rather of, "how soon." They'd have this in effect easily within a day or two. Which was good. They were still on a timer.

While Whistler went off with the twins to talk through modifying their shields, they looped in the other cadets to get started on the calculations around Argos. They would need to be precise for this to work.

Once she and Zane had the cadets starting down through various measurements from their data, Lee excused himself for a few minutes to clear his head.

She'd finally done it—finally managed to push Lee away. He'd made it very clear today that he wanted nothing to do with her.

"Why is it always us," Zane groaned.

Kat glared. She was sick and tired of being on this ship, and sick and tired of running into Zane. The first chance she got, she was going off to the farthest reaches of the Academy as she could get. And if anyone dared try to interrupt her...

"You're a bit of a mess," Zane said, pointedly.

"Tell me something I don't know." She could feel his eyes on her. It seemed like she could feel everyone's eyes on her, just waiting for her to do something else totally ignorant and reckless. But Zane might actually be the one person she could admit this to. The one person who couldn't throw this in her face, or judge her more than he already had. Besides, he already knew all of this anyway. "I messed up. He's not talking to me."

He'd know she meant Lee. And even though there was impatience and disgust on his face, still he waited while she put together the right string of words. She might even have thought him faintly curious if he'd cared more.

"I may have accidentally told him about the other night on the Lightning Track."

Something dark tremored in his eyes as he shook his head. "I thought we'd said we were past this."

She huffed, shooting daggers over at Argos.

And then Zane sighed. "Look, not that I think you deserve this. Because you really don't. But I would suggest giving him some space and letting him work through it." He nodded to her. "Both of you."

It was the best advice she'd heard in a long while. Leave it to Zane to be the clarity in the emotional wreckage she waded, that had become her life.

"If it matters," he added a moment later, "I never would have said anything."

It didn't. But she thanked him anyway.

CHAPTER 29: LEE

THEY WERE down to the last day. Less than twenty-four hours before their own shields went under, and they'd need to get back to the Academy for recharging.

Ignoring the anxious ramblings of Nikola up the observation deck from him, Lee flexed his still-throbbing hand. He hadn't pulled his punch by their bunks the other day, he'd wanted to feel every bit of the sting. And he had—for the last day and a half. His knuckles were bruised, purple and red. Instinctively, he tucked his hand back down by his side.

They were waiting on a final confirmation from Whistler on their modifications.

He knew they were close. The twins had given their okay a half hour ago and had moved on to making the minute adjustments to one of the RIMs. Now, they were just waiting on Whistler's blessing. Or Starla's, he supposed. This final inspection was for her overall performance to see how their ship was taking to the modifications.

They'd send the mod-vehicle out first to test the new frequencies. And after that, they'd take out their ship.

They were really going to attempt to pass their ship through the energy fields. Or crash their ship through it, as Nikola had so flippantly suggested in the days prior. But the cadet wasn't so off from the truth. Any number of things could still go wrong.

They'd calculated the frequency, cross-checking their assumption for the energy fields against the broader recordings, and isolated those energy waves until they had a clear target-frequency. As long as there wasn't another one of those pulses while they were going through, they should be okay.

Not to mention they had their backup. While Whistler and the twins had finished reconfiguring their main shields, he and Zane had redirected some of their energy stores from the backup. It was temporary, and would only kick into full effect if there was an issue or flagging of their main shield. But they couldn't afford any holes. Not now, and not during their attempted passage through.

A visual of burnt and flayed skin crossed through his head —he could again thank Hanna for that, for the reminder of the energy waves that really would fry them in a heartbeat.

They'd toyed around with the energy calculations for the forcefield, working through the math multiple times, trying out all types of theories, all in a *pis aller*—one final attempt to understand how something like this could exist on its own. But once again, they'd come up empty-handed.

It was too complex. Something like this had to be planned. There was no way this was some cosmic anomaly.

He supposed if this worked, they'd find out all too soon exactly what was going on.

Any minute now.

Lee picked at a speck along the smooth platform of the observation deck. Even that tiny motion sent prickles of pain up his hand.

He glanced around the cabin. Their squadron was floundering, they were lucky this was their last day.

While the twins were occupied with all the shield mechanics, the others had separated into factions. In between calculations, Jed had returned to his video game. Levy had taken to sitting with Hanna at the table in the back. And with Nikola off wherever his head went, this left he and Zane. And Kat—who was totally oblivious to everything at the moment. She sat, staring unseeing through one of the cabin's many side windows. She'd be piloting the RIM.

He still couldn't get the image of her gaunt face out of his head from a couple of days earlier. That pain had wrecked him. But it was the little things that kept getting to him, like the hushed sniffling sound she'd tried to conceal as she'd adjusted the cuff of her sleeve... He'd seen her on the verge of destruction several times over the years, though never riding so close to an edge as this. And never on account of him.

Nikola pushed back from the observation deck, sliding over more of their calculations that he'd been tinkering with over the past few hours. Lee didn't even want to look. He didn't want to learn more than they had, it was already chilling, and there were still far too many unknowns. Across from them, Zane didn't appear to be bothered by Nikola, or the drama for that matter.

Instead, he waited almost expectantly for the updates on their shields. What would it be like to just shut everyone out?

Whistler finally emerged, looking not entirely victorious; it was more of a stony-faced determination. It was time.

He and the twins met Kat by the window, where they walked her through their adjustments. There was nothing surprising there, the adjustments to the mod-vehicles were similar to those for their ship—albeit on a much smaller scale. But this would be the first test.

With Kat at the RIM controls, and Whistler standing by, Lee ushered the rest of them into a hushed, early dinner of power drinks.

He cracked one open but didn't sip it. Not yet. Not until Kat's part was through.

Her vehicle would make it, he was sure of it. They just had to get close enough to test the frequencies...

The seconds ticked by, the only sounds the tin-*chinks* and gulps as his cadets obediently downed the vile liquid. But no one made a single complaint tonight.

He knew when the RIM had reached the energy fields by the sharp intake of breath, replaced shortly after by the soft sound of static.

"I think we've lost the mod-vehicle," Kat uttered on borrowed breaths. "But we're through."

Crossing the cabin on sure-footing, she set the controls down on the table beside the observation deck. And as she and Whistler took up a couple of the power drinks lying there, the rest of the squadron seemed to gravitate closer. One final adventure.

"Are we going to hang around here all day, or are we going to fly this thing?" Whistler's voice came out a little hoarse, but he quickly coughed to clear it.

They took a few minutes to finish their drinks, Lee remaining in the cabin until the last of the cadets took their seats and fastened their harnesses. And with one last glance behind them, Lee followed the other squadron leads up to the cockpit. Like last time, Whistler would again be pilot. Kat had taken up her previous mantle with her seat on the right, with Zane on the left.

Lee placed his hands on the headrest of that fourth seat in the middle. He would stay right by Kat's side, as he always should've been. He studied the chair and his injured hand.

It was not the time for this, even if he was starting to think it never would be that time. And if anything happened to go wrong today... His hands tightened. And with a wince, he let go.

He could feel Kat's eyes on him as he slipped the headset over his ears. And gritting his teeth, he slid into position, training his eyes on the windshield ahead of him. First things first. Get through that forcefield. And then... And then they'd go from there.

"Nice night for flying," Whistler called through the headset. "You guys can thank me later."

"Cocky bastard," Zane muttered in reply. Lee grinned, and he heard Kat's shaky laugh peal through. That was a sound he'd never forget. He imagined the slash of a smile that would be on her own face. It was without a doubt something fierce.

These last couple of days had been rough. Kat was drama.

The ship grazed smoothly into a slow pull, Whistler having started them out this time on manual overdrive. Lee wouldn't have known they were moving at all, except for the flicker of stars up ahead. They seemed to grow brighter as they approached the looming, invisible energy fields ahead of them.

But the drama wasn't all bad. The countless times he and Kat had blown up in each other's faces, only to knock on her door the next morning with a green drink in hand, and find she'd also gone to his. How long had it been since he'd gotten her one of those?

He could only imagine the look on her face as they drew closer, now. But he continued to stare straight ahead. Unflinching. Unwavering.

"Nice and easy," Whistler murmured. He guided their ship towards the edge of the energy fields. Lee could see it on the radar. They were almost touching now.

Lee waited for the shaking and the jostling. The loss of control of the ship. But there was nothing. Nothing at all to let them know they were now doing the impossible and that they were going against all odds...

"I'm going to fly right through," Whistler's tight voice cut through like a razor. Lee could hear the sharp inhale.

They were all holding their breaths.

One second... Two, while they crossed through, and then—

"Holy fuck," Whistler breathed as the greatest secret the galaxy had been hiding unfolded before their eyes.

CHAPTER 30: KAT

KAT HAD forgotten how to speak. How to think. She could only stare, holding her breath as the stars melted away and they passed through that invisible barrier. In its place, a ship materialized.

She could almost feel the faint thrums pulsing around her, such as she would have expected passing through a shield of this nature; the wavelengths from their holotech were charred into her brain.

A cloak. This had not only been an energy field and a shield, but a cloaking device as well. They had trained for every possible scenario they could imagine. Except for this one.

At first, the untapped ship with its sheets of darkened windows appeared standard enough, although it wasn't a design or model she was familiar with.

But as they drew closer...

Ship? Or city planet? Whatever it was, the thing was massive. She could more fully appreciate its size as they drew nearer. And the markings she'd for some reason assumed were windows —that was all raw material—patchwork. In some places, it looked as if the pieces were barely holding together. Could that thing even fly? And if so, what was it doing all the way out here?

She didn't remember unbuckling her harness, but she'd gravitated up towards the window. Bracing her hands against the dash, she stood there, staring out at the ship, this hodge-podge collection of parts.

Her nails bit into the cool material. Behind her, someone was drumming their fingers, the sound merging with the gentle purring of the engine as they drifted steadily nearer.

And then a light began blinking on the dash.

"*Void*—switching over to our backup. Come on Starla," Whistler murmured, his hands flying fluidly across the controls.

"The shields?" Kat demanded.

"Yeah," Whistler said tightly, guiding their spacecraft with vice grips. They were barely coasting now. "This configuration is draining our shields quicker than we anticipated." He swallowed, the sound audible from both inside and out of her headset. "We should have enough if we want to abort, but..."

"Should?" Zane asked, a silent debate ensuing from the opposite side of the cockpit. But it was rhetorical. While they had technically already accomplished their mission, they were raiders. She didn't need to see the end of the debate to know they would see this thing through to the end. They'd come too far to turn back now.

With one last look out the front window, Kat slipped back into her seat, buckling in as she pushed back against the shaky feeling in her stomach. She was grateful for the small dinner she'd sipped tonight.

She tensed, her stomach clenching further as a door opened on the rogue ship up ahead. From inside, two spacecrafts emerged, cruising toward them. Coming to head them off, by the looks of them.

"No turning back now," Whistler murmured. Assuming, of course, they weren't imminently zapped into oblivion...

Her fingertips hovered over the dash, ready to put their ship's blasters to work at a moment's notice.

But the two crafts themselves didn't appear aggressive, looking closer to the size of one of their skimmers. Like the mothership behind them, the models were outdated, very likely unlicensed—and unfamiliar, like they could belong to any of the star systems in their galaxy. Perhaps beyond.

"Are we sure they'll have what we need?" She asked, not quite ready to relax her wrists yet. They would have the energy stores; the cloaked-shield alone proved that. But these ships had definitely all seen better days. She peered towards the looming mothership hesitantly.

"They'll have something," Lee said grimly. She flicked her eyes over, before turning her full attention back to the ships out front.

"Time to go greet our new friends." Whistler adjusted their speed to a glide. As they drew up close, the main ship dwarfing them, the two spacecrafts fell into place, one blitzing up ahead, and one falling behind them. Their entourage.

The intention was clear: the cruiser was now in their domain.

For the second time this mission, the Commander's words pealed through her head. But it was a little late for that. They were already engaged.

Every instinct and muscle in her body screamed as they were led up through the dark opening, and into the ship.

"Aaaaaaand.... we're in." Whistler wiped his palms on his legs. It was a simple maneuver to flip them around, settling near the middle of the antechamber—a hangar of sorts, but he didn't yet make a move to lower their landing gear.

Compared to what they'd seen of the exterior of the ship, the hangar was in relatively decent shape. And underused, if the small number of spacecrafts present was any indication. Although, for a ship of this size, there ought to be a main hangar located further up...

The two foreign crafts landed swiftly and efficiently off to one side of the chamber near the other assembled ships.

"Here goes nothing," Whistler said, mostly to himself, as he slowly lowered them down to some obscure mark on the floor he'd selected for them. For a couple of heartbeats, there was only the sound of switches as they powered down.

Then they heard the grating begin. The hangar was sealing its doors. Her pulse picked up, her instincts now begging for them to get out of there while they still could. And as that last glimpse of space disappeared behind that door, they could only stare, frozen in their seats as they waited to learn their fates.

It was dim inside. The only light came from the cabin of their ship and the streams of starlight that trickled in from the narrow windows set high along the hangar walls.

"On the bright side, we get to show our new friends our pretty faces tonight," Whistler said with measured breaths. "Chemical ratios are compatible—we won't need our atmospheric filtration systems."

Kat managed a tight smile as her pulse raced onward, squinting in the direction of the other spacecrafts as she searched for humanoid or creature alike. She thought she'd detected movement out there...

And then a beam of blue-green light spilled in from a smaller opening, a door set in the wall further up from the spacecrafts.

Two figures came through. They stopped at the edge of the light, waiting for something. It was a little unimpressive for a retinue, considering all the effort they'd apparently taken to conceal their entire existence.

"Looks like our *friends* are also anxious to meet with us," Zane said, unstrapping his harness to get a better look.

"Don't be a dick," Lee murmured, also unstrapping.

Whistler was totally unphased, already checking things out on the dashboard to see what was left of their shields. Lee slipped up there with him. "How bad is it?" He asked, stealing a glance out into the blue-green-tinted darkness.

"We'll need about two days, even with our backup... our stores are pretty low." There was a pause, while Whistler sucked in a breath. "And we'll need access to an energy source."

Awesome. So they had that fun little detail to work through as well.

Leaving the boys to secure the ship and figure out exactly how they were going to go about finding said energy source, Kat slunk to the back to update the cadets and collect a couple of blasters—and to collect herself. She could use a moment of distraction. But within minutes, the four squadron leads stood at the edge of the cabin, staring into the dimness as they lowered the ramp.

The squadron leads would go down first and evaluate. Then, collectively, they'd decide upon a plan of attack—or survival.

"What did you do to your hand?" Kat frowned, staring down at the fist Lee had balled at his side.

He grimaced, not quite mitigating the tension in his fist. "Never mind that."

She shook her head and shook him off. Whatever. Not her problem right now. Steeling her spine and locking her shoulders back, they began their descent.

It was a strangely vulnerable experience, descending down into the unknown. Kat blinked frantically, the odd, teal-colored lights of the hangar brighter than they'd appeared from inside their own spacecraft. But she kept her face otherwise blank, taking up a defensive stance as they reached the base of the ramp.

The two figures they'd seen enter the chamber earlier had since been joined by a third, who Kat would wager had come from one of the two spacecrafts now parked by the wall. Where the other pilot was now, remained to be seen.

Again, she was underwhelmed by their greeting party. Standing here, at this moment, they were nearly matched for numbers. Not that it made them equals.

The first figure on their left, with amphibian-like facial features, held a box in their hands filled with small band-like gadgets of sorts. This would be their tech guru. The pilot, messy-haired and stocky, stood in the middle. Which left the harried-looking female, her vivid indigo hair cropped closely to her head.

For the first few seconds, they both just studied each other, neither party wanting to speak that first word.

It was the harried-looking female who addressed them first. "Good afternoon," she said coolly. She spoke the words in rapid cadence but in the galaxy's common tongue. So there would be no language barrier, at least.

"Good afternoon," Zane replied, speaking for their group.

The indigo-haired female tipped her chin, acknowledging the language confirmation. "We apologize for the provisional escort. We weren't anticipating having visitors this afternoon." Kat couldn't tell if it was nerves propelling her speech or if it was her natural preference as the female again spoke in the same rapid cadence as before.

"We weren't aware of a ship or any other humanoid life-forms existing out here in the quadrant," Zane replied smoothly.

"It seems we both harbor explanations that may be of value to the other." The female's lips flattened out into a thin line as she again studied the four squadron leads and the cruiser behind them. Kat had a feeling the indigo-haired female was cataloging the scene before her, just as they were, but she could only guess at the thoughts running through the female's head. Especially as she met Kat's gaze.

The indigo-haired female's eyes narrowed, before she glanced away from Kat altogether, softly addressing her techie.

Dismissed.

Kat glared at them; she glared at the techie with their silly gadgets. She could feel the tightening in her gut, her breathing coming in very short, crisp breaths as her nostrils flared.

Someone pinched her arm and Kat muffled a yelp. She peered over sidelong at Lee, but he wasn't looking her way. He kept his face carefully blank as he continued to stare straight ahead. His pinch had been a reminder. *Keep your cool and stay the course.*

Frowning, Kat redirected her attention back towards their retinue. The indigo-haired female had turned back once more to face them. And as she took a step forward, Kat braced herself. She didn't know what she was expecting, some matter of defense, of weaponry, maybe. But it definitely wasn't the female's impatient sigh as she reached a hand into the box her techie companion was holding, and pulled out a couple of the bands. "We'd best get this over with. Dyinai, if you could."

"What—" Kat began to ask, stiffening, as a thin, flexible band was placed in her hand.

"Slip that on your wrist—that's it. This is your protection against any offshoot rays. I'm assuming you know about the dark radiation out there?"

R. LYNN HANKS

"Yessum," Whistler said, politely, examining the band around his wrist. Kat noticed a similar band, then, on the indigo-haired female's wrist as she addressed Zane on Kat's other side. "Refuse if you want, that's on you."

The dark radiation, though. So their research had been accurate; the dark rays somehow played a role in all of this... Kat still had so many questions.

"How many do you have onboard?" the techie, Dyinai asked then, their voice surprisingly high, as they pulled out another small handful of the bands. She wondered idly if their unique facial structure contributed to the higher-pitched and airier tones.

Another gamble, revealing their hand. But again, they didn't really have another option at the moment. Some tense glances were exchanged among them, mainly between Lee and Zane. If she had been in a better mood, Kat could have spliced some fun dialog to go along. Instead, she waited in silence, checking out the interesting fabric of the female's jacket and pants. All three of them wore clothing of a similar style, made of some type of dark, synthetic material.

It felt like hours, instead of mere seconds, passed. But then she heard Lee respond in a clipped tone, "Six." The most they would yield in regards to their party onboard the ship. For now, anyway.

"If you could hang onto these and distribute them to the rest of your party—" Dyinai lifted their other hand into the box, pulling out a couple more. "Then, afterward, we'll go find a more accommodating place for us to talk."

322

Kat stiffened. None of the other squadron leads had moved either.

And it was with forced calmness that their indigo-haired host again addressed them. "We can stand here all night, or we can find someplace a little more comfortable to talk—preferably where we can actually see each other." And there was something knowing in her tone.

Accepting the bands, Lee passed a couple to both Kat and Whistler. Then, with one last shared look between him and Zane, Lee started back up the ramp. Kat's eyes flickered between his retreating back, and the indigo-haired boss-lady who'd now turned to her pilot, requesting the status on 'Ned's latest blue scale rise'. Kat didn't know what that meant, and it irked her.

With Zane standing guard, his hands tucked too casually into his pockets near where Kat knew rested at least one of his preferred quick-load blasters, Kat also made for their ship.

It was almost as unnerving as before, to turn her back on the foreign party and a potential enemy. But the feeling was ameliorated slightly once she'd cleared the ramp and stood again in their brightly lit, eggshell cabin.

Kat was in no mood to answer questions, much less give orders. But thankfully she had Lee for that. And Whistler. Like Lee, Whistler had a gift for easing tension and did an effective job at dissuading any hesitation or resistance to slipping the bands around their wrists. She was listening in when Whistler gave Jed and Nikola an extremely detailed, and completely fictional run-down of how exactly the bands worked. Only the twins seemed to see through the mechanics, but they both kept their mouths shut, shooting Kat matching scrutinizing looks.

Kat peered out one of the ship's windows. From this angle, she could barely make out a portion of Zane's outline. She hadn't realized they'd been standing so close to their retinue. Out of habit, she did another scan of the hangar. For a super-secret spaceship hiding out here alone in the galaxy, its defenses seemed very low priority, and its attack force wasn't present at all. There could easily be more to it, but thus far, the logic wasn't adding up.

"What's going on down there?" Levy asked, coming up beside her, to peer out the window.

"They haven't killed us yet," Jed muttered, coming up to Kat's other side.

"They want to go somewhere to talk," Kat relayed, eyes still on Zane, who'd crossed his arms over his chest. She didn't like leaving him out there alone.

"And we're going to go with them?" Jed pressed. She let her eyes slip from the window, to glance at his face. She hadn't known him to care about anything to do with the raid. But it wasn't just him. Levy was also waiting with anxious eyes.

It was Lee who answered them. "Yeah, we are."

Kat turned away from both Jed and the window as her eyes darted first to Lee, and then to Whistler. Then she nodded, a terse motion. She supposed it was their only option, anyway. And as they weren't about to divide forces...

She beckoned with her head for the cadets to follow them. "Up and at em' guys. Let's go find us some answers."

They gathered again at the ramp, facing Lee. "As a reminder, per raid rules, no one below Gamma level travels alone." And with one last warning look, Lee strode back down, with Kat and Whistler tailing the cadets. At least this time around, she knew what to expect.

"Seems like we didn't miss all that much," she murmured, slipping smoothly up on phantom paces between Zane, an abominable force on one side, and Lee, the portrait of careful indifference, his hands slipped casually into his pockets. Their cadets pooled behind them.

"You've caught us at a good time," the indigo-haired female murmured looking at something at her wrist. "Shifts just ended." Her words came and went right through Kat's ears as she stared back at her. And only once Dyinai had conducted a quick inspection of their devices, did the female nod towards them. "Right then. This way."

There was some stiffness still as they fell into step behind the foreign boss-lady, the pilot, and the amphibious tech ambassador, with Whistler falling back to tail them and Zane taking the head.

Their chance at a quick and dirty exit was now far behind them. That only made it more eerie as they walked away from their ship and the only tangible thing within lightyears of here that held any ions of familiarity. Not to mention their lifeline back to the Academy. Oh, Starla. Who knew she'd so soon be missing those eggshell-paneled walls.

Out of habit, she glanced around to find Lee.

Levy walked at his side, glancing up at his face every couple of paces, as if hoping to find some sort of comfort or affirmation on his face. But Lee didn't seem to notice. His eyes were clear and alert, as he took in the new corner of the hangar, noting anything that could be of later use to them. Kat could almost see the gears turning in his mind. It would, of course, be not one, but a myriad of thoughts. She wished now, more than anything, that they were still on speaking terms.

They came to the doors through which that strange, blue-green light emanated. She was distracted enough wondering what Lee made of all this that she didn't bother to shove away as Zane fell into step beside her.

His gait was stiff, but he matched her step-for-step, tension drilled into his features. She glanced sidelong at him, raising her eyebrows in question. But Zane directed her eyes pointedly back to the figures directly ahead of them. The indigo-haired female was speaking in low undertones to her two companions.

It had crossed Kat's mind multiple times that they ought to be wary of the female. This could easily all be a trap and one that could be sprung on them at any moment while they followed her to the *void-knew-where.* While they'd been floating out dormant in space, their host had had days to prepare for their potential arrival. There was not a chance whatsoever, that this entire engagement hadn't been premeditated. But like before, their decision had already been made for them. They had a mission to accomplish. And their host now had a resource they needed.

So Kat nodded, turning her attention instead to what little detail she could pull from the scant passage around them as they passed from the hangar, and through the doors up ahead.

More of those teal lights flooded the roughened path they now tread, hanging over them like streetlights. The dark walls extended high above them on either side, casting shadows over everything.

It took her about a block to realize that the passage from which they had entered was an *alleyway*, behind a *block*. And those were *streetlights*.

This was a city.

CHAPTER 31: LEE

THEY ROUNDED a corner.

Lee nearly ran into the heel of Hanna's boots as he caught himself, because this—this was not what he'd expected.

The pathway had opened into what could very easily be the teetering neighborhood on the outskirts of any metropolis planet in their star system.

Modular structures towered over either side of them, stretching as far as they could see. The modules on the ground floor were all made up of identical dimensions. Some of the next levels as well. But as they went up, things got a little crafty —and cramped. Some of the structures were connected by bridges; some with wire. And some simply leaned there, haphazardly. The structures had been built upward, hastily, using more of that raw material they'd seen on the exterior of the ship, and with whatever materials they'd been able to find, by the looks of things. They were messy, but in a functional way.

And if he looked to the tops, he could see—was that stars? It couldn't be. But something had definitely been fashioned there, sealing the city in a sparkling, midnight sky. A light draft blew past their necks, but not from any natural wind. Like the stars overhead, this draft was a by-product of industry.

And as they were led deeper into that neighborhood, more of the ship's patchwork repairs made sense. This was an expansion.

And they weren't the only ones out tonight.

The city had a nightlife. Or a daylife. Lee couldn't even remember what the hour was as they passed the scenes playing out on the street. A couple of figures sat, chatting, under the makeshift porch from an overhang above; they looked up as he passed. Another humanoid figure stumbled off down the street like they'd maybe had one too many drinks after a long day. There were lights in several of the windows. And he thought he heard music coming from one of the open doorways. The cramped streets and the night sounds were so unlike their own monotone, whitewashed hallways back onboard the Academy, that it was all Lee could do not to stop and stare.

The streets seemed to empty out the longer they walked, growing quieter, and more desolate as they went. But he supposed that was to be expected. They weren't exactly invited guests, despite the familiarity their host afforded.

Those he did see wore similar clothing to their entourage, in the same dark shades. The clothes took on a slight sheen under these teal-colored lights, reflecting some of that light. The effect pulled at a thread in his brain. But that wouldn't be it... the application was all wrong...

And then something else caught his eye—he would have said a shooting star if the night sky was real. But then another came careening by, only much lower. He watched as the personal flier dodged both wire and bridge alike as it weaved around another corner.

They rounded the block. Lee had identified at least a half-dozen small shops and restaurants before he noticed the tiny sign beside the door advertising some type of juice or smoothie shop.

A little smile crinkled his lips. If they made it through the night, he'd make sure she found it, one way or another. Although, he didn't think Kat would have an issue finding her way around here.

Her hair looked almost green under this light. And it caught a fair amount of light, especially as she whipped her head this way and that, casting her eyes up about in wonderment. He couldn't remember the last time she'd had that look in her eyes. And thanks to one brash, emotion-ridden conversation, he wasn't even the one standing there with her to experience it.

They turned down another little street, stopping as a couple new figures in the dark metallic clothing strolled towards them. One of them came right up to their escort. They spoke in low voices as they conversed, but Lee didn't catch much of what they were saying as Jed pulled out his blaster and began absentmindedly polishing the grip in short, grinding strokes.

One of those fliers streaked past in a blur of light and energy. And from off to the side, nearly disguised by the city sounds, Lee caught the scratch of metal on fabric and the sudden intake of breath.

And then he heard the click.

He knew that sound.

His heart stuttered as he whirled, searching blindly for the device powering up as Jed backed toward him, now empty-handed.

Seven years of training scattered like so many lights overhead as he matched the source to the blaster, and the male now wielding it. And as the blast was released, Lee leaped. "Kat—no!"

He felt the singeing heat skim past his arm as Kat was hurled to the ground. But not by him.

Zane stood protectively over Kat, the bastard, feet braced and blaster drawn as he turned on their attacker. The air sizzled where her heart had been only milliseconds before.

Not skipping a beat, Lee moved in adrenaline-fueled fury, knocking Jed's blaster from the attacker's hands. Lee barely got a look into the male's crazed eyes before he drove his own blaster into the attacker's head. The male dropped fast.

The whole street erupted into chaos as the dome of energy snapped around them, sealing them in. Lee felt more than saw it as the smell of charred wire filled the space, the air inside seeming to vibrate as the entirety of their group was entrapped along that open street.

At the sound of multiple devices powering up, Lee launched himself backward, back beside Kat, who'd since scrambled to her feet. She snarled as she scooped up Jed's blaster from the ground.

Panting, his heartbeat still hammering in his head, Lee took up his stance at Kat's right hand, angling Jed and Levy, and as many of the cadets as he could guard behind them. Whistler did the same at Zane's other side, the four of them flanking their squadron.

He wasn't familiar with the odd-shaped devices the couple members of their host wielded, and defensive or otherwise, he wasn't anxious to find out.

Behind him, their blasters pointed in every direction, his own cadets looked a spark away from retaliation.

The tension simmered around them with each thundering heartbeat while Lee ran through the facts: Their host had them contained—and if they were smart, they had more on the way. Pushing this now would only lead to a further lack of trust, which they very badly needed.

Confirming first that Kat was still there beside him, and willing his breaths to come in at more even intervals, Lee clicked the safety back into place and lowered his blaster. He kept his eyes locked on the grounded attacker, madness still in the male's eyes as his hands grappled with the rough, manufactured pavement below him.

"Gaia, where are you going?" One of the newcomers called out. But the indigo-haired female ignored them as she pushed her way towards them, eyes flickering between both parties. "I'd hoped we wouldn't need these." And while there was caution in her eyes, she didn't appear all that flummoxed by the outcome. Something to digest later.

The rest of the cadets lowered their blasters—lowered, but didn't lose their holds, not as the pilot from before tapped something into the narrow gadget in his hands. The forcefield around them dissolved.

A few more figures had indeed arrived on the scene. Whether they'd been watching from nearby or summoned remained to be seen, but Lee was again wary of the new arrivals. He kept an eye on them while their attacker was stunned into unconsciousness, his arms locked behind him. It was only once the male was hauled off down another street, that Lee stole a glance back.

Just behind him, Zane berated Jed for his carelessness with his firearms. Next to them, Whistler studied the new party additions. And beyond him—

Kat stood quietly a meter and a half away, where her feet had carried her after the dome shield went down. She looked shaken. And he could tell from the way she held herself now, arms wrapped about her middle, that she had her guard up again, to no one's surprise. That had been a close one. Much too close.

He'd been distracted. So *zapping* distracted, trying to decipher what was going on in Kat's head, he hadn't even seen the attacker lunge for Jed's blaster.

They'd faced death before. *Fuck the void*, that was a part of their daily life; it was practically spelled out in their job description. But to be so careless as to be lost inside his own head right now... that single mistake had nearly cost him everything.

It was a tense couple of minutes while the indigo-haired female, Gaia got everything sorted out. This had very clearly not been a part of her plan. But eventually, she dismissed the last of their escort until only she and the amphibious figure remained. She turned her flustered face on them. "Come with me." It was not a request.

With a hand still on one of his blasters, and one more stolen glance over at Kat, Lee fell into line behind her, the silence a bit more prolific this time.

There appeared to be no damage to any of the structures from the loose blast. And aside from the lack of night traffic at the moment, there might not have been anything going down here at all. And when he looked up—somewhere levels up were more of those painted stars.

They'd been close to their destination, it turned out. They only went one more block before they came to another alleyway, its black wall seeming to stretch all the way up to the stars. The two hosts led them right up to a set of doors identical to the last. The doors split apart as they drew up close.

This passage was similar to the last in style, only much longer. Under the blue-green lights, the passage seemed to extend forever. The hallways were wide, wide enough to accommodate a good deal of foot traffic—and flier traffic, with doors breaking off left and right. And a soft humming accompanied their boots as they followed along that manufactured pavement worn smooth where they were led through one of the first doors on the right.

It was a makeshift meeting room with a maze of intricate piping taking up one of the walls. The ship's hydraulics system —likely water reclamation. A table had been dragged in from somewhere and set up towards the middle of the room, with mismatched chairs situated loosely around it. Like their host had indeed been expecting them.

They filed inside. Dyinai didn't hesitate as they pulled out one of the chairs to sit, but Gaia remained standing, so Lee did as well. He motioned for some of the cadets to take a seat if they wished; it had been quite the eventful evening already.

Shutting the door behind them, Gaia crossed her arms over her chest. Impatience rippled off her in waves, but she somehow managed a fairly even tone as she addressed them. "We must first apologize. This was not how we intended this initial meeting to go. The male you encountered is a long-standing inhabitant of our ship and has been taken away to be treated." Then she paused, meeting each of their eyes in turn. "We have staff on hand should any of you wish to address this interaction any further." Her gaze came to linger on Kat, but at the present moment, the latter was blank-faced. And if anything, what Kat likely needed most, was a few minutes to get out of her head.

"As to your arrival," their host again addressed their group as a whole, "would you care to explain how your party ended up inside our shields and onboard our ship this afternoon?" While her eyes again scanned them, Lee snuck a glance at both Whistler and Zane. Zane dipped his head a centimeter, feigning adjustment to the lights overhead.

Frowning slightly, Lee cleared his throat. "You assumed correctly earlier that we know of the dark rays. My companions and I have been tracking a series of radiation spikes in this quadrant. We were surprised, however, when we stumbled upon your energy fields. To have perfected something of this nature must have taken quite some time."

Gaia ignored his comment as she studied him and their squadron once more. "And yet you board our ship, fully armed."

"A precaution," Lee said, swiftly. With what just happened, he was sure she'd have more to say on the matter. But to his surprise, she did not. Not yet, anyway.

It would be obvious from a few minutes prior that their squadron had the training and the firearms. But their host had the manpower, and, evidently, means of their own, whatever their intentions. And unless the plan was to turn those means against them—they were at a stalemate. She seemed to understand that as well. "The radiation spikes you would have observed are part of a longstanding experiment. This is not our first attempt; we've been at this awhile." That still didn't explain what they were doing out here, but he'd take what he could get, especially as she waved her hand dismissively. "But if I may, how did you manage to navigate our energy fields?"

For this, Lee motioned towards Whistler.

"Reconfiguration." Whistler shot her his usual crooked grin. "We were able to adjust the frequencies of our shields in such a manner as would allow us to pass through undetected."

"Impressive," Gaia said coolly, despite her face portraying the impression that she was anything but impressed.

"If we may," Lee said, tossing her volley right back, "of what nature are the portable energy fields we just witnessed outside these halls? Identical to those outside the ship, or something else entirely?" Lee asked.

"Another experiment." Gaia's lips had pressed into a thin line.

Dyinai, however, looked thoughtful. "How did your ship's shields handle the reconfiguration?" they asked in their high, breathy voice, glancing between Lee and Whistler.

"Not great," Whistler said. His tone turned business-like as he explained their situation. "In the process of reconfiguring our shields, we also drained our energy stores."

"We need access to an energy source. As soon as our shields have re-charged, we'll be on our way." Lee kept his face neutral, careful not to meet Whistler's eye and showcase just how dire their situation had become. They were on fairly even ground. And until they got the resources they needed, they'd need to be strategic in how they played things. But if Whistler's estimates were accurate, this would give them two days to learn what they could of this ship and its energy fields.

Gaia had initially narrowed her eyes, but at their promise to depart afterward, her face relaxed a little. "I trust you'll understand our need for caution as well. As it happens, we have some room onboard. We will send someone on ahead to arrange a couple of our stacks for your personal use while you remain on our ship. Accept our hospitality. Take advantage of our amenities. And I will send someone first thing in the morning to help you access our energy resources. We should be able to figure something out there." A wry glance to her amphibious companion, then she faced them once more. "I will warn you now, take care with your *temperament.*" Her eyes flickered between them, lingering pointedly on one of their blasters. "Violence of any kind will not be tolerated onboard this ship."

She leveled them one more flat look, then, the meaning all too clear: don't cause any more disruptions. "If you have any urgent questions, ask for Gaia." She gestured to her counterpart. "Dyinai will get you taken care of and show you out."

With a parting nod, she turned to leave, but stopped herself. "Oh, and by the way, welcome to Segura."

There was the grim hint of a smile on her face as she turned away once more, as if she'd been unable to keep it from her lips. She left the room, heading further up the passageway.

In her wake, Dyinai rose nimbly to their feet, looking almost apologetic as they now addressed the squadron. "These bands are coded to our system. In addition to sending a signal through in the case of offshoot radiation, the bands will also be your access to the stacks and any other comforts you may need. And if I may, I'd like to recommend a friend's nosh, it's just around the corner..."

As Dyinai finished explaining about their friend's local delicacy, Whistler slid up to their side. "You're from the Trinities, right?"

Lee recognized the star system. One of the cadets at the Academy had originally come from out there.

"You know them?" the techie asked in their high voice.

"Of them, a friend back home," Whistler said smoothly with his usual lopsided grin.

What Lee would guess to be their brow, furrowed a little as they nodded, explaining to Whistler how they hadn't been back there since they were a small child. And as the conversation moved on to how they'd go about recharging their ship, Lee again tried to catch Kat's eye. He wanted to get a better feel for how she was taking all of this. She'd been silent throughout their meeting.

But as he took a step towards her, she wrapped her arms around herself once more and turned away.

Lee froze, stepping backward again as his gut plummeted. His hand throbbed as he clenched it again. Of course something like this would happen tonight.

Dyinai and Whistler moved their conversation back out to the passageway, the others following along behind them. But as Zane went to clear the doorway, Lee stopped him, pulling him aside with his good hand.

"Thank you," he said quietly.

Zane briefly met his gaze with a slight dip of his head. Releasing him, they rejoined the others filtering out into that passageway.

And it wasn't until they'd stepped back into that craft city, the impossible tech turning everything hues of blue-green around him, that Lee realized no one had bothered to ask who they were.

Unless they already knew.

CHAPTER 32: KAT

KAT STOOD staring up at the stacks, the levels rising up in varying heights from the rough-paved street. She'd barely listened while they'd made housing assignments. But apparently, their host had prepared four of the levels for their squadron, which was generous. More than generous. Not entirely surprising, Zane had opted not to stay in the city and had already departed for their ship. Generosity be damned.

This was another raid, another foreign landscape. Except this time, it felt different; it felt wrong. Like they were the invading predators. She hadn't been able to shake that feeling as they'd walked through the streets of this blue-green glowing city, confidently, with their blasters by their sides.

From what they'd seen, the inhabitants living on this ship were innocent. They had lives and loved ones. And then when that one attacked her...

They'd nearly blown their entire mission on that attack.

It wasn't the first time she'd had a blaster directed at her face, and it wouldn't be the last. But if there'd been any collateral damage on account of them...

Their squadron shouldn't be here, and that attack—that attack should never have happened.

She took a breath, holding it, as she let everything leading up to what had happened this afternoon sink into her. The anxiety of crossing that invisible forcefield barrier. The tension, of finding the hidden ship thrumming. And then the fear—that heart-stopping and world-shattering fear when she'd realized how quickly she may have been erased. And to go out on those terms, to leave things with Lee like that—

She let it out, slowly, taking in another breath. But this wasn't where their story was supposed to end. They weren't done writing it yet.

She took in another.

They were protectors. And this was life.

Another breath.

"You coming, Kat?"

She whipped her head around.

She hadn't realized anyone was talking to her or that they'd been making plans. Or that anything had been going on around her at all.

She blinked her eyes to find Lee staring at her, waiting for her response.

"We're going to go check out that place Dyinai told us about and find some food," Lee explained again with what must have taken infinite patience. "Maybe after we'll try to find out how we get our hands on one of those fliers..."

She'd noticed them too. And despite everything that had happened thus far, all the uncertainty and tension riding them, there was excitement in his eyes. The familiar thrill of adventure. She hadn't expected to see that emotion here.

But there was something else in his eyes too. Almost a frenzied probing, like he was also assuring himself she was still there and that she was okay. Like he'd been afraid of losing her...

Sucking in another too-sharp breath, she swallowed, looking up at the stacks. Looking elsewhere. She needed to get away from here, and away from the glare of the blue-green lights.

"That's okay, I—I'll catch up with you guys later."

Something darkened in his gaze, his brow lowering as he worked something out in his head. "I can hang back. Whistler you want to take them on ahead?" he asked, dancing in a quick step between her and Whistler who, too, seemed to be debating what to make of this change in plans.

Kat shook her head, pasting a fake smile to her lips. "No, it's okay. You two go. I'll be fine."

And she didn't dare glance Lee's way again, she didn't want to shatter the fantasy playing in her mind. Because the looks she'd thought she'd seen in his eyes just now, the looks she'd fantasized...

It was the same unrequited desperation she felt for him.

In a play of emotion that seemed to run at a tantalizingly slow pace, the rest of the squadron set off, heading back down their little side street, with Lee reluctantly following suit. And she turned away, not caring what they made of it. *The invincible Kat, turning her back on an adventure.* Her long-time restlessness smothered, for once, by the other thoughts writhing inside of her.

She began picking her way back in the general direction of the hangar. The city had been more or less built up around a grid—or a circuit.

She thought she could see more movement behind her, out of the corner of her eyes. The hints of a shadow in the streetlight. But she dismissed it as she passed by a lighted door, some humanoid figures spilling out of it. There were many figures out tonight. She didn't even bother to glance in their direction. If anyone wanted to make a go of it and come at her, let them try.

If only she carried on her person the technology that shrouded Argos, then she could just disappear for a while under a cloaking device of her own making.

"Segura," Kat breathed the name so she could hear it on her own tongue. City of safety.

They were dreamers, then. Or idealists, more like it; that is, if any still existed anymore. Besides Lee.

She smiled to herself, partially for the comfort of the thought, and partially for the truth, lying there. Whoever's dream this city and those energy fields had been, it was somehow working. The ship had survived all these years alone out here, undisturbed by the rest of the galaxy, peacefully conducting their little research projects within whatever symbiotic relationship the ship's inhabitants lived by. And albeit, their situation was a little flawed... she could still see her attacker's face, imagine the tension their mere presence had invoked. They were more or less trapped out here, surrounded by dark radiation... But even their squadron, wary as they'd been, was being permitted a small slice of the experience that was Segura.

That is, assuming they made it through the next couple of hours without causing more mayhem. The next few days would be trying with whatever moratorium the quick-tongued boss-lady had planned for them. Assuming this whole thing didn't blow up in their faces before then... There would be more to this; it was their job to find it.

A couple more of those fliers zoomed past overhead. Kat glanced up, vaguely wondering if any of their squadron had yet made it into the air; if maybe she shouldn't have gone with them for the sake of blowing off steam. A distraction. She was more than ready to just curse this whole day to the *void*.

It was a relief to get off those streets, to clamber back through the passageway and hear the door close on everything behind her. And on everyone.

A reset. That's what she most needed now. And she fully intended to take advantage of their empty ship.

Mostly empty—Zane would've already made it back. She could see a couple of lights on in the main cabin, glowing like amber in the dimness. But it would have to do.

She strode up the ramp and into the main cabin, eyes quickly adjusting to the dim overhead lights. Zane had unfurled a mat towards the back of the cabin and was working through a set of triangle push-ups. She didn't bother acknowledging him as she breezed back toward the dorms. Zane didn't say anything either, his eyes tracking to the dark mat beneath him.

She slipped into one of the spiral showers, taking her time as she scrubbed her face in the basin beside it, afterward. She was thoroughly missing good, old-school steam and water. Running a comb through her hair, she didn't bother to tie it back as she padded back out to the main cabin to make herself a green juice.

It felt a little odd to be back here already and without the others. The seamless lines of the decks and ports were not quite as cozy or welcoming as she'd hoped. But at least she could be herself in here. And, while she was here, no one else was in danger on account of her.

She ran the juice machine, the grinding reverberating around them. Tonight, it sounded too loud. Everything was too loud. Stretching her arms out wide, she shook them out, rocking on her feet.

"It's funny, you forget how much space we actually have when we aren't all crowding around," she said, turning to face outward. Zane had finished up on another set of pushups and moved on to his legs. He held his lateral lunge. And only after he'd released the hold, shifting his balance from one leg to the other to keep them warm, did he look over.

"Why are you here, Kat."

She ran her finger along the edge of the countertop. Everything was so clean in here.

"I've got the cruiser," he said, pointedly.

"We never filled out the health surveys." She pushed off from the counter, taking her time as she moved to brace her hands instead along the platform of the observation deck, sifting through the holograms on the hub.

Zane rolled up his mat, tucking it away, and closing up the ramp, before coming to perch a little further up the observation deck.

"This doesn't feel right. We shouldn't be here," she told the table.

"It was our mission," Zane countered.

"'Do not engage?'" She looked over at him, pointedly, paraphrasing the Commander.

Zane's face was unyielding as he studied her. "It's like with the blasters the other night. This is all part of uncovering whatever facade this is." He looked away, as if he could see all the way into the blue-green city, then flicked his eyes back to her. "But I agree."

She gave him a wistful smile.

She found the actual holofile for the surveys and began filling out the repetitive questions. "I'm surprised Whistler wasn't the one to volunteer to stay with the ship."

Zane snorted, the blandest sound of amusement, but it was something. "His beloved Starla. But nah, he wouldn't miss out on getting in on some of that action. I'm actually a little surprised you are."

"Yeah, well." Kat frowned. She wasn't going to follow that train of thought. Zane let it drop too.

They were quiet for a minute. The silence wasn't exactly companionable, but it could've been much worse. They could've still been fighting over their failed mess of a relationship, or whatever it'd been.

It was a short while later before Zane spoke again. "You know, you're different than I thought you'd be."

"As in, 'Wow Kat, you are actually insanely brilliant in addition to being gifted with your tongue'?"

She could feel the impatience and borderline annoyance in the air as he huffed a breath. But he still replied. "As in, 'I don't think we actually got to know each other, when we were, you know...'"

"Hooking up?" She asked. Then she winked. "I always knew you'd be a good time."

"Never mind."

"But Zane—" he glanced over at her again, somewhat warily. "It hasn't sucked working with you, either."

He was still rolling his eyes a moment later when she submitted the cadet health surveys.

"I think someone was following me back," she murmured a second later.

"I thought the same. They're likely keeping tabs on all of us —as they should," Zane added, considering. "What did you make of that greeting this evening, their defenses?" Most of the lights in the ship had been left dimmed, leaving only those shining over the observation deck.

"The 'provisional escort'." Kat nodded, thinking out loud. "The ship's inhabitants aren't without means." They had the shield, and whatever strange energy powered this whole ship.

"But as far as an attack force goes, I don't think they've really got one."

"That's what worries me the most."

An error message came up with the files she'd attempted to send out. "That's not good."

"What? What is it?" Zane came up beside her.

"'Unable to complete transmission'," Kat read.

"A result of their energy fields, I'm guessing?"

"We never did intercept any communication signals while we were out there..." This wasn't good at all. And when the Commander realized a whole squadron of cadets had simply vanished from space... "There's got to be something we can do."

"What about Nikola?"

Kat shook her head. "Worth a try."

She was grateful when Zane volunteered to go out and find him, even if the enlightened look he shot her when he offered, chafed a little.

This left her alone in the too-open spaceship and vulnerable as she stared out the windows into the dark hanger around her.

It was odd for her to find herself missing his companionship; Zane, of all people, who'd have thought. And yet, here they were, having found some common ground to stand on, for once. All it had taken was getting 'messy' as Zane had once said. And oddly, her heart felt a little lighter. If she and Zane could get passed this, then maybe she and Lee could get through this latest space-block as well. Even if it was just earning back his friendship again. She hadn't let herself admit it—not out loud at least, but she was missing her best friend terribly.

It was a good hour before Zane returned, the X cadet in tow. Kat had almost dozed off in one of the chairs beside the little translucent table there. But as the doors outside split open and the blue-green light spilled through, she slid back to her feet.

They came up the ramp, and Nikola peered about him curiously, as if he might find the solution to their problem written on one of the windows of the ship. He didn't wait for them to provide any further explanations as he picked a spot along the observation deck. Within seconds, he had the holofiles for the surveys drawn up before him.

"So here is the message that keeps coming up." Kat demonstrated the error transmission.

Nikola adjusted the frame of his glasses while they tried a second time to get the message out. When the faulty message popped up immediately after, Nikola leaned in, resting both elbows on the table. "You were correct about the energy fields being to blame—while we do have a signal, it's just having trouble getting through."

He pulled up the transmission files for the ship. "Diffraction won't work as our signal can't get through the energy fields. But I wonder if we could tunnel a communication channel through, essentially like what we did with the ship's shields..."

While Nikola mused, Kat tuned out his ramblings, head drifting back into that crafted city, to a certain Gamma now coasting underneath its painted skies.

CHAPTER 33: LEE

IT'S NOT your fault.

Those were the words he'd told Jed in a conversation earlier that evening on their way to grab some food. Those were also the words he'd been telling himself for the past few days whenever the ache in his hand fueled the ache in his gut. But that didn't mean he liked the outcomes.

Lee stood on the precipice of one of the stacks, the artificial draft brushing across his face in sweeping waves before it dipped, crashing into the pavement levels below. The room behind him was dark; the ceiling overhead was speckled with stars; and everything below him—a haze of blues and greens.

Another flier whizzed past. Lee traced its glittering path until it wound out of sight. The flier beneath him hummed, awaiting his instruction. He ran a finger along the metallic lettering stamped neatly across the middle, *Flyr6000*. As he stretched his hands around the grips, staring down the flier's transparent, head-to-toe shield, Lee could feel the fierce grin growing across his face. This was exactly what he'd needed to clear his head after the day they'd had—after the last few weeks, really.

It hadn't been difficult to locate the spacecraft mecca. The terminal resided five levels above the street, with an entire wall open to the city. How was that for taking advantage of their amenities? Like with their food earlier, all it had taken was a wave of their bands for the fliers to thrum to life.

While it had been tempting to stay and watch Whistler eat his way through a third plate of the slimy and wiggling, sesame seed delicacy Dyinai had recommended, he'd opted instead to get above ground. "Are we really doing this?" Levy had asked, excited, as she and a few of the cadets had followed him out. But Lee had only had eyes for the skies.

They'd lost the twins on their way over; Lee had pretended not to notice as they'd sidled off after catching a whiff of smoke spilling out from some bar or tavern, eager to learn what else these bands could get them. Let them enjoy this one thing for themselves. Let *him*.

Lee cast one last look behind him, towards the glowing docks on either side of the room where Levy straddled another of the fliers. Even Jed had a speck of emotion on his face at the prospect of jetting out on one of the racing spacecrafts.

Lee revved the near-silent engine, and it jettisoned to life beneath him. Leaving everything else to gravity's will, he kicked off, hurtling out into the dark sky.

He gave himself a minute or two to adjust to the weight and feel of the flier beneath him, to the faint thrumming and the polished edges as the spacecraft dipped and curved at the slightest inclinations from him. It was freedom—like the first time he'd flown one of the Academy's small training ships... Only freer. And more vulnerable. Like he could traverse the universe, and then plummet down to his death in one wrong move. The fliers were riveting.

With a whoop and a holler, he looped back around. The gusts tore at his hair as he caught up to Levy just whisking out into the skies. He tailed her for a while, touring the city from above. From these angles, its raw surfaces captured all sorts of light.

It's people, as well.

Lee still couldn't figure out the timetable for the city; their shifts or whatever. Just as when they'd walked the streets earlier, the city's inhabitants seemed to come and go, sometimes in trickles, and sometimes in floods. Some were finishing their day, like the cook from the little hole-in-the-wall they'd visited earlier. Some appeared to be just starting theirs; he'd seen a handful of figures trekking up through the side streets towards the passageway at the end of the alleyway Gaia had led them through before. And as he flew, he observed layer after layer of what was, for all intents and purposes, a fully functioning society.

It was perfectly impossible that this place could even exist, and exist undetected, completely devoid of any natural air or starlight. And yet here it was, thriving; everything here was so alive and halcyon.

Like the shields surrounding them, it was as if a living current of energy flowed all around them, running parallel to the drafts from vents he'd spied lining the edges. A city of life and energy.

Kat would've been all over this; the music, the fliers, the nightlife... she might've even found those party lights she'd talked about. This was a place where even a near-invincible cadet had been content to trail behind and stare up with wonderment. He'd seen her wear a similar look on her face once before, a few years back, on holiday with his family.

He wondered if the city reminded her of that, too, or if Segura was too tainted for her, now.

But he was done blaming her. It was time to let go of those faults and embrace them.

He was making circuits around some of the taller stacks when Whistler whooped past, a wild grin on his face. "Not bad, eh?" He skimmed by, close enough for Lee to feel the hairs on his arm stand on end. Not even food could keep Whistler from the skies for long. "We've got to get the Academy to invest in a dozen of these!"

Lee had to echo the sentiment.

It was only when Lee's fingers grew numb, his fingers cramping and his hand starting to ache again, that he slowed his flier down to a cruise. But he didn't take the flier back yet. Instead, Levy now trailing him, they flew over by one of the rooftops, a stack looking out over a smaller street they'd trodden earlier.

Discarding their fliers on the flattop behind them, they let their feet dangle into the blue-green darkness below.

She toyed with a thin, beaded bracelet around her wrist. He'd never noticed it before, but then again, not many cadets he knew wore any sort of ornamentation at all beyond their hyper-band.

His ears were still ringing, cheeks stinging from where the currents had ripped across his face. "Hey, about what I said before…"

"You don't have to say anything." Levy smiled as she shook her head in that easy, quiet way she always did everything. He traced her face in the dark. The way the blue-green lights lit up the round planes of her face. She was one of those people who just seemed to get him, who didn't feel the need to dance around things; she told it like it was.

Lee followed her gaze down to the pathway below them, his eyes snagging again on the little sign in the window for the shop selling green drinks.

And he'd been a complete fool.

Lee could feel his mouth tightening, but he swallowed, shoveling all that remorse away.

Maybe it was just to clear the air. And maybe, because he genuinely did like Levy. But he said quietly, "I'm sorry, though, if I did anything to lead you on. I really didn't intend for any of it to go down the way it did."

"Hey." She stopped him with a flick of her eyes. "I kissed you, remember?" But she frowned, guessing correctly where his mind had gone. There was something too-knowing in her dark gaze. When she spoke again, her voice was gentle. "I never meant to get in the way. But, I do really enjoy being around you, and I hope we can still be friends. All of us."

"Friends, huh?" He nudged her with one of his shoulders.

"Mmhm."

This was probably the conversation they should've had all along. He could really use a friend right now. Because even now, after the ragged ride he'd taken her on, she still breathed so much life into their mission and their squadron.

"We probably ought to get these things back before they actually accuse us of taking advantage of their hospitality," Lee said. But he made no move to get up. And he was glad when Levy was the one to propose they stay.

"A few more minutes probably wouldn't hurt."

He flashed her a smile. It had felt nice to be doing something again. Even if that something was running around the dark city carelessly with a couple of his cadets.

They returned the fliers when they saw Jed heading in a short while later.

Segura's streets were as occupied as ever. They passed a handful of figures as the three of them made their way back up the little side street to their assigned stacks.

They grew quiet as they approached the modules. Whistler was perched outside, peering up and down the streets. He nodded towards them as they drew close.

"Not exactly where we thought we'd be tonight." He had a distant look in his eyes as he gave Lee a quick update on the cadets. Hanna had come back with him, and the twins shortly after them. And Nikola was now apparently back on the ship with Zane; they were having some communication issues with the ship. One more thing for them to deal with.

Whistler didn't mention anything about Kat, and Lee didn't ask. He didn't know how to ask. But Kat would be okay; she'd be insulted by him even worrying after her. She'd likely just gone back to the ship or crashed in one of the other modules.

He thanked Whistler, heading for the stairs. Levy perched along the bottom step, rising to her feet as he reached her. "I don't want to wake anyone," she murmured.

"Here, you can crash in mine. I think it's just me, anyway." Lee motioned with his head, and she followed him up.

He unlocked a module on the second level of one of the stacks with the band at his wrist. Between the door and the plate glass window set in one of the walls, enough light filtered in from the streets below to illuminate their lodgings. The room was roughly the size of two of their Academy dorms combined, with a bed and a futon along one wall, and a narrow table on the other. He gave Levy first dibs of the little quarter room with the copper basin to freshen up. While he waited, he went over to the little table.

Several sets of clothing had been carefully arranged in neat piles. The message was clear. And although it wouldn't hide what Lee was guessing were generations of familiarity, it could buy them some moments to breathe. Lee would make sure their cadets were made aware, should they wish to accept the gesture.

He'd found an extra blanket and pillow at the foot of the little couch by the time Levy emerged.

Fresh-faced and hesitant, Lee insisted she take the bed for herself, excusing himself for a few moments to relieve himself.

The futon was stiff. He turned his neck to the side, rotating his shoulders a little. The band on his wrist felt foreign. Not tight—just, different. It was a reminder of all that lurked outside. And all they still had to accomplish. Tomorrow was going to be a long day, they'd best rest up.

But after days spent bunking on Starla, it hadn't taken him long to make himself comfortable.

Levy was quiet. He couldn't tell if she'd fallen asleep and was peacefully snoozing, or if she still lay there awake, like him.

He'd drawn the curtains, but a soft turquoise glow still seeped into the room. He wondered if the ship's inhabitants ever got used to them, or if it was always an adjustment.

And as he turned away from the window, pulling the blanket up over himself to shut out the city's glow, he noticed his hand wasn't hurting him as much anymore.

CHAPTER 34: KAT

ZANE WAS already up and sipping one of those power drinks when Kat came out from the dorms the next morning.

"Any updates?" she asked, blinking back the sleep from her eyes. The three of them had been up into the early hours of the morning, trying to find a workaround for the communication block.

"Not yet. I told Nikola to get some rest for a couple of hours while I kept at it."

She nodded, walking over to one of the windows facing the darkened doorway outside their cruiser. Gaia had said she'd send someone along this morning to help them recharge their shields. She supposed they'd find out pretty quick how badly their host wanted them gone.

But it was Whistler who came through the doors first. A flood of blue-green light cast an eerie glow across his lean form as he crossed the hangar. She half expected to see Lee climbing up the ramp after him a moment later, but Whistler was alone, his eyes bright and his long hair slightly windblown, despite the loose knot he'd tied atop his head. It wasn't hard to guess what he'd been up to.

"Busy morning?" she called as he came into the cabin.

Whistler shrugged, nodding towards her and Zane. He was murmuring something about wanting to evaluate their energy stores as he headed up to the cockpit.

It wasn't half past seven when the doors to the hanger split open once more and a long-nosed figure came through. Kat went down with Whistler to greet him. This latest arrival was lanky, and hefted an angular bag over one shoulder; he glanced over at them somewhat warily, before motioning for them to come around the ship with him.

It took a little mechanical coercion to find outfittings that would adapt to the cruiser, but he seemed to know enough about what he was doing. There was power flowing into the cruiser when Kat left Whistler and Rorin, the mechanic, to slip back into the city.

Segura.

She told herself she was just going to check up on how the others were faring. But she was curious. She wanted to see if the city felt any different this morning.

She tallied her sleep during her swift walk into the city. She'd probably only gotten three or four hours, but for once it'd been dreamless. Turns out, uncovering a secret city in the stars was good for her headspace.

Despite the early hour, the street inside was swarming. She knew the ship likely held hundreds of inhabitants—thousands even who accessed these streets. But to see them all out and walking around... She kept as close to the modules as she could while she edged her way around the blocks to where she knew their designated sleep modules to lay.

She was at the foot of one of the stacks, staring upwards before realizing she didn't even know which levels were theirs; which one might hold the Gamma cadet she so desperately hoped to see, and equally desperately needed to not see. Because what they were these days... maybe it was better that she didn't find him at all.

Her efforts at avoidance were in vain, however. Not a minute later, with the dregs of the shift change, the street traffic finally ebbing, a figure she knew came strolling toward her from the opposite end of the street. His medium brown hair was ruffled from sleep, and he carried with him a paper bag in one hand, and a tray of drinks in the other.

Lee.

He looked up, locking eyes with her.

It was just as the night before. Her breathing caught in her throat, her heartbeat scurrying about to meet him as that anxiety was once again rekindled. His eyes seemed to shudder as something like surprise, and even relief lighted them.

But both emotions were wiped clean from his face as he bridged the gap between them, blinking down as he remembered the items he'd secured in each of his hands. Lee was somewhat apologetic as he offered her one of the drinks. "Sorry, I know this isn't your preference. I didn't expect..."

Kat wrinkled her nose at the sweet-charred scent of fresh-brewed coffee, but she accepted it, her fingers curling robotically around the warm paper cup. Lee set the rest of the drinks and the bag down on the steps, rejoining her, with a coffee for himself.

"I'm guessing you made it back to the ship last night?" Lee asked carefully. He kept his face neutral; enough so, that she had no clue what he was thinking. But that was fine. They had something more important at hand, anyway.

She didn't bother to do more than dip her head in affirmation as she explained what they'd been working on last night. "We've lost all communication abilities."

He nodded. He already knew, then. "So our coordinates, the health surveys..." he asked anyway.

"Nothing has gone out since yesterday afternoon," Kat confirmed grimly. They both knew what that meant.

"How much time do you wager we have until the AMG fleet arrives outside? Another twenty hours?" Lee's green eyes were clear as they flickered outwards to the street, and whoever may be passing by within hearing range.

"If that," Kat agreed. "Zane's been working to try to get something out this morning, but no luck so far."

Lee blew out a breath.

But despite his earnestness and the relief her presence had brought him, things were just as stilted between them as ever. She cast around, searching for something, anything to say to make things right again.

She thought about asking how his night had gone with the fliers when Hanna and the twins came staggering down the stairs.

In place of their black all-terrain suits, all three wore loose-fitting trousers and jackets in those dark, synthetic fabrics of Segura. That would have been all fine and great—she was cool with it, so long as no one asked Kat to play dress up. But then she saw the dark shadows under their eyes, and the drunken way Kiara bobbed a bit on her feet. It was only too obvious just how well their nights had gone.

Her eyes narrowed.

Tired, or slightly hungover, it was hard to say. They'd definitely been up all night. She honestly would have laughed if it weren't for their already precarious situation.

Lee, likely noting the same things as she, went right over to help distribute the drinks and contents of the bags—it sounded like he'd managed to scrounge up some type of plant-based nutrition bar.

She could have hugged Jed, when he came down the stairs a few minutes later to join them, looking disgruntled as ever in his dark, all-terrain suit. He didn't speak to anyone as he went right for the coffee, helping himself to a drink and a nutrition bar.

She shook her cup, wondering if it was finally cool enough to drink. She'd never had the patience to figure that out.

As they stood around with their simple breakfasts, Kat pondered her own social complex. She wished she'd never started this with Lee to begin with. Or better yet, just forgone boys altogether. She could live like one of those flier things and just fly by the handlebars for a while, freely doing whatever it was she wanted...

But she knew, now, what she wanted. And he was standing right there next to her with an impermeable wall of I'm-trying-so-hard-not-to-flub-things-up-again still separating them.

Another of their cadets came around the corner. Kat knew that low female voice well enough, that she didn't have to look.

"Hey Lee, I wasn't sure if it needed to be bolted, so I left the room unlocked. I didn't want us—Kat." Levy came into view of their party, stopping short when she noticed Kat standing there opposite Lee.

Levy looked confused; she was slow with her smile, and slow to cover up whatever thoughts were staining her lavender skin maroon in these lights.

"I only did the first lock," she said quickly, moving over by Hanna to help herself to some breakfast.

"I trust everyone found beds last night?" she asked Lee, working to keep her voice cool. She didn't trust herself to meet his eyes again as she tried hastily to brush off everything she'd just learned, while also pleading with herself not to care about any of it.

"Everyone is accounted for," Lee said stiffly, and Kat nodded.

"You totally missed out on a fun night," Jed commented, having finished with his nutrition bar. He pushed off the stairs, coming over to them with his coffee in hand.

Reluctantly, she let her gaze trip up between him and Lee. Some of the excitement had crept back into Lee's face. His green eyes were bright, aglow with the memories of a night in the skies. Something splintered in her at the idea that she'd missed that; she could've been a part of that—even if Levy had also been involved.

Lee's joy was subdued when he met her gaze. Was that for her, or because of her? "You really should try one, Kat," he said quietly.

His directness disarmed her. It took her a few seconds to recover and stumble out a reply. And disjointed as it was, Kat was relieved that he'd addressed her directly this time. That maybe they were back on speaking terms again—almost.

"I—I'll think about it." Because yearning, or otherwise, she'd been missing their easy camaraderie and the girl she'd been with Lee by her side. They'd never had that added romantic element between them in the past, so there was nothing to miss there.

They were still meandering outside their assigned stacks later that morning when Zane came by to let them know they'd been invited to tour part of the ship. Whether that meant more of the city or engineering, they'd find out pretty quickly, here.

Rorin, the mechanic, had left, so now it was just Whistler monitoring the connection in case of energy overload. From what Whistler had said, though, with this ship's strange energy configuration, it would only be another day, not two, before their ship was ready. That didn't give them much time to check things out here. However, if they didn't get a message out to Command soon, they'd have much bigger issues to deal with anyway.

At ten to 10:00 hours, they headed deeper into the city. Gaia had asked that they meet her outside the fore-facing doors, the same ones they'd gone through the previous night.

Hanna and the twins drifted right over to try their bands out on the security system. Zane busied himself tinkering with something on his hyperband. And with Levy over, chatting with Jed, she decided it was now or never. She and Lee were going to get past this awkwardness once and for all.

Lee was studying the streetlights above them when Kat came up to his side.

"Hey," she said coolly, her hand drifting over to rest lightly on his arm before she realized she'd even touched him. His body tensed, and she quickly let her hand drop back down. But he continued to stare up at the lights for a second, shaking his head a little. Then glancing first down at his arm, as if he could feel a brand there, he turned to face her.

"Hey." His eyes were wary and his voice cool, when he finally spoke.

"Can we talk?" she asked, for what felt like the millionth time already since this raid had begun.

"Of course, what's up?"

She glanced around her, conscious of Zane only a couple meters away, and Levy and Jed beyond him.

"Over here." She pivoted, not waiting to see if Lee would follow as she strode several paces away until there was a significant distance between her and the others.

She turned to find Lee standing there, hands stuffed into his pockets, and a hint of irritation flaring in his eyes.

"What do you want, Kat?"

At his tone, her own vexation rose swiftly inside of her to meet his. She thought the hair around her face would catch fire from the searing heat as she stared back at her one-time best friend standing barely an arm's width away. But as she opened her mouth, a sigh escaped her. And just as swiftly, the heat was doused. She was tired of this.

"We probably shouldn't let on that we've been trying to get any communication out from the ship," she said flatly.

It was Lee's turn to hesitate, lost for words. His eyes were fixated on a spot in the stacks just over her head. He cleared his throat. "That's it? Sure, Kat."

As he turned to walk away, Kat blinked, starting to shake with the force of refraining from screaming, from the fury starting to erupt throughout her once more. "That's it?" she repeated, now blinking furiously. She could feel tears threatening to break at the corners.

Lee's own eyes widened. "Look, Kat—"

"Lee—" Kat pleaded at the same time.

They both stopped speaking, the tiniest laugh bubbling to her lips.

Lee's own lips turned up a bit. "You first."

Kat tried to smile, but she wasn't sure what her face was doing, so she spoke quickly. "I was just going to say that I'm sorry for how things went down between us. I never meant to hurt you or put anything above our friendship. Again, I really am sorry. I've accepted things with you and Levy. That's all fine, and I'm happy for you."

But Lee didn't smile. He didn't laugh with relief to finally have things resolved between them. He didn't show any reaction at all. Eventually, he squinted, opening his mouth as if he might say something, but then he closed it again.

"Whatever, Kat." He rolled his shoulders, loosening a stiffness there, some ache he hadn't been able to shake. And when he looked back at her, he again didn't bother pasting any looks to his face. "I'm glad our relationship is fine with you." And, shaking his head slightly, Lee walked away from her, seemingly deliberately putting some distance between them, as he went to stand beside Zane.

She stood there for a second, tongue-tied and completely dumbstruck.

Our relationship? Had he meant he and Levy? Or he and Kat?

Kat didn't linger there long. She gave herself all of thirty seconds to collect herself before striding back over to wait for their host.

They needed to get to the bottom of all of this soon and call this raid over. It was messing with her head, and it was messing with her personal life. She was ready to go home.

CHAPTER 35: LEE

LEE WAS irritated.

Mostly with himself.

Okay, a little bit with Kat.

But how she could even still think it possible that he could ever have something with Levy? After all of their years together, and after everything they'd been through together...

He knew that, while Levy was remarkable and truly a great girl, their chemistry would never compare to what he and Kat had. The fire and the chaos she brought to his heart; the seething turmoil to always being close to her, but never getting it right. And the inability to stop bringing her up in every thought he had...

He probably could have curbed his reaction a little. But the thought alone was so ridiculous, that she'd caught him off-guard.

And after yesterday... He'd woken at least twice in the night. Once thinking the energy fields still loomed up over them, taunting them. And then again, with the image of that blaster pointing right at Kat, with the terror he'd felt that evening mirrored on her own face.

And then to see her today, thinking things were fine if he chose someone else; as if anyone else could ever match her.

It irritated him more than it should have.

He'd merely nodded when Gaia arrived a few minutes later, accompanied by someone tall and dark-haired. "One of our lead scientists, Elia."

Scientist; not engineer; not operations. That was new.

They were quiet as they were led through the doors and into the long passageway. The draft continued in here, too, a soft breath at his ears. Though not nearly chilling enough to soothe the fuming in his head.

Gaia's explanations were succinct as they were led past a series of doors. He was correct about that first room being related to the ship's hydraulics. They'd had to expand as the ship's inhabitants had grown, but the basic network remained mostly unchanged.

She had to direct them back against the walls a couple of times, when fliers zipped by them, doors parting at a wave of the driver's wrists. That explained the humming sound from before... But Gaia and Elia appeared unphased, and seconds later they were walking again.

Lee had yet to gather what exactly their host's expertise was, for it definitely wasn't tour guide or diplomatic relations, but he was already starting to gauge that each of the ship's numerous inhabitants wore many, many hats—and possibly masks.

He glazed over the details as Gaia rattled off the various roles for each of the workers they passed and how they played into their little self-sustaining ecosystem. Elia occasionally chimed in with specifics to answer Zane's questions or the twins' skepticism at the processes.

"We do, in fact, do more here aside from simply zip about on our top-model fliers."

They moved deeper into the complex. For security reasons, they were not shown the main hangar. Although with how self-sustaining the rest of the ship appeared to be, maintenance aside, Lee wondered if the main hangar was used any more frequently than the one in which their own ship currently resided.

Lee actually cracked a smile when they passed through the massive corridor devoted entirely to space farming and hydroponics. The rows of dirt and crop extending for what had to be kilometers, in neat rows and boxes. He'd been missing his greenhouses. And sure enough, speckled throughout, as well as overhead, were more of the blue-green lights.

They'd made it to the conversion rooms when Gaia slipped them each a pair of glasses. The air seemed to vibrate around them with the static. The anticipation. He'd forgotten exactly how much energy they'd be dealing with.

The transformer modules were complicated. Intricately woven and powerful, they thrummed with enough wattage to power a small metropolis—about what they'd expect for a ship and a city of this size.

But beyond those, seeming to glow with an ethereal aura around them—

"Particle accelerators," Lee breathed. He'd known what he would find here, the blue-green lights were everywhere. And for the sheer amount of energy it would require to sustain the energy fields... "You're using neutrinos, right? You rely on the particles' cosmic rays for energy?"

Multiple heads turned his way, including their host.

"Basic neutrino conversion." Gaia nodded, face unreadable. "You're familiar?" From her other side, Elia had turned to scrutinize him with interest.

"Never to this scale," Lee murmured. He could feel the others watching them closely. "We do something similar in our greenhouses, for space farming," he added, more for them than their host. He wondered how they'd gotten around the stability issue, though, for a project of this size...

Gaia was nodding. "A common application. That was actually how this all started. We were searching for a sustainable energy source capable of not only withstanding the dark radiation," a nod towards them and their presumed mission, "but also with the ability to ultimately diffuse its footprint as part of a long-term project. Our research has advanced lightyears in the years since."

"You were working on a defense?" Zane asked.

"We *are* working on a defense," Gaia corrected him.

"With the energy fields," Lee said smoothly.

Gaia nodded. "And yes, before you ask. Our energy shield is also capable of withstanding a certain level of outside forces, such as loose meteoroids, lesser rays, ship blasts…"

"We meant no harm, we didn't know," Zane said, speaking quickly.

But Gaia had waved her hand, dismissively. Lee wondered if her scientists had taken to their firing blasters at the ship so cavalier at the time…

"And what of the radiation spikes we observed?" Lee asked carefully, mentally assembling the last few pieces to the puzzle in his mind.

"A bi-product of one of our experiments. We're always looking to push ourselves. The stacks, the fliers, all of what you've seen out there are not purely for comfort; rather a way to stave off the excess energy and provide for those risking their lives out here, while also expanding the proposed limits and pushing efficiency."

Elia led them through a couple of the safety measures they'd taken with the lead coating on the accelerator tubing, and the radiation monitors. They were doing everything they could on multiple fronts to make this as successful as possible. This was not some half-baked shadow market experiment, and the explanations they'd been given were all sound. So why, then, all the secrecy? Why base their operations out here? And why not bring their research to light? They could easily apply for funding.

Unless it was still too dangerous…

He studied the accelerators again, his hand grazing the band at his wrist. Everything about space was dangerous. Each time they took out the skimmers or the cruiser for a raid, they were placing themselves in danger. But what made this project so dangerous that they would go to such lengths as to base their operations in a known quadrant where dark rays flew rampant?

They'd reached the end of the passageway—at least this first one. Elia excused herself, continuing on through a set of doors off to one side.

"What do you make of our accelerators?" Gaia asked, coming up beside Lee as they made their way back down the way they'd come.

"'Basic neutrino conversion?'" Lee didn't need to exaggerate his astonishment. It was truly impressive, the scale at which they'd managed to harness this level of energy. They had taken the conversion far beyond what he'd even presumed possible. Not only were the energy fields sustainable, but there was enough residual energy to power a city and conduct what Lee would guess were an infinite number of experiments to further their research. These energy advancements would put even those of the AMG to the test.

It was all impressive. The city, the fliers, the way the energy fed into their little biome.

But for all they were doing, particularly with the energy fields, he'd expected more. Like everything in the city was just a distraction, a light show, meant to detract from the main operation. Like there was something they weren't being shown; something they weren't being permitted to see...

Their group reached the doors on the opposite end of the passageway. After offering Gaia a concise update on the status of their ship, she left them outside.

She was already heading back up the passageway as the doors closed again behind her. The same passageway where everyone seemed to keep disappearing.

They needed to get behind those doors.

He turned to Hanna and Jed. "I need your help with something."

CHAPTER 36: KAT

KAT GLANCED overhead as they stepped back into the glowing city, her eyes going instinctively to the painted stars on the domed metal. They were realistic enough, that she half-expected to see one of Command's ships painted alongside them, waiting to escort their squadron back to the Academy. Every hour they were delayed in getting a message out, there was a greater possibility of someone coming out here to find them. And those ships likely wouldn't take the same stance as they had with their investigation of Segura.

Maybe it was just the city wearing on her. And maybe that meant it had forgiven her. But it was kind of beautiful what they were trying to do with their shields, to not only withstand the dark radiation, but work to alleviate the threat as well. If it worked as well as it sounded, this scientific breakthrough could be the key to their future.

She didn't catch what Lee was saying to their cadets. She'd done her best to stay clear while he cooled down, giving him his space. He'd made it obvious he hadn't forgiven her. Instead, she found herself standing over by Zane. At least when Zane was pissed, he said it to her face. "You think Nikola's managed to make any progress with our communication?"

Zane glanced down at his hyperband, the signal that had been dead since they'd arrived. "I think he'd have come and found us."

"He can do this. If anyone could figure it out it'd be Nikola."

Zane frowned. "Let's hope you're right."

Kat matched his grim expression. "We may as well go back and see what we can do to help." But when she glanced up, she saw that Lee had already started back that way. And to have them both thrown together in that cabin, working side by side —"You know what, I'll catch up to you in a bit."

Zane gave her an impervious look, waving her off.

The rest of her squadron was mostly out of sight before she realized she didn't actually have anywhere to go. The streets were a little too empty at the moment to just wander, especially with the host's shadows following her. And she didn't want to just go sit in one of their rooms in the stacks, even though she would probably benefit from a lie-down. But maybe she could hole up somewhere, or finally go try out one of those flier things. Everyone had seemed pretty excited about them.

She started off down a random street. She was sure she'd seen a flier head this way at some point.

She'd only visited a major city, once. With Lee. During one of the weeks they got off for holidays in-between terms. Tonya had gotten three tickets to see this show—and when Lee's dad got called away last minute for work, they'd invited Kat. The show itself was frilly; it was super over-the-top, with even more outrageous costumes. But Tonya had loved it, and Kat had loved watching Tonya. And walking down that humming city street with Tonya and Lee after the show, with all the sounds, and the lights, and the architecture...

This felt like that.

A door opened up ahead, the lean figure calling out a cheerful farewell, a drink in hand as he started up the street towards Kat. Of course, some of his cheerfulness faded as they passed. He kept a wide berth between them, slopping some of his drink down onto the pavement in his haste to avoid her path.

She approached that same hammered door, hesitating. This was probably a bad idea. But it seemed welcoming enough inside, some type of alternative music wended its way out to the textured pavement. The music was a little shriller than what she and Lee would usually listen to, but it was nice to hear any sort of music at all. And at least she would be somewhere.

Sliding open the door, she went inside.

The interior was compact. Most of the tables and counter space were built of scrap. And the teal glow coming from the hanging lights still threw her. It was mostly deserted too, with only one other humanoid figure, a metallic-scaled female, sipping a drink at one of the irregular tables. She must be between shifts. But there was no one there, as far as she could see, to serve the bar. Maybe they were in the back. Or on break... she had no idea how this was supposed to work.

She'd taken a couple of steps back towards the door when someone came around the counter. He had light gold hair and a strong jaw. He looked to be about her age, too, although it was hard to say as both his face and his body lacked the tone and definition she was used to at the Academy. It was actually refreshing, for a change.

His eyes widened when he noted who stood across from him, but unlike the one on the streets who'd hurried away from her earlier, he didn't look wary, more—intrigued. She could work with that.

"What can I get you?"

"Oh—" She cast her mind about. Without a firm grasp on what sort of place she'd stumbled into, the only thing she could think to ask for was water. But that would be incredibly odd of her...

Her mind was still stumbling along when the golden-haired bartender boy pulled a tin cup from beneath the counter. Tipping his head, he motioned with the cup to the various casks lining the wall.

Kat pointed to the first one she saw.

"You'll probably want to start with something milder. Here." Going over to the cask nearest the wall, he filled her glass, setting it smoothly down on the counter.

She fiddled with the band around her wrist. She knew that techie, Dyinai, had mentioned something about these granting them access to amenities. But as to how exactly this transaction was supposed to work, she had absolutely no idea.

The bartender boy motioned to the thin dark strip that lay flat atop the surface of the counter. She'd missed that earlier... "The sensor will detect your band if you wave your wrist over it." He nodded to her drink on the slab of countertop. "I'll bring out something to go with that as well."

With a grateful smile, Kat did as she was told. Selecting a table with a clear view of the door, she set her cup down gingerly before her, and peered inside. The liquid was a vibrant orange color, with a stream of nitro bubbles.

Sniffing at it first, she tried a small sip. It had a bitter taste, with a sharp burn as it went down her throat. Not her drink. Was this the place where the others had come last night? Hanna and Kiara had certainly looked like they'd enjoyed their share of inebriation when she'd seen them first come down this morning.

It was several minutes before the bartender boy brought out a plate of some sort of thin cracker, open-faced sandwich, thing. Whatever it was, it looked good. She hadn't even realized she was hungry. But she was very unprepared when he slid into the stool opposite hers.

"I'm Cade," he said, holding out his hand.

"I—Kerali," she said, offering instead the name of one of her earlier instructors as a cadet. Kerali had always been quite friendly with the cadets—especially the male ones...

She didn't know why she'd lied. He knew nothing about her. But maybe that was the point.

Cade smiled, and Kat-Kerali gave him an easy smile in return.

"So, what led you guys here?" Cade asked.

Here—as in to their ship. "Oh, we're just here to charter supplies back to base." She assumed there was a base, off on some distant planet or outpost somewhere. With technology such as this, someone somewhere would be benefitting from their experiments, even if it was simply sharing the knowledge with a second database.

"Nice try." Cade grinned. He gestured towards her getup and the hyperband on her other wrist.

"You know who we are," Kat said carefully.

"I know there hasn't been a transport in over a year." He motioned then towards the shop, the tables. We don't exactly have a lot of extra materials floating around, so we sort of have to make do with what we do manage to get."

"So no supply charters?"

"No supply charters. Everything always comes in second-hand. Plus, most of us, myself included, don't even know where base is." So there was a base, though. Somewhere.

He nodded then towards the table, her tin cup sitting mostly abandoned there. "You get used to it."

"You actually like this stuff?"

"Wait until you feel the buzz afterward." That she could get behind; she would give it another try.

"I heard you guys are having some trouble with your ship?" Wow. Word really had gotten around.

"Just with our shields. We didn't think we'd be out here this long." All truths. "But, for what it's worth, I'm really glad we are—here, I mean." She wasn't sure what had prompted her to say it. But she almost meant it, too.

Whatever the reasoning, he seemed to like that. He nodded. "It's really incredible what we've managed to create here."

There was that 'we' again. They truly were all invested in the success of the research, as Gaia had alluded to earlier.

And because it was what Kerali would have done, Kat smiled again at him. "What about you though, you said there hasn't been a transport in over a year. Do you have family elsewhere, a home?" She hoped she didn't sound like she was prying. She was enjoying their little interaction, and it was nice to be someone else for a few minutes.

But Cade let out a subtle cough. "Pretending you hadn't just lied to me and weren't just evading answering any more questions." He cut her a slash of a smile. "But no. Everyone, my family, my friends—we're all here. I've lived on this ship my whole life. Some of us work in engineering; some in the labs; some of us split time here, or with sanitation..."

It was nice. The idea of belonging somewhere. She'd never really belonged anywhere before the Academy.

She thought back on all the years she and Lee had pushed themselves to be faster and stronger as raiders. It was constantly a competition to be the best.

But sitting here, with Cade, imagining his life on this ship, serving amongst his family, his friends, for something they were equally passionate about. He actually reminded her a bit of Lee. Or who Lee might've been, she supposed, had he chosen a different path for himself all those years ago.

"It sounds like you have everything you need right here."

"We're not unhappy." Cade surveyed her again, and she noticed the way his gaze lingered, the parts of her suit that drew his attention.

She knew he wasn't interested in her. Not as Kat, anyway. He was interested in Kerali. The girl with all the smiles, who had time to sit around at tables in exciting places and talk about her life.

Another inhabitant of the ship came in; Cade seemed somewhat reluctant to slip from their table. And when he vacated his seat, she found herself genuinely wishing he could have stayed, if only to see more of life through Cade's eyes.

But Kat had been Kerali long enough.

She stayed long enough to finish her cracker sandwich. And when she set the tin cup back on the counter, only a little of the orange liquid remained.

He'd been right—it grew on you.

CHAPTER 37: LEE

AFTER HAVING spent the night, and the better part of the day in the city, returning to their ship was a comfort. Nostalgic, even, like returning home after the holiday. How easily they'd all slid back into the rhythm of cadet and squadron lead.

Albeit, the twins weren't back yet. He'd had a special request of them. Hopefully they didn't take too much advantage of their tavern visit...

And, of course, Kat hadn't returned with the rest of them. He was trying to overlook that fact as he fitted the rest of his plan together.

Beside him, poor Nikola was doing everything he could to help them get a signal out. His frustration was evident by the smudges on his glasses. "How are we looking?" Lee asked, glancing up the platform of the observation deck, past Nikola, to where Hanna and Jed now hacked into Segura's mainframe.

"Just confirming there are no broken loops in the code..." Hanna murmured, double-checking the parameters she'd altered for their new profiles. Unsure who of their new contacts might have the clearance they'd need to get through those doors unescorted, Hanna had duplicated Gaia's own credentials, tweaking the framework of the hologram just enough that it wouldn't trigger any alarms. He just hoped no one went in between now and then and realized Gaia had suddenly had a couple of brothers added to the system.

Jed sat hunched over beside her, his eyes flying across the hologram nearly as fast as his fingers as he covered their tracks. It had taken him but a few minutes to find his way into the intricate web of their security system. In a way, it was sort of impressive to see Jed at work. Lee had heard of the cadet's hacking abilities, but up until this point, all he'd seen him do on the raid was play his way through about a dozen video games.

"And they won't be able to trace it back to us?" Lee asked, leaning over them as he studied the code.

"I mean..." Jed and Hanna exchanged a glance.

"Never mind that," Lee waved a hand. They'd be gone before it mattered.

Their shields were making incredible time. Too good. At this rate, they'd be fully charged and out of here by morning, which meant they'd have to make their time through those doors count. But that was just as well, as they still hadn't gotten any communication out. Their odds were stacking up against them, quicker and taller than the stacks that made up Segura.

"Okay, we're good," Hanna said brightly, stepping back.

"And this will get us through any door? We're sure there won't be any issues with duplication error along the way?" Zane confirmed, glancing between Hanna and Jed.

"Yep. We made sure to alter the sequencing. Anything that Gaia had access to, the two of you now do," Hanna confirmed.

"And on the off-chance of separation or detection," Jed said a tad darkly. "You'll each have a way back in—or out."

Lee wended his way over to the lone table by the kitchenette in the back. Levy had the controls to one of the RIMs open before her as she reacquainted herself with the motions, committing them to memory. "Hey," he said, sliding into one of the seats beside her.

He waited quietly so as not to disturb her, while she ran through the sequence in her head, her fingers flying across the levers. Her hands had stilled again before she sat back, shoulders relaxing. "You ready for this?"

The look she shot him was so supercilious, so in-your-face-confident, Lee had to choke back a laugh. He knew that look only too well.

"Just checking." It would be a tight fit, but she would be fine. He was still biting back a grin while he watched her run through everything one last time. She may be a VL by status. But that was it. Out here, where it actually counted—there was nothing VL about her.

Kiara and Kamata slipped back onto the ship right as Lee was ready to start drumming his fingertips on the tabletop. "What did we learn?" He asked, striding back over beside Zane.

"Shift change is coming up on the hour," Kamata said, hands behind her back.

"And these are for you." Kiara held out a neat stack of dark synthetic clothing.

Lee didn't look too closely at the haze in the twins eyes as he took the stack, distributing a set of clothing to both Levy and Zane. The clothes likely wouldn't deter any of Gaia's people for long. But if it bought them a little time...

They quickly swapped their all-terrain suits out. And with Whistler once again remaining behind with the ship to assist Nikola and Hanna; Hanna having moved on to peer over Nikola's shoulder and assist with communications; and Jed, settling into another of his dumb video games, Lee, Zane, and Levy set out. Back into the city.

They made their way as unhurriedly as they could up the streets until they reached the other end of the city. With the passage doors to the engineering wing in sight, they turned off the nearest side street, crouching in the shadows of an overhang from the level above, facing outward.

He and Zane kept guard while Levy started up the RIM.

From here, they had a good view of the crossings between streets. They could see full facets of the stacks, from the raw additions above, down to the hole-in-the-wall comforts, like the tiny bakery where he'd found them breakfast. He peered up and down the streets, watching for the shadows of whoever had been assigned to follow them. It was impressive what they had managed to create with such limited means. But was their research worth it? Did it justify the requisite burden of leaving the rest of the galaxy behind them?

Levy had the mod-vehicle up in the air before long and skimming along the midnight wall toward a couple of vents hidden up high there.

"Almost there," she said softly, her voice like the air filtering through the ducts above. Her hands only stumbled on the switches once, while she cut through one of the grates.

He let his eyes drift upwards, imagining the little mod-vehicle making its way down through the tubing.

Beside them, Levy sucked in a breath. "I think—we are in."

"Yeah?" His blood pounded through his veins as he came around to peer at the little holo-screen, Zane doing the same. They only had minutes before shift change was due, assuming the twins' tavern intel was good.

Footage was dark while the RIM made its way through the webbing of the ducts. He wasn't too concerned with the motion attracting attention in the passageways, he'd seen fliers speed through those halls. It was more the question of the mod-vehicle getting there. Lee checked the time on his hyperband. Three minutes. They had three minutes until shift change.

"And we've got light," Zane murmured as the dark screen was overtaken by 360-degree blue-green footage of the engineering passageway.

"Now to make sure the coast is clear," Lee agreed. Cruising high above walking level, the RIM roved the long passageway of the engineering wing. They would be entering under cover of a fresh shift while their replacements filtered back out. With all of that bustle, the RIM was mostly a precaution. They just needed to make sure they didn't run into Gaia or Elia waiting just inside. Rorin. Anyone they'd met already. Too many questions and the game would be over before they ever got started. But with any luck, they would just fly on past as spaceships in the night.

This would work.

The profiles Hanna had doctored were perfect, and their security clearance confirmed. But still, as his wrist displayed the new hour, he scanned the streets once more before turning to Levy. They were technically breaking their own rules leaving her here alone, but compared to where they were headed, she was in the clear. She knew the plan, but he wanted to say something anyway. "Stay down until we're in. Then you can pull the RIM out and head back to the ship. If anything happens, find Whistler. We won't be long."

And only after she nodded did he let his gaze stray once more, searching the streets. He'd stalled as long as he could. Where was Kat?

He'd made this plan with her in mind—of course he had. She added the insane to genius. The reckless and wild to the impossible. Without her here, the whole thing just felt too... tame. Safe.

He didn't care anymore if tomorrow, she chose Zane or Whistler, or even some other nameless guy, ten times over. He'd wait. For however long it took for her to realize that he wasn't going anywhere. Because at the end of the day, when the games ended, and gravity claimed its course, he would be right here waiting for her.

Within a minute or two, a couple of fliers zipped past overhead, and the new shift of workers filled the streets. He and Zane waited until there was foot traffic around them before turning from the presumed casual conversation they'd been having with their fellow Seguran friend, Levy. Joining the throng, they headed in for their shift.

He and Zane. The idea zinged around his head in odd pings as they made their way casually toward the engineering wing doors.

If he'd told himself three weeks ago what he'd be doing now —and with whom...

No one would ever mistake Zane for anything but a military guy. A raider. But with the clothes—with Lee—maybe they'd actually have a shot.

He didn't notice any cameras as they traversed the passage; it'd been the same with their previous visits. The ship really didn't have all that many security measures in place. But, he supposed, up until a few days ago, there'd been no spacecrafts lurking beyond their energy fields, and no raiders boarding their ship.

They didn't linger, letting the crowd carry them along as they wove past those leaving for the day. The draft in the passage felt stronger this time, the lights more teal; a trick of adrenaline? And the fit of the clothes was foreign, but they were fairly airy for being synthetics, although they were making him warm.

This afternoon, the passage seemed to extend even further than before. The traffic was beginning to thin out, when they at last they reached the doors at the far end.

"What would you reckon?" Lee murmured. Elia had gone through these doors earlier. And he would wager this was where Gaia had been headed the night before. They stepped back to let a couple of others scan their identification and pass through. He had to resist glancing upward to see if Levy had managed to pull the RIM yet.

And then he and Zane passed through those doors.

They were met with another long passage. Doors split off to either side. "Erm..."

Not wanting to be caught standing there in the middle of the passageway, Lee edged them off to the side, bending down to adjust the laces of boots.

Zane had just angled himself away from the passage up ahead when they heard a familiar high-pitched, wheezy voice talking to someone a couple of doors down.

Dyinai.

Lee quickly rose to his feet, also angling his head away from the upcoming passage.

He pointed wordlessly to the door on their left, and he and Zane near-stumbled through.

His pulse seemed to stab at his lungs as he waited the second and a half for the door to slide closed behind them. Another few seconds as he awaited the confirmation whether or not Dyinai had spotted them. When they at last deemed that they were safe, Lee cleared his throat, staring down at a steep, winding, industrial-style staircase.

This was not what he was expecting; their fliers would certainly struggle making their way down these flights. Out of habit, he checked the corners and doorways of the room. But once again, there were no monitors. Like they didn't care who came and went. Or maybe they didn't want the evidence.

"Shall we?" Lee motioned to the stairway.

"After you."

He took the steps evenly, one stair at a time in the hopes of keeping silent, not wanting to draw additional attention to their presence on the chance they really had managed to slip down here right under Dyinai's nose. But it seemed as if they'd succeeded thus far, no one had yet to follow them down here.

A set of double-wide doors lay at the base of the stairs. Lab coats hung on the wall beside the doors, along with a bin of coated glasses identical to the ones Gaia had handed them earlier.

"We'd better..." Lee murmured, grabbing a couple of the lab coats. He handed one to Zane.

"Yeah," Zane grunted. They weren't exactly companionable, but there was zero resistance as they pulled the lab coats over their shoulders, coming to stand a half meter from the sliding double doors. This would be it.

He slid the glasses over his eyes as they stepped forward into the light.

There was more.

There was so much more.

A particle accelerator spanning what appeared to be the entire lower half of the ship, of Segura, was suspended from the raised ceiling some ten meters off the ground.

A living thing—that's what Kat had said of the energy fields a few days ago, of the magnetism perpetually settled around the ship.

The ethereal glow emanating from the ring was amplified a thousand times over by the blue-green lights overhead; it flickered as the light caught one of the hundreds of thousands of minuscule detectors lining the walls and ceiling in a spectacle of electricity. A series of holding cells with that same glow were stacked, meters high, along the floor by one of the base walls, feeding into the energy conversion. And spread before them, amidst a flurry of hurried feet and seismic beeping, lay a whopping, smattering of holotech.

The scientists and workers manning these sections were as oblivious to the accelerator's glow as they were to the two new visitors who had crossed into the basement lab.

Lee didn't know where to look; where to walk; what to think. Not as they stepped into the conglomeration.

Each section appeared to indicate a separate study or monitor related to the accelerator's functions, but it all appeared to blur together. Like separate species of the same genus.

Lee was trying to get a better sense of what some of these sections were without appearing overly interested. Taking a few steps towards it, he read the label on one of the holographs, the Neutrino Energy Diversion model. He took a couple more steps in to get a better look at the scale there.

"First time seeing it in person?"

Lee tensed. Maybe they weren't so inconspicuous as he'd thought. His gaze slipped from the holotech, sideways, to the aged scientist in a lab coat like theirs. The scientist had come to stop beside him and Zane, but he wasn't looking at them. He'd lifted his eyes to the arc of the accelerator immediately above them.

Lee didn't know if they should admit to it being their first time seeing it, or not, and instead remained silent.

"I'd say you get used to it, but it's pretty incredible every time." The scientist finally let his eyes drop again. He looked like he was heading back to his post, but Lee stopped him.

"And this is—stable?" What he'd really wanted to ask, was if it was safe to be harvesting these levels of energy, and storing them within such close proximity and limited space.

"Everything has its risks. We know what we signed up for." This time the scientist didn't leave them time to ask any more questions, turning a steely gaze away from them.

Lee narrowed his eyes, staring as the scientist continued over to one of the nearby sections of the lab. Gaia had said something of a similar nature earlier.

They believed in the research they were doing down here, that much was clear. But what Lee couldn't believe, was that all of this had been happening right beneath them. Beneath the city with its streets and shops, and the upper labs where they had casually trodden on a tour, not an hour earlier. The entire thing subsisted, completely unbeknownst to them.

The conversion equipment they'd seen upstairs had been mere models, toys in comparison; down-scaled versions designed to feed the city its power. Whereas this—this must be the main convertor. Which meant, they were standing amidst where the majority of the energy was generated to supply the energy shields.

Zane was quiet beside him as they ambled away from the NED model, something blue on the holograph appearing to be steadily climbing. They passed a section portraying seismic models and particle magnetism, others pertaining to the conductors. They came in close again to another workstation to see exactly what levels of energy they were working with.

There was the energy in joules. And next to it, denoted in delta-grays...

No.

No, that couldn't be possible.

He strode over to the next station.

And the next.

Each of them confirmed his fear via various observations. His eyes darted around from the monitors to the thousands of holding cells lining the base wall.

"What did you see?" Zane murmured. Lee stopped them before another holotech monitor, staring pointedly at the two sets of values on the scale. They only had to stand there for a few seconds before—"Oh f—" Zane bit down on his curse as a couple of the scientists working from that post glanced their way. Lee backed away a few steps.

Dark rays. They were harnessing dark radiation.

They'd done the calculations and the math, back on their ship. They'd had a rough estimate for the amount of energy it would take to power an energy field of this size; the sheer amount of energy that would need to be accommodated. And any sort of uncertainty about the convertor's capacity had been all but dismissed after the tour this morning.

But those calculations hadn't accounted for this second presence.

Somewhere, lost in the amalgam of his brain, a report materialized involving an accident tens of decades ago. A project with an experimental nature very similar to the experiments going on inside this room. The facilities in question having imploded upon themselves... "We need to get out of here."

Zane didn't hesitate as he followed suit, striding back around the accelerator and out the doors to the stairway beyond.

They didn't bother to do more than toss their lab coats at the hooks as they made their way up the stairs and out into the city.

At this very moment, inside that lab, they were toying with dark radiation, their experiments backed by hundreds of trillions of joules.

Trillions.

Who knew how much of it they had stored in those holding cells.

CHAPTER 38: KAT

KAT MEANDERED along the shadowed stretch of city, balancing on bottom steps and bits of steel and posts, and whatever was on the ground in front of her as she thought through her conversation with the bartender boy.

She wouldn't have ever fit in here, content to roam these same streets indefinitely.

And she wouldn't be sad about it.

She didn't run into anyone from her squadron as she cleared the streets back to their ship. Perhaps there'd been an update and they were all back there with Starla. Maybe they'd managed to get a message out. She shivered a little, thinking about the growing consequences if they hadn't... And if someone like Cade got caught in the cross-hairs because of their ill-planning...

She strode up the ramp of their ship, expecting to see the cabin thrumming like those particle accelerators their host had shown them earlier. But the cabin was—not.

She could see the top of Whistler's head peeking up from one of the floor hatches near the cockpit where the twins sat, and Jed was over by the observation deck playing his game. Nikola and Hanna had their heads together, oblivious to everyone else, and both entirely absorbed in the holotech—that didn't exactly imply great news for their squadron. But she'd get to that in a moment. Levy was off by herself, staring out one of the side windows with one of the RIM vehicles discarded at her side; she came to her feet when she saw Kat, but Kat didn't immediately address the girl. Not as her eyes continued to dance across the too-relaxed cabin.

Where was Lee?

Nearly throwing herself into a panic from the juxtaposition between her racing heartbeat, and the cabin, she finally glanced over toward Levy. "Where is—"

"Lee and Zane went to see what more they could learn about the ship's energy conversion. He thinks there is something going on…"

Kat tuned out the rest of Levy's words. Of course, there was something going on. The whole operation reeked of secrets. "And they were going back through the engineering wing?"

Levy nodded.

Oh for the *love of the void*. She turned on a heel, heading back down the ramp.

She wasn't sure what her intention was. Knowing Lee, there was some intricate game plan already in place. She wasn't about to step on toes, but the fact that he'd gone in without her… And with Zane of all people…

"I'm coming with," Levy called in her low voice. She caught up with Kat at the base of the ramp.

"Fine, whatever." Kat didn't slow her pace nor look over as they headed back into the city. She shouldn't be nervous. What was the worst that could happen? Lee and Zane would have their blasters, and they'd have their instincts. This was pie for them. Strawberry pie.

But again, she wasn't there. And if anything were to happen to them... And after she'd left everything on such shitty terms... She wasn't okay with that.

She knew the way to that engineering wing from memory by now and knew exactly which streets Lee would've taken. But still, at every crossroads, she peered up both streets as far as she could see; her eyes were always frantically searching.

They were nearly there. They rounded one last corner, Kat whipping her head around to peer up another barren street when she saw him.

"Lee."

Her breathing hitched as she locked sight of his green eyes. It was all she could do not to just sprint to him, *to the void* with Levy and Zane. But she held her cool. She kept her eyes on them —on him, until they were standing face to face. Until only their differences in height, and their unknown whereabouts of the last hour created any sort of distance between her and Lee.

She searched his eyes, his face, tracking the emotion there— the worry, and the alarm.

"I was looking for you," Lee said, his breath caressing her hair.

"I'm here." And for a few heartbeats, nothing else mattered. It was just she and Lee, frozen along that intrinsic axis they shared.

She and Lee had a lot to talk about. *Void*, they'd let it all pile beneath them this time, hadn't they? There were a lot of unspoken words they needed to say, and truths they needed to face. She swallowed. *Soon?*

"You would think it's been weeks, not the hour we've been out," Zane muttered, but there was grit to his voice.

Kat continued to track Lee's lips, and his eyes, as they stole across her face.

Lee seemed to take ages to consider, deliberating her as carefully as his next response. She was buzzing slightly from whatever had been in that cask, but she could've sworn some of the anxiousness limning his body had eased a little, especially as a smile edged his lips. *Soon.*

A flood of air seemed to whoosh into Kat's lungs, flooding her heart and flooding her senses. And their world started turning again.

Lee's undercurrents of a smile faded as he broke her gaze, glancing first to Zane and Levy, then back to her.

"We need to talk about Segura's energy resources."

Kat waited in tense silence while he and Zane explained what they'd uncovered going on below deck. The hidden laboratory; its particle accelerator. All of it.

Then they got to the values.

"You're sure it's dark rays?"

"We saw the delta-grays on the monitor and the holding cells, Kat. The levels of energy they're harnessing with the dark radiation are to the moon." Lee's eyes didn't leave hers. The energy levels, she believed. She'd seen the size of the energy fields. They all had. Those diagrams they'd drawn up back on their ship before coming here were singed into her skull. But to add dark radiation to the mix...

"And so the accelerators we saw earlier...?" she asked, if only to keep her body functioning. Each new factoid penetrated the cells of her brain like the contents of those holding cells.

"A small fraction of the operations being conducted here," Zane cut in.

"This can't be right." Kat shook her head. "The levels you're reporting are astronomical. Not only would this make these operations illegal and highly dangerous, but this is something that's never been done before. To have gotten to this point, they would've had to have been working on this for—"

"Years," Lee concluded for her, his voice coming across much calmer than seemed possible given the circumstances. "Maybe even a century..."

Kat scrambled through all the research she'd done prior to their raid. About that accident, and the abandoned operations. The imploded facilities. And there'd been mention of... "A singularity." Kat's mouth went dry. "But that couldn't be the same people, the same project. They were shut down after that accident. There's been no mention in recent years of another project of that nature..."

"Unless the operations in question just hadn't been uncovered yet... or had been operating in secret ever since," Lee said, grimly.

"At least it's stable." Levy's eyes darted between the three of them, somewhat oblivious to the underhanded meaning of the situation. There was hope still in her eyes.

"For now," Zane said darkly.

"And all of this is just sitting on the ship, right beneath where we are standing?" Kat's question was rhetorical as she pulled at the band in her hair, tightening and retightening her ponytail.

In talking in the shop earlier, the ship and its inhabitants had all sounded so close-knit and comfortable with everything going on. She supposed it made sense. Nothing bonded a people together more than a dangerous secret; a dangerous secret that had survived thus far undisturbed.

But if there were ever to be a catalyst for investigation, say, a squadron of cadets suddenly gone missing...

It had been roughly seventeen hours since their coordinates had disappeared. Seventeen hours, with no reports as to their whereabouts or general well-being. "We're a ticking time bomb. Who will they send?" Kat whispered. Her mouth had gone dry; her brain, hollow. Because it wouldn't be more Academy cadets they sent this time. It would likely be a military unit.

"The Commanding General," she breathed, answering her own question.

They still didn't have insights into how, exactly, the Commanding General had come to track the radioactive signature coming from the ship's energy fields. But with the documentation from the mainframe and the evidence of the dark radiation in the holding cells, he would have the authorization to decide the fate of the operation he'd been so zealously seeking. And if that was the case, what exactly were his plans for Segura?

With what they knew of his dealings with the shadow markets and his Preservation Initiative, General Narron would see Segura in only one light: a danger to life.

Harnessing the dark radiation was not permissible. There would be no brushing this by the wayside. There would be no options for ignorance. There would be justice served, and as raider cadets, they would likely have little to no role or say in it.

She found Lee's green eyes once more, wading with her through the nothingness. He inclined his head a fraction. She wasn't alone in her thoughts, then. He'd come to the same conclusion.

"This is insane," she murmured as fact after fact rehashed itself in her head. The entire direction their mission had taken. "This is—"

"Madness?" Lee supplied with a grimace.

"Madness," she agreed.

Because whatever it was Segura was doing differently here—it was working, permissible or not. Acceptable or not; their experiments to harness the dark rays had worked.

She now knew that she'd made a mistake in chatting with Cade, in humanizing the ship and its inhabitants. These weren't rebels or rogues onboard, these were honest, hardworking scientists; people who'd lived their whole lives for Segura and the dream of a better galaxy. This place was all they were, all they lived for.

And this was going to be taken from them.

But how much was taken—that might still be in raider hands.

"So, what, the band is back together again? You two are double-teaming it now?" Zane asked, parting her thoughts. She glared, glancing over to where he stood a few meters away with Levy. She and Lee hadn't moved half a meter from where they'd met back up minutes ago.

"Leave them," Levy said, shooting her and Lee a timid grin. This time, Kat met that grin.

"We'll catch up with you in a second," Lee called. Zane and Levy could check in with their ship and see if they had any updates to share. It was all just buying them time now, anyway, before they had to man up and make the hard choices. They could steal a few more minutes.

"The band was never broken up to begin with," Lee said quietly, as they started back, moseying after the others.

"Thanks for not looping me in earlier," she said pointedly.

"Hey, you were off—" he started in defensively, huffing a laugh when he caught her grinning. His face relaxed. "Ha ha." Just because they were doing apologies, didn't mean she had to go all soft on him. But he glanced over at her again, sidelong. "I wanted you there with me." There was nothing teasing in his words or on his face.

Kat swallowed. She didn't know how to answer that in a way that would come off as sincere as his words had. Instead, she stared around at the city again, processing. What would happen to all of this if they didn't figure things out in time?

"But seriously." Lee slowed, letting the others get even further ahead of them. "Where were you?"

Hiding from you. Kat bit her cheek as she peered down at the ground. Then up at the stacks. She stuffed her hands in her pockets, feeling for loose fibers, and doing everything she could to keep from looking at him and giving herself away.

When she finally did look his way, Lee was studying her with narrowed eyes. He knew she was hiding something—he probably knew why she'd been hiding. So instead she told him about Cade. "I talked with one of the ship's inhabitants."

"Did he tell you anything?" Lee asked curiously, losing track of the fact that she was evading his question a little. Or maybe realizing she wouldn't actually tell him anyway.

"It was over drinks," Kat shrugged as if that explained anything. "He was telling me about how long they've been here, and about their different roles. They have a base," she added, almost as an afterthought.

Lee nodded, stealing a glance at her. "It sounds like you were having fun." And maybe he meant it to sound perfectly casual, but Kat could see right through it.

"It was nice to chat a little more openly with someone who knows what's going on around here." But she was tired of games. Shaking her head, she sighed. "What are you really asking, Lee?"

"Nothing. As I said, I was a little worried about you, that's all. No one knew where you'd gone."

She eyed him. And when he held her gaze, she turned up a dangerous little smile. "So you're saying that you were worried about me?"

It was Lee's turn to shrug, glancing away for a second. "Don't read into it, okay? You know I worry about you, Kat. I'll always worry about you. You're my best friend."

She didn't try to hide the ear-splitting grin that spread across her face and into her eyes. Best friends, huh? She hadn't felt this sort of playful spark in a while. And she wasn't about to let him forget about it quite yet, either. Especially not now that they had finally put the daggers back on the shelf.

Lee was muttering something about how he'd 'never worry about her again' as they neared the opposite edge of the city.

A new thing had settled between them once again. Its boundaries were still a little fuzzy, and a little unfamiliar. But it reminded her enough of their old thing, that she thought she might be okay with it.

"You know, I think about that night in the anti-gravity chamber a lot..." he said quietly.

"You do?" She asked, and when she looked over, there was no trace of their teasing, or playful banter from before. Instead she was met again with a seriousness, an earnestness that had her stopping in her tracks.

"Yeah. Maybe when we get back from Argos we could do that again sometime?"

"I'd like that," she said. Lee was wearing his own broad grin, when an annoying sound interrupted her thoughts.

She squinted, peering about them. "Do you hear that?"

"Hear what?"

"It's like a blipping..." Kat scanned the street and then her hyperband. Her eyes shot to Lee's wrist. "I think it's coming from you—"

"What in the *zapping*—" Lee's eyes dropped down to his hyperband.

There was a virtual call coming in from Tonya Waters.

CHAPTER 39: LEE

THEIR COMMUNICATION signal was working.

A little too well.

Lee hit ignore as Tonya's second call blipped through on his hyperband. Slowing to an ambling, he flicked through to his calendar. "*Void*, what day is it?"

Time had lost all meaning over the last couple of weeks. With everything they'd been doing leading up to the raid, and then everything with Kat, he'd entirely forgotten to cancel his call with his mom.

They were almost back to their ship. They only had to clear the alleyway and the passage, then they'd be through. Although at this point, he wasn't sure that was any better. He glanced upwards, gauging the teal lights overhead and the stacks at his back. What were the chances he could pretend this was some sensory room onboard the Academy...

Kat had slowed her pace to match his. "You aren't seriously thinking about taking her call."

"She's going to keep calling back."

Sure enough, seconds later, Tonya's name came through again. "She can't know about any of this," Lee said, meeting Kat's gaze.

He accepted the call, clambering backward until he was sitting on the ground with his back to the stacks. Here was one way to test just how well the communication lines were coming through.

With a sigh, Kat did the same. She was settling in next to him when his mom's bleached-blonde waves appeared in the alleyway with them. It was almost comical, the image rendered of his mother's stainless steel kitchen blended with the blue-green lights and raw materials that were Segura.

"Uh, hey Mom." Lee ran a hand through his hair. Then, remembering that he wasn't wearing his usual dark suit, crossed his arms over his chest to hide some of the synthetic fabric. If there was one thing Tonya would notice, it was—

"Wow, honey, I like your new suit!"

"Hey Mrs. Waters," Kat chirped up while Lee shot his mom a sheepish smile.

"Oh, Kat's there too! I was wondering when Lee would let you and I chat again. How are things going?"

Lee feigned rolling his eyes. Exactly the mild annoyance Tonya would expect from him for a comment of that nature.

"Things are good. Staying busy."

"They do like to keep you on your toes, don't they." Tonya squinted, spinning in a slow circle as she surveyed their surroundings. "Wait, where are you? Did I catch you at a bad time?"

"Uh yeah, we've just been hanging out down on the training floors this afternoon. There was this cadet-wide competition thing going on..." He caught the bemused expression on Kat's face, then the raised eyebrow. *How long are you going to keep this up?*

His words escaped him at the emotion dancing there in her eyes. Her pale, grey, laughing eyes.

"But we're pretty worn. I think I'm going to head back up and squeeze a shower in," he said quickly, staring into the rough pavement to keep his head straight.

"Don't let me keep you, you crazy kids." Tonya beamed at Kat, before turning a similar expression on him. "Call me soon. And Kat, it's real good to see you, honey."

"You too, Mrs. Waters."

Lee wasn't sure what to make of the look his mom shot them; the extra sparkle in her green eyes as he ended the call.

"Well, that was illuminating." Lee leapt to his feet, extending a hand for Kat, before pulling her to her feet. "We can report back that we do have a definite signal."

Kat pulled her hand from his, tucking it under her arms. But she glanced over at him sidelong as they walked.

"What's that look?" he asked.

"Why does your mom like me so much?"

"Come on, you're practically the daughter she never had," he teased. She'd said so herself only a couple of weeks prior.

Kat smiled a little at that. But she continued to peer back at him as they walked.

Lee sighed. "She knows you're important to me. And for someone like Tonya, whose son and work are everything to her, that makes you important to her, too."

Some color had crept into Kat's cheeks. He tried to ignore the appreciation, the apologetic notes in her eyes. Kat would always—always—be welcome where Tonya was concerned. Even if things never evolved for them.

The thought had already sobered him by the time they cleared the doors out of the city. They traversed the short length of the hangar and started up the ramp before Lee noticed the air seemed quite a bit more charged than when he was here last.

They stepped into the cabin. Jed still sat around one of the small tables with his game in hand, the twins having joined him, although no one was playing right now. Hanna and Nikola were both perched along the observation deck like before, although Nikola no longer had his head buried in the holotech. Nikola and Hanna both peered his way as Lee joined them and Zane and Whistler around the platform of the observation deck.

"We got a signal through," Zane said, tensely.

"This is good," Lee said slowly. "We can get the health surveys out and let everyone know to stand down..."

But Zane looked away as Whistler slid a hologram their way. "There was a message waiting for us when we got our signal through."

The message had come from Commander Yvette Blanche. It was short and to the point.

Do not engage.

"When did this come in?" Kat demanded, coming up beside him and bracing both hands against the platform. She read the message receipt aloud. The message was from 12:00 this afternoon.

Lee blew out a breath, running his hands along his temples, massaging them while he thought. "That was barely a couple of hours ago. We could be fine. Let's get something sent out in reply."

"Already done." Whistler drew up the reply with its send receipt.

Cruiser A-01 experiencing delays. Return expected by 22:00 hours.

Lee read the message, glancing back at Whistler once more. "And we can make that? 22:00 hours?" He drummed his fingers against the platform of the observation deck. That didn't give them much time, but maybe if they could get Gaia to agree to some terms, then they could bring this back to the Commander and work something out. They could find a way to present this properly to the AMG in a way that would make them actually stop and consider this project. Because he was certain that whatever the Commanding General had planned for the city-ship, it was nothing good.

They had only begun their debating on how to handle this, when Jed called across the cabin, "We have company."

411

Lee crossed the cabin to peer out one of the side windows. Gaia strode towards them with Dyinai, once again, in tow. He couldn't read their expressions from here, but they covered the hangar with such rapidness... Lee couldn't help but compare the similarities to the last time they'd met like this.

Fine, two could play that game. With a wary glance at the cabin around him, he turned to address the others. "Whistler, Zane, Kat, and I will go down to meet them. Everyone else stays on the ship."

He checked his blaster out of habit as he waited at the top of the ramp, letting his shoulders relax and his head clear. They really were doing this again—only this time, they knew what to expect. Gaia was a no-nonsense operator, which meant they would find out very quickly what she was after.

And with Kat at his side, and Zane and Whistler flanking them, they strode back down the ramp.

"We weren't anticipating visitors this afternoon," Lee said somewhat wistfully, tossing their words back to them.

"Be that as it may," Gaia said, with a grim smile. "One of our systems engineers informed us of a breach in communications. A signal was sent out earlier this hour."

Lee was careful to keep all emotions and reactions from his face as he peered back at them. It was a tense few seconds during which both parties stared from cadet to host and back.

"Did they say anything of the nature of that signal?" Zane asked, adjusting his stance.

"Only that it came from the aft hangar." Gaia frowned. "And after a couple of our scientists reported the appearance of two strange visitors in our labs, we decided to come to learn of it for ourselves."

Lee didn't confirm or deny the latter half of her statement. But as to the signal coming from that aft hanger—"We were checking in with our command post to confirm whereabouts after our ship disappeared off the grid," he said coolly. The truth.

Gaia nodded, weighing his comment. She glanced over at her companion, before looking back at the four of them. "And where do the Allies of the Mangorian Galaxy believe their raiders to be now?"

CHAPTER 40: KAT

KAT ACTUALLY gasped.

They knew—had known. For however long, she was only mildly interested. Although Dyinai's eyes had widened, their jaw going slack, so maybe Gaia had kept this news mostly to herself... but that knowledge didn't do anything to curb the fluttering under her skin, or to change the fact that this was happening.

It would not have been hard to deduce what they were for anyone at all familiar with the way the AMG operated; with their style and their methods.

And their ships.

"It was necessary that our identity remain anonymous." Whistler was unapologetic as he offered another limited explanation.

"So you'll understand about our endeavors, as well," Gaia countered, leveling them each a look. "But now that we're both out in the open, would you care to explain why the AMG is sending its raiders out here to spy on us?"

"We were tracking a series of spikes associated with the dark radiation, the words we spoke before were true," Zane said, not breaking stance. "However, what we didn't realize at the time, was that the dark radiation was coming from you."

"You do not know of what you speak," Gaia said.

"We've seen the numbers and the holding cells. We know you've somehow found a way to harness the dark rays and that its energy courses unregulated through this ship." Zane crossed his arms over his chest, daring her—daring them to counter.

Gaia continued to stare back at them, belligerent, and unwavering.

Next to Kat, Lee sighed. "As raiders," and he nodded to Gaia, acknowledging her intelligence and assumptions, "our entire mission within the AMG is to protect. We've been assigned to help ensure the stability and survival of our galaxy. Your experiments put this at risk. There's a reason the AMG has banned the harnessing of dark radiation. It's too dangerous. There have been attempts in the past—and accidents—that have proven its properties are too much of an unknown."

"We are all aware of the risks and the lives at stake. Yours included—" Gaia said, pointedly, "should our research cease to continue. I'll remind you, that we've been at this for much longer than you have. We have learned things about the dark radiation that you could only dream about. And yet you claim it's too dangerous? Tell me, what then happens to our quadrants and your little Raider Program? What happens to the Allies of the Mangorian Galaxy, when there is no life left to protect? When the entire galaxy as you know it is overrun by dark radiation—or worse?"

"This is not your call to make."

"And it is the 'AMG's'?" The hardened mask on Gaia's face slipped away, her eyes tearing into each of theirs as she stared back at them. "We know what happens if we are found out or if we turn ourselves in. We lose everything—everything. All the advancements and progress we've worked this long to build, all our sacrifice so that we might have homes in the future—all of that is lost to oblivion. We know the AMG. Our operations will be shut down and tossed aside, the same as with those other "attempts" as you so ignorantly put it, all those years ago. And as for those accidents—" Gaia shook her head, a shadow settling over her features, "You know nothing. But *we* know what's at stake. We have learned from the past and we have planned for it. We won't be making those same mistakes again." And there was that word again. Accident.

She wasn't going to back down. They needed to offer more. Show more.

"That's also not our call to make," Kat said, speaking up for the first time. "And we are not here to engage." She frowned a little at the line their Commander kept repeating to them. "We can't speak for the previous circumstances. But General Narron has been searching for you—for this," Kat motioned to the ship around her. To the *void* with secrecy. "Somehow he knew about your experiments with the dark rays and the exact radioactive signature we tracked to your ship. He's been searching for Segura."

Gaia's eyes narrowed.

"He's not going to rest until this and everything that you're doing here with your research is brought forward. Let us help decide what that narrative will be," Kat pleaded. Gaia needed to listen—for the sake of the research. For Cade and all the inhabitants of this ship. For everyone else in this *void-forsaken* galaxy.

Gaia sighed. "These aren't just experiments. With the breakthroughs we've had with our energy and our defenses... The research and work we have undergone will benefit the continuation of life—throughout all four quadrants of the galaxy, and beyond." She knew much more about raiders than she had previously let on.

"So work with us," Lee said. "Agree to submit yourself for regulation. Help us convince them to embrace this project into the light that is our future."

"It's not that simple. There is more to it, more going on here that you don't understand."

"So help us understand," Lee said swiftly, crossing his arms over his chest.

There were a few seconds during which no one spoke in the hangar, and Kat could only wait, frozen in place as each tantalizing second dripped into the next.

She wasn't sure what Gaia saw in their faces as she calculated. Nor what finally tipped her resolve in their favor. But Kat caught the moment the resignation crossed over her features.

"How long do we have?" Gaia asked, finally, the broken look in her eyes transforming into one of piercing stone as she considered their proposition. Maybe they could still see this righted.

"We need to be on our way this evening," Whistler said, the tiniest hint of that crooked grin turning up the corners of his lips.

"My people won't be easily convinced," Gaia warned.

"Then it's good we have you on our side," Zane said, with a soldier's arrogance.

The doors split open at the other end of the hangar. The blue-green lights spilled out as another figure sprinted towards them. She skidded to a halt, torn, as her eyes darted between host and squadron, squadron and host. Settling on her own, she blurted. "Some ships appeared on our radar."

"Where, exactly," Gaia demanded.

Kat's heart fell. She knew the words that would come from the sprinter's lips before she spoke them. One guess who.

"They halted just outside the energy fields."

The AMG had come. But which flag they'd wave remained to be seen.

CHAPTER 41: LEE

THEY WOULD be AMG military ships; Lee knew it in his gut. Whether Command had sent them out as a reconnaissance mission, or as something else, was still to be determined. But there was very little doubt who'd sent the ships hovering just beyond the energy field barrier.

All their hopes of leaving this operation intact had evaporated, the last dregs swirling down through the many pipes that canvased the ship's internal structure.

"I don't care how the message was transmitted. But I need to know exactly what was conveyed." Gaia's harrowed eyes darted from him to Kat to Zane and Whistler, and back. "The future of our research is at stake."

Lee stood by while Zane and Whistler explained the situation with their communications. But the timelines didn't match up. For the Commander's message to precede the ships outside, it would've had to have been sent a couple of hours earlier. "Our Commander didn't send these ships," Lee said quietly, and five heads turned his way. "I hope I'm wrong," he offered up. He truly did. But the facts all pointed to that truth. "She wouldn't have had the time to get them here this quickly."

"Then whose ships are out there now?" Gaia demanded, her eyes boring into his, her mouth a flat line.

"The General's," Zane supplied, nodding subtly at Lee. Whoever was out there now, would've had to have gone around their Commander. It would've had to have been someone higher up; someone with the authority. The same someone who'd been condemning this research for decades with his growing influence and rise to power...

Lee's eyes flickered.

"You need to stop them, whatever they're planning. You've seen our accelerators and the results, and all that we've put into this. We're so close. We've come too far to fail now, there is too much on the line." There was panic in Gaia's eyes and in that of her companion.

And in him.

And although he didn't yet comprehend the full spectrum of their research and the work they'd been doing onboard this ship, he knew enough about the dark radiation out there. And about the people trying to run from it.

And the people who still believed they had a fighting chance to save their galaxy.

His squadron might not be able to save the ship, Segura had been doomed from the start. But the knowledge they'd acquired, and the people who knew how to interpret it...

"We need to see those ships." Lee turned to address the other squadron leads. "Gaia's right. Until we know what General Narron is planning, we need to delay them as long as possible."

But Kat was all ready for him on that same wavelength they always had. "I'll cover you. I can get a message out." And for a brief second, their eyes met, and he saw a fierce spark there, a light of defiance. And then she pivoted on a heel, heading back up the ramp.

"Zane, you'll come with me?" Lee asked. Zane's dad served under the General. He'd have the most intimate knowledge of any of them of the General's ships.

Zane again dipped his head, with two fingers to his wrist. "On my lifeblood."

With Zane's sanction, Lee addressed both Gaia and Dyinai, and the remaining two of his fellow squadron leads. "We don't know what can be done for Segura. But we can save your research."

At that, Whistler's lips turned up, in a solemn, aged-up version of his usual lopsided smile. He came right up beside Dyinai. "Start evacuations. I'll give them the choice, but for everyone willing, our cadets and our resources are at your service. Tell us what we can do to help you."

And as Whistler and Dyinai ran through logistics, the thought struck Lee; yet another attack on their AMG loyalty. What if their Commander's repeat message had not been about the rogue ship, about Segura. What if it had actually been in response to a new threat that had already begun heading their way...

While they were raiders, they were also still cadets of the Academy. They answered to the Commander. And as she couldn't get here in time herself... He turned to Gaia. "Take Zane and me with you. We will help identify the ships out there."

Gaia agreed, and with a single, parting nod to her companion, led them at a breakneck pace, back into the heart of their ship.

New shades of the ship blurred past as they were led through the city and past engineering; past the greenhouses and the conversion rooms, and the concealed stairway that led down to the labs. Every second counted. Every breath, every heartbeat.

"Our main hangar is through these doors on our right," Gaia explained with a steely look, the implications clear as they reached the end of the passageway, and continued past. The outlook for Segura was grim, and narrowing.

They entered the wing beyond the hangar, the control center, where they found only a handful of the ship's inhabitants. The rest had already been called away to help with evacuations. Good. Word had spread, then.

Gaia directed them right up beside a set of windows. Lee didn't need the radar at his fingertips as he stared out. He had a clear view of Argos, and its familiar scatter of stars. Only this time around, it was from the inside looking out.

He didn't have to look too hard. Both with their size and their design... Lee knew those ships.

Something tightened in his throat as Zane dipped his head toward him, as he stared out those windows to the demarcation line drawn by the energy fields; the ships loomed far too near. Not only did those ships have firepower, fueled and supported with all the latest advancements in energy technology, they had enough of it to blast right through the shields. And once they recovered their bounty, then they would destroy this thing, Lee was sure of it.

The Commander's last warning pealed through his ears, over and over again.

Do not engage.

Because they couldn't hold them off. Once her shields were down, Segura was virtually defenseless. A glance towards Zane confirmed his thoughts.

The Commanding General had known, without a doubt, what he would find out here today. And he'd come prepared. This had not been a random mission; sending out his raiders to track errant offshoot radiation. This had been a hunt, a condemnation. And they'd merely been the messengers; scouts for the hunting party.

Lee swallowed, steadying himself as he cast his eyes down the control panel as they explained to Gaia and the others remaining in the room what awaited them outside. "We will try to buy you time to gather your people. Salvage what you can. But we will need some assistance."

A tempestuous sea of shock and panic swam in her eyes as Gaia peered between them, her beloved ship, and the stars outside. Her head bobbed a bit. But then, as if collecting herself one final time, she straightened, gathering the attention of the remaining workers in the room. "What can we do to help?"

Lee let his eyes drift, let his gaze scroll across the control room, to the energy fields outside as he thought through all they'd seen and learned of the ship this far.

The fact that the AMG attack ships hadn't yet made their move was likely the only stroke of luck they'd get. The energy shields were throwing them off. Whether from their sheer size, or the unexpected cloaking device...

But they could work with that.

They had energy. So much energy at their fingertips. And if they could somehow use that in their favor to give those ships even one more reason to stall... His eyes landed on Zane. "What about a pulse?"

"It wouldn't be any sort of a defense, not against those ships." Zane frowned.

But Lee was shaking his head. "We don't need a defense. We just need to delay them—give them enough pause that they'll think and debate before striking the energy fields."

"Like a power play."

"A really big one." Lee nodded. Hopefully, Kat and Whistler had gotten a message out. They'd need every second they could cleave from this space siege.

Zane turned to Gaia, explaining about the pulses in their shields, and how they'd played a factor in the squadron identifying the energy fields for what they were.

"A transient disturbance," Gaia said, flatly. "That's what drew you to our ship?"

"One of the things." Lee waved his hand dismissively. Although it would only have been a matter of time. "Could something like that be manufactured on demand?"

"You want us to replicate a pulse?" Gaia asked. "It won't help our case, should they break through our shields."

"Then we better all be out of here before they arrive." He cast a knowing look toward both Zane and then Gaia, holding it a second longer. This was it. No one would be coming back to Segura. And once the AMG made it through the shield's barrier, they were no longer allies. It would be up to Gaia and her people to take care of themselves.

"I will get our people out," Gaia vowed.

With a nod, Lee motioned towards the control panel. "Let's disrupt this energy flow."

It only took a few minutes for the systems crew to locate an engineer capable of stemming the currents. But each minute they waited was one more test against fate. They'd managed thus far, but he had a feeling their luck was running out.

The systems engineer was cooperative. And although he was shaking his head, confused, and a little displaced by this new direction they were taking, he didn't question Gaia. Nor did he put forth any resistance to the foreign visitors commanding at the helm as he re-entered the database, re-programming the system for the force that might be capable of halting a set of military spacecrafts set on their imminent destruction.

Pulling his hands back, the engineer nodded once towards them. It was done. They wouldn't need long before the pulse was ready. Lee just hoped their squadron would realize what was happening and take that as a sign to hurry things along. Whatever message had been transmitted—it was working thus far.

Rising from beside one of the monitors, Gaia turned to address them one last time. "Jonah will wait with you through the pulse, in the case of something going wrong. After that, he comes with us."

Trust. That was her last request. Gaia glanced down to their wrists, the radiation monitor resting on each of them. Like she could sense its monitors gauging the very threat that had led them all here in the first place.

But the fact that she was even willing to spare one of her crew; that was enough.

"Thank you," Lee said, and Zane nodded as Gaia gave them one last long look. She had an expression written on her face that Lee couldn't quite discern. Like she was seeing something in them that she hadn't expected. But then she was hurrying back out the door. She would be at the main hangar soon to help coordinate Segura's evacuation.

How quickly things had taken a turn for the worse.

They would make it. They had to.

He and Zane were quiet in the few seconds' wake following Gaia's and the rest of the control center's departure. Lee didn't risk sending any explanations for the pulse through to Kat or Whistler for risk of the messages being intercepted. The element of surprise and delay were all they had now.

The seconds ticked on. Jonah, they learned, was a newer transfer to the ship, having only been here for a handful of years. But after today, Lee wondered if the engineer would stay with them after this—assuming they managed to get away, unscathed. The odds weren't looking great. But they would try. To the last thrum of the transports' boosters.

And then Lee saw the tremor on their monitor. He watched the pulse in the data stream, as hundreds of trillions of joules were fed into the single instance Jonah had set up for them.

A man-made phenomenon, condensed and controlled by a systems engineer on a random set of holotech.

That was what they should all be afraid of.

And then the alarms sounded.

CHAPTER 42: KAT

SHE AND Whistler had gotten a message out.

There'd been little time for debate once Whistler had joined her on their ship and their cadets had swarmed. Not with blasters quite literally aimed at their demise.

There is a ship, but it is unarmed. We are working to get the energy fields down.

Their message wasn't groundbreaking; they'd transmitted the barebones of an update. Maybe less than that; a couple of select bones from a carefully worded warning. But it was the best they could do, thinking on the spot.

Their cadets had gone along up ahead with Dyinai to assist in their evacuations. All except for Nikola, who now stood across from them at the observation deck. They'd kept him behind to help monitor their communication signal on the slim possibility the Commanding General deigned to send something back.

Shaky as she was, Kat set to work operating one of the sensors while they waited for an update. Or news. For something to happen—or not happen. The shields would be the first thing to go, that was a given.

But it was almost ironic.

They'd completed their mission and uncovered the source of the radiation spikes. And in the process, they'd also uncovered the only means presently capable of combatting the nebulous dark rays. And yet, here she was, tracking the energy waves coming from the shields once again.

She wondered what Lee and Zane had found; which of General Narron's ships they'd unveiled waiting for them outside the energy fields.

It had been almost fifteen minutes since Lee and Zane had left with Gaia. Whistler was fidgeting with their tech. Nikola kept adjusting his glasses. And she was ready to get down on the floor and start doing crunches if it meant not thinking about those AMG ships and what Lee was up to now.

She'd walked in on Hanna's parting farewell to Nikola earlier—although neither had really been talking, they'd merely been staring intently into each other's eyes... When had that started up? She supposed crazier things had happened. Was that separation weighing on him, too at the moment? She could vouch for the feeling.

Then she saw the recording on the holograph.

She dove for the platform, elbows sliding across the smooth surface as she adjusted the scale on the sensor tech. She was shaking her head a little as Whistler and Nikola came over to check it out.

"Did that come from us or from them?" Nikola asked.

The 'them' would be whoever waited just outside the energy fields. She supposed the rest of them were all an 'us' now. Their squadron, the ship's inhabitants; one big happy family—in direct violation of AMG orders.

"That had to be internal." Kat adjusted the scale once more. Sure enough, the wavelengths had returned to normal.

That had certainly been one formidable disturbance. But she knew these values. "That was a pulse," she murmured.

"This one wasn't an accident, though. This was a warning," Whistler said, meeting her gaze.

"Lee?" she breathed.

"Lee," Whistler repeated, inclining his head slightly.

It had happened, then. There was no hope for this ship, they were at the end of the line. With the crinklings of a grim smile, Whistler turned to Nikola. "Our work here is done. Let's go see what we can do to help Segura."

They strode the length of the cabin, weaving around the cafe table they'd dragged over earlier in the raid. Her eyes snagged on the pair of fitness mats someone had left lying undone on the floor by the dorms, and their green juice machine—its lid overturned from its latest spin. As they reached the lowered ramp, she stole a fleeting glimpse up into the cockpit, and the aisle leading in, where she'd confessed her feelings for Lee, only to have them thrown back in her face. Back when she'd been completely ignorant as to where his heart lay.

She bid Starla a wordless adieu as their feet pounded the ramp. It likely wouldn't be them piloting her back home. She tried her best not to think of who or what would be chartering their passage home.

But for now, they had one last part to play.

The three of them were already sprinting as they tore back through the passageway and into the city. The streets had completely cleared out. A door or two had been left open. A garbage can lay abandoned on its side. And not one flier skimmed under that star-painted ceiling.

As they cleared the street, she registered the flickering of lights in some of the doorways and the faintest bellowing of an alarm that seemed to emulate from within the walls.

She hurtled past a little shop with a lighted, teal drink sign in the window, and her thoughts flitted to Cade, and his friends and family here. Where had they been when they'd learned of this new turn of events? Had he gotten to toss back one more glass of that bitter-orange nitro drink before the alarms sounded?

Up side streets and back down they went, hurtling the corners, until they found themselves back outside engineering. This is where Dyinai had said they'd go, directly past the labs they'd find the doors leading to the second hangar.

The pealing was infinitely louder here; it bellowed in synchronization with the flashing lights.

Whistler felt around the doorway, studying it a few moments, until he located the security panel along the top section of the door. With a little help from the laser on his hyperband, he gingerly removed the smooth panel, letting it clatter to the ground.

It was deja vu. Only this time they weren't going in to steal rolls.

And they didn't have time for this.

Nudging Whistler out of the way, she directed her blaster into the frame and the wires buried within. It only required one blast, and the doors split apart.

"There's one way to do it," Whistler murmured, Nikola gaping a little under the duress, but Kat was already striding through.

There were no fliers skidding past this time. The first couple of wings, like the city, were mostly deserted. But as they crossed deeper into the passage, they encountered some of the ships' inhabitants. She checked her hyperband. Roughly fifteen more minutes had passed since they'd seen the pulse on their sensor tech. They were pushing it.

A group of figures emerged from the greenhouses up ahead, arms laden with pots in all sorts of colors and shapes. They were all moving slowly, too slowly to clear the wings.

That broke her. Splitting up, she sent Nikola on up ahead to assist those carrying the plants. Whistler peeled off to go check on the status of the scientists working down in that basement lab. And although a vital part of her ached to see the acceleration and dark radiation tech as Zane and Lee had described it, an even more vital part of her—her heart—dragged her into those greenhouses.

He would have been one of those inhabitants scrounging up as many armfuls of those potted plants as he could carry.

Elbowing her way through the doors, a storm of dirt and warmth at her face, Kat began ushering them outward and onward, flashing her blaster when they wouldn't listen. And always with the same message: "You're out of time, go now!"

All through the greenhouses she wove, pushing, directing, and hastening them along until only a scant few still pushed their way out. Kat followed after them.

She did the same thing any time she found some of the ship's inhabitants lingering in the engineering and conversion rooms, herding them on and out. Her panic had long since settled inside of her, sharpened and honed into an unfaltering tool, as she did as raiders did best. Even as a coil of that panic stirred up, restlessly seeking the one face of whose whereabouts she'd become blind to...

She made it through the set of doors at the end of the hall. One of them had a panel open overhead, its wires fried and still smoking. It could have been any of them, but she liked to think it had been Nikola breaking his way in.

They reached the hangar.

She'd been right. Roughly a dozen or more massive space-crafts stood at the ready, their ramps lowered. These would be the transports the bartender boy had mentioned.

Canvassing the massive antechamber, Kat came up beside one of the transport ships. Like their mothership, the models of these spacecrafts were outdated. They'd need to get up to hyper-speed pretty quickly if they wanted to get out of this scrape. But they'd managed to evade attention thus far, and with the state-of-the-art energy resources in their arsenal, she believed they'd at least harbor a chance.

Ensuring the line into the spacecraft kept moving, she came around another of the transports. She helped as an elderly figure climbed the ramp. In her warbling hands, she held a single tin, one Kat would assume held some type of baked goods or dried fruit.

She glanced toward the next figure in line. And the next. Some, like those in the greenhouses, or the elderly passenger now in the transport, had managed to grab a possession or two. But most had nothing at all. They had themselves. The work and research they had spent years, lifetimes, even, developing, all of it reduced down to a potted plant. Or a tin of biscuits.

These were scientists; human beings.

But they were only the first of the galaxy's inhabitants who'd be uprooted if the AMG got to them today. So she put her head down to see what she could to help ease the transition.

She ran into Levy, standing alongside the opening to another of the transports, helping some of Segura's inhabitants inside the spacecraft. She was smiling.

And Jed, with no sign of his usual boredom or disdain, was doing the same.

And at another, Kiara. And Kamata. Hanna. Nikola.

And then Lee crossed into the hangar.

The weight she hadn't realized she was carrying fluttered to the scuffed hangar floor as she darted for him.

She was at his side in an instant.

"Kat." She swore something similar had lifted in him as he sighed in relief. "I just ran into Whistler. Zane is confirming with him, but we believe we got everyone out of the labs. This should be the last of them." He motioned to the last of the humanoid figures trickling through the doors. Behind them, strode the other two Gamma squadron leads.

"What did you find out?" She asked when she felt collected enough to voice her next question. The uncertainty of the last hour had been eating into her.

"He sent attack ships. The General—they're going to—"

The hairs on her arms stood up, her nerves crackling as a wave of nothingness swept over her. There was silence as all motion in the hangar stilled, and even the alarms seemed to mute as time halted its course.

And then everything blazed violet.

Time leaped forward again on overdrive as a second wave swept in, carrying with it flashes of violet and red, as the sounds from the alarms returned in full amplitude.

The energy fields were down.

Her eyes scanned over Lee, his eyes widened with the shock that mirrored her own.

It took her a couple of heartbeats to ground herself and remind herself that they were okay; that Lee was with her now. And that they weren't the ones in jeopardy here.

Then she was whirling back around to the transports and the still-too-many figures remaining outside along the hangar. "They need to go, now."

And as the hangar around them broke into a frenzy, she grasped at that cool, calculated place inside of her as they'd been trained to do. Following the examples set forth by Gaia, and Elia, and other loosely familiar faces from around Segura, Kat and the other Gamma squadron leads strode back into the havoc. They'd been trained to push aside their own fears, and maintain order to accomplish their mission.

And so they did. The rest of their cadets soon caught on, until the entire squadron was mixed back in with the fold, hollering for the last of the crews to board their transports.

They were moving so slowly, it seemed impossible that they'd ever make it off the ground. But the last of the ships' inhabitants scrambled onboard, the transport ships' doors closing. And as the hangar doors creaked and shuttered, the ships began to hover to life.

She found Lee, first. It was just after that, she heard Zane's voice roaring over the cries of the alarms. "Lee—Kat, guys, come on!"

Zane waited at the doors leading back through the ship, waving their cadets through.

"We can't be here," Lee pressed. Not just here, as in the hangar, but anywhere near here. Their very presence would be considered rebellion. Grabbing her by the hand and pulling her along with him, they sprinted off after Zane.

The transport ships were edging their way towards the opening as she and Lee reached the passageway doors.

They raced after their squadron, spurring them onward, faster, not looking back as they flew through the passages. The alarms blared all around them in a scouring reminder of what was coming.

Of what had come.

They would not get to see the former inhabitants of Segura make it out of here; Gaia and her crew were on their own now, *void*-speed. Just as the squadron was on their own.

They'd cleared the engineering passage and made it back into the city before Kat felt her breathing ease, her lungs adjusting to the adrenaline. She stole a glance over at Lee running beside her. He'd kept pace with her the entire way, never straying from her side.

The rest of their squadron raced up ahead of them, still in their sights as they followed them down one of the side streets. She could make out Levy in the pack, her lavender hands a blur.

"Just tell me," Kat said, keeping her face pointed straight ahead, her breaths even. "Are you happy with Levy?"

Their feet pounded a steady rhythm into the paved street. "Now? You want to do this now?" Lee demanded in a whoosh of sound. At the colored undertones in his voice, Kat stole another glance over. Lee either wanted to laugh or pull her hair out, she couldn't tell. But she continued to steal glances over at him, her body going lightheaded and her breathing shallow as she awaited his response.

"Yes, now," she forced out in a breathy ultimatum. She needed this now. She needed to know he was happy, and that there was something good in the world when everything else she knew was slipping out from under them.

But Lee had smoothed the emotion from his face. His breathing was even despite the long strides. "Kat, I'm not with Levy. I don't even like her—not like that."

"You don't?" Her heart stuttered. There was enough unevenness in her breathing and in her lungs, she gripped her abdomen to catch herself.

Lee's hand shot out instinctively, gripping her arm. He would not let her fall. Not now, or ever.

At his touch, she felt something glimmer inside of her. It was a trembling and fluttery thing—and that glimmer was going to refract into a thousand *zapping* glimmers if she didn't smother it down immediately.

Void. If Lee wasn't saying what she thought he was; if he had other plans in mind for himself...

But Lee was shaking his head. "It's you, Kat. It will always be you."

Up ahead, their cadets had reached the alleyway with that final passageway that would take them back to their ship. Maybe they would make it back to their beloved Starla, after all.

She grinned over broadly at him, unable to stop the squealing from her heart, from her soul. And as she caught the brightness in his eyes, that sun that overrode all logic and sanity, that glimmer inside of her radiated.

Hope. The glimmer inside of her was hope.

And then the breaching blast echoed through the city. It reverberated along the ground, and through the stacks rising up at their shoulder blades. And as the stars shook above them, glitter rained down on the city.

The AMG was here.

CHAPTER 43: LEE

THEY NEVER made it back to their ship.

Once the dust and the glass had settled, and the ground had stopped its undulations, they'd stopped running. There was nowhere to run, anyway. It was over.

Lee let his boots slow to a loose stride until his gait was barely more than a lost and dazed wander. But Kat was there, wandering with him. And Whistler and Zane. Levy. Nikola and Hanna. The twins. And Jed. Their squadron.

It was eerily still as he peered up into the stacks again, like that first time. And realized that no one would be taking those fliers out again. The Flyr6000s. And that juice shop... he'd never gotten to take Kat to that juice shop.

The shouting overwhelmed the alleyway as Lee listened for some context as to whether or not Gaia's fleet had made it out or not. May the neutrinos protect them wherever they were headed. And when the figures came around the corner, with their dark suits and heavy blasters, the sharp angles were at odds with the city and its teal lights. And its flickering alarms. Someone really needed to smother those.

"We found them." The figure at the head of the group spoke into his hyperband, as they came to a halt. Lee could identify the male-in-command as a lieutenant, by the badges on his uniform.

These weren't raiders; this was the Commanding General's unit, the attack force.

And Lee's squadron was now being identified as simply a token of honor for the force's hard work and service.

The attack unit somehow knew exactly who they were, despite the various attire of all-terrain suits and synthetic fibers the cadets wore. As if their profiles had all been uploaded as part of the attack force's directive, to ensure there was no confusion when the unit located the two parties.

"Come with me." The Lieutenant beckoned, and Lee and the rest of their squadron fell into line behind the invading force. Lee didn't bother to fight it or to ask any questions. The raid, their mission, it was all out of their hands now.

He didn't even think to inquire after their cruiser; not that it was theirs anymore.

Another figure of the General's unit joined them. The Lieutenant's next-in-command, saluted, before falling to the Lieutenant's side.

"Were we able to get into the mainframe?" the latter asked.

"We have what we need." Lee didn't bother to look their way, as the second-in-command responded. It wouldn't have been difficult to locate what they needed. Everything was there in the basement lab. Every last trace.

"And what of the rogue transports?"

"We'll find them."

Lee's blood cooled as the words settled over him. But he kept his eyes averted. Their very presence, here, would be considered evidence. And they'd likely have to talk, at some point. But until those facts came out, until they faced Commanding General Narron himself, Lee would remain silent.

Instead, Lee slipped his hand through Kat's, squeezing once. He sunk into that callused feel of her hand in his, as she squeezed back in recognition.

They hadn't won. Not today.

They wouldn't add a name to their list of adventures. He didn't want this one.

The cadets were led back across the city, up through engineering, and into that main hangar, and the smoldering wreckage that now lay there. The hangar doors had been forced open, blasted apart by sheer force. But none of the transports remained.

They'd all gotten away.

In the transports' place, a greater ship sat at the ready. Its sleek shape and streamlined design were a product of the last few years, with each bell and whistle that being the well-funded unit of the AMG afforded.

Its presence made the derelict hangar look even grungier than before.

His squadron was taciturn and subdued as they were led right up the ramp and seated in two neat rows facing each other. Lee had to squeeze his eyes shut against the glare. Everything was far too bright under the white lights.

His trousers were the wrong color. The walls, too. And the sheen on Kat's vanilla-blonde hair...

He didn't know how long they sat there, not talking, under the watchful eye of one of the Lieutenant's next-in-command, with his dark clothes and his heavy blaster. But Lee still gripped Kat's hand in his. He leaned into that touch and focused on her. His lifeline, and his tie to humanity.

A while later, some more figures boarded the ship with the Lieutenant. They reported their findings, speaking in voices too soft and too low for them to hear. Lee didn't want to listen in anyway.

The ramp was raised; and the engine started. There was barely a thrumming, a soft whisper, as they cleared the hangar, and the ship disappeared from his view. Lee thought for a moment he could feel the hair on his arms standing on end, as they crossed the invisible barriers where the energy fields would have stood, the prickles of residual energy causing his pulse to quicken. But that, too, dissipated. Maybe he'd only imagined it.

They'd been flying a while when he heard the Lieutenant radio through to another ship. "Those energy cells have been diffused?"

The reply came through. "Affirmative."

There was a pause during which the Lieutenant adjusted the cuff at his sleeve. "Let's terminate this operation. Take us to hyperspeed."

EPILOGUE: KAT

KAT RUBBED her eyes as she sat up, blinking past the too-bright lights inside the AMG ship. She must have dozed off.

Next to her, Lee sat staring down into the grates of the heavily polished floor. He still leaned towards her in his seat, his dark shoulder stiff from where her head had been resting for *void* knew how long.

They'd been given extra clothing to change into in the earlier hours of the flight. They weren't the all-terrain suits they were accustomed to back at the Academy, but they were clean. Pressed. And far too starched for her taste.

They hadn't spoken a word in the hours since leaving behind Segura. She'd been unable to speak. She was surprised she'd been able to close her eyes at all. She could still picture the flash of the blast as it was released, targeted towards the unprotected heart of the hidden spaceship, now exposed to the galaxy.

She'd only glimpsed the sparks, barely an echo of the anticipated explosion before they'd slipped swiftly and neatly back through the galaxy. The squeezing in her head had been unbearable, except for Lee, a solid force at her side, clutching her hand to his heart to ground them there. But those echoes still burned in her head. Behind her eyes.

Again. And again. And again.

They were raiders. Their mission, as defined by the Academy, was to protect and preserve the continuation of all life within the Allies of the Mangorian Galaxy.

And with the destruction of Segura, they'd also potentially sentenced the galaxy and all of its inhabitants to its own mutilated destruction.

The dark radiation was the real threat. And unless they could find another way... There had to be another way...

She was vaguely aware of the Lieutenant-in-command addressing them. Something about their imminent arrival. She hadn't even felt the ship decelerating.

They arrived in the Commander's private hangar to a flood of more bright lights. Kat released her harness as directed, no longer privy to the screaming beneath her skin, as the numbness fully settled over her.

Following a brief instruction, they were ushered across the central skywalk, ascending the Heptagon up to their dorms.

They would be speaking with Commander Blanche in the days to follow. The Commanding General and Council after that. But for now... For now...

She clenched her eyes shut as swirls and flashes of color and those blue-green lights crashed behind her eyelids. Somehow in the thrall of it all, she kept picturing the color of Lee's clear green eyes, and the feel of his heartbeat. It wasn't over. They weren't over. They were still in control.

Perching at the edge of her bed, she stared unseeing into the darkened paneled walls for long after the crashing in her head had faded again. It could have been hours or maybe minutes, she'd lost all sense of time.

She hadn't even wrapped her head around what she was waiting for until she heard the knock at her portal door.

Sliding to her feet, her heart leaping out of her chest, she tapped the button beside the door and found Lee standing outside.

Locking sight of those green eyes, the anguish consuming them, she threw her arms around his neck and gripped him tightly. She pressed her face in close, breathing him in. Feeling him, his pulse rushing alongside hers.

They had made it. Their squadron had made it. And they would get through this. All of them, together. If they banded together once more, they could withstand whatever maelstrom now awaited them with Command. And she and Lee would finally get their chance. That glimmer of hope she still clung to, even after pulling it from the rubble that now littered Argos.

She pulled back to find the pained expression still on his face as he trained those fraught green eyes on hers.

"Levy just quit the program."

"She—what?" Kat blinked back at him, eyes wavering between his as she felt out that pain, the frustrated edge of the cyclone just beginning to touch down. There was more. "Lee, what is it?"

"The General is on his way."

ACKNOWLEDGEMENTS

Where to begin? Probably where it all began. With Luke, who remembers maybe more clearly than me, the night I sat up in the middle of the night and began plotting my very first book. Years before my dreams would take me to the Mangorian Galaxy with Kat and Lee.

Thank you for too many dates sitting at coffee shops and too many late nights hanging out at the kitchen table with me so I could write. And for all the conversations and hypotheticals where you told me you weren't an astrophysicist... You shined a pretty bright star for me, babu! There's a little bit of you in here, all over the pages.

To my boys and your infinite patience as Mommy forgot to fill juice cups and grab bowls of crunchies, but we got them to you eventually. You fuel my wonderment every single day.

Thank you to my family who graciously offered to read the early drafts: you guys deserve a lifetime supply of green juice.

Ash and Laura, I loved becoming an author alongside you. I didn't know what our friendship would evolve into when we first met. But I truly don't think I could have done this without you two. Late-night writing parties for life!

And to my writing gals, Laura M. Drake, Lauren Brown, and Amanda Tullis Smith, for showing me how to write a first chapter;)

To Stevi Lynn and Steph for pushing me to capture that emotion and build those scenes. You are the dream friends and critique partners I didn't even know I was looking for.

Thank you Megan G. Mossgrove, Kenna Blaylock, A.N. Caudle, Laura Elizabeth, and Doug Pendergrast for your thoughtful comments and beta feedback. I carried your words in my head through many many revisions of Gamma Raids I!

A thanks to my editor Noah Sky, who helped me tie it all together with a pretty bow in the end. I think I'll always mix up she and her, but at least I'm consistent.

A special thanks to Split-leaf Coffee & Beans & Brews, for many an afternoon spent commandeering a table while I finished drafts and tackled never-ending rounds of edits.

To my Goal Diggers, for all the book stress you guys saved me from, kicking the ball around late at night.

And to all my new booksta friends embarking on this journey—I could fill up pages and pages listing your encouragement and love and support I felt to even get this far! Your kind words mean everything. As some of those dearest to me would say, "Go for 30!"

ALSO BY R. LYNN HANKS

Other Worlds, A sci-fi anthology
A Paper Alliance

Gamma Raids II (2026)

ABOUT THE AUTHOR

R. LYNN Hanks is a sci-fi romance author based in a little farm town in the states. When not plotting high stakes space adventures or dabbling around with poetry, you can find me at a local coffee shop or at home teaching my two little gentlemen about the stars.

If you enjoyed Gamma Raids I, I'd love it if you left me a review. You can find me everywhere on socials @rlynnhanks or come hangout on my website, www.rlynnhanks.com.

To check out Kat & Lee's infinite Playlist, follow the QR below to my website here:

www.ingramcontent.com/pod-product-compliance
Lightning Source LLC
Chambersburg PA
CBHW020003120726
47903CB00004B/1117